WITHDRAWN

by Caroline Gordon

NOVELS

PENHALLY   1931
ALECK MAURY, SPORTSMAN   1934
  (*reissued, with Afterword, 1980*)
NONE SHALL LOOK BACK   1937
THE GARDEN OF ADONIS   1937
GREEN CENTURIES   1941
THE WOMEN ON THE PORCH   1944
THE STRANGE CHILDREN   1951
THE MALEFACTORS   1956
THE GLORY OF HERA   1963
THE NARROW HEART   *work-in-progress*

STORIES

THE FOREST OF THE SOUTH   1945
OLD RED AND OTHER STORIES   1963
THE COLLECTED STORIES   1981

CRITICISM

HOW TO READ A NOVEL   1957
A GOOD SOLDIER: A KEY TO THE
  NOVELS OF FORD MADOX FORD   1963

ANTHOLOGY

THE HOUSE OF FICTION   1950
  (*edited with Allen Tate*)

The Collected Stories of

Caroline Gordon

THE
Collected Stories of
CAROLINE
GORDON

❀

With an Introduction by

ROBERT PENN WARREN

Farrar • Straus • Giroux

NEW YORK

Printed in the United States of America
Published simultaneously in Canada by McGraw-Hill Ryerson
Ltd., Toronto
Designed by Herbert H. Johnson

FIRST PRINTING, *1981*

Library of Congress Cataloging in Publication Data
Gordon, Caroline.
   The collected stories of Caroline Gordon.
   Includes bibliographical references.
PS3513.O5765A6   1981   813'.52   80-28675

Contents

INTRODUCTION *by* *Robert Penn Warren*   *ix*

I

The Petrified Woman   *3*
The Burning Eyes   *16*
Tom Rivers   *24*
Old Red   *42*
The Enemies   *61*
One More Time   *67*
The Long Day   *76*
To Thy Chamber Window, Sweet   *84*
The Last Day in the Field   *96*
The Presence   *105*
One Against Thebes   *121*

II

Hear the Nightingale Sing   *137*
The Forest of the South   *150*
The Ice House   *167*
The Captive   *175*

III

The Brilliant Leaves   *213*
Her Quaint Honor   *222*
Mr. Powers   *238*
All Lovers Love the Spring   *247*
The Waterfall   *252*

IV

A Walk with the Accuser   *287*
The Olive Garden   *306*
Emmanuele! Emmanuele!   *317*
NOTES AND SOURCES   *351*

Introduction

Henry James once said that, in writing about fiction, "one speaks best from one's own taste, and I may therefore venture to say that the air of reality (solidity of specification) seems to me the supreme virtue of a novel—the merit on which its other merits helplessly and submissively depend." Though James here refers to the novel, what he says would inevitably apply to the short story and may serve as our golden text in an introduction to the short stories of Caroline Gordon. Her stories show to a superlative degree "solidity of specification," even if the land she knows so well lies thousands of miles and hundreds of years from the great country houses, shaven lawns, family-portrait galleries, and Sèvres which so enchanted James.

Caroline Gordon's world lies in southeast Kentucky, along the Tennessee line. It is a section of considerable Revolutionary grant land, chopped up, generation by generation, despite the device of cousinly marriages—which have their abundant and casual place in Caroline Gordon's stories. It was a rolling land of good grass and stands of timber, hedgerows, tobacco fields, and barns, with a scattering of solid or even handsome brick structures, with more modest but sometimes graceful white wooden farmhouses, and inevitably the shacks of tenantry, white or black. There were winding gravel roads, some black-top, streams, and ponds. It was a world I grew up in and spent most of boyhood's free time in, and now I read Caroline Gordon's stories with nostalgia, shutting my eyes to see landscape. For progress has been at work, with four- or six-lane highways not unusual, seventy-five-thousand-dollar tractors at work to flatten hedges and fill branches or creeks, and, with the falling away of tobacco as a money crop, the gradual falling away of the ramshackle housing of tenantry. And on prosperous farms themselves, one sees more and more new houses, with no air of rurality about them, looking as though just lifted from a booming suburb at Nashville. Landholdings get larger and larger, and mechanism more obvious. As far as can be told, the relation of man to nature is more and more tenuous—except for the weather.

That was not the land of Caroline Gordon's stories. There, man—black or white, poor or rich—seemed intertwined with nature. Professor Maury (the character most frequently appearing in the stories and the hero of her finest novel, *Alec Maury, Sportsman*, probably a work made to endure), out for a day's sport, "could see the frost glistening on the north side of every [corn] stalk." So he can say later: "I knew it was going to be a good day." He sees everything, feels everything. After an August drought, followed by a rainy September, there are the elderberry bushes: "In October light frosts came. In the afternoons when I sat on the back porch going over my fishing tackle I marked their progress on the elderberry bushes that were left standing against the stable fence. The lower, spreading branches had turned yellow and were already sinking to the ground but the leaves in the top clusters still stood up stiff and straight." It is not, however, in the sense of formal bits that the sense of man in nature is most sharply felt. Rarely is it felt sharply at all—rather, pervasively, incidentally, two little girls playing happily all afternoon in a branch rushing over stones, the flicker of silver poplar leaves.

The stories in this collection may be divided into the central and peripheral. The peripheral are relatively few, with two long examples, "The Captive" (the story of a white woman captured by Indians) and "Emmanuele! Emmanuele!" (laid in North Africa and France), and some several short pieces involving the Civil War. The central stories, more numerous, refer to the land described above, and in these the enclosing sense of the land combines with the enclosing sense of family and kin. It is true that, at all levels of society in the South, the sense of kinship, of the clan, of the family, hung on long after it died elsewhere, and hung on with so strong a sense of obligation that to the outsider it seems—or not too long ago seemed—nonsense or mystique. Caroline Gordon's stories are set just before the breakdown of the sense of family. "Still," she writes in "Tom Rivers," "in a large family connection such as ours every member, no matter how remotely related or how unimportant, had his place and a sort of record in memory. . . . We sit here under the trees all afternoon and talk about people we used to know: Cousin Owen, who walked from house to house, carrying his teeth in a basket . . . Cousin Henry Hord, who was deafened by cannonading in the Civil War and lost all his property by ill-advised investments and had to live with any of the kin who would put up with him." And then there is the last great family reunion, of five hundred members from all over the country, including one who had made it rich and provided all the whiskey—this scene narrated by a little girl, who hears her father, Professor Maury (who had only "married into" the family), remark: "All these mediocre people, getting together to congratulate themselves on their mediocrity!"

But beside the absurd or pretentious side of this world flowers story after story that is humorous (directly so as in "The Petrified Woman"), touching, or shocking. The artist here, sometimes by assuming the child's vision, shows the complexity of life. Few stories can match "The Enemies" or "The Long Day" for shock, or for a more subtle kind of shock, scarcely less powerful on reflection, at the end of "The Burning Eyes," in which a child goes on his first possum hunt. Or the muted conclusion of "One More Time," with its tangle of emotion at the end, especially for Professor Maury. He is old and slow now, his whole life now given to fishing and the study of expertise of fellow sportsmen, and at a fishing resort he meets a man whose strength is failing. The story ends with the body of the frail fellow sportsman at the bottom of the Blue Pool, with dumbbells in his pockets. This, of course, is a companion piece to "The Last Day in the Field" (which we may take to be that of Professor Maury, who, feeling his age, gives up the field entirely for the stream). It is his narrative: ". . . I shot too quick. It swerved over the thicket and I let go with the second barrel. It staggered, then zoomed up. Up, up, up, over the rim of the hill and above the tallest hickories. I saw it there for a second, its wings black against the gold light, before, wings still spread, it came whirling down, like an autumn leaf, like the leaves that were everywhere about us, all over the ground." (How subtle the touch of the word *us* here! The implied identification of the dying bird rising against the gold light, and the old man in his last act of a sport he lived for.) Subtlety of effect, poetic subtlety somehow entwined with a lucent prose, is one of the qualities of this writer. And sometimes it requires more than a second casual look.

In this book there are more than a few strong or subtle stories, with several about Professor Maury. Before turning to "Old Red"— perhaps the most memorable of Caroline Gordon's stories—we may mention "To Thy Chamber Window, Sweet." Here at a boarding-house at a fishing resort, Professor Maury, long a widower, meets a widow some ten years or so his junior, a woman charming, handsome, Virginian—all the heart could ask—and he holds her entranced, on the evening veranda, as he quotes in his magnificent voice from "Lycidas" and *Atalanta in Calydon*—not to mention some Shelley, for which he is inclined to ask God to forgive him. But a fellow fisherman turns up with splendid news from another locality. So after bedtime the two conspirators drive off, leaving a letter for the Virginia charmer, and the Professor is heard to mutter as they pull away from the temptation that would cramp his art: "And snatch'd his rudder and shook out more sail"—identifying himself with the "grave Phoenician trader" who flees westward when he sees the merry Grecian coaster come and seeks the open sea.

"Old Red" is the story of a somewhat different flight, this time from the sacred bosom of the family, which he had been dodging for years, the family who sit under the trees and talk of the dead and expect him to give up a day's fishing to go to a family funeral—the funeral of a distant relative. Everything—even the beloved family, his own daughter, his new son-in-law—is a trap. Even, he realizes ambivalently, his own marriage had been a trap, for his wife had wanted him to cut some sort of figure in the world, with his talents. In his sleeplessness, he finally drifts off into a dream of his boyhood in Virginia, a fox hunt, and the first sight of "Old Red," the fox always too fast and too shrewd for the pack. Suddenly he feels himself running as though he were the fox to a last refuge "in black dark, on moist earth while the hounds' baying filled the valley and reverberated from the mountainside."

The story up to this final moment has been full of tenderness and humor, and of the affection of the family for him, but Professor Maury finally realizes that nobody, not even here, understands him. They do not realize that he is the only one of the lot to whom Time is really precious, for whom life is an art and a discipline and a continuing joy, and who cannot afford to lose a moment out of the few precious years left. In other words, even in the bosom of the family—a family that to the modern world would have been incomprehensible in its virtues and pride, with the intellectual son-in-law and beloved daughter—he realizes that no eye can see him other than strange. He is the outsider—in perpetual flight from all that might bind him—from love, from the practical, vain, professional, and ambitious world. He is in flight from all that would deny the deep aesthetic texture of life and of nature, and their interrelation. "That look! Sooner or later you met it in every human eye."

Professor Maury—sportsman and poetry lover with the beautiful voice—is, in one perspective, a wastrel, egotist, and bum. But in another he is a philosopher and a hero. He knows the most difficult truth about the process of living.

The stories gathered in *The Collected Stories of Caroline Gordon* are more than admirable examples of the "solidity of specification." They are dramatic examples of man in contact with man, and man in contact with nature; of living sympathy; of a disciplined style as unpretentious and clear as running water, but shot through with glints of wit, humor, pity, and poetry. Caroline Gordon belongs in that group of Southern women who have been enriching our literature uniquely in this century—all so different in spirit, attitude, and method, but all with the rare gift of the teller of the tale.

ROBERT PENN WARREN

January 1980

One

The Petrified Woman

We were sitting on the porch at the Fork—it is where two creeks meet—after supper, talking about our family reunion. It was to be held at a place called Arthur's Cave that year (it has the largest entrance in the world, though it is not so famous as Mammoth), and there was to be a big picnic dinner, and we expected all our kin and connections to come, some of them from as far off as California.

Hilda and I had been playing in the creek all afternoon and hadn't had time to wash our legs before we came in to supper, so we sat on the bottom step where it was dark. Cousin Eleanor was in the porch swing with Cousin Tom. She had on a long white dress. It brushed the floor a little every time the swing moved. But you had to listen hard to hear it, under the noise the creek made. Wherever you were in that house you could hear the creek running over the rocks. Hilda and I used to play in it all day long. I liked to stay at her house better than at any of my other cousins'. But they never let me stay there long at a time. That was because she didn't have any mother, just her old mammy, Aunt Rachel—till that spring, when her father, Cousin Tom, married a lady from Birmingham named Cousin Eleanor.

A mockingbird started up in the juniper tree. It was the same one sang all night long that summer; we called him Sunny Jim. Cousin Eleanor got up and went to the end of the porch to try to see him.

"Do they always sing when there's a full moon?" she asked.

"They're worse in August," Cousin Tom said. "Got their crops laid by and don't give a damn if they do stay up all night."

"And in August the Fayerlees repair to Arthur's Cave," she said.

"Five hundred people repairing en masse to the womb—what a sight it must be."

Cousin Tom went over and put his arm about her waist. "Do they look any worse than other folks, taking them by and large?" he asked.

The mockingbird burst out as if he was the one who would answer, and I heard Cousin Eleanor's dress brushing the floor again as she walked back to the swing. She had on tiny diamond earrings that night and a diamond cross that she said her father had given her. My grandmother said that she didn't like her mouth. I thought that she was the prettiest person ever lived.

"I'd rather not take them by and large," she said. "Do we *have* to go, Tom?"

"Hell!" he said. "I'm contributing three carcasses to the dinner. I'm going, to get my money's worth."

"One thing, I'm not going to let Cousin Edward Barker kiss me tomorrow," Hilda said. "He's got tobacco juice on his mustaches."

Cousin Tom hadn't sat down in the swing when Cousin Eleanor did. He came and stood on the step above us. "I'm going to shave off my mustache," he said, "and then the women won't have any excuse."

"Which one will you start with?"

"Marjorie Wrenn. She's the prettiest girl in Gloversville. No, she isn't. I'm going to start with Sally. She's living in town now. . . . Sally, you ever been kissed?"

"She's going to kiss me good night right this minute," Cousin Eleanor said, and got up from the swing and came over and bent down and put her hand on each of our shoulders and kissed us, French fashion, she said, first on one cheek and then on the other. We said good night and started for the door. Cousin Tom was there. He put his arms about our waists and bumped our heads together and kissed Hilda first, on the mouth, and then he kissed me and he said, "What about Joe Larrabee now?"

After we got in bed Hilda wanted to talk about Joe Larrabee. He was nineteen years old and the best dancer in town. That was the summer we used to take picnic suppers to the cave, and after supper the band would play and the young people would dance. Once, when we were sitting there watching, Joe Larrabee stopped and asked Hilda to dance, and after that she always wanted to sit on that same bench and when he went past, with Marjorie Wrenn or somebody, she would squeeze my hand tight, and I knew that she thought that maybe he would stop and ask her again. But I didn't think he ever would, and anyway I didn't feel like talking about him that night, so I told her I had to go to sleep.

I dreamed a funny dream. I was at the family reunion at the cave. There were a lot of other people there, but when I'd look into their faces it would be somebody I didn't know and I kept thinking that maybe I'd gone to the wrong picnic, when I saw Cousin Tom. He saw me too, and he stood still till I got to where he was and he said, "Sally, this is Tom." He didn't say Cousin Tom, just Tom. I was about to say something but somebody came in between us, and then I was in another place that wasn't like the cave and I was wondering how I'd ever get back when I heard a *knock, knock, knock*, and Hilda said, "Come on, let's get up."

The knocking was still going on. It took me a minute to know what it was: the old biscuit block was on the downstairs back porch right under our room, and Jason, Aunt Rachel's grandson, was pounding the dough for the beaten biscuits that we were going to take on the picnic.

We got to the cave around eleven o'clock. They don't start setting the dinner out till noon, so we went on down into the hollow, where Uncle Jack Dudley and Richard were tending the fires in the barbecue pits. A funny-looking wagon was standing over by the spring, but we didn't know what was in it, then, so we didn't pay any attention, just watched them barbecuing. Thirteen carcasses were roasting over the pits that day. It was the largest family reunion we ever had. There was a cousin named Robert Dale Owen Fayerlee who had gone off to St. Louis and got rich and he hadn't seen any of his kin in a long time and wanted everybody to have a good time, so he had chartered the cave and donated five cases of whiskey. There was plenty of whiskey for the Negroes too. Every now and then Uncle Jack would go off into the bushes and come back with tin cups that he would pass around. I like to be around Negroes, and so does Hilda. We were just sitting there watching them and not doing a thing, when Cousin Tom came up.

There are three or four Cousin Toms. They keep them straight by their middle names, usually, but they call him Wild Tom. He is not awfully old and has curly brown hair. I don't think his eyes would look so light if his face wasn't so red. He is out in the sun a lot.

He didn't see us at first. He went up to Uncle Jack and asked,

"Jack, how you fixed?" Uncle Jack said, "Mister Tom, I ain't fooling you. I done already fixed." "I ain't going to fool with you, then," Cousin Tom said, and he was pulling a bottle out of his pocket when he saw us. He is a man that is particular about little girls. He said, "Hilda, what are you doing here?" and when we said we weren't doing a thing he said, "You go right on up the hill."

The first person I saw up there was my father. I hadn't expected to see him because before I left home I heard him say, "All those mediocre people, getting together to congratulate themselves on their mediocrity! I ain't going a step." But I reckon he didn't want to stay home by himself and, besides, he likes to watch them making fools of themselves.

My father is not connected. He is Professor Aleck Maury and he had a boys' school in Gloversville then. There was a girls' school there too, Miss Robinson's, but he said that I wouldn't learn anything if I went there till I was blue in the face, so I had to go to school with the boys. Sometimes I think that that is what makes me so peculiar.

It takes them a long time to set out the dinner. We sat down on a top rail of one of the benches with Susie McIntyre and watched the young people dance. Joe Larrabee was dancing with Marjorie Wrenn. She had on a tan coat-suit, with buttons made out of brown braid. Her hat was brown straw, with a tan ribbon. She held it in her hand, and it flopped up and down when she danced. It wasn't twelve o'clock but Joe Larrabee already had whiskey on his breath. I smelled it when they went past.

Susie said for us to go out there and dance too. She asked me first, and I started to, and then I remembered last year when I got off on the wrong foot and Cousin Edward Barker came along and stepped on me, and I thought it was better not to try than to fail, so I let Hilda go with Susie.

I was still sitting there on top of the bench when Cousin Tom came along. He didn't seem to remember that he was mad at us. He said, "Hello, Bumps." I am not Bumps. Hilda is Bumps, so I said, "I'm just waiting for Hilda . . . want me to get her?"

He waved his hand and I smelled whiskey on his breath. "Well, hello, anyhow," he said, and I thought for a minute that he was going to kiss me. He is a man that you don't so much mind having him kiss you, even when he has whiskey on his breath. But he went on to where Cousin Eleanor was helping Aunt Rachel set out the dinner.

On the way he knocked into a lady and when he stepped back he ran into another one, so after he asked them to excuse him he went off on tiptoe. But he lifted his feet too high and put one of them down in a basket of pies. Aunt Rachel hollered out before she thought, "Lord God, he done ruint my pies!"

Cousin Eleanor just stood there and looked at him. When he got almost up to her and she still didn't say anything, he stopped and looked at her a minute and then he said, "All right!" and went off down the hill.

Susie and Hilda came back and they rang a big bell and Cousin Sidney Grassdale (they call them by the names of their places when there are too many of the same name) said a long prayer, and they all went in.

My father got his plate helped first and then he turned around to a man behind him and said, "You stick to me and you can't go wrong. I know the ropes."

The man was short and fat and had on a cream-colored Palm Beach suit and smiled a lot. I knew he was Cousin Robert Dale Owen Fayerlee, the one that gave all the whiskey.

I didn't fool with any of the barbecue, just ate ham and chicken. And then I had some chicken salad, and Susie wanted me to try some potato salad, so I tried that too, and then we had a good many hot rolls and some stuffed eggs and some pickles and some coconut cake and some chocolate cake. I had been saving myself up for Aunt Rachel's chess pies and put three on my plate when I started out, but by the time I got to them I wasn't really hungry and I let Susie eat one of mine.

After we got through, Hilda said she had a pain in her stomach and we sat down on a bench till it went away. My grandmother and Aunt Maria came and sat down too. They had on white shirtwaists and black skirts and they both had their palm-leaf fans.

Cousin Robert D. Owen got up and made a speech. It was mostly about his father. He said that he was one of nature's noblemen. My grandmother and Aunt Maria held their fans up before their faces when he said that, and Aunt Maria said, "Chh! *Jim* Fayerlee!" and my grandmother said that all that branch of the family was boastful.

Cousin Robert D. Owen got through with his father and started on back. He said that the Fayerlees were descended from Edward the Confessor and Philippe le Bel of France and the grandfather of George Washington.

My father was sitting two seats down, with Cousin Edward Barker. "Now ain't that tooting?" he said.

Cousin Edward Barker hit himself on the knee. "I be damn if I don't write to the *Tobacco Leaf* about that," he said. "The Fayerlees have been plain, honest countrymen since 1600. Don't that fool know anything about his own family?"

Susie touched me and Hilda on the shoulder, and we got up and squeezed past my grandmother and Aunt Maria. "Where you going?" my grandmother asked.

"We're just going to take a walk, Cousin Sally," Susie said.

We went out to the gate. The cave is at the foot of a hill. There are some long wooden steps leading up to the top of the hill, and right by the gate that keeps people out if they haven't paid is a refreshment stand. I thought that it would be nice to have some orange pop, but Susie said, "No, let's go to the carnival."

"There isn't any carnival," Hilda said.

"There is, too," Susie said, "but it costs a quarter."

"I haven't got but fifteen cents," Hilda said.

"Here comes Giles Allard," Susie said. "Make out you don't see him."

Cousin Giles Allard is a member of our family connection who is not quite right in the head. He doesn't have any special place to live, just roams around. Sometimes he will come and stay two or three weeks with you and sometimes he will come on the place and not come up to the house, but stay down in the cabin with some darky that he likes. He is a little warped-looking man with pale blue eyes. I reckon that before a family reunion somebody gives him one of their old suits. He had on a nice gray suit that day and looked just about like the rest of them.

He came up to us and said, "You all having a good time?" and we said, "Fine," and thought he would go on, but he stood and looked at us. "My name is Giles Allard," he said.

We couldn't think of anything to say to that. He pointed his finger at me. "You're named for your grandmother," he said, "but your name ain't Fayerlee."

"I'm Sally Maury," I said, "Professor Maury's daughter." My father being no kin to us, they always call me and my brother Sally Maury and Frank Maury, instead of plain Sally and Frank, the way they would if our blood was pure.

"Let's get away from him," Susie whispered, and she said out loud, "We've got to go down to the spring, Cousin Giles," and we hurried on as fast as we could. We didn't realize at first that Cousin Giles was coming with us.

"There comes Papa," Hilda said.

"He looks to me like he's drunk," Susie said.

Cousin Tom stood still till we got up to him, just as he did in my dream. He smiled at us then and put his hand on Hilda's head and said, "How are you, baby?" Hilda said, "I'm all right," and he said, "You are three sweet, pretty little girls. I'm going to give each one of you fifty cents," and he stuck his hand in his pocket and took out two dollar bills, and when Hilda asked how we were going to get the change out, he said, "Keep the change."

"Whoopee!" Susie said. "Now we can go to the carnival. You come, too, Cousin Tom," and we all started out toward the hollow.

The Negroes were gone, but there were still coals in the barbecue pits. That fat man was kneeling over one, cooking something.

"What you cooking for, fellow?" Cousin Tom asked. "Don't you know this is the day everybody eats free?"

The fat man turned around and smiled at us.

"Can we see the carnival?" Susie asked.

The fat man jumped up. "Yes, *ma'am*," he said, "you sure can see the carnival," and he left his cooking and we went over to the wagon.

On the way the fat man kept talking, kind of singsong: "You folks are in luck. . . . Wouldn't be here now but for a broken wheel . . . but one man's loss is another man's gain . . . I've got the greatest attraction in the world . . . yes, sir. Behind them draperies of pure silk lies the world's greatest attraction."

"Well, what is it?" Cousin Tom asked.

The fat man stopped and looked at us and then he began shouting:

> "Stell-a, Stell-a, the One and Only Stella!
> Not flesh, not bone,
> But calkypyrate stone,
> Sweet Sixteen a Hundred Years Ago
> And Sweet Sixteen Today!"

A woman sitting on a chair in front of the wagon got up and ducked around behind it. When she came out again she had on a red satin dress, with ostrich feathers on the skirt, and a red satin hat. She walked up to us and smiled and said, "Will the ladies be seated?" and the man got some little stools down, quick, from where they were hooked on to the end of the wagon, and we all sat down, except Cousin Giles Allard, and he squatted in the grass.

The wagon had green curtains draped at each end of it. Gold birds were on the sides. The man bent down and pushed a spring or something, and one side of the wagon folded back, and there, lying on a pink satin couch, was a girl.

She had on a white satin dress. It was cut so low that you could see her bosom. Her head was propped on a satin pillow. Her eyes were shut. The lashes were long and black, with a little gold on them. Her face was dark and shone a little. But her hair was gold. It waved down on each side of her face and out over the green pillow. *The pillow had gold fringe on it! . . . lightly prest . . . in palace chambers . . . far apart. . . . The fragrant tresses are not stirred . . . that lie upon her charmèd heart. . . .*

The woman went around to the other side of the wagon. The man was still shouting:

"Stell-a, Stell-a,
The One and Only Stell-a!"

Cousin Giles Allard squeaked like a rabbit. The girl's eyes had opened. Her bosom was moving up and down.

Hilda got hold of my hand and held it tight. I could feel myself breathing. . . . But *her* breathing *is not heard . . . in palace chambers, far apart.* Her eyes were no color you could name. There was a veil over them.

The man was still shouting:

"You see her now
As she was then,
Sweet Sixteen a Hundred Years Ago,
And Sweet Sixteen Today!"

"How come her bubbies move if she's been dead so long?" Cousin Giles Allard asked.

Cousin Tom stood up, quick. "She's a pretty woman," he said, "I don't know when I've seen a prettier woman . . . lies quiet, too. . . . Well, thank you, my friend," and he gave the man two or three dollars and started off across the field.

I could tell that Susie wanted to stay and watch the girl some more, and it did look like we could, after he had paid all that money, but he was walking straight off across the field and we had to go after him. Once, before we caught up with him, he put his hand into his pocket, and I saw the bottle flash in the sun as he tilted it, but he had it back in his pocket by the time we caught up with him.

"You reckon she is sort of mummied, Cousin Tom, or is she just turned to pure rock?" Susie asked.

He didn't answer her. He was frowning. All of a sudden he opened his eyes wide, as if he had just seen something he hadn't expected to see. But there wasn't anybody around or anything to look at, except that purple weed that grows all over the field. He turned around. He hollered, the way he hollers at the hands on the place: "You come on here, Giles Allard!" and Cousin Giles came running. Once he tried to turn back, but Cousin Tom wouldn't let him go till we were halfway up to the cave. He let him slip off into the bushes then.

The sun was in all our eyes. Hilda borrowed Susie's handkerchief and wiped her face. "What made you keep Cousin Giles with us, Papa?" she asked. "I'd just as soon not have him along."

Cousin Tom sat down on a rock. The sun's fiery glare was full on his face. You could see the pulse in his temple beat. A little red vein was spreading over one of his eyeballs. He pulled the bottle out of his pocket. "I don't want him snooping around Stella," he said.

"How could he hurt her, Papa, if she's already dead?" Hilda asked.

Cousin Tom held the bottle up and moved it so that it caught the sun. "Maybe she isn't dead," he said.

Susie laughed out.

Cousin Tom winked his red eye at Susie and shook the bottle. "Maybe she isn't dead," he said again. "Maybe she's just resting."

Hilda stamped her foot on the ground. "*Papa!* I believe you've had too much to drink."

He drank all there was in the bottle and let it fall to the ground. He stood up. He put his hand out, as if he could push the sun away. "And what business is that of yours?" he asked.

"I just wondered if you were going back to the cave, where everybody is," Hilda said.

He was faced toward the cave then, but he shook his head. "No," he said, "I'm not going up to the cave," and he turned around and walked off down the hill.

We stood there a minute and watched him. "Well, anyhow, he isn't going up there where everybody is," Susie said.

"Where Mama is," Hilda said. "It just drives her crazy when he drinks."

"She better get used to it," Susie said. "All the Fayerlee men drink."

The reunion was about over when we got up to the cave. I thought I had to go back to my grandmother's—I was spending the summer there—but Hilda came and said I was to spend the night at the Fork.

"But you got to behave yourselves," Aunt Rachel said. "Big doings tonight."

We rode back in the spring wagon with her and Richard and the ice-cream freezers and what was left of the dinner. Cousin Robert D. Owen and his wife, Cousin Marie, were going to spend the night at the Fork too, and they had gone on ahead in the car with the others.

Hilda and I had long-waisted dimity dresses made just alike that summer. I had a pink sash and she had a blue one. We were so excited while we were dressing for supper that night that we couldn't get our sashes tied right. "Let's get Mama to do it," Hilda said, and we went into Cousin Eleanor's room. She was sitting at her dressing table, putting rouge on her lips. Cousin Marie was in there, too, sitting on the edge of the bed. Cousin Eleanor tied our sashes—she had to do mine twice before she got it right—and then gave me a little spank and said, "Now! You'll be the belles of the ball."

They hadn't told us to go out, so we sat down on the edge of the bed too. "Mama, where is Papa?" Hilda asked.

"I have *no* idea, darling," Cousin Eleanor said. "Tom is a law unto himself." She said that to Cousin Marie. I saw her looking at her in the mirror.

Cousin Marie had bright black eyes. She didn't need to use any rouge, her face was so pink. She had a dimple in one cheek. She said, "It's a *world* unto itself. Bob's been telling me about it ever since we were married, but I didn't believe him, till I came and saw for myself. . . . These little girls, now, how are they related?"

"In about eight different ways," Cousin Eleanor said.

Cousin Marie gave a kind of little yip. "It's just like an English novel," she said.

"They are mostly Scottish people," Cousin Eleanor said, "descended from Edward the Confessor and Philippe le Bel of France . . ."

"And the grandfather of George Washington!" Cousin Marie

said, and rolled back on the bed in her good dress and giggled. "Isn't Bob priceless? But it *is* just like a book."

"I never was a great reader," Cousin Eleanor said. "I'm an outdoor girl."

She stood up. I never will forget the dress she had on that night. It was black but thin and it had a rose-colored bow right on the hip. She sort of dusted the bow off, though there wasn't a thing on it, and looked around the room as if she never had been there before. "I was, too," she said. "I was city champion for three years."

"Well, my dear, you could have a golf course here," Cousin Marie said. "Heaven knows there's all the room in creation."

"And draw off to swing, and a mule comes along and eats your golf ball up!" Cousin Eleanor said, "No, thank you, I'm through with all that."

They went down to supper. On the stairs Cousin Marie put her arm around Cousin Eleanor's waist, and I heard her say, "Wine for dinner. We don't need it." But Cousin Eleanor kept her face straight ahead. "There's no use for us to deny ourselves just because Tom can't control himself," she said.

Cousin Tom was already at the table when we got into the dining room. He had on a clean white suit. His eyes were bloodshot, and you could still see that vein beating in his temple. He sat at the head of the table, and Cousin Eleanor and Cousin Marie sat on each side of him. Cousin Sidney Grassdale and his daughter, Molly, were there. Cousin Sidney sat next to Cousin Marie, and Molly sat next to Cousin Eleanor. They had to do it that way on account of the overseer, Mr. Turner. He sat at the foot of the table, and Hilda and I sat on each side of him.

We usually played a game when we were at the table. It was keeping something going through a whole meal, without the grown folks knowing what it was. Nobody knew we did it except Aunt Rachel, and sometimes when she was passing things she would give us a dig in the ribs, to keep us quiet.

That night we were playing Petrified Woman. With everything we said we put in something from the fat man's song; like Hilda would say, "You want some butter?" and I would come back with "No, thank you, calkypyrate bone."

Cousin Marie was asking who the lady with the white hair in the blue flowered dress was.

"That is Cousin Olivia Bradshaw," Cousin Eleanor said.

"She has a pretty daughter," Cousin Robert D. Owen said.

"*Mater pulcher, filia pulchrior*," Cousin Sidney Grassdale said.

"And they live at Summer Hill?" Cousin Marie asked.

Cousin Tom laid his fork down. "I never could stand those Summer Hill folks," he said. "Pretentious."

"But the daughter has a great deal of charm," Cousin Marie said.

"Sweet Sixteen a Hundred Years Ago," Hilda said. "Give me the salt."

"And Sweet Sixteen Today," I said. "It'll thin your blood."

Cousin Tom must have heard us. He raised his head. His bloodshot eyes stared around the table. He shut his eyes. I knew that he was trying to remember.

"I saw a woman today that had real charm," he said.

Cousin Eleanor heard his voice and turned around. She looked him straight in the face and smiled, slowly. "In what did her charm consist, Tom?"

"She was petrified," Cousin Tom said.

I looked at her and then I wished I hadn't. She had blue eyes. I always thought that they were like violets. She had a way of opening them wide whenever she looked at you.

"Some women are just petrified in spots," Cousin Tom said. "She was petrified all over."

It was like the violets were freezing, there in her eyes. We all saw it. Molly Grassdale said something, and Cousin Eleanor's lips smiled and she half bent toward her and then her head gave a little shake and she straightened up so that she faced him. She was still smiling.

"In that case, how did she exert her charm?"

I thought, "Her eyes, they will freeze him, too." But he seemed to like for her to look at him like that. He was smiling, too.

"She just lay there and looked sweet," he said. "I like a woman to look sweet. . . . Hell, they ain't got anything else to do!"

Cousin Sidney's nose was working up and down, like a squirrel I had once, named Adji-Daumo. He said, "Harry Crenfew seems to be very much in love with Lucy Bradshaw."

"*I'm* in love!" Cousin Tom shouted. "I'm in love with a petrified woman."

She was still looking at him. I never saw anything as cold as her eyes.

"What is her name, Tom?"

"Stell-a!" he shouted. "The One and Only Stell-a!" He pushed his chair back and stood up, still shouting. "I'm going down to Arthur's Cave and take her away from that fellow."

He must have got his foot tangled up in Cousin Marie's dress, for she shrieked and stood up, too, and he went down on the floor, with his wineglass in his hand. Somebody noticed us after a minute and sent us out of the room. He was still lying there when we left, his arms flung out and blood on his forehead from the broken glass. . . . I never did even see him get up off the floor.

We moved away that year and so we never went to another family reunion. And I never went to the Fork again. It burned down that fall. They said that Cousin Tom set it on fire, roaming around at night, with a lighted lamp in his hand. That was after he and Cousin Eleanor got divorced. I heard that they both got married again but I never knew who it was they married. I hardly ever think of them anymore. If I do, they are still there in that house. The mockingbird has just stopped singing. Cousin Eleanor, in her long white dress, is walking over to the window, where, on moonlight nights, we used to sit, to watch the water glint on the rocks . . . But Cousin Tom is still lying there on the floor. . . .

The Burning Eyes

I do not know how I contrived to be lonely in the midst of a large family but I know now that I was a lonely child. I look back and see myself, a child of five or six, dressed still in a pinafore, wandering for hours among the huge oak trees that dotted the lawn of our old home place, Oakleigh. The ground under my feet is barren, whitish soil with rocks outbreaking here and there—grass does not grow well under oak trees. There are no flowers on the lawn, not a shrub breaks the stark outline of the house where it rises among black trunks. I know now that this was because no woman's hand had tended Oakleigh since my mother's death and I used as a child to wonder if it was because grass and flowers would not grow in that soil. I think, however, that the gloomy appearance of the house was due not so much to the absence of flowers and shrubbery as to its peculiar architecture. The wide façade was unbroken by even a portico and the windows were shutterless. I thought of the house as having an expression, not sinister, yet curiously blank, a sort of withdrawnness from which you could not escape, walk as you would in the yard or turn suddenly to observe it from a new angle.

I used to go to the far corner of the yard and, standing on a stump, survey as much of the country as revealed itself thus to the eye. There was a broad pasture immediately in front of the house, its edges already encroached upon by old-field pines. To the right was a curving stretch of dark woodland. To the left wound away the old red road that led, I knew, to Brackets, and beyond that to Hawkwood and Grassdale. I had visited at these and various other family places in the neighborhood, knew even the savor of the houses, but I could not take these features into my landscape. For me the world as seen from my dooryard was always those woods and the pasture and the old red, winding road.

I used to steal around to the back premises whenever I could. Here the aspect was not so forbidding. The out-kitchen, a comfortable two-room building, was always full of Negroes. Fire glowed in the huge, deep-set fireplace. Nancy, our fat, motherly cook, moved about in front of it, tending her vessels. And sitting in the corner, smoking his pipe, his dog at his feet, would be Ralph, her husband. He was a giant, nearly seven feet tall and correspondingly broad. I thought of him as a sort of Cyclops: he had only one eye, which some trick of my imagination always transposed to the center of his forehead. The lids and the cornea of this eye were inflamed, so that the whole eye looked red. I asked Nancy once how Ralph lost his eye, and she said scornfully that "he poked it out on them old brambles." I don't doubt that this was so. He was a headlong hunter and would stop for nothing when his dog was on the trail. I have heard visitors ask my sisters if they were not afraid to have him around the house, and indeed his appearance must have been frightening to strangers. But to us who knew him his scarred face was pleasant and homely. As a child I liked nothing better than to sit beside him, to watch his slow, assured movements or listen to the songs he sang.

I remember one song—he used to jog me on his knee while he sang it:

> "When I was young I used to wait
> On Marster's table and pass the plate
> And pass the bottle when he war dry
> And bresh away the blue-tail fly . . ."

He had a special way of talking to me when no one else was by. It was the talk of one hunter to another, comments, mostly, on the qualities of his dog, Ming. Ralph was preeminent in that community, not only as a keen hunter of both possums and coons but as the owner of Ming. For Ming was acknowledged the best possum dog in that county. Short-legged, deep-chested, lop-eared, and a little mournful of visage, he was infallible on the trail. It was his nose, Ralph said. Ne'er a nose like it had he ever seen on dog or bitch.

I think that life, the secret life, that is compacted equally of peril and deep excitement, began for me in that cabin when I was about eight years old. It was toward the close of a day in early fall. Nancy had been busy about supper for some time and had already begun to take vessels up to the house. I was sitting, legs dangling, on the bench that was pushed back against the wall so that I might be out of her way. Ralph had been lounging in his chair, but he got up now and went to the door, Ming padding softly behind him. Dog and man both had their heads lifted at the same angle, both seemed to be sniffing the air. When Ralph turned around he made one of those cryptic utterances that had already begun to stir me.

"She'll lay," he said. "She'll lay, all right."

I knew that he meant that the scent would lie along the wind. My excited imagination began to picture Ralph and Ming moving through the woods. Then I realized that Ralph was addressing me.

"I'm gwine take you with me tonight" was what he had said.

I had never before imagined myself as accompanying them. I quivered all over with excitement, then despair swept over me. "Sis Patty won't let me go."

Ralph shook his head, slowly, gently. "I'm gwine talk to her," he said. "I'm gwine set her feet in the road."

I sat there in a daze. I had perfect confidence in Ralph. When he spoke in that deep, assured tone I did not doubt for a second that I was going. But the rapture of anticipation kept flickering. I was eight years old and already knew something of the ways of the world. White people and Negroes did not look at things the same way. Even Ralph might not be able to prevail upon my sister. I could hear her speaking, scandalized: "Off in the woods at night . . . with that Negro man . . . *Aleck!*"

Ralph was lifting his milk bucket off the hook. I slid from my bench and followed him out into the yard. He turned off in the direction of the cow pen and I walked slowly through the back yard into the house. The supper bell had evidently rung without my hearing it. The family were just sitting down to the table. I took my place. It seemed a long time before I heard a door clang in the rear and knew that Ralph had brought the milk in. My sister went out to the latticed back porch. I followed her as unobtrusively as I could. My sister, as she strained the milk from one vessel to another, was asking Ralph if he was sure he had fastened the lot gate. A cow and calf had gotten together the night before and we were short of milk as a result. Ralph told her that the gate had been fastened. He laughed.

"Them calves," he said, "hit's so light these nights they thinks it's day."

My sister agreed that we had indeed been having beautiful moonlight nights. Ralph said that the nights had been so light that he had given up trying to sleep.

"I just walks around," he said.

My sister laughed. "Admiring the scenery, Ralph?"

"I takes my dog with me," Ralph said, "I don't aim to go nowhere without old Ming." He paused and his eye lit, as if by accident, on my small figure silhouetted against the light from the kitchen door. "I been promising to take this boy out," he said. "See if us can find us a possum." His hand described a short arc in the air. The possum might have been in a tree on the lawn. "I believe I'll just take him out tonight," he said.

My sister looked doubtful. Ralph laughed again, crossed the porch, and swung me up on his shoulders. "Just run him around the lot a couple of times," he said.

I have no idea what my sister was going to say. But at that moment somebody called her from the house. As she turned to go Ralph spoke again, calmly, as if the matter was settled. "Just run him around the lot a couple of times."

She nodded and hurried into the house. "You take good care of him, Ralph."

Ralph was swinging me down to the floor. He winked his one eye at me solemnly. "I gwine take good care of him." The door had swung to behind my sister. His voice changed, became abrupt, commanding:

"Git your cap. Git your cap and come now fore she change her mind."

I grabbed my cap and we rushed down the back steps and out into the moonlit yard.

Nancy was standing in the lighted doorway of the cabin. She handed us a bottle and package of sandwiches—nigger sandwiches of fried meat and cold biscuits. Ralph stuck the sandwiches and the bottle in his pocket and, Ming at heel, we started off across the yards toward the stable lot.

He walked fast. I padded close behind him. The stable lot, a gray oblong against the black woods, was something to be got across quickly. It seemed to me that a door had opened in the house behind me. Somebody might yet call me back. I scurried around to Ralph's other side, stayed in his shadow until he had opened the gate.

We traversed the lot hurriedly, passed through another gate, and came out into an open field dotted with blackberry thickets. Ming had been trotting sedately by Ralph's side but now he gave a yelp and dove for the heart of one of these thickets. I expected Ralph to follow him, but he pursued his own course steadily across the pasture, talking to Ming meanwhile, an even flow of mild remonstrance.

"What you act like that for? . . . Why'n't you go on and tend to your business? . . . What you come out here for anyway?"

I was astonished and distressed. For months now I had been listening to tales of Ming's extraordinary feats. I had expected him to dash up to the first tree he saw and pull a possum down by the tail, and here he was, running circles around a blackberry thicket, like any rabbit dog! I slipped my hand into Ralph's.

"Ain't he doing right?" I whispered.

Ralph glanced down at me. A deep, guttural noise came from his throat. This sound, which was indescribable, was both reassurance and promise. There was in it, too, a tinge of scorn for me, who had presumed to doubt the hero. A moment later, as if recollecting that I was, after all, only a little boy, he said:

"Just warmin hisself up. . . . Dog like him, takes him long time to git warmed up."

Ming, having left one thicket and dashed around another, was coming back to us, wagging his tail. We walked along in silence for a few minutes when suddenly Ming stiffened, stopped in his tracks, then began plunging about Ralph in excited circles. Ralph looked down at him and spoke almost plaintively:

"*What* you stompin around here for?"

Ming's plungings became more frenzied. A curious, low whining came from him. Ralph's voice became bland, indulgent. He made a slight, oblique motion with his right hand.

"G'wan," he said. "G'wan, dog . . ."

Ming shot off across the field. Ralph and I followed him up over a rise and were in the woods.

The moon was high and full. It was as light as day. The trunks of the saplings might have been bathed by sun instead of moonlight, yet I was conscious suddenly of being in the woods, of blackness all about me. Ralph had stopped and was lighting his lantern. Straightening up, he stood a second, head cocked on one side.

"Thar he is," he said quietly.

For Ming's voice had rung out, bold and challenging. Ralph struck off at once in a rapid jog trot in the direction of the sound. I followed as best I could. The next few minutes—it must have been minutes, though it seemed hours—were pure agony for me. I got my right foot hung in a loop of vine first off and tried to extricate myself by a series of plunges. But I succeeded only in tearing half my stocking off. I had finally to bend down and unwind the noose. When I straightened up a long blackberry briar caught me viciously across the cheek. I threw it aside and, putting my arm up before my face, plunged doggedly on through the underbrush. Ming's baying must have been going on all this time but I did not hear it. I was conscious only of Ralph's lantern, describing its erratic arc of light. My eyes fixed upon the light, I did not see a stump that rose breast high between me and Ralph. It took me cruelly in the pit of the stomach. I went down, dazed. Gold stars whirled on a black velvet sky before my shut eyes, while far off Ming still bayed coldly, as if from another world. When I opened my eyes Ralph was bending over me with the lantern. He had heard the crash and my half-faltering cry as I went down. Without a word he swung me up on his back and we started off again.

Sitting high on his broad shoulders, I looked about me while I took the breath cautiously into my bruised body. This was better. Decidedly better. Ralph was swinging along at a rapid trot and I, perched on his back, was rushed along with him. The black trunks slipped by, one after the other, faster and faster. I had only to duck my head for low-hanging branches. There was no struggling with noosed vines, no scratches from briars. I began to feel that I was really out hunting—this effortless, easy movement was what I had pictured—and I was a little disappointed when Ralph set me down abruptly on a big oak stump.

He had put the lantern down on the ground at our feet but its glow illumined his face. I thought he looked worried. The horrid thought sprang into my mind that perhaps, after all, there were no possums left in these woods. But after the reproof I had had—I considered it a reproof—I did not dare question him. I merely sat as still as I could, drawing my breath in under my still aching ribs. Very far off Ming was still baying, but only occasionally.

Ralph sighed and scratched his head. "Mighty bright," he said. "Moon mighty bright tonight."

"What does that make?" I asked. "Ralph, what difference does that make?"

But Ralph did not answer. Ming had called again, a loud, ecstatic note that reverberated through the silent woods, the very sound, I realized suddenly, with a shiver, that I had heard on so many moonlight nights, lying sleepless in my bed.

Ralph had caught up his lantern and sprung to his feet. I think he had actually forgotten me, for he rushed ahead a few steps before he turned around and lifted me up onto his shoulders again.

We were in a little more open part of the woods now. Ralph was running, long, swift steps that carried him over the ground. As he ran he talked to Ming, a coaxing, gentle voice that I had never heard from him before.

"Come on now. . . . At's the boy. . . . At's the baby. . . ." And then, suddenly, as if addressing an unseen listener: "*Ain't* he tellin' 'em?"

We emerged from a thicket of underbrush. Ming was standing before a dogwood tree. He did not turn as we approached. His music did not increase or diminish in volume, yet I felt that he knew we were there.

Ralph, coming up, spoke one word: "*Possum!*" I found out afterwards that he knew that by Ming's stand. If it had been a coon Ming would have run round and round the tree, for coons sometimes escape by jumping from one tree to another, while a possum, once treed, tends to stay put.

Ralph set his lantern down, unfastened the hatchet he carried at his belt, and loaded his gun. Ming was now in a perfect frenzy, breaking his stand every now and then to bound convulsively as high as he could up the tree trunk. But Ralph's movements were deliberate. He still talked to himself, but coolly, as if everything were now all over.

"I ain't gwine chop him down . . . I ain't gwine shake him down . . . I gwine shoot this old possum . . . I gwine shoot him once, right in the right place . . ."

I stood there, bewildered. "Where is the possum, Ralph?" I asked. "Where is he? I want to see him."

"Ain't nothin hinderin you, is they? Walk right up. Walk right up and look at him."

I approached the tree and looked up. I was aware, first, of the blackness of the foliage. I seemed to be looking down instead of up, into deep layers, shade massed on shade. My eye found the limb, followed it to the gleam of the white belly. Then I saw the eyes, round, golden. They regarded me steadily, or rather they regarded nothing. They glowed, and it was as if there was nothing in the world but whirling blackness and, set in it, those immense, those golden orbs.

A long time they glowed. The gold became fire, whirled with the blackness. Blackness was splintered suddenly by gold. I think I put my hand up to shield my eyes. Ralph, coming up from behind, jerked me aside. The gun barrel was a moving shaft of light. It came up slowly, advanced, clove the massed shade. There was a sound. A coarsely furred gray ball dropped onto the dead leaves at our feet.

Tom Rivers

I have never been able to understand it though I think about it a great deal, less and less, of course, as the years go by and his name is not often mentioned. Still, in a large family connection such as ours every member, no matter how remotely related or how unimportant, has his place and a sort of record in memory. Even now when the kin who live at a distance come visiting as they still do in the summer, come to this old place and sit with me under the same sugar tree we sat under when I was a boy, we get to talking of other days and of people we knew when we were young, many of them dead now or gone to places so far away that they seem dead.

The people who come oftenest to this place in the summer are my first cousin Richard Allard and his wife. Richard's wife is our third cousin, Emily Crenfew. She visited here a good deal when she was a girl and even stayed here one whole year when Professor Maury had his school in the office. So we are able to recall the old times together. They stay usually two days and a night, but there is a subtler cycle by which the visit might be measured.

We sit here under the trees all afternoon and talk about people we used to know: Cousin Owen, who walked from house to house, carrying his teeth in a basket; Cousin Ella, who was forced to play cards all her younger days to entertain the old folks, and so bore three sons who were gamblers; Cousin Henry Hord, who was deafened by cannonading in the Civil War and lost all his property by ill-advised investments and had to live with any of the kin who would put up with him.

We talk about cousins like these for a while, but we go on finally to people we knew more intimately, people whose characters have left us, even after all these years, something to wonder about. We speculate on how and when Robert Allard began taking morphine, and what induced Maggie McLean to turn Jim Crenfew down for a nincompoop like Edward Brewer. Somebody has seen the notice of Maggie's death in a New Orleans paper. We think of it, but we cannot take it in. We see her as she was when she first came to Merry Point to visit, a frail, high-spirited girl, who made us all indignant with her outrageous treatment of Jim Crenfew. We talk on like that until we have called to mind almost all the people who ever came here in the old days. We hold them in our minds until they seem to live again. I look up through the branches of the sugar tree to where a light burns dimly in one of the upstairs rooms. Girls might be dressing there for a party. At any moment, I may hear the rumbling, explosive laugh of Jim Crenfew.

At such a time, none of us three will stop talking. We keep up the illusion, with a name here, a name there. Seeking to make the scene more complete, we cast about on the fringes of our enormous family connection. What ever became of this cousin, or how was that person connected? It is then that Tom Rivers's name will be mentioned. Infrequently, I say. One or two summers will go by, and I may not hear his name. And then it will be spoken, and I have always that start, half pleasure, half pride, and I realize that no matter whether I hear his name or not he is never out of my memory.

There is a curious thing I have observed. If you sit day after day, summer after summer, in a chair under the same tree, you will notice how the light falls under and through the boughs to strike always in the same pattern. You notice how it falls that way year after year, changing only with the seasons, and you think how you might go away and suffer death or torture by fire or flood, and the light always at the same hour in that season will be creeping around the bole of that beech tree.

It is like that with me when I think about Tom Rivers. I cannot understand how it was that he disappeared, leaving nowhere any trace of his going. I sit here in the late afternoon, and the long lances of shadow start from the garden fence and move slowly on, past the big sugar tree and past the beech tree, to halt for a moment at the little sugar tree that stands not fifty yards from my chair.

When they have moved past, I see that the hunched, dark shadow that seemed to me a rooster standing with his back to the western light is really only a clump of dog fennel. I see it happen like that almost every afternoon, and with it comes always a fresh wonder at the restless, hurried movements of human beings. The light can fall like that evening after evening on some tree or flower, and yet a man that one has known intimately can vanish, as we always say of Tom Rivers, off the face of the earth.

Emily told me something the other night that I never knew before. She said that Tom Rivers came to this place once as a boy. The summer I was in St. Louis, old Cousin Trump drove over from Paducah with the two boys, Tom and Horace. Emily says Tom was her first sweetheart. Old Cousin Trump picked out a little cousin for each of the boys, Emily for Tom, who was then ten years old, and Emily's sister, Lida, for twelve-year-old Horace.

"I had Tom's picture somewhere for a long time," Emily says. "Cousin Trump made him give it to me." She leans back in the lounge chair that is placed between our two chairs. Her white skirt is dappled with the feathery shadow of the cinnamon vine that grows on the garden fence. I watch the minute, interlacing shadows waver across her lap, and tell myself that Tom Rivers has set foot on this ground, has walked about out there under the trees.

"He was ashamed of the picture," Emily says, "because he was so young when it was taken. He couldn't have been more than seven. And he wore his hair roached on top of his head. Horace was better-looking."

I smile, seeing an infantile Tom with roached hair. In kilts probably, as the fashion was in those days. The breeze from the garden lifts the clumps of cinnamon vine so that they sway forward on their gnarled stems. The shadows fall across Emily's skirt, as thick as the trunks of small trees. I see our tent with the thin trunks of the little locust trees striking across it, and hear Tom's voice ringing out in "Way Up on Clinch Mountain." Or that other song he sang so much:

> "Hurry up, pretty little gal,
> Hurry up, Liza Jane,
> Hurry up, poor little gal,
> SHE died on the train."

I first saw Tom Rivers when I was eighteen years old—the spring I landed in Cisco. I came there from Fort Worth, where I had been spending the winter with an uncle. I went West in the first place because I wanted to see life, see life and ride horses. The folks thought it was all right because I was going to visit some of the kin. They were stronger on kinship in those days than they are now. If you had kin in a place, you went there and stayed as long as you wanted to. I liked my cousins all right, but I didn't much like the way they lived. Uncle Robert was a town man—in that little place he was already taking on the airs of a banker, wearing a boiled shirt every day and going without boots even when the mud was ankle deep at the crossings. And he didn't much like for me to hang around the livery stable.

After he spoke to me about that several times, I got restless. I told him I thought I would go on to Cisco and stay a while. He thought that was all right, said we had a cousin there I could stay with. Rivers his name was, Tom Rivers. I didn't much like the idea of getting tied up with more cousins. Still I thought he was a young fellow and probably wouldn't pay much attention to me. And anything was better than Uncle Robert.

I landed at Cisco at three o'clock in the afternoon. As I got off the train, I didn't know at first which way to turn. There didn't seem to be anything to go to. Then I saw, off under some chinaberry trees, the little cluster of buildings that were Cisco's main street, half a dozen frame houses and, a stone's throw away from them, a larger building that might have been a barn or a stable. I picked my valise up and stepped into the yellow shack of a depot.

There was a stove in there, I remember, and a table and some chairs and, behind a barred window, the telegraph apparatus. The three men lounging in the split-bottomed chairs eyed me incuriously. I picked the operator out by his pasty face, but it was to one of the other men I spoke: "You know a man here named Tom Rivers?"

Nobody said anything for a moment. The man I addressed had sweeping blond mustaches, almost white they were against his brick-red face. While I was looking at him they moved twice, convulsively. Abrupt, nervous laughter had broken from one of the other men before he spoke, straightening himself up in his chair as if by the movement he could delay speech. "Yeah," he said, "I know him."

The man who had not laughed spoke quickly. "He works at Burnham's livery stable. Probably up there now."

I explained that I was a cousin of Rivers, from Kentucky, and that I wanted a job, riding or driving or most anything else. "Well, Rivers can get you a job," they said.

They took me to the door and pointed out the livery stable. "If Rivers ain't there," they said, "ask for Riggin, Billy Riggin. He'll know where to find him."

The runway of the stable was dark and cool after the glare. I stepped inside, into the familiar odors of horseflesh and sweat and grain. There was nobody in sight except a man who stood with his back to me, fooling with some whips that were stuck in a rack on the wall. I set my valise down and mopped my face. The man at the rack had turned around and was coming toward me. I saw his eyes, sparkling gray under light brows, and I knew he was the man I was looking for.

He was not tall, but he was broad-shouldered. You knew that the legs under his faded jeans pants were muscular, but they were a bit bowed, from much riding. I thought of Tom Faggus. I cannot at this date recall exactly how that celebrated highwayman looked, yet I can see him always walking on his bandy legs across that lawn toward the waiting boy. And in the distance the strawberry mare, Winnie. So when I think of Tom Rivers a horse is always waiting somewhere for him, Hoxie, the pinto, or the beautiful gray mare that he called Barbara. He will be swinging off his horse, and as his body makes an arc in the air I notice that the shoulders are disproportionately broad and that his legs are regrettably bowed. But the first thing I noticed about him was his eyes, a sparkling gray, set under brows that were so fair they looked white.

In those days in the West, you shook hands with a stranger when you greeted him. He saw that I was waiting to speak to him, and he had already put out his hand before I spoke.

I think I was stammering, and I called him "Cousin" before I thought. "Cousin Tom," I said, "I'm Lew Allard. Ben Allard's son."

He was smiling. "Cousin Ben at Merry Point," he said, and I realized he knew that in my father's generation there was another Ben Allard, in Louisville.

He took me over to the boardinghouse where he lived. The next day he got me a job, driving for Ed Burnham, who owned the livery stable. My job was to take the drummers out on the trips they made

from town to town. For these trips we used what we called a hack
—a light spring wagon it was, really, with an oilcloth top fastened
over hoops. These trips sometimes took as much as six weeks. The
first one I made was only a day's trip, however, out to a ranch about
thirty miles from Cisco. It was good and dark when I got back to
the livery stable that night. Tom was still there. He had finished his
work and was feeding his own horse, Hoxie.

He came and sat on a box in the runway while I fed my team.
Then we went over to his boardinghouse. The table was cleared,
but Mrs. Riggin's oldest daughter had kept a plate for me in the
warmer. I thought she was a little smitten with Tom, but he didn't
seem to pay much attention to her except to tease her about some
cowboy that he pretended she was in love with. I found out afterwards that he had a little Mexican girl in one of the houses across
the tracks.

After I had eaten supper, we walked down the street to one of the
two saloons. There were a lot of loungers around the bar, and in
the back room a big poker game was going on. I remember that I
felt a little proud to be accepted as an equal by Tom, who must
have been twenty-two or -three to my eighteen. We sat down a few
feet away from the poker game. I noticed that every man looked up
from his cards long enough to give Tom some sort of greeting. I
thought, innocently, that it was because he had lived in that part of
Texas long enough to know everybody. But I have seen that same
thing happen in towns where he was comparatively a stranger. I
have seen him walk into a saloon or gambling place, and every man
in the room would give some sort of recognition of his presence. It
might be no more than a glance or a quick batting of an eye-
lash, but there was always some sign that they knew he was there.

In the old West a man's appearance—and I mean by that the
impression he made on a stranger—counted for a great deal. Men
moved about, from ranch to ranch, town to town. Contacts were
casual and quickly established. When you hit a new place, people
were likely to take you at your valuation of yourself—if you were
able to back up that valuation. You knew when you first laid eyes
on Tom Rivers that there was some quality about him that set him
apart from other men. He was fearless—utterly fearless. Not many
men are.

It was evident in Tom's walk, a quick, impatient stride. He seemed
always to have just got off a horse, not to have time, really, for

walking. It was apparent to me also in his eyes. They were a changeable gray, mobile and so full of light that the eye at times looked liquid. I have never seen such eyes except in one other human being, an old lady back in Kentucky, Cousin Lucy Llewellyn. Crenfew eyes they are, really, not Llewellyn or Rivers.

I recognized this particular kind of fearlessness in Tom Rivers from the first. After I had been in Cisco a while, I realized that it was generally acknowledged. Tom was not quarrelsome. I think a kind of moral compunction would have prevented him from entering a quarrel too easily. It was as if he knew that his fearlessness gave him an advantage over other men. When he did go into action, he had a peculiar short, excited laugh. There was something exultant in it, as if he had been waiting for this very thing, and virtue had at last been rewarded. I don't believe any man who ever heard that laugh could forget it. The man whom I had accosted at the depot that first day had to hear it before he realized what sort of fellow Tom was. He had gone at Tom with a pitchfork. Tom had lifted him up and had thrown him over a watering trough. I saw the man frequently after that, in Tom's company, and I never noticed any sign of enmity between them, but I knew that my question and his slow answer were repeated hilariously for weeks all over town.

There were not more than five hundred people in Cisco then. There were very few girls to go to see as you went to see girls in Kentucky, but there were two fancy houses in town, Chita's and the place across the tracks run by a woman named Annie. If the boys who worked at the livery stable didn't go to Chita's or Annie's, they went to one of the two saloons, Maudrey's or the one we called simply the "other place" because it changed hands so often.

There were some pretty stiff games in the back room there at Maudrey's. A lot of professionals drifted in and out of Cisco that winter, not sharpers, exactly, but men who came to town, rented a room, slept all day, and came out at night only to play poker. Years afterwards I learned the way they worked. They would go to the various drugstores, buy up every pack of cards in town and spend a day marking them. Then they would take the cards back to the druggist, pretending that they had found some imperfection in them. The druggist would examine them and, failing to find the imperfection, would protest. There would be high words. It would end with the gamblers' throwing all the packs of cards on the counter and stalking out of the place. Nine times out of ten the druggist would put the cards back in his stock, from which they would get into circulation in the town.

I remember one of these men, Coogan his name was. A big man who wore a full beard—something unusual even in those days—flowing down to the middle of his chest. I think Coogan relied somewhat upon his formidable appearance. He was undoubtedly a bully. Shortly after Coogan's arrival, another stranger came, a little sallow man named Jackson. There was at first nothing apparent to connect these two men. Yet the conviction grew that they were working together. It was noticed that they sat whenever it was possible with a third man between them, a position favorable, to say the least, for working the old razzle-dazzle play. Nobody had ever got anything on either Coogan or Jackson, but there was a tenseness in the air. They said that Coogan had given himself a week to take all the money out of town. It looked as if he might finish the job sooner than that. There was a crowd hanging around the game till all hours every night.

I used to drift in sometimes in the evenings. I liked to watch Coogan work. There was a histrionic quality in everything he did. Unlike most of the other men, he drank only beer while he was playing. The barkeep did not wait on him fast enough. He hired a boy to rush him a glass of beer whenever he raised his great bellowing voice. The call came always suddenly, the boy would rush to the bar and then back to Coogan, who would be sitting meanwhile drumming on the table with his great fists. When the beer came he would drink it off almost at one draught, wipe his mouth on the back of his hairy hand, then settle back to his play. The glass would have been swept off the table into some corner, whence the boy would have to retrieve it.

I never have known what prompted Coogan to pick on Tom. It may have been that he recognized in Tom a man out of the ordinary, and, flushed with his own success, wanted to go up against him. It may have been merely the showman's instinct which he possessed in great degree, or it may have been merely the exigencies of his profession. The number of men in town who would play poker with him was dwindling, but the crowd still hung around, and as long as they were there they expected action. He was playing one Thursday night with Jackson and Milt Howes and Bob Burnham and a man from Dallas whose name I didn't know. Milt had had a little run of luck earlier in the evening, but he had been losing steadily for over an hour. There were two dollars' worth of chips in front of him when he filled a diamond flush. He bet a dollar on it. Burnham and the other two stayed out. Coogan called him and raised him another dollar. Milt called him. Coogan laid down a full house. Milt pushed his chair back—he had already paid for his chips during his brief run of luck and stood up to go.

That left only four men playing. Coogan looked up at Tom, who was standing on the edge of the crowd.

"Want to take a hand?" he asked.

Tom answered with a half jerk of the head. The gesture signified negation. But it was not completed. A certain contempt was apparent in it, as if Tom did not think the gambler was worth wasting words on.

Coogan leaned back slowly in his chair. I remember noticing then, as if for the first time, the man's bulk. He had his fists resting on the table. Under his wet shirt sleeves the muscles of his upper arm stood out suddenly.

Jackson laid his cards down and, slipping out of his chair, took two steps to the right. In that instant nobody doubted that he was Coogan's partner and that they had known each other a long time. There must have been a falling back of the crowd. Morgan, the pop-eyed harness man, was in the forefront. As I watched he, too, stepped back. The two men were left facing each other. I was aware that Tom was a short man and a bit bandy-legged.

Coogan spoke: "How long'd it take you to say, 'Yas, sir'?"

Morgan's pop eyes that had been on Coogan's face were shifting slowly to Tom's. I saw with excitement that Tom's eyes were glittering. They looked as if they might spill over and run down his face. He gave his short laugh. "It'd take me till hell froze over," he said.

Coogan was on his feet. The barrel of his forty-four was a gleam of blinding, intolerable light. I have always regretted that I did not look at Coogan's face then. But I could not take my eyes off the barrel of that revolver. I saw the gleam vanish as Tom's fingers closed over the barrel. I saw him take the gun away from Coogan and return it to him butt first. There was a ludicrous precision about the movement, a finickiness as of a lady being careful to hand a spoon to a guest, handle first. Somewhere in the crowd a man snorted.

I don't think I realized properly what had happened until I saw the crowd surging before me toward the bar. Coogan walked first and a few paces behind him Tom. As I watched, Tom lifted his foot and prodded Coogan gently in the behind.

"Go on," he said. "Set 'em up."

I remember I drank whiskey with the rest. I didn't want it. I could hardly get it down, but something told me I might never have another drink bought for me under such circumstances.

Years afterwards, a man who was there told me something that I never noticed at the time. He said that Coogan kept holding the gun in his hand all the time he was at the bar, that it was only after the drink had been ordered that he laid it down, limply, in a clutter of bottles and glasses.

I was ordinarily a quiet boy, with a knack for attending to my own business, but I must have got a little drunk on Tom's prowess. I know I walked after that with a sort of swagger, and I caught myself once in the saloon jostling a man whom there was no need to jostle, merely from a feeling that I, the hero's friend, couldn't be bothered to look where I was going. It was this mood that led me to boasting.

The White Caps—they were like our own Kentucky Night Riders —were active in that part of Texas then. Off toward the Staked Plain a man named Rainey had failed to make his payments on a ranch he had bought, and the Eastern company that had sold it to him were trying to get their money through government aid, taxing his cotton so much a hundred. The White Caps were determined that this tax should not be collected. Two or three outfits had gone out from Cisco, but nobody had succeeded in picking that cotton. There was a good deal of talk about it all over town.

In my new vainglorious mood I made a foolish boast about it before I thought. "If I undertook to pick cotton I bet I'd do it." I said this in a noisy group of men in the back room at Maudrey's. It was not until I had spoken that I noticed Reynolds, the government agent, having a lonely drink at the bar.

I was glad that nobody seemed to have heard me, for I knew, when I stopped to think about it, that I wouldn't have any more chance to pick that cotton than those other fellows had had. Still, I worried about it a little all that day, and I lay awake that night thinking about it. But I had forgotten all about it by morning. When I got to the livery stable, the government agent was waiting for me. He motioned toward the wagon and the team, Jerry and Tom, that stood waiting under a chinaberry tree. There was nobody else about.

"There's your outfit," Reynolds said, and when I didn't say anything for a minute, "You're the man that was going to pick cotton, aren't you?"

"Sure," I said, and walked over to the wagon. It was then that I saw Tom Rivers coming toward me from the stable. He had a holster strapped on him, and he was carrying a pistol in his hand. I knew that it was my own forty-one that I kept in the safe at the office.

He nodded to the agent and climbed up on the driver's seat beside me. Jerry and Tom broke into their swinging trot as I lifted the reins, and we turned out of town into the road that led to Rainey's ranch.

"What made you decide to go?" I asked Tom when we were out of sight of the stable. He grinned.

"Aw," he said, "that Reynolds always did make me tired."

We got to Rainey's place while it was still light—a frame house and two or three outbuildings set in the shade of some chinaberry trees. At first we thought there wasn't anybody there, everything was so quiet. Then we saw Rainey sitting under a tree mending a piece of harness. He started talking before we got to him.

Six of them had been to see him that morning. They said they didn't mean him no harm, but warn't no cotton going off that place, and they were going to watch it. It warn't nothing to him. Taxes would take all his crop anyhow. But his wife wanted to come home. She'd been staying at Clint Evans's now for over two weeks. Said she warn't going to stay on *no* place where there was shooting going on all the time. Looked to him like that government agent would quit sending 'em out here. It warn't nothing to him. Cotton could rot in the boll. Only he was tired of all this going on. His wife said might as well give the government the land and have it over with.

Tom stood there looking at him. "You got any kin in Todd County," he asked, "name of Bye?"

Rainey laid his hame string across his knee and stared. "Now how'd you know my mammy was a Bye?" he asked.

Tom laughed with his head cocked to one side. "I believe I could tell a Bye if I met him in the middle of the desert," he said.

Rainey stood up. "You better take out before it gits dark," he said. "Come on and I'll show you where to water them hosses."

He brought a bucket of water over to the wagon for us, and he stood there while we took the horses out. Then he and Tom led the horses off to the watering trough.

I started getting the stuff out of the wagon. Rainey had planted a double row of locusts on one side of the house for a windbreak. I set the cook tent up in this little alley between the trees. It's funny when you're looking for a place to put up a tent. It makes as much difference as where you built a house. I knew as soon as I saw the place that this was where we'd pitch our tent and not change it. When you live in a country like that you get to thinking about trees. I used to dream of them at night, rows and rows of trees—in the Penhally woods, mostly, where I used to go to shoot squirrels.

I pegged the tent down well—there was just room for it between the trunks of the trees. Then I got the oven out and set it up on a couple of bricks, a skillet it was, really, with an iron, closely fitted top. You heaped your coals around it and all over the top so that the heat was uniform. I've seen niggers at home cooking on the same kind of stove. You can make mighty good biscuits on it and that's a fact.

Rainey and Tom were still standing by the watering trough. The horses had quit drinking, but they would keep putting their heads down in the trough and then bring them up with the water drooling out of their mouths. Tom Rivers was standing with one arm laid across Jerry. Every now and then he would tap the horse on the shoulder or run his hand down over his back. Rainey had dropped down on a block of wood and was fooling with his hame string again, stopping every once in a while to look up at Tom. Their bodies and the bodies of the horses looked black in the clear light. I knew that in a few minutes it would be pitch dark.

I slipped over to the wood pile and got a turn of wood. Then I hunted around and found enough chips and little stuff to start the fire. It crackled right up, a good-sized flame that looked pale in the light.

I sliced the middling and had it in the pan all ready to fry before I started making my biscuits. I had the name of making good biscuits. One of the first things I learned to do in that country was to mix them in the sack. You mixed your baking powder and salt and shortening, all your dry stuff, into the flour, then you poured the water in.

I put the biscuits in the oven and heaped the coals up around them.

It was getting dark now. The flames that you could hardly see a minute ago showed up bright and would show up, you knew, for miles around. Dark falls like that in Texas. One minute you will be moving in the clear light of day, and the next it will be black dark. I heard Tom coming with the horses before I could see him. He turned them out, then came over to the fire.

"I been fooling around all this time talking to that man," he said, "and here you got supper all cooked."

"We've got molasses," I told him. "We can have hoecakes for breakfast."

He sat down with his back against a tree. "This fellow here has got plenty of chickens," he said, "but I haven't got the heart to take 'em. A feller as down in the mouth as he is, it'd be a shame to steal his chickens."

I had been frying the middling in a skillet on top of the oven. I took the skillet off now, and we got the biscuits out. They were fairly light and just brown enough. We made sandwiches out of the fried meat, and then sopped up some of the grease from the bottom of the skillet. I complained that the middling was a little rancid.

"Not any meat out here cured right," Tom said reasonably. "They ain't got the climate." He added, musing, "If I'd a known how much fat meat I was going to have to eat out here I'd a stayed at home and been poor white folks. I believe in my soul I would."

I cleaned the plates with a piece of bread and then poured them full of molasses. We sopped it up with the last of the hot biscuits. "Molasses sure takes the taste of that sowbelly out of your mouth," Tom said.

He blew on the cup of coffee that I handed him and leaned back against the tree trunk. "It's funny now about poor white folks," he said. "You reckon they look more like each other than other folks? Now that fellow Rainey, or whatever his name is. I'd a known him for a Bye if you waked me up in the middle of the night. And it turns out that he's a nephew to old man Bye used to live on our place. Seven of 'em there was, and not one of 'em worth a damn."

"This feller he isn't worth a damn either?" I asked.

"Naw," Tom said. "He might just as well stayed in Kentucky."

"Well, maybe he likes it better out here anyhow," I said. "He's not poor white folks out here."

Tom shook his head. "They don't mind it," he said. "That's what they always been. Now take you. You think you'd hate to be a woman, but if you were a woman you wouldn't think anything of it. Or a nigger. Now, a nigger wouldn't want to change with white folks—I mean a nigger that had any sense—because the way he is he don't have to make any effort. He knows somebody's going to take care of him."

I scoured the plates and skillet with sand and put them away and dragged the oven out of the coals. The fire was down, but Tom found an old log and dragged it up and laid it across the embers. I looked in the pot and found that there was another cup of coffee apiece. We drank them, leaning back on our elbows. When Tom had finished his coffee, he rolled over on his back and sang, letting his voice ring out as loud as it could:

> "I'll brew my own whiskey,
> I'll make my own stew,
> If I get drunk, madam,
> It's nothing to you."

He told me about his girl, Barbara, in Kentucky. She had turned him down because of his drinking. He had appeared drunk at a Sunday-school picnic and shot the hat off of old Mister Billy Pettigrew's head. There had been a lot of to-do about it, of course. She had wanted him to promise her never to touch another drop. "I can't do that," Tom said. "Now, you know I can't do that. I know I made a fool of myself before all those folks, and I hope I won't do it again, but as for saying I won't ever touch another drop—"

They had argued about it all one afternoon, behind drawn blinds in the parlor at the Staytons', the old folks sitting on the porch waiting to hear the outcome. The next day Tom had started for Texas. "Her mother was tickled to death. She said all along she didn't want her daughter to marry a Rivers."

We fell to talking of horses and dogs. Tom told me about a little setter bitch he'd had once. "The smallest dog I ever saw and the smartest. It was a pleasure now just to see that dog work. She'd take a field—"

I told him of old Trecho, a pointer who had remarkable powers. Tom was amazed and pleased to hear the story. "It's bad about a dog," he added. "You get attached to 'em, and you think you couldn't get along without that dog, and all the time you know they've got to die, in ten, maybe fifteen years. And if they live to be old, it's bad after their teeth fall out, and they can't chew their food. A bird dog hates it after he gets so he can't get around."

We had spread the wagon sheet on the ground and were lying back against our rolled-up blankets. The end of the log burned slowly and shot into flames. Tom went on talking—about an old Negro man named Pomp, Uncle Pomp Rivers. They called Tom Pomp when he was little because he was always going around with old Uncle Pomp.

"We used to have some good times," Tom said, "me and that old nigger. Knew how to make the best rabbit traps of anybody around there. Knew how to do most everything."

I lay listening, my head cradled in my arms. My mind raced ahead of his slow words to make bright pictures of familiar scenes: the white, plastered wall of Oak Chapel, and against it a girl's head, gold in the morning sun—her eyes had searched mine before they moved on to rest upon George Crenfew sitting beside me—they had moved on then, but now they stopped on mine; the Blue Hole on West Fork, and the sycamore tree that sprawled its shadow over the entrance to the Guthrie Fair Grounds. I had been standing under it when the man gave me the quick look, then came over and asked me to ride his horse. "I don't want to ride." I had said it stubbornly to George Crenfew and the Johnson boy standing there with me, but now I saw myself mounting the horse and felt under me his long, quick stride. . . .

"Lived to be ninety years old," Tom said, "and went fishing every day of his life. Only nigger I ever knew fished with flies—"

His voice dropped suddenly. "Hear anything?" he asked.

I sat up and looked about me. The sky that had been black was gray now and faintly peppered with stars. The sound came again—the far-off galloping of horses' hooves. I heard a man call out and another man answering him. I remember my start of surprise. It was as if I had not realized before that the horses had riders, or that there could be anybody but us under this starry sky. Here in this alley there were leaves all about, not like Texas. Once at Merry Point we had played Prisoner's Base at night, in the lower yard, where there were Japanese quince bushes. It was exciting, different from the day. You stood there quiet until the one who was making the dare was upon you. Or he would take you for a shadow sometimes and run into you.

Tom got up and stamped out the embers, then came back and sat down again. He spoke easily, confidentially, "Those fellows'll do a lot of talking before they start anything."

I moved toward him. I whispered eagerly, "Let 'em get right up on us."

He nodded. "That's it," he said, "right up on us."

I sat down beside him. Our shoulders were touching. I could hear him breathe. He had slipped his pistol out of his holster and held it resting lightly on his bent knee. I clenched my fingers on the butt of my own gun. Tom was humming under his breath:

> "Hurry up, Liza,
> Hurry up, Liza Jane—"

We could see the massed, moving outline of the riders now, could hear the jerk and creak of saddle leather as they pulled their horses up not a hundred yards from where we sat.

A man rode out a little way from the group. "That Bill Andrews?" he asked, calling the name of one of the men who had come out earlier in the season to try to pick the cotton.

Tom got to his feet. "Andrews is over in the wagon asleep," he said. "Want me to wake him up?"

"Joe Flynn?"

"He's here too," Tom said.

The leader wheeled his horse back into the crowd. "Well, now, boys," he said, "we don't know who you are, and we don't want to make you any trouble, but you can't pick this cotton, and that's a fact. Better start to town right now."

I had got to my feet and was standing shoulder to shoulder with Tom. He whispered: "Count three before we start, and when we start keep shooting."

We ran headlong through the dark toward the waiting horsemen. My eyes were fixed on the white peaked cap of the man on the edge of the crowd. When I stumbled once and went down, I was afraid for a moment that he would get away. I was not ten feet away from him when he broke and ran. His horse's hooves spattered my face with moist earth. I stopped short and looked about me. There were only three left and they, too, were running.

It was absurdly like starting a covey of birds, the whiteness and the flight and the pounding of hooves as sudden as the whir of a partridge's wing. We stood and watched them disappear into the dark. Tom broke out into a great laugh. I laughed, too. Our laughter rang out over the plain. It was as if we were still pursuing the flying horsemen, until the last hoofbeat had died away.

Tom turned to me then. "I know those fellows!" he said.

The next morning we walked over to the spot where they had halted, and guessed at the number of men by the hoofprints. Twenty or thirty in the crowd, we thought. In one place, the earth was spotted lightly with blood. Dried now and dusted with sand. We walked round and round studying the flecks.

"He couldn't a been hurt much," Tom said.

I agreed. "Now, he couldn't a been hurt much or he wouldn't a traveled away from here so fast."

We stayed out there two weeks. The morning after the shooting I stayed in camp, and Tom got on his horse and rode over to the nearest neighbor's. A man named Jeffreys. He had eleven children under sixteen. That afternoon ten of them came over to pick cotton. They picked cotton for us all the rest of the time we were there.

We got back to town one Saturday afternoon. We washed up, and had an early supper and started downtown. It was an afternoon in late November, rather mild. Yellow leaves were spattering down onto the trampled earth in front of the livery stable. I remember thinking that at home the trees must have been bare for a long time. Tom and I were standing around in front of the stables watching a game of horseshoes when a man named Savell rode up. He lingered on the outskirts of the group a moment. Then he came up to Tom and asked if he could borrow his gun a few minutes. Tom looked at him curiously. "What you want with my gun?" he asked.

The man laughed. "They's a fellow down the road here I want to shoot," he said.

"It's more likely to be a cat," Tom said.

The man did not answer. Tom slipped his gun out of its holster and handed it to him. I remember we stood there and watched him ride off toward town before we turned back into the livery stable office. We were sitting there playing seven-up when the sheriff came. A fat man named Faris. He was wheezing, and the rims showed all around his pale blue eyes. He stood there looking at us. We went on putting our cards down as if we didn't know he was there.

"Now look here, Rivers," he said, "why'n't you leave town?"

Tom took my queen before he looked up. "What I want to leave town for?" he asked.

The sheriff took a step down into the room. "That fellow you shot has got a bad arm," he said, "and they're all saying I ought to do something." His voice rose petulantly. "Why'n't you leave town? You know I got to arrest you if you keep on hanging around."

Tom stood up. The cracker barrel that had been between our knees rolled over, the cards flying off onto the floor. "You going to arrest me?" Tom said.

The sheriff was stepping backwards out of the office. "I deputize Lew Allard and Billy Riggin to arrest you," he said, and was gone, walking with his short, uneven steps around the corner of the livery stable.

Tom stood there. He was whistling, then he broke the sound off short between his teeth. "Aw, hell!" he said, and turned and walked back into the stable. For a few minutes we heard him moving about in one of the stalls, heard him speak once to his mare Barbara. There was the creak of a girth being cinched, and then he was gone, out the back way of the stable, which gave on to another road.

I never saw him again.

Old Red

When the door had closed behind his daughter, Mr. Maury went
to the window and stood a few moments looking out. The roses that
had grown in a riot all along that side of the fence had died or been
cleared away, but the sun lay across the garden in the same level
lances of light that he remembered. He turned back into the room.
The shadows had gathered until it was nearly all in gloom. The top
of his minnow bucket just emerging from his duffel bag glinted in
the last rays of the sun. He stood looking down at his traps all
gathered neatly in a heap at the foot of the bed. He would leave
them like that. Even if they came in here sweeping and cleaning up
—it was only in hotels that a man was master of his own room—
even if they came in here cleaning up he would tell them to leave all
his things exactly as they were. It was reassuring to see them all
there together, ready to be taken up in the hand, to be carried down
and put into a car, to be driven off to some railroad station at a
moment's notice.

As he moved toward the door he spoke aloud, a habit that was
growing on him:

"Anyhow I won't stay but a week. . . . I ain't going to stay but
a week, no matter what they say. . . ."

Downstairs in the dining room they were already gathered at the
supper table: his white-haired, shrunken mother-in-law; his tall
sister-in-law who had the proud carriage of the head, the aquiline

nose, but not the spirit of his dead wife; his lean, blond, new son-in-law; his black eyed daughter who, but that she was thin, looked so much like him, all of them gathered there waiting for him, Alexander Maury. It occurred to him that this was the first time he had sat down in the bosom of the family for some years. They were always writing saying that he must make a visit this summer or certainly next summer—". . . all had a happy Christmas together, but missed you. . . ." They had even made the pretext that he ought to come up to inspect his new son-in-law. As if he hadn't always known exactly the kind of young man Sarah would marry! What was the boy's name? Stephen, yes, Stephen. He must be sure and remember that.

He sat down and, shaking out his napkin, spread it over his capacious paunch and tucked it well up under his chin in the way his wife had never allowed him to do. He let his eyes rove over the table and released a long sigh.

"Hot batter bread," he said, "and ham. Merry Point ham. I sure am glad to taste them one more time before I die."

The old lady was sending the little Negro girl scurrying back to the kitchen for a hot plate of batter bread. He pushed aside the cold plate and waited. She had bridled when he spoke of the batter bread and a faint flush had dawned on her withered cheeks. Vain she had always been as a peacock, of her housekeeping, her children, anything that belonged to her. She went on now, even at her advanced age, making her batter bread, smoking her hams according to that old recipe she was so proud of, but who came here now to this old house to eat or to praise?

He helped himself to a generous slice of batter bread, buttered it, took the first mouthful and chewed it slowly. He shook his head.

"There ain't anything like it," he said. "There ain't anything else like it in the world."

His dark eye roving over the table fell on his son-in-law. "You like batter bread?" he inquired.

Stephen nodded, smiling. Mr. Maury, still masticating slowly, regarded his face, measured the space between the eyes—his favorite test for man, horse, or dog. Yes, there was room enough for sense between the eyes. How young the boy looked! And infected already with the fatal germ, the *cacoëthes scribendi*. Well, their children—if he and Sarah ever had any children—would probably escape. It was like certain diseases of the eye, skipped every other generation.

His own father had had it badly all his life. He could see him now sitting at the head of the table spouting his own poetry—or Shakespeare's—while the children watched the preserve dish to see if it was going around. He, Aleck Maury, had been lucky to be born in the generation he had. He had escaped that at least. A few translations from Heine in his courting days, a few fragments from the Greek; but no, he had kept clear of that on the whole. . . .

His sister-in-law's eyes were fixed on him. She was smiling faintly. "You don't look much like dying, Aleck. Florida must agree with you."

The old lady spoke from the head of the table. "I can't see what you do with yourself all winter long. Doesn't time hang heavy on your hands?"

Time, he thought, *time!* They were always mouthing the word, and what did they know about it? Nothing in God's world! He saw time suddenly, a dull, leaden-colored fabric depending from the old lady's hands, from the hands of all of them, a blanket that they pulled about between them, now here, now there, trying to cover up their nakedness. Or they would cast it on the ground and creep in among the folds, finding one day a little more tightly rolled than another, but all of it everywhere the same dull gray substance. But time was a banner that whipped before him always in the wind! He stood on tiptoe to catch at the bright folds, to strain them to his bosom. They were bright and glittering. But they whipped by so fast and were whipping always ever faster. The tears came into his eyes. Where, for instance, had this year gone? He could swear he had not wasted a minute of it, for no man living, he thought, knew better how to make each day a pleasure to him. Not a minute wasted and yet here it was already May. If he lived to the biblical threescore-and-ten, which was all he ever allowed himself in his calculations, he had before him only nine more Mays. Only nine more Mays out of all eternity and they wanted him to waste one of them sitting on the front porch at Merry Point!

The butter plate which had seemed to swim before him in a glittering mist was coming solidly to rest upon the white tablecloth. He winked his eyes rapidly and, laying down his knife and fork, squared himself about in his chair to address his mother-in-law:

"Well, ma'am, you know I'm a man that always likes to be learning something. Now this year I learned how to smell out fish." He glanced around the table, holding his head high and allowing his well-cut nostrils to flutter slightly with his indrawn breaths. "Yes, sir," he said, "I'm probably the only white man in this country knows how to smell out feesh."

There was a discreet smile on the faces of the others. Sarah was laughing outright. "Did you have to learn how or did it just come to you?"

"I learned it from an old nigger woman," her father said. He shook his head reminiscently. "It's wonderful how much you can learn from niggers. But you have to know how to handle them. I was half the winter wooing that old Fanny. . . ."

He waited until their laughter had died down. "We used to start off every morning from the same little cove and we'd drift in there together at night. I noticed how she always brought in a good string, so I says to her: 'Fanny, you just lemme go 'long with you.' But she wouldn't have nothing to do with me. I saw she was going to be a hard nut to crack, but I kept right on. Finally I began giving her presents. . . ."

Laura was regarding him fixedly, a queer glint in her eyes. Seeing outrageous pictures in her mind's eye, doubtless. Poor Laura. Fifty years old if she was a day. More than half her lifetime gone and all of it spent drying up here in the old lady's shadow. She was speaking with a gasping little titter:

"What sort of presents did you give her, Aleck?"

He made his tones hearty in answer. "I give her a fine string of fish one day and I give her fifty cents. And finally I made her a present of a Barlow knife. That was when she broke down. She took me with her that morning. . . ."

"Could she really *smell* fish?" the old lady asked curiously.

"You ought to a seen her," Mr. Maury said. "She'd sail over that lake like a hound on the scent. She'd row right along and then all of a sudden she'd stop rowing." He bent over and peered into the depths of imaginary water. " 'Thar they are, White Folks, thar they are. Cain't you smell 'em?' "

Stephen was leaning forward, eyeing his father-in-law intently. "Could you?" he asked.

"I got so I could smell feesh," Mr. Maury told him. "I could smell out the feesh but I couldn't tell which kind they were. Now Fanny could row over a bed and tell just by the smell whether it was bass or bream. But she'd been at it all her life." He paused, sigh-ing. "You can't just pick these things up. . . . Who was it said, 'Genius is an infinite capacity for taking pains'?"

Sarah was rising briskly. Her eyes sought her husband's across the table. She was laughing. "Sir Izaak Walton," she said. "We'd better go in the other room. Mandy wants to clear the table."

The two older ladies remained in the dining room. Mr. Maury walked across the hall to the sitting room, accompanied by Steve and Sarah. He lowered himself cautiously into the most solid-looking of the rocking chairs that were drawn up around the fire. Steve stood on the hearthrug, his back to the fire.

Mr. Maury glanced up at him curiously. "What you thinking about, feller?" he asked.

Steve looked down. He smiled but his gaze was still contemplative. "I was thinking about the sonnet," he said, "in the form in which it first came to England."

Mr. Maury shook his head. "Wyatt and Surrey," he said. "Hey, nonny, nonny. . . . You'll have hardening of the liver long before you're my age." He looked past Steve's shoulder at the picture that hung over the mantelshelf: Cupid and Psyche holding between them a fluttering veil and running along a rocky path toward the beholder. It had been hanging there ever since he could remember; would hang there, he thought, till the house fell down or burned down, as it was more likely to do with the old lady wandering around at night carrying lighted lamps the way she did. "Old Merry Point," he said. "It don't change much, does it?"

He settled himself more solidly in his chair. His mind veered from the old house to his own wanderings in brighter places. He regarded his daughter and son-in-law affably.

"Yes, sir," he said, "this winter in Florida was valuable to me just for the acquaintances I made. Take my friend Jim Yost. Just to live in the same hotel with that man is an education." He paused, smiling reminiscently into the fire. "I'll never forget the first time I saw him. He came up to me there in the lobby of the hotel. 'Professor Maury,' he says, 'you been hearin' about me for twenty years and I been hearin' about you for twenty years. And now we've done met.'"

Sarah had sat down in the little rocking chair by the fire. She leaned toward him now, laughing. "They ought to have put down a cloth of gold for the meeting," she said.

Mr. Maury regarded her critically. It occurred to him that

she was, after all, not so much like himself as the sister whom, as a child, he had particularly disliked. A smart girl, Sarah, but too quick always on the uptake. For his own part he preferred a softer-natured woman.

He shook his head. "Nature does that in Florida," he said. "I knew right off the reel it was him. There were half a dozen men standing around. I made 'em witness. 'Jim Yost,' I says, 'Jim Yost of Maysville or I'll eat my hat.' "

"Why is he so famous?" Sarah asked.

Mr. Maury took out his knife and cut off a plug of tobacco. When he had offered a plug to his son-in-law and it had been refused, he put the tobacco back in his pocket. "He's a man of imagination," he said slowly. "There ain't many in this world."

He took a small tin box out of his pocket and set it on the little table that held the lamp. Removing the top, he tilted the box so that they could see its contents: an artificial lure, a bug with a dark body and a red, bulbous head, a hook protruding from what might be considered its vitals.

"Look at her," he said. "Ain't she a killer?"

Sarah leaned forward to look and Steve, still standing on the hearthrug, bent above them. The three heads ringed the light. Mr. Maury disregarded Sarah and addressed himself to Steve. "She takes nine strips of pork rind," he said, "nine strips cut just thick enough." He marked off the width of the strips with his two fingers on the table, then, picking up the lure and cupping it in his palm, he moved it back and forth quickly so that the painted eyes caught the light.

"Look at her," he said, "look at the wicked way she sets forward."

Sarah was poking at the lure with the tip of her finger. "Wanton," she said, "simply wanton. What does he call her?"

"This is his Devil Bug," Mr. Maury said. "He's the only man in this country makes it. I myself had the idea thirty years ago and let it slip by me the way I do with so many of my ideas." He sighed, then, elevating his tremendous bulk slightly above the table level and continuing to hold Steve with his gaze, he produced from his coat pocket the oilskin book that held his flies. He spread it open on the table and began to turn the pages. His eyes sought his son-in-law's as his hand paused before a gray, rather draggled-looking lure.

"Old Speck," he said. "I've had that fly for twenty years. I reckon she's taken five hundred pounds of fish in her day. . . ."

The fire burned lower. A fiery coal rolled from the grate and fell onto the hearthrug. Sarah scooped it up with a shovel and threw it among the ashes. In the circle of the lamplight the two men still bent over the table looking at the flies. Steve was absorbed in them, but he spoke seldom. It was her father's voice that, rising and falling, filled the room. He talked a great deal but he had a beautiful speaking voice. He was telling Steve now about Little West Fork, the first stream ever he put a fly in. "My first love," he kept calling it. It sounded rather pretty, she thought, in his mellow voice. "My first love. . . ."

II

When Mr. Maury came downstairs the next morning the dining room was empty except for his daughter, Sarah, who sat dawdling over a cup of coffee and a cigarette. Mr. Maury sat down opposite her. To the little Negro girl who presented herself at his elbow he outlined his wants briefly: "A cup of coffee and some hot batter bread, just like we had last night." He turned to his daughter. "Where's Steve?"

"He's working," she said. "He was up at eight and he's been working ever since."

Mr. Maury accepted the cup of coffee from the little girl, poured half of it into his saucer, set it aside to cool. "Ain't it wonderful," he said, "the way a man can sit down and work day after day? When I think of all the work I've done in my time . . . Can he work *every* morning?"

"He sits down at his desk every morning," she said, "but of course he gets more done some mornings than others."

Mr. Maury picked up his saucer, found the coffee cool enough for his taste. He sipped it slowly, looking out of the window. His mind was already busy with his day's program. No water—no running water—nearer than West Fork, three miles away. He couldn't drive a car and Steve was going to be busy writing all morning. There was nothing for it but a pond. The Willow Sink. It was not much, but it was better than nothing. He pushed his chair back and rose.

"Well," he said, "I'd better be starting."

When he came downstairs with his rod a few minutes later the hall was still full of the sound of measured typing. Sarah sat in the dining room in the same position in which he had left her, smoking. Mr.

Maury paused in the doorway while he slung his canvas bag over his shoulders. "How you ever going to get anything done if you don't take advantage of the morning hours?" he asked. He glanced at the door opposite as if it had been the entrance to a sick chamber. "What's he writing about?" he inquired in a whisper.

"It's an essay on John Skelton."

Mr. Maury looked out at the new green leaves framed in the doorway. "John Skelton," he said, "God Almighty!"

He went through the hall and stepped down off the porch onto the ground that was still moist with spring rains. As he crossed the lower yard he looked up into the branches of the maples. Yes, the leaves were full-grown already even on the late trees. The year, how swiftly, how steadily it advanced! He had come to the far corner of the yard. Grown up it was in pokeberry shoots and honeysuckle, but there was a place to get through. The top strand of wire had been pulled down and fastened to the others with a ragged piece of rope. He rested his weight on his good leg and swung himself over onto the game one. It gave him a good, sharp twinge when he came down on it. It was getting worse all the time, that leg, but on the other hand he was learning better all the time how to handle it. His mind flew back to a dark, startled moment, that day when the cramp first came on him. He had been sitting still in the boat all day long and that evening when he stood up to get out his leg had failed him utterly. He had pitched forward among the reeds, had lain there a second, face downward, before it came to him what had happened. With the realization came a sharp picture out of his faraway youth. Uncle James, lowering himself ponderously out of the saddle after a hard day's hunting, had fallen forward in exactly the same way, into a knot of yowling little Negroes. He had got up and cursed them all out of the lot. It had scared the old boy to death, coming down like that. The black dog he had had on his shoulder all that fall. But he himself had never lost one day's fishing on account of his leg. He had known from the start how to handle it. It meant simply that he was slowed down that much. It hadn't really made much difference in fishing. He didn't do as much wading but he got around just about as well on the whole. Hunting, of course, had had to go. You couldn't walk all day shooting birds, dragging a game leg. He had just given it up right off the reel, though it was a shame when a man was as good a shot as he was. That day he was out with Tom Kensington, last November, the only day he got out during the bird season. Nine shots he'd had and he'd bagged nine birds. Yes, it was a shame. But a man couldn't do everything. He had to limit himself. . . .

He was up over the little rise now. The field slanted straight down before him to where the pond lay, silver in the morning sun. A Negro cabin was perched halfway up the opposite slope. A woman was hanging out washing on a line stretched between two trees. From the open door little Negroes spilled down the path toward the pond. Mr. Maury surveyed the scene, spoke aloud:

"Ain't it funny now? Niggers always live in the good places."

He stopped under a wild cherry tree to light his pipe. It had been hot crossing the field, but the sunlight here was agreeably tempered by the branches. And that pond down there was fringed with willows. His eyes sought the bright disc of the water, then rose to where the smoke from the cabin chimney lay in a soft plume along the crest of the hill.

When he stooped to pick up his rod again it was with a feeling of sudden keen elation. An image had risen in his memory, an image that was familiar but came to him infrequently of late and that only in moments of elation: the wide field in front of his uncle's house in Albemarle, on one side the dark line of undergrowth that marked the Rivanna River, on the other the blue of Peters' Mountain. They would be waiting there in that broad plain when they had the first sight of the fox. On that little rise by the river, loping steadily, not yet alarmed. The sun would glint on his bright coat, on his quick turning head as he dove into the dark of the woods. There would be hullabaloo after that and shouting and riding. Sometimes there was the tailing of the fox—that time Old Whiskey was brought home on a mattress! All of that to come afterwards, but none of it ever like that first sight of the fox there on the broad plain between the river and the mountain.

There was one fox, they grew to know him in time, to call him affectionately by name. Old Red it was who showed himself always like that there on the crest of the hill. "There he goes, the damn, impudent scoundrel. . . ." Uncle James would shout and slap his thigh and yell himself hoarse at Whiskey and Mag and the pups, but they would already have settled to their work. They knew his course, every turn of it, by heart. Through the woods and then down again to the river. Their hope was always to cut him off before he could circle back to the mountain. If he got in there among those old field pines it was all up. But he always made it. Lost 'em every time and dodged through to his hole in Pinnacle Rock. A smart fox, Old Red. . . .

He descended the slope and paused in the shade of a clump of willows. The little Negroes who squatted, dabbling in the water, watched him out of round eyes as he unslung his canvas bag and laid it on a stump. He looked down at them gravely.

"D'you ever see a white man that could conjure?" he asked.

The oldest boy laid the brick he was fashioning out of mud down on a plank. He ran the tip of his tongue over his lower lip to moisten it before he spoke. "Naw, suh."

"I'm the man," Mr. Maury told him. "You chillun better quit that playin' and dig me some worms."

He drew his rod out of the case, jointed it up, and laid it down on a stump. Taking out his book of flies, he turned the pages, considering. "Silver Spinner," he said aloud. "They ought to take that . . . in May. Naw, I'll just give Old Speck a chance. It's a long time now since we had her out."

The little Negroes had risen and were stepping quietly off along the path toward the cabin, the two little boys hand in hand, the little girl following, the baby astride her hip. They were pausing now before a dilapidated building that might long ago have been a hen house. Mr. Maury shouted at them: "Look under them old boards. That's the place for worms." The biggest boy was turning around. His treble "Yassuh" quavered over the water. Then their voices died away. There was no sound except the light turning of the willow boughs in the wind.

Mr. Maury walked along the bank, rod in hand, humming: "Bangum's gone to the wild boar's den. . . . *Bangum's* gone to the wild boar's den. . . ." He stopped where a white, peeled log protruded six or seven feet into the water. The pond made a little turn here. He stepped out squarely upon the log, still humming. The line rose smoothly, soared against the blue, and curved sweetly back upon the still water. His quick ear caught the little whish that the fly made when it clove the surface, his eye followed the tiny ripples made by its flight. He cast again, leaning a little backwards as he did sometimes when the mood was on him. Again and again his line soared out over the water. His eye rested now and then on his wrist. He noted with detachment the expert play of the muscles, admired each time the accuracy of his aim. It occurred to him that it was four days now since he had wet a line. Four days. One whole day packing up, parts of two days on the train, and yesterday wasted sitting there on that front porch with the family. But the abstinence had done him good. He had never cast better than he was casting this morning.

There was a rustling along the bank, a glimpse of blue through the trees. Mr. Maury leaned forward and peered around the clump of willows. A hundred yards away Steve, hatless, in an old blue shirt and khaki pants, stood jointing up a rod.

Mr. Maury backed off his log and advanced along the path. He called out cheerfully: "Well, feller, do any good?"

Steve looked up. His face had lightened for a moment but the abstracted expression stole over it again when he spoke. "Oh, I fiddled with it all morning," he said, "but I didn't do much good."

Mr. Maury nodded sympathetically. *"Minerva invita erat,"* he said. "You can do nothing unless Minerva perches on the roof tree. Why, I been castin' here all morning and not a strike. But there's a boat tied up over on the other side. What say we get in it and just drift around?" He paused, looked at the rod Steve had finished jointing up. "I brought another rod along," he said. "You want to use it?"

Steve shook his head. "I'm used to this one," he said.

An expression of relief came over Mr. Maury's face. "That's right," he said, "a man always does better with his own rod."

The boat was only a quarter full of water. They heaved her over and dumped it out, then dragged her down to the bank. The little Negroes had come up, bringing a can of worms. Mr. Maury threw them each a nickel and set the can in the bottom of the boat. "I always like to have a few worms handy," he told Steve, "ever since I was a boy." He lowered himself ponderously into the bow and Steve pushed off and dropped down behind him.

The little Negroes still stood on the bank staring. When the boat was a little distance out on the water the boldest of them spoke: "You reckon 'at ole jawnboat going to hold you up, Cap'm?"

Mr. Maury turned his head to call over his shoulder. "Go 'way, boy. Ain't I done tole you I's a conjure?"

The boat dipped ominously. Steve changed his position a little and she settled to the water. Sitting well forward, Mr. Maury made graceful casts, now to this side, now to that. Steve, in the stern, made occasional casts but he laid his rod down every now and then to paddle though there was really no use in it. The boat drifted well enough with the wind. At the end of half an hour seven sizable bass lay on the bottom of the boat. Mr. Maury had caught five of them. He reflected that perhaps he really ought to change places with Steve. The man in the bow certainly had the best chance at the fish. "But no," he thought, "it don't make no difference. He don't hardly know where he is now."

He stole a glance over his shoulder at the young man's serious, abstracted face. It was like that of a person submerged. Steve seemed to float up to the surface every now and then, his expression would lighten, he would make some observation that showed he knew where he was, then he would sink again. If you asked him a question he answered punctiliously, two minutes later. Poor boy, dead to the world and would probably be that way the rest of his life. A pang of pity shot through Mr. Maury and on the heels of it a gust of that black fear that occasionally shook him. It was he, not Steve, that was the queer one. The world was full of people like this boy, all of them going around with their heads so full of this and that they hardly knew what they were doing. They were all like that. There was hardly anybody—there was *nobody* really in the whole world like him. . . .

Steve, coming out of his abstraction, spoke politely. He had heard that Mr. Maury was a fine shot. Did he like to fish better than hunt?

Mr. Maury reflected. "Well," he said, "they's something about a covey of birds rising up in front of you . . . they's something . . . and a good dog. Now they ain't anything in this world that I like better than a good bird dog." He stopped and sighed. "A man has got to come to himself early in life if he's going to amount to anything. Now I was smart, even as a boy. I could look around me and see all the men of my family, Uncle Jeems, Uncle Quent, my father, every one of 'em weighed two hundred by the time he was fifty. You get as heavy on your feet as all that and you can't do any good shooting. But a man can fish as long as he lives. . . . Why, one place I stayed last summer there was an old man ninety years old had himself carried down to the river every morning. Yes, sir, a man can fish as long as he can get down to the water's edge. . . ."

There was a little plop to the right. He turned just in time to see the fish flash out of the water. He watched Steve take it off the hook and drop it on top of the pile in the bottom of the boat. Seven bass that made and one bream. The old lady would be pleased. "Aleck always catches me fish," she'd say.

The boat glided over the still water. There was no wind at all now.

The willows that fringed the bank might have been cut out of paper. The plume of smoke hung perfectly horizontal over the roof of the Negro cabin. Mr. Maury watched it stream out in little eddies and disappear into the bright blue.

He spoke softly: "Ain't it wonderful . . . ain't it wonderful now that a man of my gifts can content himself a whole morning on this here little old pond?"

III

Mr. Maury woke with a start. He realized that he had been sleeping on his left side again. A bad idea. It always gave him palpitations of the heart. It must be that that had waked him up. He had gone to sleep almost immediately after his head hit the pillow. He rolled over, cautiously, as he always did since that bed in Leesburg had given down with him and, lying flat on his back, stared at the opposite wall.

The moon rose late. It must be at its height now. That patch of light was so brilliant he could almost discern the pattern of the wallpaper. It hung there, wavering, bitten by the shadows into a semblance of a human figure, a man striding with bent head and swinging arms. All the shadows in the room seemed to be moving toward him. The protruding corner of the washstand was an arrow aimed at his heart, the clumsy old-fashioned dresser was a giant towering above him.

They had put him to sleep in this same room the night after his wife died. In the summer it had been, too, in June; and there must have been a full moon, for the same giant shadows had struggled there with the same towering monsters. It would be like that here on this wall every full moon, for the pieces of furniture would never change their position, had never been changed, probably, since the house was built.

He turned back on his side. The wall before him was dark but he knew every flower in the pattern of the wallpaper, interlacing pink roses with, thrusting up between every third cluster, the enormous, spreading fronds of ferns. The wallpaper in the room across the hall was like it too. The old lady slept there, and in the room next to his own, Laura, his sister-in-law, and in the east bedroom downstairs, the young couple. He and Mary had slept there when they were first married, when they were the young couple in the house.

He tried to remember Mary as she must have looked that day he first saw her, the day he arrived from Virginia to open his school in the old office that used to stand there in the corner of the yard. He could see Mr. Allard plainly, sitting there under the sugar tree with his chair tilted back, could discern the old lady—young she had been then!—hospitably poised in the doorway, hand extended, could hear her voice: "Well, here are two of your pupils to start with. . . ." He remembered Laura, a shy child of nine hiding her face in her mother's skirts, but Mary that day was only a shadow in the dark hall. He could not even remember how her voice had sounded. "Professor Maury," she would have said, and her mother would have corrected her with "Cousin Aleck. . . ."

That day she got off her horse at the stile blocks she had turned as she walked across the lawn to look back at him. Her white sunbonnet had fallen on her shoulders. Her eyes, meeting his, had been dark and startled. He had gone on and had hitched both the horses before he leaped over the stile to join her. But he had known in that moment that she was the woman he was going to have. He could not remember all the rest of it, only that moment stood out. He had won her, she had become his wife, but the woman he had won was not the woman he had sought. It was as if he had had her only in that moment there on the lawn. As if she had paused there only for that one moment and was ever after retreating before him down a devious, a dark way that he would never have chosen.

The death of the first baby had been the start of it, of course. It had been a relief when she took so definitely to religion. Before that there had been those sudden, unaccountable forays out of some dark lurking place that she had. Guerrilla warfare and trying to the nerves, but that had been only at first. For many years they had been two enemies contending in the open. . . . Toward the last she had taken mightily to prayer. He would wake often to find her kneeling by the side of the bed in the dark. It had gone on for years. She had never given up hope. . . .

Ah, a stouthearted one, Mary! She had never given up hope of changing him, of making him over into the man she thought he ought to be. Time and again she almost had him. And there were long periods, of course, during which he had been worn down by the conflict, one spring when he himself said, when she had told all the neighbors, that he was too old now to go fishing anymore. . . . But he had made a comeback. She had had to resort to stratagem. His lips curved in a smile, remembering the trick.

It had come over him suddenly, a general lassitude, an odd faintness in the mornings, the time when his spirits ordinarily were at their highest. He had sat there by the window, almost wishing to have some ache or pain, something definite to account for his condition. But he did not feel sick in his body. It was rather a dulling of all his senses. There were no longer the reactions to the visible world that made his days a series of adventures. He had looked out of the window at the woods glistening with spring rain; he had not even taken down his gun to shoot a squirrel.

Remembering Uncle Quent's last days he had been alarmed, had decided finally that he must tell her so that they might begin preparations for the future—he had shuddered at the thought of eventual confinement, perhaps in some institution. She had looked up from her sewing, unable to repress a smile.

"You think it's your mind, Aleck. . . . It's coffee. . . . I've been giving you a coffee substitute every morning. . . ."

They had laughed together over her cleverness. He had not gone back to coffee but the lassitude had worn off. She had gone back to the attack with redoubled vigor. In the afternoons she would stand on the porch calling after him as he slipped down to the creek. "Now, don't stay long enough to get that cramp. You remember how you suffered last time. . . ." He would have forgotten all about the cramp until that moment but it would hang over him then through the whole afternoon's sport and it would descend upon him inevitably when he left the river and started for the house.

Yes, he thought with pride. She was wearing him down—he did not believe there was a man living who could withstand her a lifetime—she was wearing him down and would have had him in another few months, another year certainly. But she had been struck down just as victory was in her grasp. The paralysis had come on her in the night. It was as if a curtain had descended, dividing their life sharply into two parts. In the bewildered year and a half that followed he had found himself forlornly trying to reconstruct the Mary he had known. The pressure she had so constantly exerted upon him had become for him a part of her personality. This new, calm Mary was not the woman he had lived with all these years. She had lain there—heroically they all said—waiting for death. And lying there, waiting, all her faculties engaged now in defensive warfare, she had raised, as it were, her lifelong siege; she had lost interest in his comings and goings, had once even encouraged him to go for an afternoon's sport! He felt a rush of warm pity. Poor Mary! She must have realized toward the last that she had wasted herself in conflict. She had spent her arms and her strength against an inglorious foe when all the time the real, the invincible adversary waited. . . .

He turned over on his back again. The moonlight was waning, the contending shadows paler now and retreating toward the door. From across the hall came the sound of long, sibilant breaths, ending each one on a little upward groan. The old lady. . . . She would maintain till her dying day that she did not snore. He fancied now that he could hear from the next room Laura's light, regular breathing and downstairs were the young couple asleep in each other's arms. . . .

All of them quiet and relaxed now, but they had been lively enough at dinnertime. It had started with the talk about Aunt Sally Crenfew's funeral tomorrow. Living now, as he had for some years, away from women of his family, he had forgotten the need to be cautious. He had spoken up before he thought:

"But that's the day Steve and I were going to Barker's Mill. . . ."

Sarah had cried out at the idea. "Barker's Mill!" she had said. "Right on the Crenfew land . . . well, if not on the very farm, in the very next field. It would be a scandal if he, Professor Maury, known by everybody to be in the neighborhood, could not spare one afternoon, one insignificant summer afternoon, from his fishing long enough to attend the funeral of his cousin, the cousin of all of them, the oldest lady in the whole family connection. . . ."

Looking around the table he had caught the same look in every eye; he had felt a gust of that same fright that had shaken him there on the pond. That look! Sooner or later you met it in every human eye. The thing was to be up and ready, ready to run for your life at a moment's notice. Yes, it had always been like that. It always would be. His fear of them was shot through suddenly with contempt. It was as if Mary were there laughing with him. *She* knew that there was not one of them who could have survived as he had survived, could have paid the price for freedom that he had paid. . . .

Sarah had come to a stop. He had to say something. He shook his head.

"You think we just go fishing to have a good time. The boy and I hold high converse on that pond. I'm starved for intellectual companionship, I tell you. . . . In Florida I never see anybody but niggers. . . ."

They had all laughed out at that. "As if you didn't *prefer* the society of niggers!" Sarah said scornfully.

The old lady had been moved to anecdote:

"I remember when Aleck first came out here from Virginia, Cousin Sophy said: 'Professor Maury is so well educated. Now Cousin Cave Maynor is dead who is there in the neighborhood for him to associate with?' 'Well,' I said, 'I don't know about that. He seems perfectly satisfied with Ben Hooser. They're off to the creek together every evening soon as school is out.' "

Ben Hooser. . . . He could see now the wrinkled face, overlaid with that ashy pallor of the aged Negro, smiling eyes, the pendulous lower lip that, drooping away, showed always some of the rotten teeth. A fine nigger, Ben, and on to a lot of tricks, the only man really that he'd ever cared to take fishing with him.

But the first real friend of his bosom had been old Uncle Teague, the factotum at Hawkwood. Once a week or more likely every ten days he fed the hounds on the carcass of a calf that had had time to get pretty high. They would drive the spring wagon out into the lot; he, a boy of ten, beside Uncle Teague on the driver's seat. The hounds would come in a great rush and rear their slobbering jowls against the wagon wheels. Uncle Teague would wield his whip, chuckling while he threw the first hunk of meat to Old Mag, his favorite.

"Dey goin' run on dis," he'd say. "Dey goin' run like a shadow. . . ."

He shifted his position again, cautiously. People, he thought . . . people . . . so bone ignorant, all of them. Not one person in a thousand realized that a foxhound remains at heart a wild beast and must kill and gorge and then, when he is ravenous, kill and gorge again. . . . Or that the channel cat is a night feeder. . . . Or . . . His daughter had told him once that he ought to set all his knowledge down in a book. "Why?" he had asked. "So everybody else can know as much as I do?"

If he allowed his mind to get active, really active, he would never get any sleep. He was fighting an inclination now to get up and find a cigarette. He relaxed again upon his pillows, deliberately summoned pictures before his mind's eye. Landscapes—and streams. He observed their outlines, watched one flow into another. The Black River into West Fork, that in turn into Spring Creek and Spring Creek into the Withlicoochee. Then they were all flowing together, merging into one broad plain. He watched it take form slowly: the wide field in front of Hawkwood, the Rivanna River on one side, on the other Peters' Mountain. They would be waiting there till the fox showed himself on that little rise by the river. The young men would hold back till Uncle James had wheeled Old Filly, then they would all be off pell-mell across the plain. He himself would be mounted on Jonesboro. Almost blind, but she would take anything you put her at. That first thicket on the edge of the woods. They would break there, one half of them going around, the other half streaking it through the woods. He was always of those going around to try to cut the fox off on the other side. No, he was down off his horse. He was coursing with the fox through the trees. He could hear the sharp, pointed feet padding on the dead leaves, see the quick head turned now and then over the shoulder. The trees kept flashing by, one black trunk after another. And now it was a ragged mountain field and the sage grass running before them in waves to where a narrow stream curved in between the ridges. The fox's feet were light in the water. He moved forward steadily, head down. The hounds' baying grew louder. Old Mag knew the trick. She had stopped to give tongue by that big rock and now they had all leaped the gulch and were scrambling up through the pines. But the fox's feet were already hard on the mountain path. He ran slowly, past the big boulder, past the blasted pine to where the shadow of the Pinnacle Rock was black across the path. He ran on and the shadow swayed and rose to meet him. Its cool touch was on his hot tongue, his heaving flanks. He had slipped in under it. He was sinking down, panting, in black dark, on moist earth while the hounds' baying filled the valley and reverberated from the mountainside.

Mr. Maury got up and lit a cigarette. He smoked it quietly, lying back upon his pillows. When he had finished smoking he rolled over on his side and closed his eyes. It was still a good while till morning, but perhaps he could get some sleep. His mind played quietly over the scene that would be enacted in the morning. He would be sitting on the porch after breakfast, smoking, when Sarah came out. She would ask him how he felt, how he had slept.

He would heave a groan, not looking at her for fear of catching that smile on her face—the girl had little sense of decency. He would heave a groan, not too loud or overdone. "My kidney trouble," he would say, shaking his head. "It's come back on me, daughter, in the night."

She would express sympathy and go on to talk of something else. She never took any stock in his kidney trouble. He would ask her finally if she reckoned Steve had time to drive him to the train that morning. He'd been thinking about how much good the chalybeate water of Estill Springs had done him last year. He might heave another groan here to drown her protests. "No. . . . I better be getting on to the Springs. . . . I need the water. . . ."

She would talk on a lot after that. He would not need to listen. He would be sitting there thinking about Elk River, where it runs through the village of Estill Springs. He could see that place by the bridge now: a wide, deep pool with plenty of lay-bys under the willows.

The train would get in around one o'clock. That nigger, Ed, would hustle his bags up to the boardinghouse for him. He would tell Mrs. Rogers he must have the same room. He would have his bags packed so he could get at everything quick. He would be into his black shirt and fishing pants before you could say Jack Robinson. . . . Thirty minutes after he got off the train he would have a fly in that water.

The Enemies

The sheriff met the two dark figures at the head of the stairway. "Step up, boy," he said kindly.

The attendant fell back. The Negro, manacled at wrist and ankle, took his place on the iron trap. His arms were already handcuffed behind his back. A deputy was about to slip the black hood over his head when the sheriff motioned him aside and, hand on the lever, bent forward. "Anything to say, boy?"

The Negro's eyes remained fixed on the opposite wall. He spoke in a full, throaty voice: "I ain't got nothing to say, boss."

The deputy approached, slipped the hood over the man's head, and fitted the noose well up under the ears. The sheriff wiped the perspiration from his face and pulled the lever. The man's body lurched forward and dropped with a thud to the floor below.

The three or four spectators turned away before the black, hooded figure on the floor had stopped twitching. The *Press-Scimitar* reporter, reaching the outer steps, drew a deep draught of cold March air into his lungs and lit a cigarette.

"I've covered twenty-three hangings in my time," he said. "I never saw a nigger step up on the trap before without singing."

His colleague on the morning paper nodded. "Or preaching a sermon. Don't seem natural." He leaned forward to the match the other was holding, then drew back as a slight, crouching figure broke from the shrubbery in front of him. "What do you want?" he asked roughly.

A Negro boy turned his yellow, working face up to the light. "Is he dead, boss?" he quavered.

The *Press-Scimitar* man flipped the flaring match into the leaves. "As a doornail," he said, "or will be in another minute."

"Two," the other said judicially. "They say five or six minutes but it takes nearer seven, I've noticed. Come on, Smith, I got to get to a phone."

They swung down the street. The boy, left alone at the jail door, straightened to his puny height, drew a long, sobbing breath, and then, half crouching, half running, darted off down the empty street.

In the Magnolia Café three people watched the night out. In her corner the aged proprietress hovered over a dying fire. Behind her in the light of a kerosene lamp a lean, grizzled Negro paced up and down. These two, as the night turned into day, addressed each other occasionally in monosyllables. The third occupant of the room, a gigantic Negro man, sat silent, his head in his hands, a coon dog dozing at his feet.

As the town clock struck five old Aunt Perea laid aside the turkey wing with which she had been fanning the embers. "Done turned toward day, Lias," she muttered, "I felt it."

The lean Negro, with a glance at their silent companion, went to the window and drew the dingy curtains aside. "Hit's some streaks showing," he said.

Aunt Perea got up and went over to the table. She turned up the lamp wick, then, reaching into a cupboard, drew forth a jug. "I aches," she moaned. "I got to have a dram . . . Lias?"

She poured herself a drink, then with one hand on the jug motioned toward the fire.

Lias filled another glass and walked softly toward the rocking chair's occupant. "Gunter," he said, "you want a dram? Gunter?"

The man in the chair raised up. His head, held rigid on its bull neck, turned until his bloodshot eyes looked full into the other Negro's face. Without lowering his gaze he took the glass, drained it at a gulp, then slumped back in his chair.

In the middle of the room Aunt Perea steadied herself with a shaking hand laid on the table as the door opened and the little yellow boy who had been at the jailhouse burst in. He came in the same half-crouching, dog-like fashion and fell into the chair at the head of the table. For a moment there was no sound in the room except his labored breaths. Then Lias filled a glass and walked toward him.

"Is he gone, Eugene?"

Eugene sat up and reached for the extended glass. "I heerd him drop," he said in an odd singsong. "I heerd him drop and I run around to the jailhouse. They was two white men standin' on the steps. I ask um if he's gone and they say he be dead in five, six minutes."

Aunt Perea went over and sat down in her chair by the hearth. She rocked back and forth for several minutes, then "What'd he sing?" she asked grimly. "What'd he sing when he stepped up on the trap? Tell me. I wants to remember it."

Eugene drained his glass and set it on the table. "He didn't sing nothing," he said.

There was silence, then Uncle Lias, with a glance at the silent figure by the hearth, said gently, "Go on, boy, you better tell us about it now. Did they 'low you to go up? Did they 'low you to talk to him?"

"They 'lowed me to go up," the boy said in the same remote listless tone. "They 'lowed me to stay thar in the hall till 'twas most time for him to go."

"Who else come?" Aunt Perea asked fiercely. "That yellow gal from Memphis, I bound she's thar."

"She come," the boy said, "but he wouldn't have no talk with her. Say he ain't got no time to be foolin' with women."

The big Negro turned suddenly in his chair by the fire.

"What'd he say about Mamie?"

The boy made his eyes meet the smoky brown ones. "Say he ain't got no time to be foolin' with women," he repeated.

Aunt Perea burst out sobbing. "Mamie! Kill my chile, cut 'er th'oat en ain't even say he sorry before he go to meet Jesus. Oh, my God!" She threw herself back in her chair and lay, her mouth half open, the cords in her withered neck twitching.

Uncle Lias half rose to go to his wife, then sank back as if dazed. "Ain't got no repentance," he murmured. "Steal this man's wife and cut 'er th'oat for a little yaller fly-up-the-creek and then ain't got no repentance!"

Eugene looked at the two moaning figures, then looked away. His lips moved. He seemed to be talking to himself. "He sont fer me. He sont fer me or I wouldn't a went to that jailhouse. Me and the doctor. We was the onliest ones. He *conjured* us to come."

The big Negro, Gunter, had risen and was walking toward the boy. "What'd he want wid the doctor?"

The boy shrank back, whining. "He ask the doctor how long hit take a man to die after they done broke his neck."

Gunter paused, one foot still uplifted. "And how long do hit take?" he asked softly.

"Hit take six or seven minutes." The boy threw his hand up, palm forward. "Don't you come no fu'ther," he cried shrilly. "He sont fer me and I gives you the message but I ain't tech you and I ain't let you tech me."

The big Negro stood still. "I takes the message," he said in the same soft tone.

The boy heaved himself up in his chair, his hand pressed against his throat as if to help the words out. "He says that ar posse wouldn't never found him if hadn't been fer you and your ole coon dog. Say you give that ole Ming one of his shoes and he tek that posse right to the log he's hidin' in. He say tell you and that ole coon dog to give him ten minutes. Say give him ten minutes and he be with you." He threw himself forward against the table, his shoulders twitching. "Oh, my Jesus," he moaned. "He put his hand through them bars and laid it on my arm."

The big Negro's eyes shone tawny in the light. His nostrils flared. He began to pace up and down the room, moving as quiet as a cat on his huge feet. From his lips came soft murmurings: "Me and Mamie. Ma'ied in the springtime and ne'er a cross word between us twel he come on Big Bend. Slep in my bed and sop out my skillet, then run off with my wife. Run off with my wife, then cut 'er th'oat for a little yaller fly-up-the-creek. . . ." He whirled sharply as slow footfalls sounded down the street and stood with his shining eyes fixed on the door. "Ming," he whispered, "*Ming!*"

The dog was on his feet in an instant and crouched at his master's knee. His hackles had risen and low growls came from his throat.

The boy, with a groan, slipped to the floor and lay face downward under the table. Uncle Lias leaned forward, his hand cupped over his ear, his wrinkled face ashen. "I hears 'im," he muttered.

The big Negro's hand went swiftly inside his shirt, brought up a black cord. His fingers played upon it while his soft murmurings still ran on: "Ma'ied in the springtime and ne'er a cross word between us twel he come on Big Bend. . . ." He ceased abruptly. For a second there was no sound in the room except the dog's low whining. Then Uncle Lias fell back limply against the wall. "Done gone by," he cried. "Oh, my sweet Saviour!"

The big Negro stood without moving until the footsteps had died away down the quiet street. He put up his hand and wiped the beads of sweat from his forehead. Suddenly he smiled through stiff lips. "Hit's more'n a mile to the jailhouse."

Uncle Lias, erect now against the wall, did not answer. His eyes left the man's form, traveled to the window where the morning light was growing. A sunbeam slipped through the dingy curtains, traversed the floor to fall on Eugene's outstretched hand. Uncle Lias leaned over, stirred the prostrate form with the toe of his boot. "Git up, boy. Git up and sit at 'at table."

Eugene got to his feet and crossed over to the hearth. Uncle Lias followed him. Arrived at the hearth, he threw a chunk of wood on the fire and rearranged the back log. Beside Aunt Perea's chair he paused, leaned over, and shook her by the shoulder. "Git up," he said in a low voice, "git up and cook us some breakfast."

The old woman rose from her chair, took a skillet from its hook on the mantel, and began cutting slices from the side of meat she got out of the cupboard. The smell of frying meat rose on the air, mingled after a little with the fragrance of boiling coffee.

In the middle of the room the big Negro stood, seemingly oblivious of the actions of the other three. The muscles in his arms bulged under his shirt sleeves as he clenched and unclenched his hands. He threw his head sharply back. Words poured from him:

"Thirty-four years old, sound as a nut. Ain't no man on Big Bend can put me on my back. Ain't no man anywhere on the river. . . ."

Uncle Lias turned from the fire, a tin plate in his hand. "Gunter," he said in a pleading voice, "Gunter!"

The big Negro's eyes, fixed now on the ceiling, did not waver. His voice rose higher and higher. "Ain't no man in 'is world can do it. Ain't no man *anywhere.* . . ."

Uncle Lias's eyes went to the window, vivid now with morning light. He drew a long breath, set the tin plate on Eugene's knee. "Eat 'at, boy," he commanded. The boy, never taking his eyes from Gunter, lifted the slice of fat meat mechanically to his mouth. His jaws moved once, then opened wide. The bitten-off morsel lay for a second on his tongue, then fell to the plate. Uncle Lias, turning, followed the gaze of the starting eyes.

The dog lay flat on the floor, paws limp, head thrown back at an unnaturally sharp angle. As Uncle Lias watched, the thin line of red at his throat widened and suddenly spilled over into blood.

Uncle Lias took a step forward. "Put that razor down, Gunter!"

The big Negro was straightening up to his full height. His rapt eyes gazed over their heads. One hand was thrust out as if to ward off approach. The other wove bright circles in the smoky air.

"Coming!" he shouted. "Coming. I gives you your time and you didn't get here. Now I'm coming!"

The circling hand drew in, hovered a moment. Then the razor dropped to the floor as the man staggered and fell face forward across the table.

Uncle Lias shrank back into the chimney corner. A woman's shrill cry rose:

"*Done gone to meet him!* Oh, my baby. She can res' easy now!"

One More Time

There wasn't anybody in sight on the veranda or in the front hall when I got to the inn. I went around through the crape myrtles and the quince bushes to the little back enclosure. Mrs. Rogers was standing with her back to me turning over some peaches that had been put on a table to dry and Aunt Zilphy was in her chair by the steps picking a chicken. She saw me and her little eyes went beady but she didn't say anything.

I stood there by the big quince bush and made my voice deep: "Madam, I want a night's lodging."

Mrs. Rogers flung up her hands and screamed.

"Lawd God," Aunt Zilphy said. "Come up here and skeer us to death!"

I went over and clapped her on the shoulder. "Burgoo for supper," I said, "and apple pie."

She looked at me out of her little sunk bright eyes. "Man, wheah I gwine git any squirrels?"

Mrs. Rogers hadn't let go of my hand. "I thought you weren't coming this year. You wrote and said you weren't coming."

"Somebody got my room?"

She shook her head, smiling. "But the inn's pretty full. Lord, Mr. Maury, you ought to been here Labor Day. I had a cot set up in every hall."

"I'd rather be here this weekend," I said.

We went in the back way and up the hall that was still covered with matting and she threw open the door of Number 22. The bed was still pulled over between the east windows and the same picture was over the washstand: an eye staring straight ahead and under it a hand holding a bunch of pencils.

I sat down on the edge of the bed and took my shoes off and put on the canvas sneakers I had in my bag and changed into my black shirt and fishing pants. It was four o'clock now but I'd have time for a short turn on the river. I slipped my tin tackle box in my pocket, got my rod and my waders, and went out the back way and around to the side of the house where the paddles stood against the wall. There were two or three dozen, some of them very fancy. I hefted them till I found one that suited my hand, then started down the path to the river.

You come down that path and the first thing you strike is a long, deep pool, the Blue Pool the natives call it. Must be twenty feet deep and ten or twelve from bank to bank. There's a lot of elder growing around it and in summer the surface of the water is white with the little blooms. I think of Elk River in winter when I can't get out to do any fishing and it's this part that comes back to me. And I remember old Bob Reynolds sitting in a boat in the middle of that long pool and looking up to the top of the gorge and then down to the last bend before the Big Eddy and saying that from this one spot you can see nearly a whole mile of the Elk.

The boat was tied up at the old place. I stowed my stuff in the bottom and shoved off. I started out the usual way, paddling with my right hand and then laying the paddle down to take up the rod when I saw a likely bit of water, but it is wearisome continually laying down the rod and taking up the paddle and you lose a lot of water too, so I shifted to paddling with my right and casting with my left. You can only do that on this river. It's the paddle the natives make. Lightest in the world. Of sassafras with a heart oak board for the blade, fastened with sixpenny nails driven flush and clinched. The one I had was a beauty.

I made good time up the river and came pretty soon to one of my favorite holes, a place where a big sycamore had fallen quartering upstream. It was bass water, all right. I put on Old Speck and cast every likely inch of it. Not even a strike. I tried a Johnson's Fancy; no better luck. I'd about decided to push on when I saw a native coming around the bend. He was making time, putting his back into it but paddling with only one hand. I thought at first he was going right by me but he stopped, bringing her around with a big swish the way they do.

I saw his red hair and pinched-in mouth and thought he was one of Squire Haynes's boys. "How're you, Ben?" I asked.

He shook his head. " 'Tain't Ben. It's Tom."

"Well, Tom, what're you catching?"

He grinned. "I got one little ole pyerch."

I put my hand in my pocket. "Give you two bits for him."

He threw the fish over, caught the quarter, and paddled off.

I got my knife out, slit the fish's belly open, and took out the maw. It was full of little shining green things. I sat there looking at them. "Great Scott!" I said. "He's full of willow flies."

I turned around and shouted, "Where'd you catch this fish?"

There was a second or so before his voice came back: "Other side of Big Eddy."

I looked up. The sun was out of sight behind the walls of the gorge and the mists already rising from the river. The Big Eddy was more than two miles away. I couldn't hope to make it there before dark. I put my tackle up, moored the boat, and started up the path. I hadn't caught a single fish and yet I was happy. I was here, when I'd thought up to the last minute I wouldn't get to come—and they were taking willow flies. Tomorrow was *bound* to be a good day.

Mrs. Rogers was still at the table when I got into the dining room but everybody else was gone. She called to Aunt Zilphy to bring the burgoo that she'd been keeping hot for me. I watched Aunt Zilphy set the big bowl of steaming burgoo down in front of me and it seemed to me I could hardly wait to take up my spoon.

"There ain't anything like it," I said when I'd had a few spoonfuls. "There ain't anything else like it in this world."

Mrs. Rogers had been sitting there, turned away from the table, looking out over the valley. She smiled when her eyes met mine. "Apple dumplings," she said. "You always say that about apple dumplings."

"Apple dumplings are all right," I said, "in their place."

I saw Aunt Zilphy looking at me from the doorway and I called her in and told her she ought to write it down. She sniffed and tossed her head like she always does. "Cain't do no cooking with a pencil."

Mrs. Rogers was looking at me, still smiling. "Guess who's here?"

I shook my head. "Hope it's nobody I know."

"It's Mr. Reynolds."

I stopped with my spoon halfway to my mouth. "You mean old Bob Reynolds is *here*?"

"He's out on the porch now. His wife's with him."

I finished my second bowl of burgoo and pulled the apple pie toward me. It was hot, just the way I like it, with a dash of nutmeg and a piece of cheese on the side. I was glad old Bob was here but I didn't see why he'd brought his wife and then I thought maybe he couldn't help it. Women take notions sometimes.

Aunt Zilphy brought me another cup of coffee and I drank it, wondering if it would keep me awake. Mrs. Rogers had gone out to see about something and I was by myself in the dining room. I lit my pipe and tilted my chair back against the wall. In a minute I would go out on the porch and see old Bob. At first I hadn't wanted anybody else to be here but I was glad now he'd come. I began planning which way we'd go tomorrow. The Big Eddy, first, of course. Then Bob would want to turn up Rocky Creek the way he always did. Stubborn cuss if ever there was one. Still I was first on the ground this time. He'd have to do what I said.

I got up and went out on the porch. Coming out of the lighted dining room everything looked black but after a second I made out two people sitting in chairs beside the rail. I went toward them.

"Well," I said, "old Bob!"

His deep voice came out of the dark. "You old son of a gun! What you doing here?"

There was a rustle. The woman beside him was putting out her hand. "They told us you were here, Mr. Maury. Bob's been telling me about Elk River so long I told him I'd just have to come along this time and see it for myself."

She had one of those twittery voices and I had an idea that she was little and blond and dumpy. Now that I came to think of it I'd never heard Bob mention his wife.

I dragged a chair up and sat down beside them. "Bob," I said, "they're taking willow flies. Now we got to get an early start in the morning. . . ."

The woman spoke: "Bob isn't equal to a trip like that. He hasn't been at all well lately."

Bob was knocking his pipe out on the railing. "That's right, Maury. I've been on the sick list, all fall."

The woman spoke up again before I could answer: "But he's so much better. The doctor says it's wonderful the way he's gaining."

Bob bent forward to strike a match. I could see his big beak of a nose and long jutting chin and I saw too that he had some sort of muffler up around his neck though the night was warm. His pipe was going now. It made a little purring noise in the dark.

"So you're going to try willow flies," he said. "Well, don't bank on 'em too much. Here today, you know, and gone tomorrow. Now if I were you I'd start out at that place below the second bridge. Splendid rock bass water. . . ."

We talked there for half an hour, about the time we went to Logan's Ferry and another big day we'd had together up Rocky Creek in the spring.

Once Mrs. Reynolds, restless, no doubt, at being left out of the conversation, suggested that even if Bob couldn't go off with me tomorrow he might do a little fishing. "Just stand on the bank and cast. I could carry all the things down for you."

Bob laughed, sort of short. "Maury, d'you ever know a woman knew anything about fishing?"

"No," I said, "I never did."

They were still sitting there when I got up to go in the house. I didn't feel like sitting there with them any longer and yet I wasn't ready to go to bed. There wasn't anybody in the parlor or halls but through the half-open door I could see Aunt Zilphy pottering around in the dining room. I went in and sat on the edge of a table and smoked and watched her change tablecloths and shift pepper and salt stands. "What's become of that half-grown girl you had around here?" I asked, seeing how slow she moved.

She sniffed. "Tuck some of the boarders' stockings and Miss Aggie done sont her whar she b'longs."

I shook my head like I thought that was mighty bad. "Well, I don't know what Miss Aggie'll do when you get too old to work. How old *are* you, Aunt Zilph?"

She had taken a soiled cloth from a table and held it stretched out in her hands. Usually she rose to a question about her age like a bass to a mayfly but now she was looking over my head out into the hall. I turned around. There was the sound of feet on the stairs but I couldn't see anybody. Whoever it was must have gone on up to the second landing.

Aunt Zilphy still stood there gazing. "If that woman any 'count she'd keep that man at home."

I knew then it was the Reynoldses. "Aunt Zilph," I said, "what's the matter with Bob?"

Her eyes went beady the way they always did when she talked about sickness. "Doctor say it's his liver. He ain't got but a piece of liver. Some little something been eatin' on it. Done et all of it but one little piece and when that's gone he'll be dead."

"Who told you that?"

"Didn't nobody need to tell me. Didn't you see his hand? Didn't you see where the flesh done fretted off his cheeks? Didn't you see how he looks out of his eye?" She had folded the bundle of table-cloths up and was moving toward the pantry door. The door swung to behind her, then swung and swung again. I stood there till it was quiet, then I went over and got some matches from the little glass holder on the mantel and left the dining room.

There were half a dozen magazines in the rack in the hall. I took a *Rod and Gun* and went upstairs. I undressed and got into bed and read for a while, propped up against the pillows. But the magazine was old and I never could read that stuff, anyhow, and after a while I switched off the light and just lay there, still propped against the pillows. My bed faced the gorge. You couldn't see the water, of course. It was too deep down but you could see the light from the hotel windows shining in two broad shafts on the leaves and you could see the black trunks of the poplars going down, down to where the water was, way below. I looked away from the open window at the picture that was hung up high toward the ceiling. The eye gazed straight at me the way it always did. It came to me suddenly what it was: Brotherhood of Railway Conductors, of course. Jim Rogers, Miss Aggie's husband, had been a conductor. He had been dead a long time now. I thought of Bob Reynolds and wondered whether it was his liver as Aunt Zilphy had said. She was a morbid old crow and loved to tell of people she had known that died of cancer. And then I wondered how it would be to know that there was something inside you that would give soon and that you could only live as long as it lasted, a year, six months, three. . . . Would you want to stay very quiet so you might live longer or would you tell yourself there was nothing the matter and try to have as good a time as you could? The other shaft of light had disappeared from the dark slope outside. I could hear the man next door snoring. I slipped down so that I lay flat in the bed and sent myself to sleep the way I do sometimes, just seeing a pool of water somewhere around a bend and myself coming up to it, all set, the Tucker Special in my hand, a Black Gnat all ready to put on. . . .

I was up before day the next morning—had to light a match to get the lines through the guides. I didn't waste any time on other pools but paddled hard as I could clip it up to the Big Eddy. It was a three-mile pull. The sun was well up when I came around the bend to where the big willows were. The flies were still there, hundreds of 'em, shining in the sun. There was one branch hanging way over the water where a great cluster had settled, almost like a swarm of bees. A streak of light ran there under the willows. I could see the water dimpling as the fish took the flies just as they'd hit the surface. I stopped paddling and sat there a few minutes, sizing things up, then I eased the boat up to the bank and made it fast just about thirty feet from the willows. I went into my tackle box and got out my willow fly and made my first cast just on the edge of that dimpling water. I was on to a pound bream right away. I put on all the pressure I dared so as to get him away from the hole and not disturb the others but it was a hard fight for a three-and-a-half-ounce rod. I landed him, all right, downstream, two feet from the bank. I didn't take time to string him, just threw him into the bottom of the boat and went back to it. The next was a pound-and-a-half little mouth— they're chicken hawk and chain lightning. I didn't get him out into the stream quick enough and he churned that hole up so that I had to wait another hour before the water started dimpling again. I cast then, taking pains to make the fly hit the water before the leader touched it and took another good-sized little mouth. There were some crappie after that and several bream and then suddenly it was all off. They'd quit. Full up. You've seen it happen often but you never can quite believe it. I wasted another hour there by those willows, then I paddled on upstream. There were plenty more willows swarming with flies but it was the same thing all along. They weren't taking 'em. I thought of what old Bob had said about willow flies: "Here today and gone tomorrow." Well, it was tomorrow now. I'd have to try something else.

I must have been five or six miles from the head of the gorge by this time. I ate my lunch and rested awhile in the shade, then started back. I fished slowly downstream, picking up some fine bream and some little mouth. Once I saw a man ahead of me in a boat, drifting along, not fishing. It looked like Bob Reynolds but I didn't think it could be; he'd said himself he could hardly make it down to the river. It was five o'clock when I came out at the head of the Blue Pool and saw the sun at the top of the gorge and knew that the day was nearly over. The man in the boat was at the other end of the long pool by this time, a tall man with a peaked cap pulled down over his face. I looked up from putting on a fly and saw him round the bend there by the big sycamore and then I forgot all about him. The Blue Pool is wonderful rock bass water. I put on a Johnson's Fancy with a South Bend Trix-Oreno, a quick-sinking bait, weedless, and cast right in the middle of the current. If he strikes going from you he'll hang himself. If he strikes either to the right or left you'll see the movement of the line. I began to retrieve slowly, vibrating the tip of the rod to give action. The line twisted sharply to the left and I knew I was on to a big one. The next one I took was going from me, a splendid little mouth. There were two or three more bass after that and then it was too dark to see, so I put up my tackle and drifted back to the landing.

It was good dark when I got up to the inn. People were running around in the halls. Somewhere upstairs a woman was screaming. I stood there on the lower veranda and listened to her scream and then stop and scream again. After a while Mrs. Rogers came down the back way. She said Bob Reynolds had taken a boat and gone off by himself early in the afternoon. His wife wanted to go with him but he wouldn't let her. They had found the boat two hours ago stuck in some willows but Bob had never come back.

That was eight o'clock. They went down half an hour later with searchlights and lanterns and hunted all over the banks of the creek. But they couldn't do any good, of course, in the dark. The next afternoon they found his body. In the Blue Pool. There was an iron dumbbell weighing five pounds in each pocket. Lida Reynolds said she had intended all along asking him what that odd-looking bundle was he was carrying when they got on the train. Now that it was all over she remembered that he had had a queer look on his face when they first started talking about the trip—when he said he wanted to see the old place one more time.

The Long Day

They were talking on the back porch when Henry went into the dining room to get his breakfast.

"Let him go," Uncle Fergus said. "Joe'll take care of him."

"I know Joe'll take care of him to the best of his ability," Henry's mother said, "but suppose something else comes up. Suppose Sarah follows them down to the creek."

Uncle Fergus laughed. "Sarah won't be up to any more didoes today," he said. "Joe gave her a good larruping before he came up to the house."

"I hope he did," she said. "I hope he beat her within an inch of her life. It's outrageous, really it is."

Uncle Fergus laughed again. "Joe likes his mamas hot," he said. "Georgy was no sucking dove."

"Georgy behaved herself very well while she was on this place. At any rate she never attacked Joe with a razor. This razor business is really too much, Fergus. If I were you I'd tell her to leave."

Henry got up and went out on the porch.

"Mama," he said, "what's the matter with Joe?"

"He had an accident," she said. "Got a little cut on his cheek. Darling, wouldn't you just as soon go fishing next Saturday?"

"I'd rather go today. Joe said we'd go today."

"I know, darling, but that was before he got cut. He might not feel like going now."

"Can I go down to the cabin and see how he's feeling?"

"Oh, Joe's all right," Uncle Fergus said. "I tell you it wasn't anything. Just barely laid the skin open."

"You can go down to the cabin," she said, "but you mustn't go inside. And you mustn't stay."

"Can I take my lunch and go down to the creek if Joe feels like going fishing?"

His mother looked at Uncle Fergus.

"Let him go," Uncle Fergus said. "It'll be a good thing to get Joe off the place for the day."

"Can I, Mama?" Henry said.

"I suppose so, darling. I suppose it'll be all right. But don't make Joe go unless he feels like it. And don't hang around the cabin."

"No'm," Henry said. "I won't."

He kissed his mother, then he got the package of lunch from the refrigerator and went out the back door and down the path to the cabin. It was a pretty day, the kind you get in August sometimes when the drought breaks, cool, but without any wind stirring, and the sun shining steadily in a bright sky.

He parted the strands of the barbed-wire fence and slipped through into the field. He walked slowly across the open ground, but when he got to the path through the tall weeds he struck a dogtrot, and he ran until he came to the hollow where the nigger cabin was. Joe was standing in the door of the cabin looking out. You couldn't see any blood on him anywhere, but he had a long strip of court plaster down one side of his cheek and a little round piece on his forehead.

Henry stopped under the sycamore tree.

"Joe," he said, "you want to go fishing?"

"Yes," Joe said, "I'd like to go fishing." He stepped down from the porch and walked a little way toward the sycamore tree, then stopped. "I can't go fishing right now, Hinry," he said. "I have to stay round here a while and wait on Sarah. She's feeling po'ly."

"All right," Henry said. "I'll go dig some worms."

He picked up a can and went around the back to the hen house. The hen house hadn't been used for so long that it was all falling to pieces. The best worms were there under the fallen planks. He turned one of the planks over and began digging with the no-handled spade. Inside the cabin Joe walked to and fro. Blang—blang—blang! There was one loose board that flopped up and down every time he stepped on it. All that walking around was to wait on Sarah. But how could he wait on her? There wasn't anything in the cabin but the pallet that Sarah was lying on and a table that Joe had made and one chair. There was a closet in one corner, though. Maybe they kept their clothes there. Sarah changed her dress sometimes, and Joe had some Sunday clothes.

The can was full of worms. He put a chunk of soft black dirt on top, dropped the plank back in place, and took the can around to the front of the house. The door was shut. Joe was sitting on the steps that went down to the porch, rolling a cigarette. He looked sick. Maybe he had lost too much blood. It must be bad to have somebody jumping at you with a razor. A razor was so quick. It sliced clean through you before you even knew you were cut. Uncle Fergus said Sarah was the worst little hellcat he'd ever seen, but he didn't believe she meant to cut Joe. She thought a lot of Joe.

Joe finished rolling his cigarette. "You want to feed that possum?" he asked.

"Yes," Henry said, "I'll feed him."

Joe went in the cabin and got a piece of corn pone. "You crumple that in the cage," he said. "That old possum's hungry."

Henry took the corn bread and threw it on the floor of the cage. "Come on, baby," he said. "Come on, now, and eat your dinner."

The possum put his paw out and flicked a crumb of bread toward him, but he would not eat while anybody was looking. Henry picked the cage up and set it down under the sycamore tree. Then he went back and sat down on the porch. Joe came and sat down beside him. He did not say anything, though, and he kept his head turned as if he were listening for Sarah to call him. In a minute he got up and went into the cabin. Henry could hear him talking, in a soft voice, to Sarah, and he could hear Sarah crying, not a loud crying like a grown person's, but a tiny, low moaning, almost like a little baby's. She must be feeling pretty bad to be crying like that.

Joe came out of the cabin and walked to the end of the porch. He looked up at the sun. "It's long past noon," he said.

"I'm hungry," Henry said. "Are you hungry, Joe?"

"I could eat something," Joe said.

Henry got the package of lunch and spread it on the floor. There was plenty: five ham sandwiches, some potato salad in a little glass jar, some sweet pickles, four deviled eggs, four oatmeal cookies, and two big Elberta peaches.

They ate two sandwiches apiece and all the potato salad and eggs; then they started in on the peaches. Henry picked up the sandwich that was left. "How about Sarah?" he asked. "Doesn't she want anything to eat?"

Joe shook his head. "She don't want nothin'," he said. "Her stomach's upset." He took out his tobacco pouch. "If we had some coffee now," he said, "if we had some good hot coffee!"

"I tell you," Henry said, "I'll go up to the house and get some. Ella always sets the coffeepot back on the stove after breakfast. I'll just slip in the kitchen an' get what's left."

"If Ella's there she won't let you," Joe said. "Ella's ornery."

"She'll be down in her room taking a nap," Henry said. "She always takes a nap after dinner." He started up the path.

"Hinry . . ." Joe said.

Henry turned around. Joe was sitting there looking after him as if he wanted to ask him something. He came back a few steps. "What you want?" he asked. "You want me to get something else?"

"Yo ma has got some old rags up at the house, hasn't she?" Joe said. "Clean, white rags?"

"Yes," Henry said, she's got a whole drawerful. In the entry."

"Can you get 'em without anybody seein' you?" Joe asked.

"Yes," Henry said. "I'll just slip in the side door and get 'em."

He ran along the path until he got to the place where the open ground began. He stopped there a moment, under cover of the weeds. There was no one in sight. He slid through the fence and went softly up the back steps and into the kitchen.

Ella was sitting just inside the door, with her back to him, shelling peas. She turned around when he came in.

"What you want now?" she asked.

He walked over to the stove. The coffeepot was in its place at the back. "Sarah's sick," he said. "Joe sent me up here to get her some coffee."

"You better not be takin' that coffee," Ella said. "Yo' mama'll be comin' in here wantin' to know what's become of it."

He set the coffeepot down and looked at her. "Mama told me I could have that old leather pillow that was on the porch for a haversack," he said. "You know where it is?"

Ella laughed.

"I like to know how you goin' to use it for a haversack," she said. "It's got a hole in it big as my head."

"I could fix it so it'd be all right," he said.

Ella set the pan of peas down on the table. "How'm I going to know where everything on this place is?" she said. "I got all I can do to cook. I can't be keepin' up with everything on this place." She took a bucket down from the rack and poured it half full of coffee. "Now you bring this bucket back when you get through with it," she said.

He took the bucket and went out on the back porch. There was no one in the hall. His mother always went upstairs to lie down this time of day, and Uncle Fergus usually went to town. He tiptoed into the back entry. Opening the top drawer of the chest, he took out a ragged shirt and a couple of old napkins, then he shut the drawer softly and tiptoed through the back door and down the steps.

Joe was sitting on the porch, leaning forward, with his head in his hands. He did not look up or move. Henry thought he was asleep. He waited until he was right at him, then he gave a sharp whistle. Joe opened his eyes and jumped as if he had been shot.

"What's the matter with you?" he asked.

Henry laughed. "I thought you were asleep," he said.

"I wasn't asleep," Joe said, "and if I was you needn't go hootin' at me like an owl." He stood up. "I bet you forgot the sugar."

"I sure did," Henry said. "I forgot all about that sugar." He felt in his pockets. "Here are the rags, anyhow," he said.

Joe took them and went into the cabin, shutting the door behind him. In a few minutes he came out with a bag of sugar and two tin cups. "It didn't make no difference," he said. "Sarah had some in the cupboard."

They went over and sat under the sycamore tree while they drank the coffee. It was hot and strong. There were two cups apiece and a little over. Henry poured what was left into Joe's cup. "You drink that, Joe," he said. "I've had all I want."

Joe drained the coffee, then ate the sugar that was in the bottom of the cup. "That's good coffee," he said.

"Yes," Henry said. "It sure is."

He leaned back against the tree trunk, with his hands clasped behind his neck. It was cool here in the shade, but the day had turned out hot after all. Out in the field you could see the heat simmering over the tops of the goldenrod. He sat up suddenly. The goldenrod in the middle of the field kept moving.

"Joe," he said, "there's somebody coming along the path."

Joe got up and went in the cabin. When he came back he had an old seine and a ball of twine. He sat down on the steps and began cutting off pieces of twine and tying up broken places in the seine. Henry went over and sat down beside him.

"I bet that's Mama," he said.

Joe did not say anything.

Henry watched his mother come up out of the hollow and start along the path to the cabin. She came a little way, then stopped.

"Why, Henry!" she said. "I thought you were down at the creek."

Joe spoke up. "We been tryin' to mend this old seine," he said, "but it looks like we been wastin' our time. We goin' along directly now."

She came on, past the sycamore tree; past the possum's cage. "Ella told me Sarah was sick," she said. "I thought I'd better see how she was. What's the matter with her, Joe?"

"Her stomach's upset," Joe said.

She started to step up on the porch. "Well," she said, "I reckon I better go in and see how she is."

Joe put the seine down. "You better not go in there now, Miss Mamie," he said. "Sarah done throw up, all over the floor. I ain't got it cleaned up good yet."

She took her foot down from the step. "You better clean it up now," she said. "It'll be easier to clean it up now than later. I'm going to send Sarah some phosphate of soda. And some clean sheets. Now you fix her bed up nice, Joe. You know how to do things like that."

"Yas'm," Joe said. "I got a cake of soap."

She looked at Henry.

"You better come on up to the house now," she said.

"Please let me stay, Mama," Henry said. "Joe and I got to get this seine mended. We can't ever get any minnows if we don't get our seine mended."

She laid her hand on his arm. "You come walk a little way with me," she said.

They went up over the edge of the field. When they came to the path through the weeds she stopped, still holding his arm. "I don't mind you staying down here with Joe if you don't go inside the cabin," she said. "Now you won't go inside that cabin?"

Henry shook his head. "No'm," he said. "I'll just sit out there in the yard till we're ready to go."

She let go of his arm. "Don't stay long," she said. "And, Henry, don't be late for supper."

"No'm," Henry said, "I won't."

He ran back to the cabin. Joe was sitting under the sycamore tree by the possum's cage. The possum was rolled up in a ball, asleep, with one paw stuck through the broken place in the bars.

"Joe," Henry said, "less start now. Can't we start now?"

Joe sat looking straight in front of him.

"I never cut that woman," he said. "Before God, I never cut that woman!"

"Is she cut?" Henry said. "Joe, is she cut?"

"She cut herself," Joe said, "tryin' to do me harm."

"She cut you too, Joe," Henry said. "She cut you first."

"She never meant to cut me," Joe said. "She wouldn't a cut me for nothin' . . . And now she's done cut herself."

"Is she cut bad?" Henry said.

"Naw," Joe said, "she ain't cut bad." He looked down at the cage. "That old possum's going to get away from us if we don't fix up that cage," he said.

"I'll fix it," Henry said. "I know how to fix it. Joe, have you still got that old axe?"

"It's in there in the cupboard," Joe said.

He got up and went into the house. Henry sat where he was a minute, then he got up too and went over to the hen house. There was one plank there that was thinner than the others. He thought he would make a bar for the cage out of that. He picked the plank up and started back to the sycamore tree. As he came around the corner of the house, Joe stepped down on the porch.

"Joe," Henry said, "less go possum hunting one night soon."

Joe did not answer. He stood there a second, then he jumped off the porch and ran toward the field. He ran, crouching like a dog, until he got to the edge of the field. He straightened up then and dived into the tall weeds. The goldenrod rippled where he made his way. Henry watched the yellow ripple spread slowly across the field. When the whole field was still he turned around. The cabin door was open. He could see Sarah lying on a pallet on the floor. The white cloths that were about her head and neck were stained with blood. Her eyes were wide open. He took one look at her, then he ran as fast as he could to the house.

To Thy
Chamber Window, Sweet

Mr. Maury regarded the smoking dish which Carrie, the colored waitress, had just set before him: an oval, pale yellow, quivering, and sprinkled with what appeared to be shavings of fine greens, the whole reposing upon a silver platter and flanked by two slices of thin, unbuttered toast. Mr. Maury prodded the yellow substance distastefully with his fork, then looked up at the waitress. "What's all this flummery?"

Carrie pursed her lips. "They calls it omelette feens zebs."

Mr. Maury, in turn, pursed his lips. "Omelette feens zebs. If that ain't a helluva note!"

A sparely built man of about forty-five who had just taken his place at the next table broke into a laugh. "Beats me how they think up all that fancy stuff," he said.

Mr. Maury nodded. *"Omelette fines herbes!"* he said. "I like fried ham for breakfast." He eyed the newcomer, noting that though he was slim he was strongly built and that he had under heavy brows a pair of fine gray eyes. "Yep," he repeated, "I could eat fried ham for breakfast every morning of my life— What's your name?"

The stranger turned from his contemplation of the view: Lake Harris, blue-green, willow-fringed, its waters dancing in the morning light.

"Jim Yost," he said.

"And what you doing here?" Mr. Maury inquired as he unfolded his napkin.

"I thought I'd do a little fishing."

Mr. Maury waved his hand toward the window. "It's a delusion," he said. "A delusion and a snare. I been here two months now. I might as well a been on the Gobi Desert."

The stranger knit his black brows. "You mean there aren't any fish in that lake?"

Mr. Maury took a mouthful of omelette, made a face, then swallowed. "They're there," he said. "Hundreds of 'em. Hundreds? Thousands. Man—" He pushed his plate back, rose, and, going to the window, went through the motions of a man delivering a cast. "You put on the best you got, Black Gnat on a Number Four hook if you're like me." He made another imaginary cast. "Whoopee! Zip! You got him. Three-pound littlemouth." He stepped backwards, almost upsetting the table behind him, flexed his wrist ostentatiously in the play, and landed the imaginary bass on the table beside the silver platter. "There he is. There he is. Two feet of your nose but you can't take him."

The stranger's gray eyes were incredulous. "Why can't you?"

"Because," Mr. Maury explained, "he's snarled up in eelgrass so tight he can't budge." He waved his hand again at the lake, shimmering among its encircling willows. "That whole damn lake, nine miles of it, is covered two feet down with eelgrass thick as the hair on a dog's back. You can catch bass till the world looks level but you can't take 'em out."

Yost's handsome face had resumed its ordinary calm. He pushed his plate back. "Well, that's hard if you like to cast. I do mostly bait fishing."

Mr. Maury, for some years now, had not taken the trouble to disguise any emotion that visited him. He allowed his mouth to drop open as he regarded the stranger.

"I wouldn't have thought it, to look at you," he said.

Yost, on his feet now, nodded pleasantly and left the dining room. Mr. Maury had finished his breakfast but he sat on for some minutes smoking. The dining room, vacant now save for himself and filled with fresh morning sun, was agreeable. He hummed a little tune as he smoked and drummed on the tablecloth with his fork. There was a rustle in the passage outside, the sound of a feminine voice, contralto, agreeably pitched: "Good morning, Carrie."

Mr. Maury rose suddenly and, catching up his hat from where he had placed it on the corner of the table, tiptoed through the swinging door, through the pantry, and on out into the kitchen.

Aunt Fanny, standing beside the rolling block, turned a broad, good-humored face. "Biscuits all right this morning?"

"I don't know," Mr. Maury said glumly. "I never had any. Nothing but two little old pieces of toast."

Aunt Fanny left the rolling block. Her arms akimbo on her hips, she leaned slightly toward him. "You know why?" she inquired in a resonant whisper. " 'Cause you's too fat!"

Mr. Maury glanced down over his protuberant middle. "I ain't so fat," he said. "And I've fallen off since I've come here."

Aunt Fanny compressed her lips. "Miz Carter say you overweight. She show me how to fix them aigs so they won't be any grease in 'em. Say you eat too much starch too."

Mr. Maury gazed at her in silence for some seconds. His lips were closed but a slight humming sound came from behind his clenched teeth. Finally he released a long sigh and picked up his minnow bucket from where he had set it behind the kitchen stove. "I'll be down a little earlier in the morning from now on, Fanny," he said. "You can fix up all them omelettes you want to but I want my fried ham. And three eggs, fried *hard*."

He went out onto the back porch, took up his poles and his traps, and started down to the lake. Ahead of him somebody was moving through the mimosa branches. As Mr. Maury came out onto the beach he caught a glimpse of the man: the same broad-shouldered, athletic-looking fellow that he had been talking to at breakfast.

He shook his head, addressing an invisible companion. "Now would you take him for a mumble-pegger?"

The boathouse keeper was maneuvering the *Sally M.* out from the flotilla into the open water at the foot of the dock. Mr. Maury went ponderously down the steps and ensconced himself in the boat, poles ready to hand, live well between his spread legs. He raised his hand in salute to Old Tom and, taking up his paddle, sent the boat forward with sure, practiced strokes. When he was well out into the middle of the lake he laid his paddle down and, glancing around involuntarily—he could never get over a tight sense of shame at engaging in such proceedings—he rigged up his pole, baited it with a live minnow, and made a long cast to the left side of the boat. The cork bobbed on the waves only a moment before it went down. Mr.

Maury reeled the line in, took a sizable bass off the hook, and laid him in the live well in the bottom of the boat. He performed these motions abstractedly, his thoughts seeming to be still on his conversation with the invisible auditor. Once he spoke aloud, a high, derisive tone that carried far over the lake.

"*Cyarter—*" he said, "*Cyarter—*"

Carter was the name of the lady whose voice, heard in the hall a few minutes ago, had sent Mr. Maury hurrying out into the kitchen. As he uttered her name she was clearly visible to him as she had appeared on his first meeting with her, two, could it already be three months ago? He had had a hard day on the lake—that was when he was still trying to cast in that eelgrass—and he had fallen asleep in his chair on the east veranda almost immediately after dinner. The two ladies, Mrs. Bellows, the proprietress of the hotel, and the new guest, Mrs. Carter, were already deep in conversation when he came to himself. He must have been confused by his nap: he had had for a moment the feeling that he was a boy back in Virginia, at Brackets, Hawkwood, any of those places. He had not known what it was until Mrs. Carter spoke again; the voice might have been Cousin Ellen's or Aunt Vic's. He had chuckled to himself in the dark, then, leaning back in his chair, had given himself over to his reflections. But the crisp Virginia accents had gone on. He had heard them with the top part of his mind as it were. It was a pure spirit of mischief that had prompted him when the ladies rose to go into the house to lean forward and speak out of the dark:

"Mrs. Cyarter, how do you pronounce 'c-o-w p-e-n'?"

The handsome, gray-haired woman had given an amused little toss of the head. "Cuppen," she said briskly as she turned into the house.

It was the next afternoon when he was coming up from the lake, ragged, dirty, his black shirt open at the throat, that he had encountered Mrs. Carter on the mimosa-bordered path. He had stepped back into the shrubbery to let her pass but she had stopped, smiling:

"What county in Virginia do you come from, Mr. Maury?"

Startled, he had yet retained some presence of mind. "I'm a Kentuckian, ma'am. Born in Todd County."

She had raised her brows but she had passed on. All would have been well if he had let it go at that. It was his vanity that had betrayed him that night on the porch—it must have been a week later. Alf Bellows had been talking for half an hour: a tedious, confused account of an adventure that he had had on one of the Great

Lakes. Mr. Maury had listened with the ill-concealed impatience of the born raconteur. In the pause that followed Alf's recital he cleared his throat gently.

"My uncle, James Morris, had the finest pack of hounds in Piedmont Virginia. Old Mag, Old Whiskey and the pups—" He told them about the death of Old Red and the tailing of another fox, of the time one of Old Mag's pups was brought home on a mattress. And of old Judge Rives, who was so book-learned that he could hardly converse with ordinary folks and, when it was time to cut corn, would ask of his colored overseer if the maize had a uniform aspect. And for grace notes, as it were, a tale in the vernacular, of Uncle Sam Bunch and Lias Jones's breachy sow: "Thar she was, Billy, right in the middle of my sweet 'tater patch, a-nuzzlin' and a-guzzlin'. I went in the house and I got Old Betsy down off the rack and I drapped her in her tracks, eleven paces from the back door to the smokehouse. And now he's a-lawin' of me—"

He shifted his bulk on the hard seat. "I'm like my father," he thought complacently, "finest speaking voice in the state." His grandfather before him had had that mellow voice too. In the old days, when erudition counted for something, where other lawyers would argue a case he would simply quote a little Shakespeare to the jury and have 'em crying in no time—

The cork went down again. A redbreast this time. Mr. Maury reeled him in methodically, tossed him into the live well. It was like picking them up in the middle of the street. Or like the Eskimos. He had read somewhere that they merely made a hole in the ice and took the fish out. He got out his tobacco pouch and, staring ruminatively over the water, filled his pipe. It was the next night, really, that the mischief had been done. Alf Bellows again. He had had the nerve to tell some more of his tedious stories in a rasping, halting voice. It was Alf's voice that had broken down Mr. Maury's resistance. It had been with surprise that he heard his own sonorous tones:

"Bitter constraint and sad occasion dear,
Compels me to disturb thy season due:
For Lycidas is dead—"

That might have been considered an accident; he had not intended to recite any poetry to them. It was vanity, sheer vanity, that had led him to recite from *Atalanta in Calydon*, and, not content with quoting Swinburne, he had gone on to Shelley:

> "And a spirit in my feet
> Hath led me—who knows how?
> To thy chamber window, sweet—"

When they rose to go Mrs. Bellows had thanked him for reciting so beautifully but Mrs. Carter, allowing him to press her soft, well-kept hand in good-night, had not spoken. But he had had a glimpse of her face in the light as she turned up the stairs. He shook his head now as he replaced the tobacco pouch that he had all this time been holding in his hand.

"*Shelley!*" he said and took up his paddle. "Any man that'd quote Shelley—"

His pipe had gone out. He relit it, sighing. That old line! As infallible as Old Speck, in May. But it was not May with him—December, rather. In a few months he would have turned seventy. And Mrs. Carter might be said to be in the ripe September of her life. A handsome woman with those wide-set blue eyes and gray hair waving softly back from a really beautiful brow. She had a spirited way of tossing her hair back to keep that brow clear. Well, he liked a bit of spirit. His dead wife, all the women of his family, had had a thought too much perhaps. He seemed to have spent the greater part of his life in soothing them down. Still, a man got used to that, he supposed, like having too much pepper in his food.

It was the afternoon after the poetry session that Mrs. Carter had sent Henry upstairs to know if Professor Maury would like to drive out to Rainbow Springs with her. Henry, he thought, and shook his head again. Henry . . . Any man, living even as retired a life as he himself lived, was bound to come up against manifestations of the injustice of Providence that were, to say the least, shocking. Henry was the exact shade of chocolate brown that Mr. Maury liked in a nigger, six feet tall and correspondingly broad. Smart, too, with a ready tongue in his head and capable, mechanic's fingers. Make anything. Only yesterday he had soldered Mr. Maury's minnow bucket beautifully. It was a crying shame for such a valuable nigger to be wasted on a woman. He had told Mrs. Carter so, too, roundly: "I could take Henry here and make something of him."

Henry had glanced back over his shoulder, grinning: "Yas, *suh!*"

Mrs. Carter had smiled too. "Henry's been with us since he was sixteen," she said. "Mr. Carter thought a lot of him."

The boat, drifting now for some minutes, had arrived on the west side of the lake. It was a place Mr. Maury usually avoided. Cypress trees fringed the lake on every side but on this west bank they extended in solid formation far out into the water. Mr. Maury, taking up his paddle, was arrested by the sight of a man in a boat, paddling, it seemed, straight for the cypress thicket. Mr. Maury laid his paddle down and watched, chuckling.

"Fool," he said, "he'll come out o' there faster'n he went in."

Minutes passed, however, and the man did not emerge. Mr. Maury paddled closer until he could see the man's figure dodging in and out among the cypress trees. The man disappeared for some seconds, reappeared again. Mr. Maury leaned forward to get a better view. Suddenly he brought his hand down on the side of the boat.

"I don't believe it," he said. "Yep, that's what he's doing— Naw— yep!" And with the words he took up his paddle and sent the *Sally M.* racing over the water toward the cypress thicket.

At five o'clock Mrs. Carter came down the stairs and out onto the veranda. She was all in pale gray and a cluster of some delicate purple blossom was pinned at her shoulder. Mr. Maury—he was attired more formally than usual in a baggy suit of white Panama cloth but he wore his broad-brimmed fishing hat—arose and escorted her to where her automobile awaited them under the porte cochère.

As he took his place beside her Mrs. Carter gave a fleeting glance upward. "You couldn't find your hat?" she murmured.

Mr. Maury shook his head. "Musta mislaid it. I like this one better anyhow."

Mrs. Carter smiled indulgently. "You look so nice when you're dressed up," she said. "You ought to do it oftener."

Mr. Maury did not answer. The car wheeled from out of the drive and out onto the wide boulevard. They drove past the courthouse with its fountains, past the cluster of bright-awninged shops and out into the open country. Mr. Maury cleared his throat.

"I understand you think I'm too fat?"

Mrs. Carter regarded him composedly. "You'd feel better if you weighed a little less. It's all a matter of diet."

"No, it ain't," Mr. Maury retorted. "It runs in families. There was my father and my Uncle James and my Uncle Quent. Every one of 'em weighed two hundred by the time they were fifty."

Mrs. Carter sighed. "Mr. Carter came of a family that was inclined to stoutness, but he always kept his weight down to one hundred and seventy-five."

"How'd he do it?" Mr. Maury inquired.

"Diet. He rarely ate starches, or any fattening foods, in fact. Fortunately he was a great lover of fruits. Prunes, figs, plums; there was hardly any fruit that he didn't like."

"I never had any use for prunes," Mr. Maury said gloomily. "Figs either. Might as well be eating so much hay. Besides a man naturally takes on weight when he gets old."

Mrs. Carter leaned forward suddenly. She allowed her gray-gloved fingers to rest for a moment on his brown, wrinkled hand. "A man is as old as he feels," she said softly. "You have the heart of a little child."

Mr. Maury gazed straight before him to where the road, banked on either side with roses, seemed to disappear in a tunnel of live oak branches. There was silence for some minutes. It was broken by Mr. Maury. "The older I get," he said reflectively, "the more I believe in the working of a Divine Providence."

Mrs. Carter nodded. "If one only has faith."

"Now take me," said Mr. Maury. "Here I been sitting around for two months griping because I came to the wrong place and all the time a revelation was being prepared for me."

Mrs. Carter's luminous blue eyes met his. He looked away.

"This fellow, Jim Yost," he said. "I first saw him I couldn't believe my eyes. I says, 'That fellow's crazy.' But there was something about the way he was handling that rod— There was something— I paddled over there fast as I could clip it and what did I see?"

"What did you see?" Mrs. Carter asked crisply.

"Well," said Mr. Maury, "he was using a two-handed rod, his own invention. Only combination rod ever made. Eight feet long. First two joints bait rod joints, top joints fly rod joints. *Bait casting and that rod'd deliver the lure like it was a fly.* I just stopped paddling and sat there and watched him. Finally he turns around. 'You know where I could get a boy to paddle me?' 'Sure,' I says. 'Well, where is he and what's his name?' 'Name's Aleck,' I says, and I beached my boat and paddled him all afternoon."

"That was certainly very kind of you," Mrs. Carter observed.

"Hunh," said Mr. Maury. "One thing about me I ain't vain. Yes, sir, I was proud to sit at his feet. Well, we started off. In three hours he'd caught forty-eight. Catch 'em on one side of the boat and turn 'em loose on the other. Along in the evening we got back to that place where all that cypress grows out in the lake. 'Go into them cypress,' he says. 'Man, you can't cast in there.' He looked at me. 'When I get a boy to paddle me he usually goes where I tell him.' 'You're the doctor,' I says, and I put him right into the thick of 'em. 'Now,' he says, 'I'll hook a lot of fish I can't land. They'll hang themselves in the tree roots. But I'll get the strikes.' He'd throw that lure through a twelve-inch opening thirty feet off and bring out a five-pound bass. *Hard*-casting he calls it. He uses an invincible line, twelve-pound test, and he never uses but one a week. Casts so much the line wears out going through the guides. I asked him—just for devilment—why he didn't get a level wind reel. 'Why don't I get a seine?' he says."

Henry, who had been listening intently, turned his head to look at Mr. Maury. "What kind of bait do he use, Cap'm?"

"Henry," Mr. Maury said, "it's a shame for a smart boy like you to have to spend his time driving a lady around the country. It ain't all the rod and his casting. It's the *lures*."

"What are they like?" asked Mrs. Carter.

"They're like nothing in the heavens above or the earth beneath or the waters under the earth," said Mr. Maury. "Take his Devil Bug. You want to know how he makes it?"

Mrs. Carter said that she thought it would be very interesting to hear.

"Well, of course the body of the bug don't amount to anything. It's the pork rind. Get you a piece half an inch wide and three inches long, preferably from the belly of a sow. Put it down on a smooth board, drive a small tack in the head of it, and with a razor blade (new; nothing is too good for the angler) cut the rind into strips. The rind is tough and will hold up under the blade. A beginner, such as you or Henry here, will not be able to cut more than five or six strips. Jim Yost can cut twelve, smaller than a broom straw."

Mrs. Carter said that she thought Mr. Yost must be a highly intelligent man.

Mr. Maury waved his hand. "It ain't so much intelligence. It's genius, untutored genius. Now take me. I'm weighed down by my learning. It cripples my imagination. But this fellow, knowing nothing of the art, will rush in where angels fear to tread. At one stroke he's bridged the gap between bait fishing and fly casting. A Christopher Columbus, that's what he is—" He drew out his watch. "Seven o'clock. Don't you think we been out long enough? I want to find out how he makes his Skeeter Hawk."

It was ten o'clock but a light shone from over the transom of Number 18. Mr. Maury knocked. There was no answer but the sound of moving footsteps continued. Mr. Maury knocked again. The door opened and Jim Yost put his head out.

"I thought I'd come up and get you to show me how you made that Skeeter Hawk," Mr. Maury said.

Jim Yost smiled. "Sure. Come in and sit down. If you can find a place to sit." He removed two suits of clothes from a chair, then knelt before a yawning suitcase. "That Skeeter Hawk," he said. "You know, it was funny. I never could get the right kind of hair for the feelers till one night I was camping up in the Smokies." He raised his head and regarded Mr. Maury seriously. "I was laying on an old bearskin in front of the fire and I happened to throw my hand back. You know those stiff bristles around the nose were just the thing I'd been looking for. But I never would have found 'em if I hadn't happened to lay down on that old bearskin—"

Mr. Maury's eyes roved over the room. "It looks like you're going away?"

Yost nodded. "The notion just struck me about an hour ago, and I got a telegram from a pal of mine. He's up on the Suwannee River. I figure I can make it by tomorrow afternoon if I get a head start tonight."

"Suwannee River—" Mr. Maury said. "Fishing any good there?"

"It's as good as I want," Yost said. "You ought to try it sometime. Man, I made a run of a hundred and fifty bass there one day last fall."

Mr. Maury rose. "I'll be going along," he said. "You got to pack."

Yost, balancing on his haunches, looked up. "I won't be out of here for another hour," he said. "Say, I got an extra one of those

Skeeter Hawks. I'll come across it in a minute in one of these bags and I'll bring it over to you."

Mr. Maury nodded. "Much obliged," he said.

Back in his own room he sat down heavily in the big chair that was always pulled up to the lake window. Once he spoke aloud. "I might have known it," he said. "I might have known it." He got up and paced slowly about the room. Suddenly he paused, snapping his second finger and thumb together. "Aleck Maury," he said, "you're an old fool."

He went out into the corridor and knocked again on the door of Number 18.

"Come in," Yost called.

Mr. Maury entered and shut the door hurriedly behind him. "You got room in that car for a passenger?" he asked.

"Sure," Yost said. "Like to have you come along."

Mr. Maury nodded. "I ain't got much baggage. And that boat—Well, I ain't going to be tied down by any boat, no matter how good it is." He approached Yost and laid a hand on his arm. "They stay up late sometimes," he whispered, "but if Mrs. Bellows or any of 'em say anything to you, you don't know anything. You understand? You don't know anything."

Yost looked a little mystified. "Sure," he said.

Mr. Maury stepped out into the corridor once more. It was when he was halfway toward his own room that he met Henry. Mr. Maury stopped short. Henry, too, paused. "You want anything, Cap'm?"

Mr. Maury shook his head slowly from side to side. He glanced over Henry's shoulder at a door that was farther down the corridor. "Henry," he said, "what did you have to come along here now for?"

Henry grinned. "I just stepped up. Thought maybe that gentleman'd show me some of them baits you was telling about."

Mr. Maury shook his head again. Suddenly he drew out his wallet, took from it a five-dollar bill. "Henry," he said sharply. "You put that in your pocket. And don't you go thanking me. 'Nough noise round here now as 'tis."

Henry followed him in silence into his room. When they emerged forty-five minutes later Mr. Maury was carrying his three rod cases and a bunch of cane poles. A dip net was slung over Henry's shoulders and he staggered under the weight of two heavy bags. When he lost his footing and slipped on the landing Mr. Maury turned on him angrily. "You want to wake up the whole house?" he demanded.

They went softly through the hall and out onto the back porch. In the black shadow of the porte cochere ahead there was a faint red gleam: the taillight on Yost's roadster. Mr. Maury tiptoed across the dew-wet grass, sank into his seat. Henry was stowing the bags in the rumble. Mr. Maury took two white envelopes out of his pocket. "Henry," he said, "you give this envelope to Mrs. Bellows and you give this one to your mistress. I wouldn't want to be waking either of those ladies up this time of night to say goodbye."

Yost was climbing in beside him. "All set?" he asked.

They moved out from under the porte cochere onto the faintly lit street. Mr. Maury looked back. The wide façade of the house was pale under its black tracery of mimosa boughs. On the second floor there was one window where a light still gleamed. Mr. Maury raised his hand. His lips parted. He murmured:

" '*And snatch'd his rudder and shook out more sail—*' "

Jim Yost turned. "What'd you say?"

Mr. Maury leaned back. His fingers closed on his rod case. He kicked the minnow bucket into better place between his feet. "Nothing," he said. "How long'll it take us to get to that Suwannee River?"

The Last Day in the Field

That was the fall when the leaves stayed green so long. We had a drought in August and the ponds everywhere were dry and the watercourses shrunken. Then in September heavy rains came. Things greened up. It looked like winter was never coming.

"You aren't going to hunt this year, Aleck?" Molly said. "Remember how you stayed awake nights last fall with that pain in your leg."

In October light frosts came. In the afternoons when I sat on the back porch going over my fishing tackle I marked their progress on the elderberry bushes that were left standing against the stable fence. The lower, spreading branches had turned yellow and were already sinking to the ground but the leaves in the top clusters still stood up stiff and straight.

"Ah-ha, it'll get you yet!" I said, thinking how frost creeps higher and higher out of the ground each night of fall.

The dogs next door felt it and would thrust their noses through the wire fence scenting the wind from the north. When I walked in the back yard they would bound twice their height and whine, for meat scraps Molly said, but it was because they smelled blood on my old hunting coat.

They were almost matched liver-and-white pointers. The big dog had a beautiful, square muzzle and was deep-chested and rangy. The bitch, Judy, had a smaller head and not so good a muzzle but she was springy-loined too and had one of the merriest tails I've ever watched.

When Joe Thomas, the boy that owned them, came home from the hardware store he would change his clothes and then come down the back way and we would stand there watching the dogs and wondering how they would work. They had just been with a trainer up in Kentucky for three months. Joe said they were keen as mustard. He was going to take them out the first good Saturday and he wanted me to come along.

"I can't make it," I said. "My leg's worse this fall than it was last."

The fifteenth of November was clear and so warm that we sat out on the porch till nine o'clock. It was still warm when we went to bed toward eleven. The change must have come in the middle of the night. I woke once, hearing the clock strike two, and felt the air cold on my face and thought before I went back to sleep that the weather had broken at last. When I woke again toward dawn the cold air slapped my face hard. I came wide awake, turned over in bed, and looked out of the window. The sun was just coming up behind a wall of purple clouds streaked with amber. As I watched, it burned through and the light everywhere got bright.

There was a scaly bark hickory tree growing on the east side of the house. You could see its upper branches from the bedroom window. The leaves had turned yellow a week ago. But yesterday evening when I walked out there in the yard they had still been flat, with green streaks showing in them. Now they were curled up tight and a lot of leaves had fallen to the ground.

I got out of bed quietly so as not to wake Molly, dressed, and went down the back way over to the Thomas house. There was no one stirring but I knew which room Joe's was. The window was open and I could hear him snoring. I went up and stuck my head in.

"Hey," I said, "killing frost!"

He opened his eyes and looked at me and then his eyes went shut. I reached my arm through the window and shook him. "Get up," I said. "We got to start right away."

He was awake now and out on the floor stretching. I told him to dress and be over at the house as quick as he could. I'd have breakfast ready for us both.

Aunt Martha had a way of leaving fire in the kitchen stove at night. There were red embers there now. I poked the ashes out and piled kindling on top of them. When the flame came up I put some heavier wood on, filled the coffeepot, and put some grease on in a skillet. By the time Joe got there I had coffee ready and had stirred up some hoecakes to go with our fried eggs. Joe had brought a thermos bottle. We put the rest of the coffee in it and I found a ham in the pantry and made some sandwiches.

While I was fixing the lunch Joe went down to the lot to hitch up. He was just driving the buggy out of the stable when I came down the back steps. The dogs knew what was up, all right. They were whining and surging against the fence and Bob, the big dog, thrust his paw through and into the pocket of my hunting coat as I passed. While Joe was snapping on the leashes I got a few handfuls of straw from the rack and put it in the foot of the buggy. It was twelve miles where we were going; the dogs would need to ride warm coming back.

Joe said he would drive. We got in the buggy and started out, up Seventh Street, on over to College, and out through Scufftown. When we got into the nigger section we could see what a killing frost it had been. A light shimmer over all the ground still and the weeds around all the cabins dark and matted the way they are when the frost hits them hard and twists them.

We drove on over the Red River bridge and out into the open country. At Jim Gill's place the cows had come up and were standing there waiting to be milked but nobody was stirring yet from the house. I looked back from the top of the hill and saw that the frost mists still hung heavy in the bottom and thought it was a good sign. A day like this when the earth is warmer than the air currents is good for the hunter. Scent particles are borne on the warm air; and birds will forage far on such a day.

It took us over an hour to get from Gloversville to Spring Creek. Joe wanted to get out as soon as we hit the big bottom there but I held him down and we drove on through and up Rollow's hill to the top of the ridge. We got out there, unhitched Old Dick and turned him into one of Rob Fayerlee's pastures—I thought how surprised Rob would be when he looked out and saw him grazing there—put our guns together, and started out, with the dogs still on leash.

It was rough, broken ground, scrub oak with a few gum trees and lots of buckberry bushes. One place a patch of corn ran clear up to the top of the ridge. As we passed along between the rows, I could see the frost glistening on the north side of every stalk. I knew it was going to be a good day.

I walked over to the brow of the hill. From there you could see off over the whole valley—I've hunted over every foot of it in my time—tobacco land, mostly. One or two patches of cowpeas there on the side of the ridge. I thought we might start there and then I knew that wouldn't do. Quail will linger on the roost a cold day and feed in shelter during the morning. It is only in the afternoon that they will work out well into the open.

The dogs' whining made me turn around. Joe had bent down and was about to slip the leashes. "Hey, boy," I said, "wait a minute."

I turned around and looked down the other side of the hill. It looked better that way. The corn land of the bottoms ran high up onto the ridge in several places there and where the corn stopped there were big patches of ironweed and buckberry. I stooped and knocked my pipe out on a stump.

"Let's go that way," I said.

Joe was looking at my old buckhorn whistle that I had slung around my neck. "I forgot to bring mine," he said.

"All right," I said, "I'll handle 'em."

He unfastened their collars and cast off. They broke away, racing for the first hundred yards and barking, then suddenly swerved. The big dog took off to the right along the hillside. The bitch, Judy, skirted a belt of corn along the upper bottomlands. I kept my eye on the big dog. A dog that has bird sense knows cover when he sees it. This big Bob was an independent hunter. I could see him moving fast through the scrub oaks, working his way down toward a patch of ironweed. He caught the first scent traces just on the edge of the weed patch and froze. Judy, meanwhile, had been following the line of the cornfield. A hundred yards away she caught sight of Bob's point and backed him.

We went up and flushed the birds. They got up in two bunches. I heard Joe's shot while I was in the act of raising my gun and I saw his bird fall not thirty paces from where I stood. I had covered a middle bird of the larger bunch—that's the one led by the boss cock—the way I usually do. He fell, whirling head over heels, driven a little forward by the impact. A well-centered shot. I could tell by the way the feathers fluffed as he tumbled.

The dogs were off through the grass. They had retrieved both birds. Joe stuck his in his pocket. He laughed. "I thought there for a minute you were going to let him get away."

I looked at him but I didn't say anything. It's a wonderful thing to be twenty years old.

The majority of the singles had flown straight ahead to settle in the rank grass that jutted out from the bottomland. Judy got down to work at once but the big dog broke off to the left, wanting to get footloose to find another covey. I thought of how Gyges, the best dog I ever had—the best dog any man ever had—used always to want to do the same thing, and I laughed.

"Naw, you won't," I said. "Come back here, you scoundrel, and hunt these singles."

He stopped on the edge of a briar patch, looked at me, and heeled up promptly. I clucked him out again. He gave me another look. I thought we were beginning to understand each other better. We got some nice points among those singles and I found him reasonably steady to both wing and shot, needing only a little control.

We followed that valley along the creek bed through two or three more cornfields without finding another covey. Joe was disappointed but I wasn't worrying yet; you always make your bag in the afternoon.

It was twelve o'clock by this time. We turned up the ravine toward Buck Springs. They had cleared out some of the big trees on the sides of the ravine but the spring itself was just the same: the tall sycamore tree and the water pouring in a thin stream over the slick rocks. I unwrapped the sandwiches and the pieces of cake and laid them on a stump. Joe had got the thermos bottle out of his pocket. Something had gone wrong with it and the coffee was stone cold. We were about to drink it that way when Joe saw a good tin can flung down beside the spring. He made a trash fire and we put the coffee in the can and heated it to boiling.

Joe finished his last sandwich and reached for the cake. "Good ham," he said.

"It's John Ferguson's," I said. I was watching the dogs. They were tired, all right. Judy had scooped out a soft place between the roots of a sycamore but the big dog, Bob, lay there with his forepaws stretched out before him, never taking his eyes off our faces. I looked at him and thought how different he was from his mate and like some dogs I had known—and men, too—who lived only for hunting and could never get enough no matter how long the day was. There was something about his head and his markings that reminded me of another dog I used to hunt with a long time ago and I asked the boy who had trained him. He said the old fellow he bought the dogs from had been killed last spring, over in Trigg: Charley Morrison.

Charley Morrison. I remembered how he died. Out hunting by himself and the gun had gone off, accidentally, they said. Charley had called the dog to him, got blood all over him, and sent him home. The dog went, all right, but when they got there Charley was dead. Two years ago that was and now I was hunting the last dogs he'd ever trained. . . .

Joe lifted the thermos bottle. "Another cup?"

I held my cup out and he filled it. The coffee was still good and hot. I lit my pipe and ran my eye over the country in front of us. I always enjoy figuring out which way they'll go. This afternoon with the hot coffee in me and the ache gone from my leg I felt like I could do it. It's not as hard as it looks. A well-organized covey has a range, like chickens. I knew what they'd be doing this time of day: in a thicket, dusting—sometimes they'll get up in grapevine swings. Then after they've fed and rested they'll start out again, working always toward the open.

Joe was stamping out his cigarette. "Let's go."

The dogs were already out of sight but I could see the sedge grass ahead moving and I knew they'd be making for the same thing that took my eye: a spearhead of thicket that ran far out into this open field. We came up over a little rise. There they were. Bob on a point and Judy, the staunch little devil, backing him, not fifty feet from the thicket. I saw it was going to be tough shooting. No way to tell whether the birds were between the dog and the thicket or in the thicket itself. Then I saw that the cover was more open along the side of the thicket and I thought that that was the way they'd go if they were in the thicket. But Joe had already broken away to the left. He got too far to the side. The birds flushed to the right and left him standing, flat-footed, without a shot.

He looked sort of foolish and grinned.

I thought I wouldn't say anything and then found myself speaking:

"Trouble with you, you try to outthink the dog."

There was nothing to do about it now, though, and the chances were that the singles had pitched through the trees below. We went down there. It was hard hunting. The woods were open, the ground heavily carpeted everywhere with leaves. Dead leaves make a tremendous rustle when the dogs surge through them; it takes a good nose to cut scent keenly in such dry, noisy cover. I kept my eye on Bob. He never faltered, getting over the ground in big, springy strides but combing every inch of it. We came to an open place in the woods. Nothing but big hickory trees and bramble thickets overhung with trailing vines. Bob passed the first thicket and came to a beautiful point. We went up. He stood perfectly steady but the bird flushed out fifteen or twenty steps ahead of him. I saw it swing to the right, gaining altitude very quickly, and it came to me how it would be.

I called to Joe: "Don't shoot yet."

He nodded and raised his gun, following the bird with the barrel. It was directly over the treetops when I gave the word and he shot, scoring a clean kill.

He laughed excitedly as he stuck the bird in his pocket. "*Man!* I didn't know you could take that much time!"

We went on through the open woods. I was thinking about a day I'd had years ago, in the woods at Grassdale, with my uncle James Morris and his son Julian. Uncle James had given Julian and me hell for missing just such a shot. I can see him now, standing up against a big pine tree, his face red from liquor and his gray hair ruffling in the wind: "*Let him alone. Let him alone!* And establish your lead as he *climbs!*"

Joe was still talking about the shot he'd made. "Lord, I wish I could get another one like that."

"You won't," I said. "We're getting out of the woods now."

We struck a path that led through the woods. My leg was stiff from the hip down and every time I brought it over the pain would start in my knee, zing, and travel up and settle in the small of my back. I walked with my head down, watching the light catch on the ridges of Joe's brown corduroy trousers and then shift and catch again as he moved forward. Sometimes he would get on ahead and then there would be nothing but the black tree trunks coming up out of the dead leaves that were all over the ground.

Joe was talking about that wild land up on the Cumberland. We could get up there some Saturday on an early train. Have a good day. Might even spend the night. When I didn't answer he turned around. "Man, you're sweating!"

I pulled my handkerchief out and wiped my face. "Hot work," I said.

He had stopped and was looking about him. "Used to be a spring somewhere around here."

He had found the path and was off. I sat down on a stump and mopped my face some more. The sun was halfway down through the trees, the whole west woods ablaze with light. I sat there and thought that in another hour it would be good dark and I wished that the day could go on and not end so soon and yet I didn't see how I could make it much farther with my leg the way it was.

Joe was coming up the path with his folding cup full of water. I hadn't thought I was thirsty but the cold water tasted good. We sat there awhile and smoked. It was Joe said we ought to be starting back, that we must be a good piece from the rig by this time.

We set out, working north through the edge of the woods. It was rough going and I was thinking that it would be all I could do to make it back to the rig when we climbed a fence and came out at one end of a long field. It sloped down to a wooded ravine, broken ground badly gullied and covered with sedge everywhere except where sumac thickets had sprung up—as birdy a place as ever I saw. I looked it over and I knew I'd have to hunt it, leg or no leg, but it would be close work, for me and the dogs too.

I blew them in a bit and we stood there watching them cut up the cover. The sun was down now; there was just enough light left to see the dogs work. The big dog circled the far wall of the basin and came upwind just off the drain, then stiffened to a point. We walked down to it. The birds had obviously run a bit, into the scraggly sumac stalks that bordered the ditch. My mind was so much on the dogs that I forgot Joe. He took one step too many and the fullest-blown bevy of the day roared up through the tangle. It had to be fast work. I raised my gun and scored with the only barrel I had time to peg. Joe shouted: I knew he had got one too.

We stood awhile trying to figure out which way the singles had gone. But they had fanned out too quick for us and after beating around the thicket for fifteen minutes or so we gave up and went on.

We came to the rim of the swale, eased over it, crossed the dry creek bed that was drifted thick with leaves, and started up the other side. I had blown in the dogs, thinking there was no use for them to run their heads off now we'd started home, but they didn't come. I walked a little way, then I looked back and saw Bob's white shoulders through a tangle of cinnamon vines.

Joe had turned around too. "Look a yonder! They've pinned a single out of that last covey."

"Your shot, " I told him.

He shook his head. "No, you take it."

I went back and flushed the bird. It went skimming along the buckberry bushes that covered that side of the swale. In the fading light I could hardly make it out and I shot too quick. It swerved over the thicket and I let go with the second barrel. It staggered, then zoomed up. Up, up, up, over the rim of the hill and above the tallest hickories. I saw it there for a second, its wings black against the gold light, before, wings still spread, it came whirling down, like an autumn leaf, like the leaves that were everywhere about us, all over the ground.

The Presence

Mr. Maury woke from his nap late. When he came downstairs Miss Gilbert was already settled in his big wicker chair at the north end of the porch. Mr. Maury stood in the doorway and waved his palm-leaf fan. The leaves of the hibiscus vine fluttered. Miss Gilbert inclined her aquiline nose. Mr. Maury waited. The nose disappeared into a great scarlet cup, then tilted upward again, unpolluted by any golden grain.

"Damned hummingbird!" Mr. Maury said under his breath as he took his seat in the chair next to hers, sighing to feel the wooden slats pressing into the fleshy part of his back. Some lines from an old song came into his head:

> "All dressed in white linen,
> As cold as the clay . . ."

She dressed in white, winter and summer, to set off her white hair and blue eyes; she would ask to be dressed in white when it came time to lay her out. But that was a long way off. Take her all in all, liver, lights, kidneys—he winced—she was sounder than he was.

Miss Gilbert looked up from her book. "Jenny's train was two hours late," she said.

"Well, she got here," Mr. Maury said. "It was time. Life's not worth living without her. At least my life isn't. . . . But my life's hardly worth living, anyhow." He sighed again.

Miss Gilbert's pince-nez glittered as she turned toward him. "Oh, how I wish I could persuade you to read this book!" she said earnestly. She held it up. Gold letters were incised on its limp white leather cover: *In Tune with the Infinite*, by Ralph Waldo Trine.

Mr. Maury shook his head. "I can't hardly stand Ralph Waldo Emerson." He leaned forward suddenly. "You rascal!" he shouted. "You come out of those bushes."

A blue-ticked setter burst through the shrubbery and, rushing up to him, stood, panting, saliva drooling from her open jaws onto his knee. Mr. Maury held her in the crook of his arm and pulled the cockleburs from her ears.

A big, sunburned man in hunting clothes came up on the porch. He slid a game bag from his shoulder. Mr. Maury released the dog and, bending over, his legs spread wide apart, emptied the bag of birds. "Nine," he said, and, bending farther forward, touched a warm, speckled feather with the tip of his finger. "Nine, not counting what you got in your pockets, you scoundrel! . . . Well, which way'd you go?"

The hunter sat down at the foot of one of the big columns that supported the gallery. "You know that biggest stand of pine out at Tom Sullivan's?"

Mr. Maury nodded eagerly. "There's a branch runs through it, southeast. Grapevines thick as fleas on a dog's back. . . . But you didn't find anything there?"

"That big dog of Joe's found our first covey in the next field."

"She back him?"

"I'll say. I brought down two birds."

Mr. Maury pulled the dog's ear ecstatically. "That old big dog, how'd he work?"

"He sure gets over the ground, but he ain't got the nose she's got."

"How was she on the singles?"

"Man, you ought to seen her!"

Mr. Maury let out a whistle. "You got something, Jim!"

Jim Mowbray leaned back against the column. His brown eyes, mottled, Mr. Maury had always thought, like the sides of a trout, met Mr. Maury's in a long, companionable look. "Just give me another season on her!"

"You're tired, man," Mr. Maury said solicitously. "You go and take a hot bath. I'll feed her."

Jim Mowbray was stuffing the birds back into the bag. Mr.

Maury took it from him and went down the steps and along the path, edged with night-blooming jasmine, to the kitchen quarters. In the twilight the blossoms were already giving off a faint fragrance. But there was a sharper smell in the air. He came to the old pine tree, where the paths forked, one path going on to the little back court, the other leading into the grove. Mingled with the mimosas and cork bark trees were clusters of bamboo shoots which Mrs. Mowbray had allowed Mr. Maury to root there when he had first come to board with her ten years ago. Mr. Maury paused beside the pine tree and let the game bag trail on the ground. The bruised, brown needles gave off a smell of resin. A mimosa bough ahead of him was suddenly feathered with light; the new moon was rising behind the grove. He slung the game bag up over his shoulder by its canvas strap. His nostrils widened. The grove ended, he knew, at the fence which divided the Mowbray lot from the Hamlins', yet as he stood there, the pine needles crisp under his feet, their smell sharp in his nostrils, the grove seemed larger. That dark round at his right was not the ridged column of a bamboo shoot but the smooth bole of a beech. There were elms and oaks and hickories ahead. He might have been making his way home, at day's end, by the slanting rays of the sun, his game bag heavy on his shoulder. . . .

The setter whined and pressed against his leg. "Come on," he said, and turned back toward the kitchen.

The cook looked up from the electric mixer she was operating. "Doctor, git that dog off my clean floor," she said plaintively.

Mr. Maury took a quarter from his pocket and tossed it on the table. "Go on, get me that ham bone you got in the refrigerator. This is a big day in this dog's life."

"Big day in *my* life," she said. "Be picking birds here till midnight." She stilled her machine and, opening the refrigerator, drew the remains of a ham out of a cellophane wrapper. The dog leaped up, whining. She kicked her aside. "You better cut it off," she said, "I got my mayonnaise to make."

Mr. Maury swiftly stripped the bone of meat and threw it through the open doorway. The dog whirled after it. "Now give me some more scraps," he said. She pointed to a garbage can. He bent and patiently disentangled some scraps of meat from the vegetable refuse, heaped them on a plate, and, going to the door, called the setter. A growl came from the shrubbery. Mr. Maury laughed as he set the plate on the ground. He glanced overhead. The moon had climbed over the mimosas and was riding into the branches of the pine. They said it was bad luck to look at the new moon through the leaves, but he was not engaged now—had not been engaged since those wharf rats had reported to Miss Jenny that he had almost drowned getting in and out of his boat, and she had made him stop fishing—in any enterprise that called for the favor of the gods. . . . But what a night for high emprise! The dog growled again from her cover. He stood and gazed into the grove. A cloud was sailing toward the moon. They met in the branches of the pine. The cloud passed. Light welled from the moon, ran quicksilver down a bamboo shoot, splashed onto the brown earth. What he had thought was the trunk of a tree stirred. Another shape was moving toward it. They merged into one. The dark mass remained motionless for several seconds, then resolved into two blunt columns that passed slowly between the trunks of the trees. One was shorter than the other.

"Jim?" he shouted.

There was no answer. In the kitchen Daisy was singing, loud enough to drown the whir of the mixer. The bushes rustled. The setter had finished burying her bone and, wagging her tail, now approached her plate. He patted her on the head and turned back into the house.

There was no one in the living room. He went out on the porch. Miss Gilbert still had his chair. The streetlight at the corner had come on. He dragged the clumsy wooden chair back into the shadow of the vines. "That Jim Mowbray is a remarkable fellow," he said meditatively.

A sound came from Miss Gilbert. A sniff? Or was she merely clearing her throat? "I have no doubt that he's a competent game warden," she said.

"*Game warden?*" Mr. Maury repeated. "Any fool can be a game warden. This fellow's one of the greatest trainers ever lived. Good as Uncle Jim Avent, if you ask me. And he was the greatest trainer and handler this country ever produced, till he got mixed up with those rich Yankee women. . . ."

"What happened to him?" Miss Gilbert asked.

"Oh, he didn't lose his virtue," Mr. Maury said coarsely, "they just took him to the cleaner's. . . . But this Mowbray now, he's got as much natural talent as Uncle Jim and I be dog if I don't find him more inventive. He's worked out some shortcuts that'd astonish you. At least they astonish *me*. . . . Take this little bitch. He got her only last September, and look at her . . . just look at her!"

Miss Gilbert made the same sound. A sniff, or he was a Dutchman. "I am no judge of his sportsmanship," she said. "I could never bear to take the life of any fellow creature." And she got up and went into the house.

"No," Mr. Maury said aloud to the semitropical night. "No, but Nature is sure red in your tooth and claw. Nose, too, if you ask me."

The supper bell rang. He entered the dining room before its last peal had died away. Jenny Mowbray, who had been away in Kentucky visiting her father for the last three weeks, was already in her place at the head of the table. She wore a camellia in her brown hair; her face, flushed from the ardors of the kitchen, was almost as pink as the petals of the flower. She made a face at him as he sat down beside her. "You haven't said a word about being glad to see me," she told him, and took his fan from him and fanned herself so vigorously that the damp tendrils of hair curling about her forehead quivered.

"My heart is too full for words," Mr. Maury said.

She gave a childlike giggle and looked about the table with bright eyes; a bantam hen, counting her chickens. She took a fierce, motherly interest in all her boarders. But there was malice in her, too. She had him and the cook in stitches sometimes at her imitation of the way old Mr. Sloane walked, one hand curved over the small of his back, protecting his kidneys, Jenny said. She kept a straight face whenever Miss Gilbert's name was mentioned—"She's really a very kind person, Doctor"—but you couldn't tell *him* that she didn't see through that old sack of acid.

The other boarders had assembled. Phyllis, the waitress, brought a great platter through the swinging door. "Chicken and dumplings," Mr. Maury said with satisfaction. He looked at Riva Gaines, the young divorcée who had kept the boardinghouse while Miss Jenny was away. One Sunday Riva had given them hash, baked, it is true, and crusted with cheese, but hash, for all that, from the remains of Friday's roast. Miss Jenny would never do a thing like that. He helped himself to a piece of breast and three tender dumplings and detained Phyllis until he had poured out four ladlefuls of the delicate golden gravy, but before he took a bite he turned to Jenny. "Those shots do your father's arthritis any good?" he asked.

She shook her head. Her soft, red mouth drooped. "Papa's hands are so crippled up he can't even hold the paper to read. But his mind's failed so now he can't remember what he reads. . . . It's a terrible thing to lose your faculties, Doctor."

A pang shot through the knuckle bone of Mr. Maury's right index finger. Before him a vista seemed to open, a tunnel, whose low, arched side oozed dark mist. At the far end a stooping, shawled figure slowly raised a clumsy, bandaged hand. From the dank walls the moisture poured faster; the figure was dissolving in gray mist; he could no longer see even the feebly raised right hand. . . . A terrible thing to lose your faculties. . . . What a terrible thing it would be if he lost his mind that to him such a kingdom was! He turned to Jenny, his lip trembling. "I haven't been so well," he said. "My kidneys trouble me a great deal."

She gave his arm a quick pressure. "Dr. Weathers wrote me out a prescription for you."

"Now that was clever of him," he said. "I'll get it filled first thing in the morning."

Riva Gaines asked Mr. Maury to pass her the salt.

"You'd better not eat so much salt," Mr. Maury said. "Don't you know it's fattening?"

Riva shook her long bob back and sat up straighter. "You think I need to diet?" she asked.

Mr. Maury looked at the narrow gray belt that set off a waist that a man might almost have spanned with one hand. She had on her pearl necklace tonight and every blond, sinuously waved hair shone as if it had been polished. "You going juking tonight?" he inquired.

"You going to the movies?" she parried.

"It's Dorothy Lamour," Mr. Maury said. "I'm kind of tired of her."

"If you don't go, will you keep an eye on Benny?"

Mr. Maury allowed his dark, crafty eye to rest on the breasts showing under the gray sweater as firm and pointed as new hickory buds. "You ought to get married again," he said, "then you wouldn't run around so much, nights."

Her full mouth widened in its ready smile as her gray eyes engaged his, but her glance was abstracted; she was thinking of her unhappy marriage. Joe Gaines had had the best-equipped service station in town and the Cadillac agency to boot, but he had got to running with a tough gang and neglected his business and one day walked out, owing everybody in town. Riva had had to go to work at the packing plant, handling the payroll, working overtime two or three nights a week. Still, nobody ever heard her complain. Her eyes were brightening, her smile turned arch. "You didn't need to say that in front of everybody!" she said.

Jim Mowbray came in, greeted the guests, and took his place at the foot of the table.

"You heard that, Jim?" Mr. Maury called.

Jim looked up. "You want to watch her," he said. He had changed into a fresh white suit and wore a new tie in a striking pattern of brown and yellow, but an outdoor air still clung about him. His face was ordinarily the color of cured tobacco but tonight his nose and his forehead—he always pushed his cap to one side when he got excited—carried a fresh burn, and the handsome tie, knotted loosely across his unbuttoned shirt collar, did not conceal the raw, brick-red patch at the base of his powerful neck.

"She's trying to back me into a corner, Jim," Mr. Maury said, elaborating the agreeable fiction that the attractive twenty-eight-year-old woman was attempting to extract an offer of marriage from him in order that she might sue him for breach of promise. "Now what would *you* do in a case like that?"

Jim looked up again, briefly. Mr. Maury had never noticed before how long and thick his lashes were, long enough for a woman. "I wouldn't hardly know how to advise a fellow in a case like that," he said, and looked down at his plate and began to eat, steadily and silently.

The dessert came on: lemon pudding. Mr. Maury shook his head at Phyllis. "You know I can't eat anything with lemon in it."

Mrs. Mowbray started and spoke quietly. "Phyllis, bring Doctor some of that new quince preserves."

Phyllis took the pudding away and set a small glass preserve dish before Mr. Maury. He regarded it with delight and called for more hot biscuits and butter. Miss Gilbert was eyeing the golden crescents, which seemed, so delicate was Miss Jenny's art, to swim in their own honey. He pushed the dish a little to one side of his plate. "How much of these preserves have you got?" he inquired.

Jenny laughed. "A gallon. Enough to last you all winter." She looked at Miss Gilbert. "Miss Anna, I didn't stay on that diet but two days. My brother had a fresh Jersey cow. I declare, the cream was as thick as butter."

"I thought you'd taken on a little weight," Miss Gilbert said, stiffening her slender back.

Mr. Maury pulled the butter plate toward him. "Miss Jenny don't want to get lean and stringy," he said. "She's the Junoesque type."

"Now you know I'd look better if I fell off about ten pounds," Jenny said.

"Fifteen," Miss Gilbert said.

Mr. Maury helped himself again to preserves. "A woman gets too thin, her better nature dries up," he said. He looked about the table. " 'Who can find a virtuous woman,' " he asked. " 'for her price is far above rubies . . . She seeketh wool, and flax, and worketh willingly with her hands. . . .' "

"I do know how to knit . . ." Jenny said.

" 'She looketh well to the ways of her household, and eateth not the bread of idleness,' " Mr. Maury said. He shook a fork, dripping with golden syrup, at Riva Gaines. "You'd better learn how to make preserves like this if you want me to marry you."

She rose from the table, laughing. The two drugstore clerks and old Mr. Sloane followed her out into the hall. Jim, Miss Gilbert, and the Jacksons went, too. There was no one left in the room except himself and Jenny. He pushed his chair back from the table but did not rise, the words he had just spoken still echoing in his mind: ". . . The heart of her husband doth safely trust in her . . . Her children arise up and call her blessed . . ." Jim and Jenny had no children, no young to cherish, unless you could count the bird dogs; there were always half a dozen back there in the yard. Jenny was as crazy about them as Jim was. And she did not spoil them, one of the few women he had ever known who knew how to treat a bird dog. Phyllis moved softly about, loading her tray with dishes. Jenny, who ordinarily, at this hour of the day, was all bustle and directions, sat, leaning her elbow on the table, her dark blue eyes fixed on his face. He met her gaze with surprise. She had never looked at him like that before, as if she had for a long time taken him on his own recommendation and was only now asking herself what manner of man he really was. "You tired?" he asked.

She arched her dark, silky brows. Her expression became lively, though still a little tinged with melancholy. "I've got to go out to see Betty Slocomb with Miss Anna. . . . She can't even sit up in bed now. It's a sad world, Doctor."

"It is, for a fact," Mr. Maury said. "I'm glad I'm not long for it."
"Oh, *you!*" she said. "All the friends you've got!"

"What's friends?" Mr. Maury inquired gloomily. "You say I'm too old to go hunting or fishing. What am I going to do? I'm like Milton in his blindness. 'That one talent it were death to hide, lodged in me useless.' . . . Miss Jenny, you don't know what it is to sit around all day, doing nothing. . . ."

She patted him on the shoulder. "You know I couldn't run this boardinghouse without you. All these people, with all their temperaments. . . ."

"They are a set of catamounts," Mr. Maury said. "Takes somebody to keep 'em in order." He cut himself a plug of tobacco and went out on the porch.

There was no one there except old Mr. Sloane. He asked Mr. Maury if he would like a game of checkers. "I'm not in the mood for it," Mr. Maury said. Mr. Sloane said that he himself didn't care whether he played or not. The two old men sat and silently gazed out on the street where the young people passed, on their way to the movies or the juke joints.

After a little, Riva Gaines came down. Mr. Maury told her that he had decided not to go to the movies and would take care of Benny if he woke. "But he ought not to go waking up so much at night," he added irritably. Riva thanked him in what was for her an unusually subdued tone and went on through the gate, to the house of her intimate friend, Mabel Turner, he supposed. A few minutes later Jim Mowbray came out, with his wife and Miss Gilbert.

"Well, Jim, we got her back," Mr. Maury said.

Jenny steadied herself with a hand on her husband's arm while she pinned a fresh camellia in her hair. "Doctor, he didn't write to me but once while I was in Kentucky. Does that look like he wanted me back?"

"He was afraid you would find out how things were going here," Mr. Maury said.

She laughed. "Was it all that bad?"

"Scandalous," Mr. Maury said. "I was about to move over to Wares'," naming the rival boardinghouse of the town.

Jim took a step forward. "Jim," Mr. Maury said, "where'd you go from Tom's place?"

"Over to Tillot's. Started two coveys there."

"That big live oak still standing in his east field?"

"Hurricane seems to have got it." He was turning off on the path to the garage.

"Where you going?" Mr. Maury asked.

"Thought I'd shoot a little pool."

The two women went down the front walk. "Where *you* going?" Mr. Maury called.

Jenny turned around. "Out to Betty Slocomb's. If anybody calls, will you answer the phone, Doctor?"

Mr. Maury assured her that he would. Jim Mowbray brought the car around from the garage and halted it at the gate. He climbed out and held the door open while the women got in. The car moved off down the quiet street.

Mr. Sloane yawned and said he thought he would go up to bed. Mr. Maury rose and dragged his chair over to where a gap in the vines gave a better view of the street. While they had been indoors the night had come closer. The sky was a deep gentian blue. His eyes, as always—for he could not believe that he would rise to a dawn whose doings took no account of fair or foul weather—roamed the heavens until they found the elongated diamond shape, rough with small stars: Cygnus, the Swan, who always flies west in fair weather. He had first seen it when he was ten or eleven years old, coming home from duck hunting with Uncle James. They had been wondering whether it would rain tomorrow, when Uncle James looked up and saw the Bird flying west. He had stopped and made him crane his neck and stare until he saw it, too: "Cygnus, the Swan, Aleck, the shape Zeus took when he wooed Leda. . . ." But Zeus had wooed Io, too, and many another mortal. His wife, Juno, who suffered from jealousy, for all that she was Queen of Heaven, had set her servant, Argus, to spy on them. When Argus fell asleep Juno was so enraged that she tore out his hundred eyes and cast them, not into the heavens, but onto the peacock's tail. . . . Was it in the *Iliad* or the *Odyssey* that Zeus had hung her up for three days in a golden net of old Vulcan's contriving and called on all the gods to come and taunt her? As a boy he had been distressed by the figure she cut. In his childish mind pagan and Christian symbols had mingled. He had always thought of Uncle James's wife, Aunt Victoria, the tall, statuesque, blue-eyed woman who had brought him up, as a sort of queen of heaven. Was that because she was noted for her piety and her good works or because Uncle James sometimes referred to her as "Junoesque"?

Soft, bare feet brushed the hall carpet. Mr. Maury did not turn around.

"Where's my mother?" the little boy asked.

"Said she's going over to Mabel Turner's. . . . What you want?"

"I want a drink of water."

Mr. Maury turned around. "When a big man like you wants a drink of water, what's to keep him from getting it out of the cooler himself?"

A thin, towheaded child came slowly through the doorway and fixed Mr. Maury's face with glittering, accusing eyes. "You tell me about Br'er Rabbit," he said.

"I ain't going to do anything of the kind," Mr. Maury said.

The child pressed up against his knee, shaking it a little. "Why?"

Mr. Maury set his hand on the fragile shoulder and held the child's body still. "What you reckon Br'er Rabbit's got them long ears for? He can hear every word we say."

The child tossed his head. In his faded, shrunken pajamas, his shock of almost white hair shining faintly in the moonlight, he looked like some albino woods creature, strayed from its burrow. "We ain't saying anything," he said defiantly.

"He don't like to hear *no* kind of talking at night," Mr. Maury said. He got up. The child caught at his hand. "Where you going?"

Mr. Maury went through the hall and started up the stairs. "I'm going to leave my door open a crack," he said, "and if I hear one peep out of you I ain't going to tell you another story as long as I live."

They were at the head of the stairs. The boy halted at the door of the bedroom he shared with his mother. "Which one you going to tell me in the morning?"

Mr. Maury, in his room, sat down heavily in a chair. "Might be about the time Br'er Fox lost his tail. But it ain't no use talking about it. You ain't going to be quiet." He bent and began unlacing his shoes. The child slipped away. Mr. Maury could hear the door to his bedroom creaking as he stood and swung it to and fro. Mr. Maury went to the closet and got out his bedroom slippers. "Good night," he said. There was a subdued "Good night" and then light, skittering sounds; the little creature was hurling himself into bed. Mr. Maury finished undressing, put on his nightshirt, got into bed, and, propping himself up on two pillows, took up his book, *The Light of Western Stars*, and began to read.

But he had read this book three times before. And Zane Grey, he reflected, was poor pabulum for a man who had known the real thing. Why, he himself, in his faraway youth, had roved all over the West, had seen all that Zane Grey had seen, and more, and could tell about it better. But that was long ago. Now he could only lie in bed and read about what other men did . . . or sit on the porch till they came home and told you what kind of day they had had in the field. . . . Jim Mowbray, out hunting since sunup and going off, after supper, as fresh as a daisy, to shoot pool! A good fellow, Jim, a real Florida cracker, to hear him talk, but he came, like his wife, of good Kentucky stock. It showed, in unexpected reticences, in little deferential ways toward women. . . . He was blessed with a good wife, the daughter of old Judge Beckitt, who had emigrated here in '98 and then, when he went broke in '32, had gone back to Kentucky to die. She was forty-five to Jim's forty-seven, but she looked older, because she was plump. Miss Gilbert was always at her to reduce, but there was no need for a settled woman to starve herself and get as lean and nervous as a cat, like Riva Gaines, for instance. Jenny Mowbray relished her own food—you could tell that from her rosy complexion—and why shouldn't she, for where could you find a better cook?

The front door opened. There was the sound of voices and steps on the stairs. Two women were ascending. One of them seemed to have to be urged to mount, for he heard a whisper, "Come on. Come *on*, now!"

He leaned forward but could see nothing except the sliver of light from the hall shining through the crack in his door. The steps passed his door, stopped. At the Mowbrays' bedroom or Miss Gilbert's? A door closed. A murmuring, low but ominous, like the gathering hum of bees, was interrupted by a moan. It lasted only a second but it rang on in his head after it had died away.

He got out of bed and took a bottle down from the glass shelf over his washbowl. He had forgotten to take his medicine before he went to bed. This was as good a time as any to take it, now that they had roused him. That was the trouble with a boardinghouse. People came in at all hours of the night. Riva Gaines had probably had too much to drink and some of her gang were seeing her home.

There was a tap on his door. "Well, what is it?" he called, and moved forward, glass in hand.

Miss Gilbert put her head in. "Have you got any spirits of ammonia?"

He shook his head. "Ring up the drugstore."

She seemed not to realize that he was in his nightshirt. She advanced into the room. Her eyes stared palely into his. She wrung her long bird's claws and then with one of them caught at the back of a chair. "I'm afraid to leave her," she said.

Mr. Maury hastily slipped on his trousers. "Who's sick?" he asked when he had finished buttoning the last button.

She raised her head. The cry had come again, a faint, sharp, anguished question. . . . Where had he heard that cry before?

He went with her into the hall. She paused before the door of Mrs. Mowbray's bedroom, opened the door a little, paused again. "Jenny," she said in a low voice, "Doctor Maury wants to see you."

Mr. Maury pushed her aside and entered the room. The ceiling light was on. Jenny lay on the bed, on her back, her arms flung out on each side of her. Her jaw was slack, her mouth a little open. Her eyes fixed the ceiling widely. He had the feeling that she was trying to stare it down on top of them.

He went nearer the bed. "Miss Jenny . . ." he said gently.

Miss Gilbert was at his side. "*Pool!*" she whispered. "Shooting a little pool!"

Mr. Maury drew back. "There isn't any law against that."

She came closer. "Jenny wanted to get some raspberry ice, to take home, so we stopped at the Mayfair and there they were, out on the floor, *dancing.* . . ."

"Dancing . . ." Mr. Maury said slowly. "Jim and that Gaines woman . . ."

Her eyes shone tigerishly into his. "I wondered how long it would take you to see it. All the time Jenny was in Kentucky. I started to write her. Oh, I was never so torn! There's no faith in men."

Jenny sat up. She passed her hands over her face, hiding her eyes for a second behind her cupped palms, then her hands went to her disordered hair. "You all will have to excuse me," she said, "you'll just have to excuse me." Her voice broke. She shuddered and flung herself face downward on the bed.

"Miss Gilbert," Mr. Maury said, "you go downstairs and fix Miss Jenny a hot toddy."

She hesitated, looking from him to the prone figure. "Make it plenty hot," he said calmly, as if he were speaking to a recalcitrant boy in the schoolroom. "It'll cool off some before you get it upstairs."

She was gone. He crossed the room and sat down in a chair beside the open window. The heap on the bed stirred.

"Doctor, you go on to bed," Jenny said weakly.

He shook his head. "You sat up with me when I was sick."

He had been ill with influenza for two weeks. She had nursed him well and he had recovered. . . . But here was a kind of death. She lay there like a shot bird.

"Did you have any talk with him?" he asked.

She sat up on the side of the bed. "He came out to the car. . . . Doctor, he wants to marry that woman."

"He don't want to do anything of the kind," he said.

"Oh, yes," she said, and twisted her delicate mouth that he had always thought so pretty. "I hope they'll be happy. She must want him mighty bad." Her low, hoarse voice broke into a sob. She crossed the room heavily, went behind a screen. He could hear her washing her face and hands. She came out from behind the screen. The pale yellow towel was still crumpled in her hands. She looked at it in a kind of surprise and flung it from her onto the floor. "It doesn't take long in Florida," she said.

"I wouldn't do anything in a hurry," he said.

She began to cry again. She put her empty hands down at her sides and walked to the window. "To think of her staying here . . . letting me keep her child, nights . . ."

"Women'll do anything these days," Mr. Maury said.

She turned toward him a face stonier for having been bathed in fresh tears. "I'm going to call Mr. Murphy in the morning."

Sanders Murphy had been her father's law partner. He had influence with the circuit judge. Jim Mowbray would be divorced and married again before he knew what had happened to him.

"You don't need to go so fast," he said. "Listen . . . Miss Jenny . . ."

She left the window. Her head cocked on one side, her eyes bright with tears, she spoke musingly: "I think I'll sell this place and go to Kentucky. . . ."

"What about me?" his heart cried out. "You'll run off to Kentucky. I'll have to find some other place to live." And he could not live just anywhere. She knew that.

"Yes," she said, "I'll list it—tomorrow."

"You could get your money out, all right," he said drearily.

Miss Gilbert came back with the toddy. He said good night and went to his room, put his coat on over his nightshirt, and went down the stairs, stumbling on the last step, and out onto the porch.

There was no sound anywhere on the street. The town slept. He wondered where Jim and that girl were. They would not dare to come back to the house tonight. In some tourist cabin, probably, some place that took fly-by-nighters. Well, they might as well get used to being on the bum. Jim Mowbray was not a man to stand up to women . . . as fine a wing shot as ever lived, as gifted a handler! His heavy hand fell slack on his knee. There were places on this earth's surface that he would never revisit. . . . Oh, the light on the long grass, on the green, willowy pool! They did not know why you went or where, but let a man break the lockstep and go over the hill and they grew frightened and watched his return with implacable eyes; sometimes they denied him the privilege of resuming his chains. . . .

Miss Gilbert came out on the porch and sat down in the chair next to his. She had on a white, woolly wrap and held a glass full of some milky fluid in her hand. "Will you have a glass of Theno-Malt?" she asked.

"No," Mr. Maury said. *Sthenos, the Greek word for strength. As a man's days, so is his strength . . . Seventy-five years old and no place to lay his head.*

"She got quieter before I left. I read to her a little."

"And what, pray, did you select to read to her?"

She turned a cold, bird's eye on him as she held up her book—she had as many litanies as an orthodox Catholic. She said: "It is at a time like this, when the hard core of the personality is shattered, that the real self has a chance to emerge . . ."

"*Women!*" Mr. Maury cried passionately. "I've been watching them. They'll rock the world if they don't look out!"

Her white-shod feet rustled on the worn boards. Her shawl fluttered as she passed, bearing the empty glass before her like a chalice. He turned his face up to the night. The heavens were dark, for all their gold stars. It would be a long time till morning. When it came they would shut their eyes against the light and lie quiet until the brain, rattling inside the cold skull, set them moving about the hateful business of the day. . . . There were no women in his life now, and yet he seemed to have been in servitude to them all his life.

He had loved his wife. Until the day of her death the mere touch of her hand could stir him. But she had been dead for fifteen years. He seldom saw his daughter, a dark, flighty girl, bound for an unhappy life. He had never known his mother. Orphaned at four and raised by Uncle James and Aunt Vic . . . Aunt Vic had pretended that she was taking him to Grassdale to live to teach him Latin and mathematics, but it was really to save his immortal soul. The prayers, morning and evening! Uncle James said that she trained him and Julian, her son, like bird dogs, to charge, that is, to kneel, at one word of command, to point in prayer at another. And it was a fact that they used to kneel at one wave of her fine, long-fingered hand and start praying at the next. He had been kneeling at her bedside, praying, when she died. She had been ill so long that the family was worn out. He had been called in to sit with her while old Aunt Beck got some sleep. She had seemed better that evening and had talked to him for a while about his soul. It grew dark. Her voice trailed off. Her hand moved restlessly on the counterpane. He slid to his knees and began mumbling the Angelic Salutation:

Hail, Mary, full of grace! The Lord is with thee: blessed art thou among women . . .

She uttered a cry and raised her head from the pillow. Her eyes fixed a point beyond his shoulder. He turned and saw nothing. Another, softer sound broke from her and her head fell back on the pillow and she was still. As he ran, weeping, to tell the others that she was gone, he had wondered what it was that he could not see. But that had been a long time ago, when he was a boy of thirteen. He had not thought about such things often since that time. . . . Holy Mary, Mother of God, pray for us sinners, now and at the *hour* . . . of our death.

One Against Thebes

A child is walking along a road, a dusty road which runs from one end of a farm to the other. It is an afternoon in midsummer. The dust is hot and lies so thick on the road that each time she puts her bare foot down it sinks out of sight in the soft, fine dust. From time to time she glances to the other side of the road where a Negro girl, a little older than she is, walks, so briskly that the dust stirred by her feet rises in a cloud as high as her head. In front of them a Negro woman strides, a basket over her arm. A Negro boy, older than either of the girls, runs behind the woman. He lurches from side to side as he runs and occasionally looks down over his shoulder to smile at the trail his own feet have left in the dust. The child gazes at it, too, and thinks how it might have been made by a great snake, a serpent as large as any one of them, hurling itself now to one side of the road, now to the other, and thinks, too, how she and the other girl and the boy and even the old woman seem to move in its coils.

There is a row of peach trees on one side of the road, a pasture filled with grazing cattle on the other. A moment ago the Negro boy, who is called "Son," stopped and picked a yellow clingstone peach up from where it lay in the grass and handed it to her. The child had been about to bite into it when she saw by his face that it had a worm in it and threw it down to hurry after the others.

A cow that has been grazing near the road suddenly lifts her head and stares at the little girl out of great, luminous dark eyes. Her body is grayish white but her face is almost black. The tip of her nose is black, too, and would feel wet if you touched it. . . . An old woman in a fairy story she had been reading that morning lived alone in a deep forest in a hut made all of peach stones. She had a cow that would come and stand before her when she sat in the doorway of her hut, but that cow was no color; you could see through her body to the black trunks of the trees that grew about the hut. Why were the tree trunks black and the cow no color?

They have come to a house. It is old and gray, because it has never been painted and trees grow thick about it. Their trunks are stout and twisted, as if, the child thinks, a giant passing through the grove had bent them carelessly to his pleasure. She knows that the bark of the tree trunks is white but it is so deeply pitted that from where she stands it looks black.

A gate bars the entrance to the yard. Aunt Maria has lifted the chain and the gate swings open. Aunt Maria takes little shining buckets out of her basket and gives one to each child, then walks over to the corner of the yard where the peach trees grow. Olivia and Son move after her. Olivia stoops to pick up some of the peaches that have fallen on the ground. Son has climbed up into one of the trees.

The child nodded docilely when she was handed one of the buckets but she has not moved to join the others. She is staring up into the boughs of the silver poplar trees that rise high above the house. Their leaves are a glossy green on top but the child knows that if you tear a leaf in two it will show white—as if the leaf were made of cotton. She has been told that she herself was born in this house but she has no memory of ever having lived here. All her memories cluster around the tall, ugly gray house at the other end of the farm. That house stands in a grove, too. Sugar maples, planted by her grandfather, "after he got back from the War," have grown so thick about it that now all the rooms are dark. When they set out from that house a little while ago a woman was standing on the porch. Her grandmother, whose name she bears, had come out to give the old Negro woman some directions. They were about the people who lived in this gray house. (You called them "croppers"—but not to their faces.) The child had listened at first, and, then, wearying of the sound of the rapid impatient voice, sank down on the grass to think about something else.

She takes a slow step forward now and halts. A woman has come out of this house, too, and is standing on the edge of the porch. A thin woman, wearing a faded sunbonnet, whose grayish dress is almost the same color as her face. She has just said something to Aunt Maria, who smiles and points to her basket. The sallow woman says that they cannot have the peaches, that they are her peaches. Aunt Maria smiles again and says that the peaches belong to the child's grandmother and uncle. The child will always remember how the woman on the ramshackle porch turned her face away for a second to look at the peaches hanging heavy on the brittle boughs, saying, as if to herself: "*I wisht I'd picked 'em yesterday . . . I wisht I had! . . . I was just letting them sun one more day. . . .*" and turns and walks into the dark hall, then pauses on the threshold to put her hand up to her writhing lips but spread fingers cannot keep back the anguished shrieks and the names, names the woman is calling her grandmother and uncle, whereupon the old Negro woman smiles and says that they may be what the white woman has called them but they like peaches and gives one of the trees a light shake and bends over and begins filling her basket with the rosy fruit that now lies scattered all over the ground.

The child bends, too, and, trailing her hand among the grasses, pretends to be gathering the fruit which she now has no heart to touch. The Negro woman and her two children move swiftly and silently from tree to tree. When their basket and buckets are full they leave the yard and walk along the dusty road and out onto another, larger road and down into the hollow where it is always cool because the branch runs through there under a little wooden bridge and then up the rise along the big road whose dust is dry again and hot until they come to a house larger than the other houses, built of brick, and set far back on a lawn that has tall oak trees growing on it.

There is a double row of cedar trees on one side of the lane where buggies and carriages go on the way to the stable. But people who are not going to stay long hitch their horses to the long rack in front. Aunt Maria and Son and Olivia have already started down the cedar drive but the child lingers, looking back over her shoulder at the hitching rack. She knows every horse that is hitched there. Susy is the old pony. Susy's coat is red and shines in the sun but her mane and foretop and tail are yellowish white. Lather is dried white on her rump and there is a dark, wet place under her mane; Tom and Wallace Brewer had trotted her every step of the way over here. In August, too, when you are not supposed to lather horses. . . . Wallace

Brewer had been at Merry Point two weeks and he was going to stay another week. That was because his father and mother lived in town. He was two years older than Tom and every day he thought of something to do that nobody had ever thought of before—like stringing telephone wires from the big sugar tree they climbed into that old gum tree over by the fence. He made the receivers out of tin cans and he asked her to go and sit on the limb of the gum tree while he talked the first message and last night when she was sitting on the steps after supper, watching the lightning bugs, he came and sat down beside her on the steps and asked her if she ever caught lightning bugs and put them in a bottle and she said, no, because she wouldn't want anybody to put her in a bottle and he said he wouldn't, either, and he didn't say anything for a while and then he asked, "*What you like to do better than anything?*" and she thought how she liked to wade in the branch and then she thought of how in the spring she and one of the white girls on the place, Ada, used to take along a wooden spoon apiece and go to the woods, hunting guinea nests, and she was about to tell him how guinea eggs were different from hen or turkey eggs, smaller and covered all over with tiny brown spots, and how you had to lift each one out with a spoon and not touch the nest or the guinea would never come there again, when Marjorie called from the bay window and asked Wallace if he didn't want to play seven-up—she was fourteen years old and already wore a Ferris waist. Wallace said he did and he got up and went in the house and the child sat on the steps and watched the lightning bugs till somebody came along and told her it was time for her to go to bed and to be sure and wash her feet. . . . She could have driven over here with them in the pony cart today if she had had her slippers on when Tom got ready to go. She was about to go upstairs and see if she couldn't find her black slippers when Tom looked at a little bit of blood she had on her foot and said that if she would look where she was going on she wouldn't stub her toe so much and she thought how just last summer he always had a bloody rag on *his* big toe and before she thought, she said, "*What?*" and he said, "What? Riggety Rut! . . . I'M going to a birthday party. That's what!" and he knew and she knew that the party was for Alice, who is the same age she is, and she said, "You old fool!" and he said, "She who calleth her brother a fool is in danger of hellfire" and she said, "I never called you a fool. I called you a crool," and he started toward her and said, "What's a crool? Whoever heard of a crool?"

and she shut her eyes and when he got close to her she opened them and said, "There are more things in Heaven and earth, Horatio, than are dreamt of in thy philosophy," and he knew that if he came any closer she would tell her father, so he backed off and Wallace laughed and said, "She always talk like that?" and Tom said, "She don't know what she's saying half the time," and they got in the pony cart and drove off and she wouldn't have driven with them to save either of their necks or a single bone in their bodies. . . .

There is a table made out of a millstone in the shade of a tall tree over at one side of the house and the children are all gathered around the table, laughing and talking. But this child cannot join them until she and Aunt Maria and Son and Olivia have gone up the steps of the big house. A woman is sitting in a rocking chair on the porch and she gets up when she sees them and comes and stands on the top steps and smiles as she takes the basket of peaches from Aunt Maria's hand, then smiles again and, descending a step, lays her hand lightly on the child's shoulder and makes a gesture toward the rear of the house, uttering the words the child has heard every time she has come to this house.

The child nods and goes down the steps and walks off alone. Aunt Maria and Son and Olivia are still standing there on the steps while Aunt Maria and the woman talk but there is no need for her to wait for them, for even if they were walking along beside her now it would be only for a little way; nobody ever goes with her all the way to the place she has to go before she can join the ones who are laughing and talking under the trees.

The cabins are in a row back of the big house. They are white-washed. The trees that grow around them are whitewashed, too, and so are the stones that edge the flower beds in front of each cabin. The cabin she is going to is the first one in the row. One time she came here and people were sitting on the porch, laughing and talking, but there is nobody on the porch now. The porch slants a little and is so narrow that she covers it in two steps and at once is plunged into the darkness (which when she tries to recall it always seems to be compacted more of fetid smells than the absence of light), and the expected sound comes and she walks toward it and it comes again in a rising note and she murmurs something and feels her own hand grasped by another hand which is hot and dry and somehow brittle but yet has strength enough to force her to her knees for a moment, a moment during which the voice creaks harshly, complainingly in her ears until she, murmuring back, finds strength from the all at once blessed darkness to rise to her feet, so suddenly that the dry, reptilian clasp is broken and she runs through the room, which does not now seem so dark, across the threshold and out into the blinding light and is about to plunge toward the big house when a voice speaks from the next cabin:

"How Aunt Emily making out today?"

Aunt Maria is sitting in a split-bottomed chair on the porch. When the child does not answer she leans forward and calls her name. The child says, "All right," aware that Son and Olivia have come up behind her and are sitting down, side by side, on the edge of the porch.

Aunt Maria inclines her heavy body forward. "How her rheumatism?"

"She didn't say . . . I reckon it's all right."

The woman rocking beside Aunt Maria laughs. "She had a hollerin' spell towards daybreak. You'd a thought she was dying . . . Sometimes I think I ask Mister Richard to move me away from that old lady. . . ."

"You better not do that," Aunt Maria says sharply. "You better stay right where the Lord flung you."

The woman laughs again and calls the child's name. "You run on to the house . . . They got peach ice cream."

The child says, "Yes, ma'am . . ."

She has been looking from one woman to the other but all the time she can feel Son's and Olivia's eyes on her face. Son's skin is only a little darker than the dust of the road they have been walking on. That may be what makes his eyes seem so dark. They are larger than Olivia's or Aunt Maria's or her own, which, she heard some grown person say the other day, are too small and set too deep in her head. Son can look at you a long time and you will not know what he is thinking. . . . He is not looking at her now but before he looked away a change come over his eyes, as if something as bright and quick as a snake had flashed up from a deep pool, shimmered for a second over its surface, and then, before you could be certain of what you had seen, flashed back again into the depths.

She turns and runs toward the house and as she runs it seems to her that she can feel on her back the heavy-lidded, incurious gaze of the four who sit on the porch.

A mock orange bush grows at the corner of the house. She steps back into the shadow and stares through the green, pointed leaves at the row of whitewashed cabins. Rebecca gets up from her chair and walks heavily across the porch. She is going to sit with Aunt Emily awhile. . . . Aunt Emily is a hundred years old. Is it because she has lived such a long ti.ne that she always has to come first? . . . "Have you been to see Mammy yet?" Cousin Margaret will ask almost before she knows you are there. . . . Or is there another reason? "*Blood*," Tom was saying the other night when he was sitting on the porch between Billy and Jimmy and it was so dark he didn't know who had come out of the house. "*She eats blood . . . She likes it fresh, too. . . . That's why they all time losing some of them little nigger babies. . . .*" She shivered slightly as she stood in the cool shade, then deliberately steadied her nerves, as she often contrived to do, by reflecting on the inconsistencies, the illogicalities, and the injustice which she found embodied in her older brother. If he heard *you* say "nigger" he'd go and tell some grown person but *he* said it any time he got ready.

But that wasn't why Son had smiled—for that was what had flicked across his eyes: a smile. He was smiling because she had said, "Yes, ma'am" to Rebecca. You didn't even say "Yes, ma'am" to Aunt Maria all the time and she had gone and said "Yes, ma'am" to Rebecca, whom she had heard Aunt Maria call "a flighty chap"! . . . But Rebecca said "Yes, ma'am" to Aunt Maria and *everybody* said "Yes, ma'am" to Aunt Emily. They were all alike, said one thing one time and one another. . . .

She stepped out from behind the mock orange bush and walked slowly across the lawn. They had finished the game and were sitting down around the table that had been a millstone once down at Barker's Mill. Alice saw her coming and tried to get Janie Ellis to move over but Janie wouldn't move till the grown person who was ladling out the ice cream called to her and she had to stand up and the child slipped in where Janie had been sitting and Janie turned around and made a face but she had to go and sit somewhere else after she got her ice cream. It was peach ice cream as Rebecca had said it would be. The child had three helpings. There was cake, too, and after that lemonade. She could have had as many glasses of lemonade as she wanted but they were choosing sides for "Stealing Sticks" and she and Alice wanted to be on the same side, so she set her glass down before she had drunk it dry and ran over to where Wallace Brewer was choosing sides. They played "I Spy" after that.

Tom was the first to hide his eyes: "*Honey, Honey, Bee Ball.... I can't see y'all.... All sheep scattooed? ..."*

Alice and Ellen wanted to hide in the mock orange bush but she didn't want to go back on that side of the house where she knew Olivia and Son were still sitting on the porch—unless they had gone down to the sinkhole to chunk turtles—so she persuaded them to hide between two box bushes on the side walk and Alice tore her dress and while they were trying to see how bad it was Wallace Brewer came around the corner of a bush and tagged all three of them. She had to be "It" twice and was just shutting her eyes to be "It" again when she saw Aunt Maria and Son and Olivia standing under the cedar trees on the drive and she told Cousin Margaret and the others goodbye and was starting down the drive with them when Tom called to her: "What you come over here barefoot for?" She didn't say anything but he kept on hollering. "Wait a minute and you can ride home with us." She turned around then and stuck her tongue out at him. He waited a second and then he hollered again: "All right. Go ahead! Burn your feet off . . . See if I care!"

They turn out of the cedar drive onto the big road. "He don't care for nothing or nobody but himself," the child mutters. The words are words she has heard on Aunt Maria's lips many times but Aunt Maria does not seem to like to hear them from other lips. She looks down at the child's stiffly starched white piqué skirt and says: "That dress do all right, but no use talking, you'd look a lot better if you'd put your slippers on."

"I don't care," the child mutters again. "It's summertime!"

Hooves beat on the road behind them. Suddenly they are breathing acrid dust. The old woman makes a peremptory gesture and she and the three children step quickly to the side of the road and press their bodies back among the tall reeds as the pony cart whirls past. None of them move for several minutes, then Aunt Maria gives a short laugh as they step back onto the road, where the dust is still settling slowly in little eddies. "It summertime, all right," she says.

They stand at the top of the rise a moment, then start down into the hollow. At the bridge the pony cart is drawn off to the side of the road but you cannot see Tom or Wallace Brewer anywhere. Then the willows that grow up against the bridge shake and Susy's head comes up and parts the leaves and her eyes look straight into yours a second before her head sinks and you hear that long, sucking sound they make when they drink. Susy's eyes are all dark except for that one point of light in each eye . . . *Why is it that they can look straight into your eyes and never see you—except when they want you to do something for them? Like the way Susy will come up and push at you with her nose and even sometimes look at you for a second when she knows you are holding an ear of corn behind your back?*

"Glad they took time to water that poor horse," Aunt Maria says, and starts up the hill. Olivia follows her. Son has already gone on ahead. The child lingers on the bridge, dipping one foot into the cool yellow water, thinking how Tom and Wallace Brewer do not know that she is standing there on the bridge but she knows that they are sitting on the bank beyond the big willow, because, even if she cannot see them for the leaves, she can hear them talking. About Ada, that white girl on the place that Mammy used to send to the woods to see where the turkeys had stolen their nests. Guineas, too. Ada said you had to go early in the morning. Once she and Ada started before it was quite light. That was summer before last. The summer she was six years old. Ada was fourteen. She said she would be fifteen next summer.

"Was Ada there?" Wallace Brewer asked.

"Sure, she was there," Tom said. "With the baby."

She wondered where Ada got the baby but there was no use asking Tom, smart aleck as he was, ever since they started letting him go to town by himself.

"How about old Vergil Stokes?" Wallace Brewer said. "Was he there?" Tom laughed. "He was there," he said. "Old Vergil was there, all right."

"What'd the judge say? What'd he tell old Vergil?"

"Said he reckoned Vergil'd know what the age of consent was next time. Told him next time he reckoned he'd be able to figure *that* out."

They both laughed, so loud it started the echo in the woods. The child waited until the echo died, then started up the little hill. Aunt Maria and Olivia are just turning into the road that leads through the place. Son is so far on ahead now that you can't see anything of him except the cloud of dust his feet are raising.

Son lives with his father and mother and brother and sisters in a cabin back of the tall, ugly gray house the child lives in during the summers. There are two rooms in the cabin and a little room they call "the lean-to" tucked on at the back. There is a window in each of the rooms but some of the panes of glass are broken and Aunt Maria has stuffed rags into them to keep the wind and the rain out in winter. The rags stay in the windows in the summertime, too, because, the child's grandmother says, Aunt Maria is too lazy to take them out. There are two beds in one room of the cabin. Son's father, Uncle Jim, sleeps in one bed, with two of the boys. The two girls sleep in the other bed. Son sleeps on a pallet on the floor. So does Aunt Maria. She says she is not going to sleep in the bed with any old man. The child did something once that she is ashamed to remember. She is not yet clear how it came about but one day she told her grandmother where each person slept in the cabin. Her grandmother laughed and said it was too bad Aunt Maria didn't practice what she preached.

Her grandmother calls Son "Sawney." She says she will not call any nigger "Son." . . . The house girl, Leota, has a baby that is exactly the kind of baby the child thinks she would like to have as her own as soon as she is old enough to do as she pleases. Her name is Ellabelle and she is one and a half years old. Leota dresses her in a clean white, starched dress every morning and brings her up to the house and she will let you hold her in your arms a long time if you are careful. Yesterday the child sat on the doorstep of the out-kitchen and held the baby in her arms till she went fast asleep. Son was over in the shade of the big sugar tree, turning the handle of the ice-cream freezer. He had on his white coat that he wore when he worked around the house. Her grandmother came out in the yard and said, "Sawney, you get through freezing that cream, you better bring up some ice."

The ice got low this time of the year and you had to go down a ladder to reach it. Son did not like to go down that far into the ice house. He said snakes lived there. He said "Yes'm" to her grandmother but he did not look at the child, even after her grandmother had gone back into the house. Leota came out and when she saw that the baby was asleep she picked her up and took her into the kitchen to lay her down in the big split basket that had mosquito netting all over it so the flies couldn't get at her.

The child had been reading in her *Green Fairy Book* before Leota told her she could hold the baby. It was still lying there beside her on the doorsill. She picked it up and went over and held it out to Son. He kept on turning the freezer and did not look up. She bent over and slipped the book down into the pocket of his jacket. When she thought of the book now she saw the green cover that had gold letters and a picture of a fairy on it in gold sliding down into the white pocket. She would not ever see it again. . . .

They were passing the Old Place. She left the road and, going over to the fence, plucked a leaf from one of the sprouts that sprang up around the roots of all the trees and tore the leaf in two and held the broken parts in her hand a second, then let them drift down into the dust and walked on. Sometimes she and Alice and Ellen picked clover blossoms and tied them together to make wreaths to wear on their heads but the first wreath that anybody ever made was of silver poplar leaves. Heracles and Prometheus each made one and then each one gave his wreath to the other. Her father had told them that last night. When she asked why grown men were making wreaths to wear on their heads he said, "It was for a pact they made," and when she asked "What pact?" he said, "Oh, I forgot . . . Why'n't you read about it yourself?"

That was when they were all sitting on the porch after supper and Cousin Joseph had been talking for a long time. "You listen up to the Punic Wars," Auntie told Cousin Kate, "and I'll take over then. I swear I will," but Auntie didn't come out of the house and Cousin Joseph kept on talking. When he got to Hamilcar Barca and how he was probably related to the Barkers here in the neighborhood her father had started talking right over him, the way he did sometimes. He was whittling on a stick he kept over in the corner and whittled on when somebody else got to talking. He said that as soon as Heracles was grown he went out in the woods and got himself a stick, only he called it a club, and it was about the size of one of those silver poplars in the yard at the Old Place. Wallace wanted to know what kind of tree Heracles cut down to make his club. Her father said it was wild olive. "He didn't cut it down, either. Just broke it off. Might have trimmed it down a little, but it was a whole tree trunk. Carried it all his life. Must have had it with him when he climbed up on his pyre."

"What did he climb up on that pyre for?" Jimmy asked.

"To get rid of that Nessus shirt, boy. It was burning him to death. He couldn't stand it no longer. He preferred to be burnt up, himself."

Wallace said he didn't see why he put it on, anyway.

Her father said that Heracles put the shirt on because it was his Sunday shirt that his wife, Deianira, had made for him. "What made her put poison on it?" Wallace asked.

Her father said that Deianira didn't know it was poison. The centaur, Nessus, gave it to her after Heracles shot him with an arrow when he was carrying Deianira across the river and tried to run away with her.

Wallace wanted to know why Heracles didn't carry her across the river himself. Her father said that that was an error in judgment on Heracles' part. He thought that she would be safer riding on the centaur's back than for him to carry her in his arms, because horses can always swim.

"Was he a *horse?*" Jimmy asked.

"He was half horse and half man," her father said.

Tom said he didn't believe there ever was a man that was half horse. Sometimes her father's voice could cut like a knife and yet sound soft as silk. He said: "I suppose, sir, that you don't believe in Scylla or Charybdis or Medusa or Lamia or the Sphinx that had the head and shoulders of a woman and the body of a lion? . . . Has it ever been called to your attention that Erechtheus, the ancestor of the Athenians, had legs that ended in coiled serpents . . . or that the Labdacidae were descended from the dragon's teeth that Cadmus sowed?"

Tom never gave up right away. He said: "I wouldn't want to be made out of no old snake's teeth . . . and I wouldn't want to be named Labdaky, either."

"It's none of your business, sir, how you were made," her father said. "Snaps and snails and puppy dogs' tails I've been told. The origins of the House of Labdacus are none of your concern, either, but you will have to know who the Labdacidae are—and the Atreidae, too—unless you want to be branded as an ignoramus." He couldn't talk to children long at a time without getting tired, but then he couldn't talk to grown people long, either. . . .

Son still ran on ahead. He had stopped at the branch and had broken off one of the big cattails that grew there. Sometimes he carried the stalk slung over his shoulder and sometimes he swung it from side to side as he ran. When he came to a place where the trail his feet had made earlier in the afternoon still showed he would whack the dust—as if he were trying to beat a snake to death. . . .

Aunt Maria always sat in the brick breezeway to churn. Yesterday the child's grandmother had brought a chair out and sat there, too, stringing snaps. Aunt Maria said that when Son was a year old she put him under a tree on his pallet and the next time she looked out he was holding a black thing in his hands and whipping it up and down and when she got out there it was a black snake. Her grandmother said, "Humph! An infant Hercules!" and when Aunt Maria asked who that was she said that Hercules strangled two serpents in his cradle. "I never seen any serpents," Aunt Maria said, "but I sure don't like snakes. Son don't either. Looks like that experience turned him against them, though he too little to know what he doing, warn't he?" "Dunno," her grandmother said. "My experience they never too young to do meanness."

She stepped to one side of the road to avoid the serpentine trail that Son's feet had left in the dust. . . . Her father said Heracles and her grandmother said Hercules but they were the same person . . . Aunt Maria didn't know that serpents were the same as snakes . . . Sometimes they were called monsters instead of serpents and sometimes they were called dragons and were big enough to cover a whole acre and when they threw their heads back fire came out instead of breath—enough to burn up the whole countryside. But no matter how large they were or where they lived they always had tails like snakes. And their heads were snaky, too. Sometimes there would be seven or nine serpent heads on one body. Like the Lernaean Hydra. That was the first monster that Heracles killed. . . .

She walked faster, fast enough to bring the dust up around her in a cloud, the way Olivia did, the way Son did. . . . She would never see *The Green Fairy Book* again but she remembered some of the words and said them to herself as she walked along in her cloud of dust: *But where will we go? asked the Little Princess. We will ride on this cloud, the Fairy Godmother said. To my crystal palace in the wood. There is a gold crown laid out on a bed for you there and silver slippers and a veil of silver tissue, embroidered with the sun and the moon and the stars . . . the sun . . . and the moon . . . and the stars. . . .*

Two

Hear the Nightingale Sing

It was so dark in the ravine that at first she could not see the horses. Then her eyes grew accustomed to the gloom. She caught a gleam of white through the branches. She worked her way through the thicket and came upon Bess and Old Gray tethered to the ring that had been fixed in the trunk of a big pine. But the mule was not there.

She looked at the broken tether. "Where's Lightning?" she asked.

The horses pressed up to her, nudging at the sack that was slung over her shoulders. She took hold of their halters and led them down the hill to the branch and up the stream to a place where the hazel bushes grew higher than her head. She let them drink their fill, then left them tethered to a little cottonwood, while she went on up the hill to look for the mule.

The woods were thin between here and the pike. She moved slowly, keeping a tree always between her and the road. At the top of the hill she climbed up on a stump to look down on the pike. There was a cloud of dust off in the direction of Gordonsville but she could not see any soldiers moving along the road. She could remember times—in the first year of the war, just after all the boys had gone away—when she used to walk in the late afternoons up to the top of this hill in the hope that somebody might be passing. There had hardly ever been anybody then. Now there was almost always something moving along the road—great, lumbering army wagons, regiments of infantry marching, squads of cavalry sweeping by in clouds of dust.

There was a rustling in the bushes along the fence. There the mule stood, looking at her. He ducked his head when he saw that she was looking at him, and moved off quickly. She got down off the stump, clumsily, in her homemade shoes, and went toward him, holding out an ear of corn. "Cu-up! Cu-up!" she called in a whisper. He wheeled; his little hooves clattered against the rails. She turned and walked the other way, holding the nubbin of corn behind her back. When she felt him take hold of it she whirled and grasped his foretop. The nubbin had fallen to the ground. She stooped and retrieved it and held it before him on her open palm. "Lightning!" she said, "*Lightning!*" and slipped her arms down about his neck and closed her eyes and laid her cheek against his side.

A long time ago—winter before last—she used to go down to the stable lot early after breakfast on cold mornings and, finding him standing in his corner, his breath steaming in the frosty air, she would cry out to Uncle Joe that her little mule was freezing and put her arms about him and bury her face in his shaggy hair. Uncle Joe would laugh, saying that that mule had enough hair to keep both of them warm. "Ain't no 'count, nohow."

Once Tom Ladd had come up behind them without their hearing him. "I don't believe I'd have given you that mule if I'd known how you were going to raise him," he said. "You can't get him back now," she had told him. "I'm raising him to be the no 'countest mule in the country."

He laughed. They walked in silence over the lightly frozen ground up to the house. He had what her father called "the gift of silence." But sometimes, sitting in company, you would look up and find him watching you and it would seem that he had just said something or was about to say something. But what it was she never knew. And it might be that he never had any particularity for her. It might be that he noticed her more than the other girls only because she had the mule for a pet. He liked all animals.

She, too, had always been overfond of animals. When she was a little girl and Uncle Joe would bring a team in to plow the garden in the spring, she would look at the mules standing with their heads hung, their great, dark eyes fixing nothing, and she would think how, like Negroes, they were born into the world for nothing but labor, and her heart would seem to break in her bosom and she would run barefoot down the rows and when Uncle Joe cracked his whip she would clutch his elbow, shrieking, "You, Uncle Joe. Don't you hit that mule!" until the old man would leave his team standing and, going to the window where her mother sat, sewing, would ask her to please make Miss Barbara come in the house.

When she became a young lady it had tickled her fancy to have a mule for a pet. Lightning, nosing unreproved at the kitchen door or walking across the flower beds, seemed, somehow, to make up for the pangs she had suffered as a child. But even then, in those far-off days, when her father was still alive and the servants were all still on the place and you had only to call from the upper gallery to have somebody come and lead him back to the pasture when he trespassed—even then in those days that were so hard to remember now, he had been a trouble and a care.

He was old Lightfoot's colt. Lightfoot had gone blind in her last days. Tom Ladd had turned her over to Jake Robinson to take care of. Jake had taken good care of her but he could not resist the temptation to get one more colt out of her. Tom had some business with her father and had been spending the night at their house. A Negro boy brought word from Jake that Lightfoot had foaled in the night. They were at breakfast. Her mother had just asked her to go to the kitchen to get some hot bread. Tom Ladd said, "Miss Barbara, how'd you like to have one of Lightfoot's colts?" She was so taken aback that she did not answer. She came back with the biscuits and sat down and would have let what he had said pass unnoticed. But he looked at her as she came in and he spoke again. "It'll be her last colt."

Tom Ladd came to their house two or three times a week. A bed was kept ready for him in the office whenever he cared to spend the night. But he had never danced with her or with her sister and if he sat on the porch with them in the evenings it was to talk with her father about the crops or the stock. Tom Ladd loved horses better than people, her mother said, and he loved liquor better than he loved horses. Her father said that was because he was a bachelor, living alone in that big house, but her mother said it was in the blood: all the Ladds drank themselves to death.

She had felt her color rising, knowing that her mother's eyes were upon her. But it was no crime to love horses, and as for liquor, she had seen her father sprawling on the cellar steps, a jug in his hand.

She said, "I'll have to see the colt first, Mr. Ladd."

Everybody laughed and the moment passed. After breakfast they drove over to Robinson's to see the new colt. Jake was sitting on the front steps, mending some harness. He did not quit his work, saying only, "I'll be out there in a minute, Mister Tom."

They walked out into the pasture. The mare stood at the far end, beside a willow sink. They could see, under her belly, the long, thin legs and little, wobbly feet. "Sorrel," Tom Ladd said, "Lightfoot always breeds true," and walked around the mare's hindquarters and stopped and swore out loud.

Her father laughed until he had to put a hand on her shoulder to steady himself. "You never told him not to breed her," he said, wiping his eyes.

"I never thought he'd breed her to a jackass with ears as long as his," Tom Ladd said.

The colt stopped sucking and flung his head up and stared at them. His ears were so long that they looked as if they might tip him over. He had eyes as large and dark and mournful as a Negro baby's. The fawn color about his muzzle gave him the look of a little clown. She put her arms about his furry rump and he kicked feebly, nuzzling against his mother's side.

"Hush," she said, "you'll hurt his feelings."

It was a year later that Tom Ladd had given him to her, after Jake Robinson had had to give up trying to break him.

She led the mule down the hill. The horses heard them coming and whinnied. She led him up to them, so close that they could touch noses. Then she made a halter out of the broken rope and led the three of them back to the thicket. The old mare and the horse went quietly to their places beside the big pine but Lightning kept sidestepping and shaking his head. She led him off a little way and tied him to another tree and opened the sack and gave Bess and Gray four nubbins apiece and the clover that she had gathered in the orchard. When they had finished eating she tethered them again and mounted Lightning and rode him down the ravine.

The sun had set. Here in the thick woods it was dark. But she could see the light from the house, shining through the trees. They did not use the path at all now. No use in keeping your horses hid off in the woods if there was a path leading to them. But it was hard, riding through the underbrush. She had to lie flat on the mule's back to keep from being scraped off.

At the edge of the wood she dismounted and was about to open the gate when a sound down the road made her stop, chain in hand Somebody was walking along the road, whistling softly. She let the chain fall with a little click against the post and led Lightning back a little way into the bushes. The sound grew. The man, or whoever it was, walked steadily, whistling as he came.

She pressed close against the mule, her arm over his withers. He stood quietly but the sound of his breathing seemed to fill all the thicket. Light from the house fell in a great fan across the road. A man's visored cap and the knapsack that bulged at his shoulder showed black against it for a second and then he passed on. But the sound of his whistling was all around her still. An old tune that she had always known:

> "One morning, one morning, one morning in May
> I met a fair lady a-wending her way . . ."

She stood there until the sound had quite died away, then, lifting the chain with infinite care, she opened the gate and led the mule across the road and into the yard.

The front door opened. Her sister stood on the porch. "Barbara!" she called.

Barbara did not answer. After a little Sophy went inside and shut the door. Barbara drew Lightning swiftly through the yard and toward the stable. Halfway there she stopped. The stable wouldn't do. That was the first place they went. Nor the hen house, though it was big enough. None of the outbuildings would do. They always searched outbuildings, to make sure they didn't miss anything. They would search an outbuilding when they wouldn't search the house itself. She turned back into the yard and ran down the cellar steps, the mule lumbering behind her.

He came down the last two steps so fast that he ran over her.

She felt the impact of his chest between her shoulders and knew that his forefoot had grazed her ankle before she went sprawling down in the dark. She lay there a moment, wondering how badly she was hurt, then got to her feet and felt her way to where he stood. She stroked his neck and talked to him gently. "Poor little Lightning. Him have a hard time. Mammy *know* him have a hard time."

A ray of light struck on the wall. Sophy stood at the head of the steps, a lighted lamp in her hand. She peered down into the cellar, then came a little way down the steps, holding the lamp high over her head.

"Have you gone distracted?" she asked.

"Why don't you see after the stock?" Barbara asked coldly. "He's not hurting your old cellar."

She poured what corn was left in the sack out upon the earthen floor, fastened the cellar doors, and followed Sophy up the steps.

Her twelve-year-old brother sat beside the stove, whittling. He looked up eagerly as she came in. "You going to keep that mule in the cellar, sister? You going to keep him in there all the time?"

Barbara sat down in the big chair by the window. She lifted her skirt to examine her leg. Blood was caked on her shin and the flesh of the ankle was bruised and discolored. She felt her lip trembling. She spoke brusquely:

"I saw a soldier going past the house just as I was getting ready to cross the road."

Sophy did not seem to have heard her. "Why didn't you leave that mule out in the hollow?" she asked.

"He slipped his halter," Barbara said. "I had to walk all over the woods to find him."

"It would have been a good thing if you couldn't find him," Sophy said.

Barbara looked at her steadily. "I'm going to keep him," she said. "I don't care what you say. I'm going to keep him."

Sophy, compressing her lips, did not answer. Cummy had gone over and sat down at the kitchen table, where they always ate nowadays. "Aren't we going to have any supper?" he asked.

Sophy went out on the back porch and returned with two covered dishes. "There's some black-eyed peas," she said. "And Mrs. Thomas sent us a pat of butter. I thought we might as well have it while it was fresh."

She bent over the table, arranging knives and forks and plates. A frail woman of twenty-seven, who looked, Barbara thought suddenly, at least thirty-five. That was because she was just recovering from one of her asthmatic attacks. No, it was because she was so thin. She had never noticed until tonight how sunken her sister's temples were. And under her cheekbones, where even as a young girl she had had hollows, were deep wells of shadow.

"She can't stand it," she thought. "She's not strong like me. She can't stand it. . . . I ought not to keep him. Those nubbins I gave him today. I could have taken them to the mill and had them ground into meal."

"There's two jars of preserves left," she said, "a jar of quince and a jar of peach."

Cummy was up from the table and halfway down the cellar steps before she had stopped speaking. He brought up the two jars.

Sophy nodded. "Might as well have them now. Preserves aren't any good without buttered bread, and no telling when we'll have butter again."

Barbara did not answer. She was looking through the open door into the hall. "Isn't that somebody on the porch?" she asked.

Cummy half rose from his chair. "You sit still," Barbara said sharply.

She got up and went through the hall toward the front door. When she was halfway there she stopped. "Who is it?" she called.

The door swung slowly open. A man stepped into the hall. A tall, red-faced man in a dark cloak and cavalryman's boots. He looked at Barbara a moment before he took off his visored cap.

"Good evening, miss," he said. "This the way to Gordonsville?"

"Yes," Barbara said, and stepped out onto the porch. "You keep on down this lane till you hit the pike. It isn't more than a quarter of a mile."

The soldier was looking back through the hall into the lighted kitchen. "How about a bite of supper?" he asked, smiling a little.

Barbara moved past him to the door. She put her hand on the knob. "I'm sorry but we haven't got a thing."

He thrust his foot swiftly forward just before the door closed. He was laughing. "That's too bad," he said, and pushed past her into the kitchen.

Sophy got up slowly from her chair. Her face had gone dead white. Her mouth was open and then it shut, quivering like a rabbit's. She was always like that. In a minute she would be crying and telling him it was all right, the way she did last spring when the soldiers took all the meat out of the smokehouse.

Barbara thought of that time and her right hand clenched in the folds of her skirt. She put the other hand on Sophy's shoulder and pointed to the door. "Go on," she said, "you go on and take Cummy with you."

The soldier had sat down at the table and, pulling the dish of peas toward him, looked up at her, shaking his head a little. "I'm mighty sorry," he said, "but I'm so hungry I could eat a horse." He laughed. "Horse gave out on me way back up the road. I must have walked three miles."

Barbara leaned forward until her face was on a level with his. A vein in her forehead stood out, swollen and tinged faintly with purple. She spoke through clenched teeth.

"*Aren't you ashamed to take the bread out of the mouths of women and children?*"

The soldier stared. He seemed about to rise from his chair, but he sank back, shaking his head again, laughing. After a moment he spoke, his mouth full of peas. "Lady, you got any pie?"

"We haven't got anything," Barbara said. "There isn't anything left on this place worth the taking. It doesn't make any difference which side they're on. They come and take everything."

The soldier nodded. A mischievous light came in his eyes. "Those damn Rebs," he said. "You turn 'em loose on a place and they'll strip it."

"Don't you say 'damn Reb' to me!" Barbara cried.

He put his knife and fork down and sat looking at her. His eyes sparkled. "Damn Reb," he said. "Damn Reb. Damn Reb. . . . If you aren't the feistiest Reb I ever saw!"

Barbara left the room. Sophy and Cummy were on the front porch. She walked up and down a few minutes, then went into the deserted parlor and stood before one of the darkened windows. "I wish I could kill him," she said aloud. "God! I wish I could kill him."

"Hush!" came a fierce whisper. "Here he comes."

The soldier stood in the doorway. "That was a fine dinner," he said. He made a little bow. "I'm much obliged to you."

No one spoke. He lingered, fastened his cloak. He was humming that same tune.

> "One morning, one morning, one morning in May
> I met a fair lady a-wending her way . . ."

"Very *much* obliged," he said. His eyes sought Barbara's. She did not answer, staring at Sophy, who had moved over and was lighting one of the lamps that stood on the mantel, as if, Barbara thought, they had come in here to entertain a welcome guest. Sophy finished lighting the lamp and sat down on the old love seat, her hands folded in her lap. Cummy had slipped into the room and sat down beside her. On the mantel the lamp burned steadily, revealing objects unfamiliar from long disuse: the walnut chairs, upholstered in faded red, the mute piano, the damask curtains. Their mother had been proud of her parlor when all those things were new. The soldier was looking about him as calmly as if he had been invited to spend the evening in their company. A little smile played about the corners of his mouth. He walked over to a whatnot in the corner. Dresden figurines were on the top shelf and on the shelf below a hand-painted Japanese fan lay among a pile of Indian arrowheads that Cummy had picked up on the old chipping ground. He took one in his hand. The bits of mica embedded in the flint gleamed as he turned it over slowly. "We get 'em like that on our home place," he said, and looked into her eyes and smiled. "Up in Indiana." He laid the arrowhead down and picked up a larger flint. "That's not for an arrow," he said. "That's a sword. A ceremonial sword. My grandfather knew an old Indian once told him what all the different kinds were."

He spoke in a low, casual tone, as if to somebody who stood beside him, somebody who was listening and in a minute would say something back. But there was not anybody here who would listen to anything that he might ever say. And the room itself was not used to the sound of human voices. There had not been anybody in it for a long time, not since that night, two years ago, the night of Marie's wedding. They had pushed the chairs back and danced till dawn broke at the windows. Gil Lathrop played the fiddle. Sometimes he sang as he played:

"And the voice that I heard made the valleys all ring;
  It was fairer than the music when the nightingale sings."

The soldier was humming again. That song, the song they all sang that night, seemed to go on inside him, and now he had to have something to listen to and words rang out in the still room:

"And if ever I return it will be in the spring
  For to see the waters flowing, hear the nightingale sing."

He had a clear tenor voice. At home, among his own people, he would be the one to sing at the gatherings. He picked up the little, bright-colored fan. Over its rim his eyes sought hers again. "Now which one of you ladies does this belong to?"

"For to see the waters flowing, hear the nightingale sing . . ."

But that night you could not tell who was singing: the song was on every lip. "Look!" Ruth Emory said. "There's Tom Ladd. I never saw him at a dance before." He would have asked me to marry him, but for all their talk. "It will be in the spring." No, I will never see him again. There are some men do not come home from a war. If the music could only have gone on that night . . .

The man's eyes were blue, really, not gray. Blue, overlaid with white, like frozen water. There was no song in the room now. Black pinpoints grew in his eyes, glinted as he slowly turned his head. "Now what was that?" he asked.

Barbara whirled and stood with her back to the window, her hands locked tight in front of her. She thought at first that she had not heard anything, that it was only the blood pounding in her ears. Then it came again, the slow beat–beat of the mule's hoof against the brick wall of the cellar.

She left the window and walked across the room. As she passed the fireplace she pushed the shovel with her foot. It fell to the floor with a clatter, taking the tongs with it. The Yankee picked them up and stood them on the hearth. He looked at her, his eyes grave and speculative.

"What was that?" he asked again.

She took a step toward him. "It's my brother," she said. "He's armed." She took another step. "He'll shoot you."

The Yankee laughed, cocking his head on one side. "Now what good would it do you to get me shot?"

He walked in his heavy boots out into the hall and back into the kitchen. They followed him. He lifted the lighted lantern that sat on the table and beckoned to Cummy. "Come here, son. I've got an errand for you."

Cummy's face took on its stubborn look. "I don't want to go down there," he said.

Sophy was crying. "Poor little motherless boy. Don't make him go."

The Yankee put his arm about Cummy's shoulders. "You come along with me, son. Nothing's going to hurt you."

He opened the door into the cellar and, holding the lantern, leaned over Cummy's shoulder, to look down the stairs. He straightened up, laughing. "That's a mighty peculiar brother you've got down there," he said.

He handed the lantern to Cummy. "You hold on to that, son, and don't get in the way of my right arm. I wouldn't be surprised if you had another brother down there."

They started down the steps. The Yankee walked slowly, a step behind Cummy, his arm still about Cummy's shoulder. Barbara watched them until they were halfway down, then she ran out through the back door and around the side of the house.

The double cellar doors were still closed when she got there, but she could hear the Yankee fumbling with the bolt. He had pulled it out. The doors slammed back. Lightning came slowly up the steps. She waited until his head and shoulders were level with the ground before she reached up and caught the halter.

"This is my mule," she said.

Lightning snorted and tossed his head. The whites of his eyes showed. His ears were laid back. She tugged at the halter again. "You let him go," she sobbed. "You better let him go!"

The Yankee raised his arm and pushed her, so hard that she spun away from him to fall on the grass. He brought Lightning up the last two steps, then came and stood over her while she was getting to her feet. His hand was on her arm. The fingers pressed it for a moment, the firm, friendly, admonitory pressure a man might give your arm—at a dance, if there was some secret understanding between you that he wanted to remind you of. "I didn't mean to hurt you," he said, "but you oughtn't to have come interfering. Between us we might have broken that mule's legs on those steps."

She did not answer, staring past him at the mule where he stood in the wash of light from the window, gazing before him out of great, dark eyes. His coat and his little bristling mane shone red in the light. His nostrils were ringed with palest fawn color. If she went over now and cupped his nose in her hands, the nostrils, snuffing gently in and out, would beat against her palm like butter-flies' wings.

She looked up into gray eyes that sparkled in the light. The soldier had a broad mouth that slanted a little to one side. The blunt lips seemed always just about to stretch into a smile. She looked away, thinking how you could set your thumbs at the corners of those lips and rend the mouth from side to side and then, grasping in your hands the head—the head that you had severed from the body—you would beat it up and down on the boards of the well sweep until you cast it, a battered bloody pulp, into those grasses that sprang up there beside the well.

She walked over and sat down on the wooden platform. The planks were cool and wet. She gripped them hard with both hands. The man was still there, making a throat latch out of a piece of twine. He was turning around. "You haven't got a bridle to spare, Bud?"

Cummy spoke up shrilly. "You better not take that mule. I'm telling you now. You better not take him. Can't anybody do anything with him but Tom Ladd and he's joined the army."

The Yankee had thrown a leg over Lightning's back and was sitting there looking down at them. "I'm swapping you a good mare for this mule," he said. "She gave out on me . . . About three miles up the road . . ."

Lightning had stood quiet while the man mounted but he reared suddenly and plunged forward, his small, wicked head tucked down, his ears flat on his neck. And now he plunged on, turned the corner into the lane, and broke into a mad gallop. The soldier's voice drifted back above the pounding of hooves. "I'd be glad for you to have her . . . Lying down under a big oak . . . About three miles up the road."

Cummy caught hold of Barbara's arm. "Come on, sister. Let's go see if we can find that mare."

Barbara did not move. Cummy waited a moment, and sat down beside her. "One thing," he said, "he won't ever get Lightning through those woods. Lightning'll rub him off on the branches."

Barbara had been sitting with her head lifted, staring off into the lane. When he began to speak again she raised her hand. "Hush!" she said sharply and then: "What's that?"

Cummy jumped to his feet. "It's that Yankee," he said. "He's in trouble."

He bounded across the yard and through the open gate. Barbara followed him. It was black dark in the lane. They could not see their hands before them. There was no sound except the thudding of their own feet and then it came again, the cry which rose and swelled and broke finally into hideous shrieks. Barbara caught up with Cummy and pulled him to the left. "It's this way," she panted, "over in the woods."

They crashed through the underbrush and came out in a little glade. They could not see anything at first, then they made out the white trunk of a sycamore and beside it, Lightning, stock-still under a low-hanging bough, his head sharply lifted, his forefeet planted wide apart. The dark mass between his spread legs was too dense for shadow.

Cummy was holding on to Barbara's hand. "Somebody's coming," he whispered.

Barbara did not look around. "It's Sis Sophy," she said. "She's bringing the lantern."

She stood motionless. The long rays of the lantern flickered across the tree trunk and fell on the soldier's face, on the place where his eyes had been, on the blood that oozed from the torn mouth onto the dead leaves.

Sophy was whimpering softly. The lantern shook in her hand. "We'll have to bury him . . . We'll have to get somebody to help us bury him."

Barbara's eyes came away from the dead man to rest on Sophy's face. "I'm not going to help bury him," she said.

She walked past Sophy to where the mule stood. She put her hand up and cupped it over his quivering nostrils. He gave a long sigh and stepped clear of the body. She slid her arm down to rest on his withers.

"Come on," she said, "let's go home."

The Forest of the South

Major Reilly and Lieutenant Munford stood on the upper gallery of Villa Rose and watched the blowing up of Clifton. They knew the time it was to happen, knew the hour, even the minute. An orderly had ridden out from Natchez that morning with the news. A fort was to be built. Its line would cut through the mansion of Clifton. The house and its garden were to be blown up within the hour.

Major Reilly and Lieutenant Munford were in the major's office at Villa Rose, making out reports—there had been a brush with Confederate cavalry over near Lake St. John the night before. One of Reilly's men had been killed, another wounded. He was glad to be back at this old house with the rest of his squadron safe.

He read the papers the orderly brought. When the soldier had left the room he turned to John Munford. His dark mustache lifted to disclose gleaming teeth.

"Mr. Surget of Clifton would never make a diplomat."

John Munford turned serious blue eyes on his chief. "A diplomat?"

The major leaned back in his chair. "Mr. Surget of Clifton has given a series of dinners for Federal officers. But he has never had the wit to invite the Chief Engineer."

John Munford said, "Ah!" and tried to look knowing. But he still did not understand. "Do you mean, sir, that the Chief Engineer is going to blow the place up because he was not invited to dinner?"

"He is going to blow it clean to hell," the major said. He looked at his watch. "In about three minutes, I should say. Come on, boy, we might as well see the explosion."

They went out through the hall and up the winding stairway into an upper hall and then up another short flight of steps and emerged on a balcony. John Munford had stepped out on this balcony before and always with astonishment. Villa Rose, a squat house built in the old manorial style, stood on a hill high for that part of the country. Below them on the right lay the Mississippi and four or five miles away as the crow flies was the town. Munford's eyes sought and found the tall spire of St. Mary's Cathedral, white in the morning sun, then moved on. There was the river again and, dark against it, masses of green: the famous gardens of Clifton. His eye roved on. More white. That would be the columns of the house or perhaps one of the pavilions. It was hard to tell at this distance just where the house stood.

He summoned up the picture of the house as he had seen it two days before when he had gone in to town with a message from Major Reilly. The Indiana colonel whom he was seeking was an ardent botanist. He had been told to look for him in the gardens of Clifton. He had traversed graveled walks, between box hedges, through scented arbors, and at last had found the colonel standing with Mr. Surget beside a great star-shaped flower bed. There had been an expanse of placid water beyond them with, as he lived, swans floating upon it. Returning through a vine-hung pavilion he had had to put up his hand to brush away masses of bloom. He had made a mental note of the lake, of the swans, of the oleanders for the letter he wrote home each week.

Major Reilly drew in his breath with a whistle. "There she goes!"

A great column of smoke rose and wavered over the trees. A few seconds later they heard the detonation. It jarred the earth beneath them and rattled against the distant woods. Reilly was turning away. John Munford followed him down the stairs. In his mind was a dull wonder. The flowers and the fountains he had seen two days before, the camellias, the Cape jessamines, the late roses, the marble of the grottoes and the pavilions—all those shining, rose-colored things had vanished in that plume of dull smoke!

In the hall below, the two men faced each other a second, then crossed the gallery and went out into the garden. Major Reilly was breathing hard as if to clear his lungs. "A great pity, Munford. As handsome a gentleman's estate as I've seen, here or in the old country." He had found his cigars at last and was offering Munford one. He drew on his cigar and suddenly was himself again. He remembered an engagement in town. "I'll let you finish up those requisitions by yourself, boy. You can manage, eh?"

John said that he could. The major motioned to an orderly to bring his horse, and strode toward the gate. Halfway there he turned. "You'd better look in on the old lady. See if she wants anything."

John said, "Yes, sir," again. After the major had ridden off he stood there a few minutes, the unlit cigar in his hand. There was an acrid smell of smoke in the air but the garden—this garden in which he stood—was just as it had been when he came out on the gallery into the fresh morning air an hour ago. The walks, branching out from the graveled circular drive, straggled off into dense greenery. The greenery was starred here and there with the pink of japonicas and off to the right a low hedge of Cape jessamine was popcorn-white with bloom.

His thoughts went to his Connecticut home. He had had a letter that morning from his sister, Eunice. She reported that the first big snow of the winter had come the night before. She was driving in to Danbury that afternoon, but she would have to go by sleigh, and over the winter road. Snow was drifted five feet deep between their house and the Robinsons'.

A hummingbird was hovering over a vine nearby. Munford watched the tiny wings which never for a second stopped their beating, then raised his eyes. Everywhere about him light fell, on glossy green leaves, on a scarlet flower, on the scarlet of the bird's breast. The fancy came to him that this light might have been filtered through the wings of birds, so shimmering it was, so iridescent. Off toward the stables some men were shouting to each other but their distant voices only served to emphasize the quiet of the garden. He had never known it so quiet before. But the stillness was oppressive and the landscape, he thought suddenly, too bright. This shining air held a menace.

A soldier came down the steps and made off toward the stables. Munford, recalled to his duty, followed the man around to the back of the house. A wide gallery ran the length of the ell. At the end of the ell up a short flight of steps there was a little room. It had been the overseer's room, originally. Now Mrs. Mazereau and her daughter, the owners of the house, lived in it.

In the shadow of one of the columns a soldier sat in a low, split-bottomed chair picking a chicken. Munford paused beside him a second to watch how deftly he was pulling the pinfeathers out from the wings. A good forager, Bill Morehouse. A good man at everything. Munford wished that Morehouse had the job of looking after the old lady instead of himself.

He went up the short flight of steps and knocked at the door. There was the sound of footsteps. The door opened a little way. He put the palm of his hand against it and pushed. It opened a little wider. He stepped inside the room. The blinds were drawn and the air was oppressive with stale odors. A young woman confronted him. She stood erect at first, then shrank a little back. Her hands came up in front of her face. She did not speak.

Impatience and embarrassment made his voice brusque. He said: "It is Lieutenant Munford, Miss Mazereau. Major Reilly's compliments. He wants to know how your mother is this morning."

The girl, still moving backwards, let her hands drop to her sides. "She didn't sleep," she said in a low voice.

He glanced toward the closed blinds. "Perhaps if you had more light . . ."

She halted at that. "I had the blinds open when we first got up but she saw some men going by. . . ." Suddenly she was coming toward him. He could not be sure in that half light but he thought that there was a smile on her face. "She thinks she's a girl," she said. "And I'm another girl. We're on our way to her old home . . . to the Green Springs, in Virginia. . . ." Damn it, she was laughing! Laughing at her old mother for being crazy. He would have to tell Reilly that.

A harsh voice came from the bed in the corner. "Eugénie!"

"Yes, Mama!"

The old woman was out of the bed and was coming toward them. A fierce, incredibly fat white cockatoo. The quilt from the bed was half hanging from her shoulders. She wore a nightgown which he, John Munford, had bought for her in a shop in Natchez-under-the-Hill. Clutching the quilt about her as if it had been a bed gown, she fixed him with her bloodshot blue eyes. "Young man, where are you going?"

Munford bowed his fair head. He said patiently, "I wasn't going anywhere this morning, ma'am. Major Reilly has gone to town and has left me in command."

She said, "*Major!*" She closed her eyes, pursed her lips. "*Soldiers,*" she whispered. She leaned forward, so close that her foul breath fanned his cheek. She went on whispering. "Two women in distress. . . . Trying to find our way home. . . . I knew this country well once but it has changed. . . . So many roads . . . and the people . . ." Her voice sank lower. Her lower lip was wry with cunning. "I will give you a barrel of flour if you will conduct us to our home. It is in the Green Springs. . . ."

"We haven't any barrel of flour, Mama!"

Munford felt the girl's eyes upon him. He bowed and said, "I am sorry, ma'am, but I don't know the country. I can't conduct you to your home." He went out, shutting the door behind him.

As he reached the foot of the stairs a cur pup, the soldiers' pet, came scampering toward him, then fell on her back with her habitual gesture of outstretched paws. He thrust out his toe to poke her gently in the belly and then withdrew his foot, frowning. "Get up!" he said harshly.

He walked the length of the gallery and entered the wide front hall. At the far end the open door disclosed vistas of green. Patches of quivering light fell on the broad boards. There was one place where the oak was discolored in a great splotch. Munford, as he approached it, slowed his steps. Always when he passed this spot he had to stop and look down. Colonel Mazereau's blood, gushing from his cloven chest, had made that dark, greasy-looking place there by the newel post.

Munford's thoughts went to that night. He had had the story from Major Reilly, who in turn had had it from Eugénie Mazereau. Reilly, when he told it to Munford, had used what must have been the girl's words.

"The Negroes all ran away. Then the soldiers came. Mama said not to worry. She talked to the captain and she said he was a gentleman. But he rode off somewhere. He left three or four soldiers. There was one kept walking through the house. He came and looked in the library where we were. Mama said not to notice. We worked on our embroidery.

"Then we heard somebody step up on the porch. Mama said, 'Eugénie, it's your father.'

"I went to the door. I could see the soldier hiding there by the post and I could see Papa. He had on a long cloak and he was all splashed with mud. He stood there and he kept calling: 'Josephine! Eugénie! Josephine!'

"I went back into the room. I said, 'Mama, Papa is there and he keeps calling.'

"She went to the door. She said, 'Arsène, for God's sake . . . Arsène,' she said, 'I beg of you. For God's sake, go away!'

"He didn't listen. He started toward her. He got as far as the post. The soldier came up from behind. He had the axe in his hand." Major Reilly, telling the story, would put his hand to his breast. "It was like felling an ox. He went back, very slow, on his heels. Then he was standing straight and then he fell over. The blood was on the floor even before he fell."

John Munford had wanted to know what the women did then.

Colonel Mazereau, the major reported, had lived for several hours, until nearly sundown. "The thing that worried the girl most was that her mother kept trying to get the cloth out of the wound. The cloth of his uniform, Munford, was driven down into his breastbone and he was spouting blood like a whale. Unconscious, of course, from the moment of the blow. Finally, toward sundown, they were convinced that he was dead. The old lady was all for getting him buried before the soldiers came back. She made the girl go out and dig the grave. The girl said she dug all over the garden, but the ground was too hard. At last she persuaded the old lady to bury him temporarily under a pile of rotting leaves. Just as they finished Slocomb's men came back. The women ran and hid in the overseer's room and stayed there till those damned Dutchmen set the house on fire.

"I found them wandering around in the yard after the fire was put out and Slocomb's men had gone. The old lady was perfectly quiet then. It was the girl that was hard to handle. She kept coming up to me and saying they wouldn't do any harm and when I said I didn't expect them to she kept thanking me. I said, 'My God, madam, the exigencies of war have made it necessary for me to commandeer your house but you needn't be grateful to me. . . .' A queer girl, Munford. I wonder what she'd be like in other circumstances."

It was a subject that Major Reilly often speculated on: the character and personality of Miss Eugénie Mazereau. "In my opinion she's loonier than the old lady." Or "She's still scared out of her wits. You ought to do something about that, Munford. Take her for a buggy ride. Convince her we're not ogres."

John Munford, following the major's suggestion, had invited Miss Mazereau to walk with him in the garden and had even taken her driving several times in a trap that had been found in the stables. She came with him whenever he invited her, wearing always the same black dress and a voluminous black shawl that must have been her mother's. She never wore a bonnet. She had been bareheaded when she escaped from the house.

She talked to him as they drove along the river road. "Yes, Lieutenant Munford, the weather has been delightful for the past week . . . You say your home is in Connecticut . . . No, I have never been farther north than Memphis . . ."

Once he halted his horse before a gate set in a tall hedge. He motioned with his whip. "All those people who lived here. What has become of them?"

"They have all gone away, Lieutenant Munford."

But as they drove on she had turned to look back at the gate. "The Macrae place," she said. "That is the Macrae place." Her tone struck Munford as strange. It was the tone that might have been used by a traveler returning to his old haunts after years of absence.

He went now through the hall and turned right, into the great room that was used as an office for the cavalry squadron. It was barely furnished: two field desks, six or seven pine chairs, and an old sofa in one corner where Major Reilly sometimes napped. The major had a grudge against the officer whom he had relieved. Once, walking in the garden with Munford, Reilly had kicked at the charred pieces of a mahogany dining table. "Those damned Dutchmen! They might at least have left that for the officers to eat on."

Young Slater was pushing a sheaf of requisition blanks toward Munford. He took them and began signing them mechanically. They worked for two hours. At twelve o'clock Munford put his pen down and went out on the gallery. Young Slater stood with him for a few minutes, then went back into the house. Munford began pacing up and down the gallery. Once he stopped to stare into the windows that ran on each side of the doorway. The glass was full of imperfections; some of the whorls had opalescent tints. When he was a child he used to press his nose against just such cloudy panes of glass—in his grandfather's house at Danbury. A white house with a steep, gabled roof, twin "bride" trees—elms—on each side of the stoop. He could see it all clearly but it seemed unreal, like something he had seen in a picture rather than something he remembered. He fell to pacing again and as he went was conscious of greenery pressing in there beyond the graveled walks, of sunshine on the gravel, of pink and white blossoms. And yet it was a hushed land-scape. Moving about these grounds he had sometimes the feeling that he imagined a man might have on a desert island. Here in this smiling land he was lonely. It came to him that there was one person lonelier than he. That girl in the little back room. There was not, he supposed, anybody in the world lonelier than she. Colonel Mazereau, before he was killed, had quarreled with all his relations, Reilly said. The girl's mother, her companion in misfortune, had deserted her to wander in memory along the road that led to the Green Springs in Virginia. Yes, she was quite alone, that girl.

The call for mess sounded. Young Slater spoke to him from the doorway. He told the boy that he was coming, but before he went into the mess hall he turned back into the office. Sitting down at his desk, he drew a sheet of paper toward him and wrote a note. It presented Lieutenant Munford's compliments to Miss Mazereau and inquired if she would drive with him that afternoon.

II

At three o'clock Lieutenant Munford and Miss Mazereau were driving north along the river road. She sat with her hands folded, one over the other, in her lap. She was wearing a pair of gloves, lace gloves or rather mitts, for they left the tips of her fingers bare. Munford wondered where in the world she had got them. Some old trunk, probably, that had escaped Slocomb's men.

He stared ahead of him. The bit of road visible between the horse's forward-pricked ears was not unlike a stretch of road on the way to Gaylordsville with the dark trees and that old rail fence riding against the skyline. He had driven young ladies along that road often enough—in sleighs at this time of year. That New Year's party at the Robinsons'. He had escorted Jane Scoville, and Sam Dillon and Roberta Jennings had been in the back seat. He was not in love with Jane Scoville now but he would like to have her beside him with her furs and her perfume and her chatter. Well, he was on pleasure bent this afternoon, with a pretty girl beside him. He had always flattered himself that he could keep a pretty girl entertained, but how could you make yourself agreeable to a girl when you were occupying the house that by rights should have been hers?

By rights? His thoughts went, as they often did these days, to the conflict in which he was engaged. Major Reilly said that he himself was not opposed to slavery. Certain types of civilization, he said, were always founded on slavery, and he had cited ancient Athens and God knows what other countries—the major was a graduate of the University of Dublin. Well, he, John Munford, was not a highly educated man. But he knew right from wrong. He would do it all over again, to strike the shackles from the wrists of slaves. And yet it was all so different from what he had pictured.

The girl was turning toward him. Her eyes—unusually large, luminous eyes—were the color of the chestnuts that used to fall from the great tree in his grandfather's yard. The lids were heavy, so heavy that they dimmed the brilliance of her glance. And the lids themselves had a peculiar pallor. Wax-white, like the petals of the magnolia blossom. When he had first come into this country he had gathered one of those creamy blossoms only to see it turn brown in his grasp. She was saying something about a letter. ". . . It may be we can leave."

He said, "*Leave* Villa Rose?"

She nodded, still with those large strange-colored eyes fixed on his. "My cousin in Kentucky says we can come there."

He said, "I should not think you would want to go to Kentucky, Miss Mazereau. They are fighting there too."

She did not answer. As they drove on he considered what she had said. If he or Major Reilly went away—and they might be ordered away at any time—what would become of this girl and her mother? He turned to her abruptly. "Perhaps you would be better advised to go to Kentucky—if you can get through the lines."

She looked up at him, then suddenly shrank back as, he thought savagely, she might have done if he had menaced her with the whip he held in his hand. "I don't want to go where they're fighting."

He compressed his lips, feeling the angry blood surge to his forehead. "I don't know where you'll go then," he said curtly.

She did not answer.

They were at the top of a little rise, descending toward a stream. The horse's hooves splashed little drops of water in their faces as they crossed it. And now they were on a rise again. He looked at the pines crowding close on each side of the road and wondered if they would come to any hilltop which would command a view. "What is the name of that stream we have just crossed?" he asked.

"Sand Creek," she said.

He checked the horse. Before them was the tall hedge and the gate where they had paused the other day. She was looking about her with more animation than he had ever seen her display. On an impulse he pulled the horse up short and motioned with his whip at the gate. "Shall we go in there?"

"Yes," she said.

He got down and opened the gate; then, as she did not pick up the reins from where he had hung them over the dashboard, he led the horse through. He closed the gate and went up to the trap. "Shall we hitch the horse and walk for a little?"

"Yes," she said.

He assisted her down, then turned the trap about and hitched the horse to one of the bars of the gate. They started up the avenue. It was broader than the one at Villa Rose and lined on each side with live oaks. At the end of the avenue a square gray structure with a dilapidated double gallery was visible through the drooping wreaths of Spanish moss. They paused beside the carriage block to look up at it.

"A dreary place," Munford said.

She did not say anything.

"What is the name of the family that lived here?"

"Macrae," she said dreamily. Suddenly she took a few steps away from him, then looked back over her shoulder. "There is a fountain over here in the shrubbery," she said.

He followed her silently between the unclipped hedges into an abandoned garden. Once she had to stand aside while he dragged away a great, fallen branch. Suddenly the path widened and they emerged into what had once been a circle of flower beds. In the center was a fountain, a great basin, and standing beside it the marble figure of a woman. The woman was bending a little forward. Water from the pitcher which she carried had once run into the basin but no water had run there for a long time now. The basin was green with moss up to its rim.

The girl had walked over and was standing beside the fountain in much the same attitude as that of the marble figure. He studied the pale, down-bent face, wondering wherein lay its attraction. For it had come to that. She was the most attractive woman he had ever seen. The conviction had been growing on him for months. He remembered now his first sight of her, the day after he had been transferred to Reilly's squadron. A small figure in black, hurrying around the corner of the house—she had been gathering chips and was carrying them in her upturned skirt. He had thought that she must be the wife of one of the soldiers or perhaps a camp follower— Reilly was lenient with them. Then he had seen slim ankles swinging out from under a ragged petticoat and the thought had come to him that she might be a lady. A lady! He had not seen a woman—a respectable woman—in weeks. He hurried on and caught up with her. She had looked up at him just as she had looked at him a moment ago, but he had insisted on gathering some more wood for her and had carried it up to the little room. He had followed her at first because he had been attracted by the sight of a woman. After he caught up with her he was repelled by her manner—the slight favor he proposed doing her did not deserve such effusive thanks. He had gone on, however, finding the wood for her, showing her all the courtesy he would have shown any respectable woman. He might never have thought of her again if Reilly had not told him her story that night.

He had seen her often since, and though he felt that he understood her better he still found her manner strange. He thought of another girl, a girl he had seen for one brief evening only, in Tennessee. When she was asked to play the piano for some Federal officers she had asked to be excused for a moment and had returned to the parlor with an axe. She had hurled it high above her head and had brought it down on the keyboard, saying she would make matchwood of the instrument before it should play a tune for despised "Yankees." . . . The word "Yankee" was never on Eugénie Mazereau's lips. She seemed to have no concern for the Confederate cause, and yet, he thought, she might be patriotic, and proud too, in other circumstances. . . .

She had put out her hand and with the tip of her index finger was tracking the rim of the basin. Her head, with its smoothly banded black hair, was still down-bent. There was a faint, mysterious smile on her lips.

Munford found this smile maddening. He took two steps and was beside her. "Why are you doing that?"

She looked up. Her eyes were blue! He had thought them brown. That was because of the stain of light brown about the iris but the eye itself was blue. Blue, that is, if you stood there and looked into her eyes but if you stepped back a few paces you would say, "This girl's eyes are brown, pale brown," and you would say, too, "She looks at me but she never sees me." Why should an eye look out and not see? Does it look within? Has it seen something it cannot look away from?

She had not spoken. He laid his finger on that part of the marble her finger had touched.

She smiled. "The fountain? You mean why did I touch the fountain?"

He said hoarsely, "Miss Mazereau . . . Eugénie . . . you must know my sentiments."

She gazed at him, still smiling. He could not tell whether she had heard what he said.

A sudden thought turned him scarlet. He took a turn around the fountain and came back. He bowed. "I have the honor to ask for your hand in marriage."

She said, "My hand!" and moved a little away so that a tuft of long grass she had been standing on sprang up between them.

"I would have spoken to your mother," he said stiffly, "if circumstances had been different."

"No," she whispered. "Don't speak to my mother."

"I understand that," he said. "The point is . . . will you marry me? I . . . Is the prospect agreeable to you, Miss Mazereau?"

"Agreeable?" she said.

He stammered, "Eugénie. *Look* at me!"

She put out a hand and fearfully touched his face. He seized her. He kissed her lips, her brow, her throat, her lips again. "I will send you home," he whispered. "To my people. To Connecticut."

She drew back at that. "Connecticut? Is it a long way?"

"Yes," he said impatiently, and went on to tell her that his mother would welcome her as a daughter. His sister, Eunice, would be a sister to her, for there was a special bond of affection between him and his sister. In place of the family she had lost she should have his family. He swore that he would make her so happy that she would forget everything that had happened.

She did not say anything, only put up her hand again and touched his cheek. They went over and sat down on a bench near the fountain. Munford's arm was about her waist. She allowed her head to rest on his shoulder. All around them was a tangle of green but they could see rising about the hedge a slanting roof, a red chimney.

"What is that?" he asked.

"The old schoolhouse."

"Did you go to school there?"

"Yes, with the Macrae children."

He had been thinking that very soon, in a few days at most, he would have to send her North. Yes, three days at most, and he did not know how she had looked as a child, what nickname she had had, what paths she had taken when she came here to school. He was even curious about the Macraes, the departed owners of this place. "How many children were there?" he asked.

"Mary and Ellen. And there was Frank."

Some impulse made him repeat the name he was never afterwards to forget. "Frank . . . ?"

She tilted her head away from his caressing hand. The strange eyes gleamed under the heavy lids. "Frank . . . He was always playing jokes. He put Cousin Maria's crinoline on that statue there and he put a bonnet on it and painted its face with pokeberry juice and put a prayer book in its hand. He said she was going to church."

He laughed. "Where is Frank now?"

"He joined the army. . . ."

The shadows were getting longer. He roused himself and said that they must go back. They walked slowly along the path past the fountain. Munford smiled, seeing a mischievous boy coming through the hedge, his arms heaped with women's wear. The boy's eyes were gray and lively. He was laughing as he went up to the statue. Suddenly Munford was jealous of that boy who had played here in this garden. He stopped and, taking Eugénie's face between his hands, looked deep into her eyes before he kissed her.

"Say you love me."

"I love you," she said.

III

Major Reilly was silent when Munford told him of his engagement. Finally he shook his head. "You are a rash man. You seem to forget that Miss Mazereau's father was killed here in this hall. Her brothers, if she has any, certainly many of her cousins, are in the Confederate service."

"I shall be able to answer for my wife's loyalty," Munford said stiffly.

The major's brown face broke up into crisscross lines as it did when he laughed, and yet he wasn't laughing. "I wasn't thinking of her loyalty," he said.

Munford left the room. Later that night, lying on his cot in the officers' quarters, he thought of the expression that had been on Reilly's face. Yet Reilly, on the whole, had been as sympathetic, as considerate as a man could be. Munford and Eugénie Mazereau were to be married in Reilly's office tomorrow afternoon at four o'clock —Reilly had already sent a message to the chaplain. It would be all right for Eugénie to stay at Villa Rose a few days, Reilly said, but it could be only a few days. She and her mother ought to be on their way north as soon as the trip could be arranged for. Munford wondered what his mother and sister would think when they were confronted with the old woman and had to listen to her ravings. Would it not perhaps be better to let the two women stay in the South; if not at Villa Rose, at some safe quarters nearby?

His head felt hot. There was little air in the room. He got up and went to the open window. There was a full moon over the garden. In its light every leaf, every twig stood out as bright as if in noonday light. "Too bright, too light," he thought irritably. He stayed at the window long enough to smoke a cigar, then went back to bed and finally slept.

Major Reilly rode off to town early the next morning and Munford was again left in command. He was engaged with Ralph Slater in making out company reports when the guard at the door suddenly advanced into the room and told him that Miss Mazereau wanted to see him on business.

He told young Slater he would be gone for a little while and went, half smiling at the word "business," through the hall and out onto the back gallery. Eugénie Mazereau was waiting for him there. She had her black shawl drawn close about her shoulders. Her face was pale. Her eyes had a curious, intent look.

She came up to him, whispering, "Could you come with me a minute?"

He had given a cautious glance over his shoulder and, seeing that no one was in sight, was about to lean over to kiss her when something in her expression checked him. "Yes," he said quietly, and followed her down the steps and out through the yard. They passed through a side gate and took a path through the woods. They had progressed some distance along it before Munford saw the gray outline of a house through the trees and realized that this was a shortcut to the Macrae place.

The girl walked on before him in silence. And yet when they had stopped there in the woods a moment ago she had yielded herself to his embraces more freely than at any time yesterday. She had even put her arm up about his neck to draw his head down to hers. He had thought when they first started out that she had changed her mind about their engagement and was bringing him back to the same place they had visited yesterday to tell him that she would not marry him. He smiled. If that was the case he would be able to persuade her to change her mind back to what it had been yesterday. They were entering the ground by a side entrance. She did not go toward the garden but walked instead toward the house. On the gallery she paused a moment, then slipped quietly inside the half-open door, motioning to him to follow her. He hesitated a second. He was armed but he was only one man. But he put the thought of ambush away from him and walked resolutely after her.

The hall smelled musty. The blinds at both ends were drawn. What light there was came from a window high on the landing. Munford's eyes went to this window and then to the stairs below. The steps were thick with dust. He stiffened suddenly as he saw places where that dust had been disturbed, by boot soles. At the same moment there was the sound of steps above him. A face appeared over the railing.

Munford drew back, his hand on his revolver. But the girl was already starting up the steps. She looked back at him over her shoulder. "You can come," she said; "he's alone."

Munford drew his revolver. He pushed past her and went up, taking the stairs two at a time. The best way, he told himself mechanically. To rush the man was the only chance now. He came to the landing, made the turn, and stopped dead still. A man in a Federal uniform stood at the head of the stairs.

Eugénie had come up behind him. She stretched out her hand. "Lieutenant Munford, this is my cousin, Captain Macrae," she said, calmly, as if she were making an introduction in a drawing room.

Frank Macrae stood on the top step, staring down at them. He looked exactly as Munford had pictured him. Blond, with a handsome, well-fleshed face, made red by exposure to wind and weather, an aquiline nose, steady gray eyes set under fair brows.

He did not seem to see Munford. He was staring at the girl.

"Eugénie," he said in a low voice, "have you gone crazy?"

Her laugh rang out. "It's Mama . . . She thinks she's a girl and she thinks she's back in the Green Springs. . . . Ever since Papa was killed."

Munford said stiffly, "I regret to say that Mrs. Mazereau suffers from hallucinations . . ."

Eugénie interrupted him. "He came in the hall and a soldier killed him, with an axe." She looked at her cousin. "The blood was all over everything, Frank."

Frank Macrae, as if suddenly recollecting himself, took a step backwards. He looked at Munford, then stood aside while the other two ascended the stairs. Munford, his revolver cocked, went up to Macrae, laid his hand on his arm. "Captain Macrae, you are my prisoner," he said sternly. He paused a moment, then added, "It is unfortunate that you are in Federal uniform."

Frank Macrae laughed. "It is indeed unfortunate," he said. But he did not start down the stairs. Instead he turned into one of the great dim rooms opening off the upper hall. Munford, a little bewildered, followed him. The girl came too. She advanced toward her cousin but he motioned her back. "Go over there and stand by the window, Eugénie," he said curtly.

She went obediently and stood in the place he had indicated. The two men confronted each other. Macrae was very pale and his brows were drawn. He had been staring at the girl and now he still kept glancing at her though he had turned to Munford. Absent-mindedly, in the manner of a man making conversation, he asked Munford some questions about recent movements of the Federal squadron. Munford answered them. But he was conscious that time was passing. Perhaps he was in a trap. The Confederate officer might be trying to delay him until help came. He was about to speak when Macrae gave a long sigh.

"Well, we had better get on with it . . . Lieutenant, before your court meets there is a matter I must attend to."

Munford bowed. "I am at your service, Captain."

"Will you secure for me a license and the services of a chaplain? I want to go through a marriage ceremony with my cousin. I . . . there is certain property that will then be automatically at her disposal!"

Munford lifted his fair head haughtily. "That is impossible, Captain. Your cousin has promised to marry me."

Macrae stared. "You are engaged to marry my cousin?"
Munford bowed again.

There was a long silence. The girl laughed suddenly, left the window, and started toward the two men. Macrae lifted his hand, gently, in the gesture he might have used to a child or a puppy. "Stay where you are, Eugénie." He turned to Munford. "Lieutenant Munford, I know you by reputation. I believe you to be a man of honor. I do not envy you the privilege of marrying my cousin. . . . Do you fully understand the responsibilities you assume?"

The two men gazed at each other. Macrae's eyes were gray and hard as steel. It came to Munford that in a few hours this man would be dead, hanged as a spy. He looked away, to where the girl was standing beside the open window. Her strange, incurious eyes were fixed upon him, Munford. There was a smile on her lips. It was the smile that had so wrought upon him in the garden. It was not mysterious now. He averted his gaze. The window frame was dark and gauzy with cobwebs but beyond stretched a green meadow. Light played everywhere upon it, the same luminous, quivering light that yesterday at this hour had struck through the leaves at Villa Rose.

He withdrew his eyes from the scene. When he lifted them it was to meet the prisoner's hard, victorious glance.

"Yes," he said dully, "I understand."

The Ice House

Doug was waiting where the paths forked as Raeburn came through the woods. He had his Barlow out and was whittling a stick, but he threw it away and started striding along the path as soon as he saw Raeburn.

"I thought you wasn't coming," he said. "I thought you'd just about give it out and decided you wasn't coming."

"I had to get my breakfast," Raeburn told him. "I ain't going to work for nobody on a empty stomach." He cast an eye at the sun. "'Tain't more'n six o'clock anyhow."

Doug slackened his pace a little. "Well," he said, "the way I look at it if you going to work for a man you ought to work for him. We don't know nothin' about this man. If we get there late he may not pay us what he said he would."

Raeburn watched his own skinny shadow racing with him, over the new green shoots of pokeberry and sassafras. It occurred to him that it was the middle of April. The dogwoods were in full flower. Channel cat ought to be biting.

"Wilmer was over to our house last night," he said. "He wanted to know if that man had asked us to work for him. He said *he* wouldn't tech it. He said he wouldn't tech it for *no* amount of money."

Doug laughed. "I don't reckon he would," he said. "I don't reckon anybody that once took a look at Wilmer would hire him for *this* job. He couldn't hold out to handle a pick . . ."

"You reckon we'll have to use a pick, Doug?"

Doug stopped short in the path. "You know who's in that ice house?" he asked.

"I don't know none of their names."

"I reckon you don't. They's Yankees. Every last one of 'em's Yankees. Course now if you don't want to you don't have to do it. I can git somebody else. Handlin' a dead Yankee ain't no more to *me* than handlin' a dead hawg, but of course now you don't have to go if you don't want to."

"Oh, I'll go," Raeburn said. "It ain't nothin' to me."

They emerged from the woods into the clearing. A hundred yards away the ice house stood, with around it the black, straight trunks of half a dozen oak trees. There were no leaves as yet on any of their branches, but a sugar tree at one corner of the house cast its yellowish green tassels low on the sloping roof.

The man was standing before the ice house door looking down into the pit. A short man, so plump that the waistband of his trousers seemed on the verge of bursting. He heard them coming and turned around. His eyes were gray. They looked pale in the creases of his red, round face.

"Well, boys," he said affably, "I see you're like me. Early risers."

He waved his hand at the unpainted pine coffins that curved in a long glistening line around one whole side of the ice house and back behind the sugar tree. "Now what we got to do is fill them boxes up. The sooner we get them boxes filled up the sooner we get done and the sooner we get done the sooner you get your money. . . . Ain't that right, Bud?"

"That's right," Doug said. He took a pick and stepped over the threshold of the ice house onto the little ledge of earth that ran all around the circular pit. Raeburn followed him.

The skeletons were level with the earth. There was a man's skull on top of the pile. The eye sockets turned toward the door, the ribs and long leg bones slanting away diagonally across the heap, as if the man had flung himself down face forward to look out over the field. Where the light from the open door fell the bones were pale, almost white, but the bones that showed here and there underneath were darker. There was moss on some of them.

Doug picked up one of the fingers. The joints still stuck together. But as he held them in his hand the little joint dropped from its socket and a wisp of dried tendon fell out on the heap.

Doug stooped and with both hands lifted the curved grayish

ribs where they were joined to the backbone. "Here," he said, "I'll give 'em to you and you put 'em outside. That's the best way to do it."

Raeburn laid the ribs in the wheelbarrow that the contractor had drawn up to the door. When he turned around Doug had more bones ready to hand him. They worked there that way for a long while. When the barrow was full the contractor wheeled it around the corner and deposited the load in the pine boxes. Raeburn could hear the light clatter as the more fragile bones fell from the barrow into the coffin and could hear the contractor whistling as he went the rounds of the boxes arranging the skeletons.

Once when he knew the contractor was at the creek getting a drink Raeburn called down into the pit cautiously:

"Doug, how you reckon he knows when he's got a whole skeleton in one of them coffins?"

Doug raised a face curiously striped by the greenish light that filtered down through cracks in the planking. "I'd know," he said. "He can put a skull in each box, I reckon, even if he don't know where all them little bones belong. . . . Naw, he can't, either. Some of them fellers was put in here without any head!"

"Some of 'em was blowed clean to pieces," Raeburn said.

He looked out over the field where the new green was creeping up through the clumps of brown sedge grass. They had fought all over that field, and in the woods. In December. In the snow. When they went to bury the dead the next day the ground was frozen. A foot deep. They had to dig them out with pickaxes. They had buried a lot of them on the battlefield. In two big trenches. And then they had put all the rest in this ice house. . . . In 1862 that had been. Four years ago. . . .

The contractor's round, red face showed in the doorway. "Well, boys," he said, "time for a little snack, ain't it?"

Doug had heard him and was clambering up the side of the pit. Raeburn gave him a hand and pulled him up beside him. They walked around the side of the ice house and down the path to the creek. Both boys stretched themselves on the ground and lowered their faces into the water. It was clear and very cold. Raeburn gulped some down, then thrust his hands in wrist deep and let the cold water run over them. Doug was wiping his on some water grasses. "Wish I'd brought some soap," he said. He looked at Raeburn. "It ain't so hard when you just have to stand there and let me hand 'em up to you. It's getting 'em dug out and getting 'em loose from each other that's so hard."

"I'll get down in the pit after dinner," Raeburn told him.

The contractor was on his knees in the shade of the sugar tree when they came up the path. He had a trash fire going and was boiling coffee in a little bucket. Doug and Raeburn took their cold meat and biscuits and sat down on the grass. The contractor poured coffee into tin cups.

Raeburn drank the hot coffee down at a gulp. It warmed his insides and invigorated him. He decided that he would be able to eat something, after all, and bit into a biscuit, but the sick feeling swept over him again and he had to put it down quickly. He stretched out in the grass, supporting his head on one hand. Through a rift in the bushes he could see the creek shining in the noonday sun. It ran swiftly along here just above the falls, but there were good pools, all along here and higher up, too.

Doug was asking the man questions about his business. Had he ever worked for the government before? And how was he paid? By the day or so much for the job?

The contractor had finished eating his lunch and was lighting his pipe. "I ain't had much experience working for the government. Fact is, this is the first job I ever did fer 'em. Now on this job they pay me every time I take in a load of them boxes. Every time I take in a load of them boxes they count 'em and pay me so much a head." He took his pipe out of his mouth. "So much a head," he repeated meditatively.

"Channel cat ought to be biting now," Raeburn said. His voice that was not through changing yet, though he was nearly sixteen, broke unexpectedly into a deep bass. "I know a way to catch channel cat till the world looks level."

The contractor had got up and was standing beside one of the boxes. He had his stubby fingers spread out as if he were counting. "How's that?" he asked.

"Well," Raeburn said, "you have to do it at night." He fixed his large brown eyes intently on the man's face. "The channel cat, he's a night feeder, so you have to fix for him at night. . . ."

The contractor was looking at the boxes again, but he nodded politely. "What do you have to do, son?"

"Well, you fix you some limb lines. Get you a tree that has a branch over the creek, and just tie half a dozen lines on the limbs and leave 'em. Don't use too much sinker, because the channel cat he feeds on top of the water. Just fix 'em and leave 'em there and in the morning you'll have all the fish you can eat for breakfast."

The contractor came back and sat down. "Now that's right noticing, for a boy your age," he said.

"I'm fifteen," Raeburn told him. "I'm fifteen and Doug'll be sixteen next month."

"Well now . . ." the contractor said, "and what do you boys aim to do when you get through with this job?"

"Work for Mr. Foster out on the aidge of town here," Doug said, "if he needs any hands. Folks ain't hirin' many hands now, though."

The contractor shook his head. "Farm work's all right," he said. "Farm work's all right if you can't get nothing else to do, but a smart young feller like you wants to be looking out fer oppertunity. . . . Ain't everybody knows oppertunity when they see it. The folks at home all thought I was mighty foolish when I come down in this country, but I knew they was oppertunity in the South . . . bound to be." He put out his pipe and rose briskly. "Well," he said, "I reckon we better be gettin' back to work."

Doug stood up. "One thing," he said, "we got to have a ladder. They're way down in there now. I don't know as I can get 'em up to Raeburn without a ladder."

The contractor looked at the Porter house, just visible through the trees. "Maybe them folks would lend us a ladder. . . . Supposing I walk over and see if they'd lend us a ladder."

"You reckon they'll lend him a ladder?" Raeburn asked when he was gone.

"Shore they will," Doug said. " 'Tain't nothin' to lend anybody a ladder."

Raeburn watched the rotund figure disappear in the bushes that fringed the slope. "Mrs. Porter hates Yankees," he said. "They was three of her boys killed by the Yankees."

Doug laughed. "This feller never killed no Confederates."

He stepped back into the ice house and slid quickly down into the pit.

Raeburn protested as he took his stand on the ledge. "I told you I was going to get down there after dinner."

Doug shook his head. "I'm used to it now. You have to kind of get the hang of it. It'd just be wasting time now if we changed places."

He stirred the bones vigorously with his pick and a rank odor rose and floated in the chill air. Raeburn drew it into his nostrils, wondering. It was several minutes before he knew where he had smelled it before—in the wooden walls and flooring of an abandoned slaughterhouse that had stood for a long time in one of Foster's fields.

The bones that Doug was piling up on the ledge now were different from the ones on top, grayish-green, matted, some of them, with strange fungus growths. Water had stood in the ice house a good deal of the time, it seemed. Doug had to keep shifting about to find a dry place to stand on.

He did not like it if Raeburn kept his face turned away from the pit to look over the field. He talked incessantly:

"You know what that Yankee done? . . . He went down there in Blue Gum Hollow and asked Uncle Hooser's boys to work for him." He laughed. "Uncle Hooser told him them boys sho would be glad to make that money, but every one of them was away from home." He laughed again, so hard that he shook all over. "Every last one of them niggers was away from home!"

"Niggers is funny," Raeburn agreed. "When my Uncle Rod was killed . . . over in Caroline County . . . killed right there on his front porch . . . there was a old nigger man standing there in the front yard. Old Uncle Lias Sims. And he wouldn't even help my mother carry Uncle Rod in the house. Naw, sir, he just turned around and ran. Niggers don't like to have nothin' to do with dead people."

"How come your Uncle Rod to get killed settin' on his front porch?" Doug inquired.

"He was so deaf he couldn't hear 'em shelling. The rest of the folks they all got down in the cellar, then somebody got to asking where Uncle Rod was. After it was over they went out on the front porch and there he was, settin' bolt up in his chair . . ."

"Dead?"

"Dead as a herring." Raeburn looked off across the field. "There's that man coming," he said, "but he ain't got no ladder. How long you reckon he expects us to work? It'll be gettin' dark pretty soon."

"Must be past seven o'clock," Doug said. "I ain't going to work no longer."

The man came up just as Doug was climbing out of the ice house. He was panting and his round face wore a harassed look. "Them folks didn't have no ladder," he said; "more'n that they sent me off on a fool errant . . . said the Widow Hickman might have a ladder. And when I get to where they say the Widow Hickman lives there ain't nothing but an old house looks like nobody ain't lived in it these thirty years. . . . Either you boys ever hear of the Widow Hickman?"

"I don't know many folks over this way," Doug said. He laid his pick up against a tree. "Well," he said, "I reckon it's about quittin' time."

The man took a leather wallet from his pocket and counted silver out into their hands. "I don't believe I'll be needin' you boys tomorrow, after all," he said.

Doug stood looking at him a minute as if he wasn't sure he'd heard right, then he said, "Suit yourself," and started off across the field. Raeburn ran and caught up with him at the edge of the woods.

"I thought you said he wanted us to work three, four days, Doug. I thought you said he wanted us to get *all* of them skeletons out of that ice house."

"Hunh," Doug said.

He stopped and looked about him a minute, then turned off into the woods. Raeburn stood there waiting. When Doug did not come back he whistled, the soft, slow whistle that they used for calling each other. Doug's head appeared suddenly over a clump of buckberry bushes. "Shh!" he said, and beckoned Raeburn to come.

Raeburn made his way through the bushes. Doug was lying flat on his stomach behind the buckberries. Raeburn lay down beside him.

"What you doing this for?" he whispered.

Doug pushed a spray of buckberry a little to one side. "Look at that," he said.

The man was standing with his back to them. In front of the coffins. He had his hat off. They could see his bald head and the fringe of gray hair that came down on his blue shirt collar. He put his hand up and scratched his bald head, then he leaned over and lifted some bones out of one of the coffins. He held them in his hands a minute as if he didn't know what to do with them, then he laid them in one of the boxes farther down the line. He kept on doing this until he had put some bones in each of the empty boxes. Then he began fastening the lids and hammering them down.

"What you reckon he's doing, Doug?" Raeburn said.

Doug put his lips up close to Raeburn's ear. "He's dividing up them skeletons," he whispered. "He's dividing up them skeletons so he can git paid double."

He got to his feet and slipped off silently through the underbrush. Raeburn followed him. When they came to where the paths forked Doug stopped. "There ain't a whole man in ary one of them boxes," he said. He slapped his leg and rocked with laughter.

"If that ain't a Yankee fer ye!"

The Captive

I

We were up long before day and were loading the horses at first dawn streak. Even then Tom didn't want to go.

"This ginseng don't have to get to the station," he said, "and as for the money it'll bring, we can get along without that."

"We've been without salt for three weeks now," I told him.

"There's worse things than doing without salt," Tom said.

I knew if he got to studying about it he wouldn't go and I was bound he should make the trip, Indians or no Indians. I slapped the lead horse on the rump. "Go along," I said. "I'd as soon be scalped now and have done with it as keep on thinking about it all the time."

Tom rode off without saying anything more, and I went on in the house and set about my morning work. The children were all stirring by that time. Joe felt mighty big to be the only man on the place. He was telling them what he'd do if Indians came.

"You'd better hush that up," I said. "Can't you get your mind off Indians a minute?"

All that morning, though, I was thinking about what Tom had said and wishing he hadn't had to go. It seemed like I was riding with him most of the day.

"Now he's at West Fork," I'd say to myself, and then after I'd done some more chores, "He'll be about at the crossroads now or maybe Sayler's Tavern." I knew, though, it wasn't much use to be following him that way in my mind. It'd be good dark before he could get home, and my thinking about it wouldn't hurry him.

It was around ten o'clock that I heard the first owl hooting. Over on the mountain, it seemed. Joe was in the yard feeding the chickens and he stopped stock-still and threw his head back.

"You hear that, Mammy?" he asked.

I knew then that there must be something wrong with the call, or a boy like Joe wouldn't have noticed it.

I spoke up sharp, though. "I heard it," I said, "and I could hear a heap of other things if I had time to stand around with my ears open. How long you reckon it's going to take you to get those chickens fed?"

We both went on about our business without more talk, but all the time I was saying to myself that if I could get through this and see Tom Wiley riding in at the gate one more time I'd be content to bide without salt the rest of my natural life. I knew it wouldn't do to let down before the children, though, and I kept them busy doing one thing and another till dinnertime. It began to rain while we were eating and it rained a long time. After it stopped raining the fog settled down, so thick you could hardly see your hand before you. And all the time the owls were calling. Calling back and forth from one mountain to another. My littlest girl, Martha, got scared, so I made all the children stay in the house and play by the fire whilst I started in on a piece of cloth I'd had in the loom a long time and never could seem to finish. I'd put a stripe through it and I was going to dye it red and make both the girls a dress out of that piece before the winter set in.

By that time the fog had risen as high as the top of the ridges and the whole house was swallowed up in it. The children kept teasing, saying it was good dark now and couldn't they have a candle.

"Yes," I said, "we're here all by ourselves and you want to go lighting candles, so they can't help finding the house."

One of the girls got to crying. "Who's coming?" she said. "Mammy, who you think's coming?"

I saw I'd got them stirred up and I'd have to settle them, for I couldn't stand to be worrying like I was and have the children crying. I gave them all a lump of sugar around and got them started on a play-party. I made out that I had the headache and if they were going to sing they'd have to sing low. It was "Hog Drovers" they were playing.

> "Hog-drovers, hog-drovers, hog-drovers we air,
> A-courtin' your daughter so sweet and so fair.
> Kin we git lodgin' here, O here,
> Kin we git lodgin' here?"

I got them started to frolicking and went back to my work. But I couldn't get my mind off something a man said to me once when we were out hunting on the Hurricane, and I made him to go right in on a bear without waiting for the other menfolks to come up.

"You're brash, Jinny," he said, "and you always been lucky, but one of these times you going to be too brash."

Sitting there listening to them owls calling, and wondering how much longer it would be before Tom got home, I got to thinking that maybe this was the time I was too brash. For I knew well there wasn't another woman in the settlements would have undertaken to stay on that place all day with nothing but a parcel of children. Still, I said to myself, it's done now and there's no undoing it. And the first thing I know, Tom will be back, and tomorrow morning it'll fair up, and I'll be thinking what a goose I was to get scared over nothing.

The children were still singing:

> "Oh, this is my daughter that sets by my lap.
> No pig-stealing drover kin git her from Pap.
> You can't git lodgin' here, O here,
> You can't git lodgin' here."

I got up and looked out of the window. It seemed to me that the fog was lifting a little. A man was coming up the path. I knew it was a white man by the walk, but I didn't know it was John Borders till he stepped up to the door.

The first thing he asked was where was Tom.

"Gone to the station with a load of ginseng," I told him. "I'm looking for him back now any minute."

He stood there looking off toward the mountain. "How long them owls been calling?" he asked.

"Off and on all evening," I said, "but owls'll hoot, dark days like this."

"Yes," he said, "and some owls'll holler like wolves and gobble like turkeys and every other kind of varmint. Jinny, you better git them children and come over to our house. Ain't no telling when Tom'll be back."

Just then an owl hooted and another one answered him from somewhere on top of the ridge. We both listened hard. It sounded like a real owl calling to his mate, but I was good and scared by that time and I thought I'd best go over to the Borderses'. It was my judgment, though, that there wasn't any hurry. Indians hardly ever come round before nightfall.

I told John that if he'd wait till I'd fastened up the stock I'd go back with him. He said that while I was doing that he'd walk out in the woods a little way. He'd been looking all day for some strayed sheep and hadn't found trace of them, but he thought they might be herded up in that gully by the spring. He went off down the path and I fastened the front door and went out the back way. I didn't fasten the back door, but I kept my eye on it all the time I was worrying with the cattle. Joe was along helping me. The cow was standing there at the pen; so I stopped and milked her while Joe went up in the triangle to look for the heifer. He found her and brought her up to the cow pen just as I finished milking. We fastened both cows up in the stable and Joe went over and saw that all the chickens were up and fastened the door on them. Then we started back to the house with the milk.

We were halfway up the path when we heard the Indians holler. We started for the house on a dead run. I could see Indians in the yard, and one Indian was coming around the house to the back door. I ran faster and slipped in the door ahead of him. Joe was right behind me. The room was so full of Indians that at first I couldn't see any of my children. The Indians was dancing around and hollering and hacking with their tomahawks. I heard one of the children screaming but I didn't know which one it was. An Indian caught me around the waist but I got away from him. I thought, I had got to do something. I fell down on my knees and crawled around between the Indians' legs, they striking at me all the time, till I found Martha, my littlest one, in the corner by the loom. She was dead and I crawled on a little way and found Sadie. She was dead, too, with her skull split open. The baby was just sitting there holding on to the bar of the loom. I caught him in my bosom and held him up to me tight; then I got to my feet. Joe was right behind me all the time and he stood up when I did. But an Indian come up and brained him with a tomahawk. I saw him go down and I knew I couldn't get any more help from him. I couldn't think of anything to do; so I worked my way over toward the door, but there was two or three Indians standing on the porch and I knew there was no use running for it. I just stood there holding the baby while the Indians pulled burning logs out of the fire onto the floor. When the blaze had sprung up they all come out onto the porch.

I made a break and got some way down the path, but an Indian run after me and caught me. He stood there, holding me tight till the other Indians come up; then he laid his hand on my head and he touched the baby too. It seemed he was claiming me for his prisoner. He had rings on his arms and ankles, and trinkets in his ear. I knew he was a chief and I thought he must be a Shawnee. I could understand some of what he said.

He was telling them they better hurry and get away before Tice Harman came home. Another Indian stepped up. I knew him—a Cherokee that come sometimes to the station. Mad Dog they called him. Tice Harman had killed his son. It come to me that they had been thinking all along that they was at Tice Harman's. I jerked my arm away from the Shawnee chief.

"You think you're burning Tice Harman's house," I said. "This ain't Tice Harman's house. It's Tom Wiley's. Tom Wiley. Tom Wiley never killed any Indians."

They looked at each other and I think they was feared. Feared because they had burned the wrong house, but feared too of Tice Harman. Mad Dog said something and laid his hand on his tomahawk, but the old chief shook his head and took hold of my arm again. He spoke, too, but so fast I couldn't tell what he was saying. The Cherokee looked mad but he turned around after a minute and called to the other Indians, and they all left the house and started off through the woods. Mad Dog went first and half a dozen young Indians after him. The old chief and I came last. He had hold of my arm and was hurrying me along, and all the time he kept talking, telling me that he had saved my life, that I was to go with him to his town to be a daughter to him to take the place of a daughter that had died.

I didn't take in much that he was saying. I kept looking back toward the burning house, thinking maybe they wasn't all dead before the Indians set fire to it. Finally I couldn't stand it no longer and I asked the old Shawnee. He pointed to one of the young Indians who was going up the ridge ahead of us. I saw something dangling from his belt and I looked away quick. I knew it was the scalps of my children.

II

We went up over the ridge and then struck north through the woods. I didn't take much notice of where we was going. I had all I could do to keep Dinny quiet—he warn't but ten months old. I let him suck all the way but it didn't do much good. We went so fast it'd jolt out of his mouth and he'd cry louder than ever. The Shawnee would grab my arm and say the other Indians would kill him sure if he kept that up. Finally I got his head down inside the waist of my dress and I held him up against me so tight he couldn't cry, and then I was scared he'd smother, but the Shawnee wouldn't let me stop to find out.

We went on, up one valley and down another, till finally we come out on level land at the foot of a mountain. The old chief made me go first, right up the mountainside. It was worse there than it was in the woods. The laurel and the ivy was so thick that sometimes he'd have to reach ahead of me and break a way through. My arms got numb and wouldn't hold the baby up. It was lucky for me I was crawling up a mountain. I would put him up ahead of me and then crawl to him, and in this way my arms would get a little ease of the burden. The old chief didn't like this, though, and every time it happened he'd slap me and tell me to go faster, go faster or they would surely kill the baby.

We got to the top of the mountain, somehow, and started down. My legs were hurting me now worse than my arms. It was going so straight down the mountainside. The back of my legs got stiff and would jerk me up every time I set my foot down, what they call stifled in a horse. I got on, somehow, though, all through that night and for most of the next day. It was near sundown when we stopped, in a rockhouse[1] at the head of a creek. The Indians must have thought they were too far for any white men to follow them. They made up a big fire and walked around it pretty careless. Two of the young Indians went off in the woods. I heard a shot and they come back dragging a little deer. They butchered it and sliced it down the middle, and slung the two haunches over the fire on forked sticks. The tenderer parts they broiled on rocks that they heated red-hot in the coals. A young buck squatted down by the fire and kept the venison turning. Soon the smell of rich meat cooking rose up in the

[1] A rockhouse is not a cave, but a place sheltered by an overhanging ledge of rock.

air. The juices began dripping down into the blaze and I thought it was a shame for all that gravy to go to waste. I asked the Shawnee to lend me a little kettle he had, and I hung it on a forked stick and caught the juices as they fell, and then poured them back over the meat. When they turned brown and rich I caught the gravy in the little kettle and sopped my fingers in it and let the baby suck them.

The old chief, Crowmocker, smiled like he thought a lot of me. "White woman know," he said. "White woman teach Indian women. You make rum?"

I said I didn't know how to make rum, but there was plenty in the settlements and if he would take me back, take me just within a mile or two of the clearing, I'd undertake to furnish him and his men with all the rum they could drink.

He laughed. "White people promise," he said. "You in your cabin you forget poor Indian."

The Cherokee, Mad Dog, had been sitting there broiling the deer nose on a rock that he had got red-hot in the flames. When it was brown he brought it over and gave it to me. Then he went back and sat down, sullen like, not saying anything. The fire shone on his black eyes and on his long beak of a nose. When he moved, you could see the muscles moving, too, in his big chest and up and down his naked legs. An Indian woman would have thought him a fine-looking man, tall and well formed in every way, but it frightened me to look at him. I was glad it was the old chief and not him that had taken me prisoner. I was glad, too, that the chief was old. I'd heard tell how particular the Indians are about things like that. I thought the old chief would likely do what he said and keep me for his daughter, but if it was Mad Dog he would have me for his wife.

I thought the meat never would get done, but it finally did. The Indians give me a good-size piece off the haunch and I ate it all, except a little piece I put in Dinny's mouth. He spit it out, but I kept putting it back till he got some good of it. Then I took him down to the creek and scooped up water in my hands for him. He'd been fretting because my milk was giving out, but the water and the juice from the meat quieted him a little. After we'd both had all the water we could drink I went back up the hill and sat down on a log with Dinny laying across my knees. It felt good to have his weight off my arms, but I was afraid to take my hands off him. I was feared one of them might come up and snatch him away from me any minute.

He laid there a while a-fretting and then he put his little hand up and felt my face.

"Sadie . . ." he said. "Sadie . . ."

Sadie was the oldest girl. She played with him a lot and fondled him. He'd go to her any time out of my arms.

I hugged him up close and sang him the song Sadie used to get him to sleep by. "Lord Lovell, he stood at the castle gate," I sang, and the tears a-running down my face.

"Hush, my pretty," I said, "hush. Sadie's gone, but Mammy's here. Mammy's here with Baby."

He cried, though, for Sadie and wouldn't nothing I could do comfort him. He cried himself hoarse and then he'd keep opening his little mouth but wouldn't no sound come. I felt him and he was hot to the touch. I was feared he'd fret himself into a fever, but there wasn't nothing I could do. I held his arms and legs to the blaze and got him as warm as I could, and then I went off from the fire a little way and laid down with him in my arms.

The Indians kept putting fresh wood to the fire till it blazed up and lit the whole hollow. They squatted around it, talking. After a while half a dozen of them got up and went off in the woods. The light fell far out through the trees. I could see their naked legs moving between the black trunks. Some of them was dragging up down timber for the fire and some kept reaching up and tearing boughs off the trees. They came back trailing the green boughs behind them. Two or three other Indians come over and they all squatted down and begun stripping the leaves off the switches and binding them into hoops. An Indian took one of the scalps off his belt—Sadie's light hair, curling a little at the ends and speckled now all over with blood. I watched it fall across the bough of the maple. I watched till they began stretching the scalp on the hoop and then I shut my eyes.

After a while Crowmocker come over and tied me with some rawhide thongs that he took off his belt. He tied me up tight and it felt good to have the keen thongs cutting into me. I strained against them for a while and then I must have dropped off to sleep. I woke myself up hollering. I thought at first it was the Indians hollering, and then I knew it was me. I tried to stop but I couldn't. It would start way down inside me and I would fight to hold it in, but before I knew it my mouth would be wide open and as soon as I'd loose one shriek another would start working its way up and there wasn't nothing I could do to hold it back. I was shaking, too, so hard that the baby rolled out of my arms and started crying.

The old chief got up from where he was sleeping and come over. He stood there looking down at me and then he lighted a torch and went off in the woods a little way. He brought some leaves back with him and he put them to boil in his little kettle. He made me drink some tea from the leaves and he gave the baby some too, and after a while we both went off to sleep.

III

I woke with the old chief shaking me by the arm and telling me it was time to get up. I was still sort of light-headed and for a minute I didn't know where I was. It was raining hard and so dark you couldn't tell whether it was good day. The Indians had built a fire up under the ledge and were broiling the rest of the venison. I laid there and I saw the light shine on their naked legs and the tomahawks hanging from their belts, and I knew where I was and all that had happened.

The old chief untied the thongs and I stood up with Dinny in my arms. They gave me a little piece of venison and some parched corn. My lips were so swelled I couldn't chew, but I swallowed the corn and I put the meat in my mouth and sucked it till it went away. I felt milk in my breasts and I was glad for the baby. I gave him his dinny but he wouldn't suck. He wouldn't hardly open his eyes. I thought that was from the tea the old Indian had given us and I feared he'd got too much. He was still hot to the touch and I thought he might have got a fever from laying out all night in the rain. I tore off part of my top skirt and I made a sort of sling that I put around my shoulders to carry him in; and I made a cover, too, out of part of the cloth to keep the rain off his little face.

Soon as we had finished eating, the Indians stomped out the fire and scattered the ashes so you couldn't have told there had ever been a camp there, and we started off through the woods.

We hadn't gone far before two of the young Indians left us. I thought they was most likely going back over the trail to watch if anybody was following us. I heard them saying that the folks at the settlement would be sure to send out a party. Some of the Indians thought it wouldn't do no good because the heavy rains had washed out the trail so nobody could find it. But Mad Dog said Tice Harman could follow any trail. I never knew before the Indians was so feared of Harman. They said he was the best hunter among the Long Knives, that he could go as far and stand as much as any Indian, and that they would like for him to come and live with them and be one of their warriors. Mad Dog said now that the only thing was to go so fast and go so far that even Tice Harman couldn't come up with us. He said "O-hi-yo" several times and I judged they meant to make for one of the towns on the river.

It stopped raining after a while but it didn't do much good. It was level ground we was traveling over and the water was standing everywhere, so that half the time you was wading. I knew we was some place high up in the hills, but afterwards I couldn't have told what country I had passed over. I went with my head down most of the time, not seeing anything but the black trunks of the trees going by and the yellow leaves floating in the puddles. Beech woods we must have been in because the leaves was all yellow and little.

We went on like that all day, not stopping to eat anything except some parched corn that the old chief took out of his bag and handed around to us still traveling. Late that evening we come to a water hole. One of the Indians shot a bear and we stopped and built a fire under a cliff. The Indians hadn't no more'n butchered the meat when two scouts come running into camp. They said that white men were following us, on horseback. The Indians all looked scared at this. Crowmocker stood there talking to Mad Dog about what we had best do. I went over and stood by them. Mad Dog said that they ought to kill the child and change the course, that they would have to go faster than ever now and I couldn't keep up, carrying the baby. Crowmocker showed him the sling I had made and said the baby wasn't no burden to me now. He said he had brought me this far and was going to carry me on to his town to teach his women how to weave cloth like the dress I had on.

He told Mad Dog that and then he motioned to me and said, "Go!" I started off, top speed, through the trees. Behind me I could hear the Indians stomping around in the leaves to cover up the signs of the fire. I went on as fast as I could, but every now and then an Indian would shoot past me. Pretty soon they was all ahead except the old chief.

We went downhill toward a hollow that had a little branch running through it. Mad Dog was in the lead, the other Indians right on his heels, jumping over down logs and bushes quick as cats. The old chief stayed by me, and when I'd slow up getting over a log or fall down in the bushes he'd jerk me onto my feet again.

The branch was narrow but running deep with the rains. Mad Dog started wading downstream and the other Indians after him, single file. They hadn't slowed up much and water splashed high. I could see their legs moving through the splashing water. The old chief by my side was breathing hard. I knew he was winded but I thought he would wind quicker than the others. I thought I would keep moving as long as I saw the Indians' legs going on.

The Indian that was in front of me stepped in a hole up to his waist. When he come out of it he took two, three steps and stood still. I knew then that Mad Dog had stopped and I knew he would be coming back down the line. I looked up, but the sides of the gully was too steep. I turned and ran back upstream fast as I could. I heard the breathing close behind me and I knew it was the old chief, and then there was a big splashing. Mad Dog was after me.

I left the water and ran sideways up the gully. The breathing was closer now. I tried to run faster and I caught my foot in a root. They were on me as soon as I went down. Mad Dog grabbed me by both arms. Crowmocker got there a second after, but Mad Dog already had hold of Dinny. I caught at his legs and tried to push them out from under him but he kicked me away. I got up and went at him again but he kicked me down. He kicked me again and then he went on up the side of the gully till he came to a big tree and he held the baby by the feet and dashed his brains out.

I rolled over on my face and I laid there flat on the ground till the old chief come up. He pulled me to my feet and said we would have to run on fast, that the white men were following us on horses. I said no, I wouldn't go, I would stay there with my baby; but he and another Indian took me by the arms and drug me down the stream spite of all I could do.

We went on down the branch a good way. Toward dark we came out on the banks of a river. Water was standing halfway up the trunks of big trees. I saw the current, running fast and covered with black drift, and I didn't believe even an Indian could get across that raging river. But they didn't stop a minute. Crowmocker fell back and two young Indians took hold of my arms and carried me out into the water. The current caught us and swept us off our feet. I couldn't swim much on account of my clothes, but the two young Indians held on to my wrists and carried me on between them. The other Indians come right in after us. They held their guns up high over their heads and swum like boys treading water. I could see their heads bobbing all around me through the black drift and I couldn't see nothing to keep all of us from drowning. They managed to keep out of the drift somehow, though, and all the time they were working toward the other bank till finally we come out in dead water at the mouth of a creek. The Indians that were holding me up stopped swimming all of a sudden, and I knew that we must have got across. It was so dark by that time I couldn't see anything. I got out of the water as best I could and a little way up the creek bank. I fell down there 'mongst some willows. I saw the Indians come up out of the water shaking themselves like dogs, and I saw them falling down all around me, and then my eyes went shut.

IV

The old chief woke me up at the first dawn streak. I heard him and I felt him shaking me, but I didn't get up. As soon as I opened my eyes the pain in my feet started up. I touched one foot to the ground and it throbbed worse'n toothache. I knew I couldn't travel any that day and I didn't care. I turned over on my back and laid there looking up at the sky. It had cleared off during the night and the stars was shining. The sky was all a pale gray except for one long sulphur-colored streak where day was getting ready to break. Behind me the Indians was looking to their guns and settling their tomahawks in their belts. I watched their heads and shoulders moving against that yellow light, and I saw one of them take his tomahawk out and heft it and then try the blade with his finger. I thought that if I just kept on laying there that maybe he would be the one to finish me off, and then I thought Mad Dog was quicker and would beat him to it.

The old chief was still shaking me. "Get up, Jinny. Day come."

"No," I said, "I ain't going to get up."

He took me by the shoulders and tried to pull me to my feet but I slumped back on the ground. I spoke to him in Shawnee.

"My feet bleed and I cannot travel. Let me die."

He leaned over and looked at my feet and then he called to one of the young Indians to bring him some white oak bark. When the bark come he boiled it over the fire and then he took the liquor from the bark and cooled it with more water and poured it over my feet.

The other Indians had finished scattering the fire and was starting out through the willows, but Crowmocker just sat there pouring that stuff on my feet. I could feel the swelling going down and after a while I touched my feet to the ground. It didn't hurt like it had, and I got up and we started off. He give me some parched corn and I ate it, walking. He said we would have to travel fast to catch up with the other Indians. I asked him if the white people were still following us and he laughed and said no white men could get across that river. I owned to myself that they couldn't, and I didn't think any more about them coming after me. I thought the Indians would probably take me so far away that I'd never again see a white face.

We caught up with the other Indians toward dark. That night we slept in a canebrake by a little river. A buffalo was wallowing in the river as we come up. One of the Indians shot him. They butchered him there in the water and drug big slabs of the meat up the bank with ropes cut from the hide. We must have been in Indian country by this time. They didn't seem to think it made any difference how much noise they made. They made up a big fire to one side of the brake and they were half the night cooking the meat and eating. I went to sleep under a tree with them singing and yelling all around me.

When I woke up the next morning they were having a council. They talked till the sun was high and then they split up into two parties. Mad Dog and three of the young bucks left us and swum across the river. The rest of us kept on up the bank. We traveled all that day through the cane and then we struck a divide and followed it into another valley. We had run out of everything to eat by this time except the strings of jerked meat that they all carried slung around their necks. We stayed two, three days at a buffalo lick, hoping to kill some game, but none came and we went on.

Most of the leaves were off the trees by this time and the nights were cold. I knew it was sometime in October that the Indians come and burned our house, but I didn't know how long we'd been on the trail and I didn't have any idea what country we were in.

One morning we come out in some deep narrows just above where two creeks flowed together. A wild-looking place with tumbling falls and big rocks laying around everywhere. I looked up at the cliffs over our heads and I couldn't believe my eyes. They were *painted*: deer and buffalo and turtles big as a man, painted in red and in black on the rock. Some of the young Indians acted like they had never been there before either. They would keep walking around looking at things and sometimes stand and stare at the pictures of wild beasts that were painted everywhere on the smooth rock.

The old chief took a way up the side of the cliffs, the rest of us following. The young Indians went up like deer, but I had to pull myself up by the laurel that grew down in between the rocks. We walked along a narrow ledge and come to a rockhouse. It was the biggest rockhouse ever I saw, run all along one side of the cliff. The old chief uncovered an iron pot from where it was hid in a lot of trash in one corner of the cave and showed me how to set it up on forked sticks. He said that I would have to do all the work around the camp from now on, the way Indian women did, and when the spring rains come and melted the snows he would take me to his town on the Tenassee and I would learn more about Indian ways and be adopted into the tribe in place of his dead daughter.

I thought if he took me there I would never get away and I had it in mind to make a break for it first chance I got. I got hold of two strings of jerked meat and I kept them tied around my waist so I'd be ready when the time came. I thought I would wait, though, and maybe I would find out how far it was to the settlements. I would lie there in my corner of the cave at night, making out I was asleep, and listen to them talking around the fire. I heard them call the names of the creeks that flowed through that valley—Big Paint and Little Mudlick; and farther off was another creek, Big Mudlick, where they went sometimes to hunt. The names were strange to me and I never could tell from their talk how far it was to the settlements or even which way to go. I had an idea that the place I was in was secret to the Indians, for it was a wonder to see and yet I had never heard any white body tell of it. I asked Crowmocker what the pictures of deer and buffalo and bear were for and he said they were the Indians' fathers and that I would learn about them when I was adopted into the tribe. Once he pointed some mounds out to me and said they were graves. He said that he and his people always stopped when they come this way to visit the graves of their fathers that was all over the valley.

A spell of fine weather come, late in the fall. Indian summer they call it. We looked out one day and bees were swarming on the cliffside. Crowmocker was mad when he saw them. He said it meant that the white people were coming; that when bees swarmed out of season they were running away from the white people who had scared all the game out of the country and made it so that even bees couldn't live in it. I asked would the white people find their way into this valley and he said they couldn't—that it was a way known only to Indians; that if a white man ever set foot in it the great bear would come down off the wall and crush him in his paws. He said, though, that there would be fighting soon over all the land and a lot of bloodshed.

I knew that was all foolishness about the bear, but I thought likely as not there would be fighting and I wanted to get away worse than ever. One morning I was down in the hollow by myself, gathering wood, and I thought that was the time. Three of the Indians had gone off hunting and I knew the others were laying up in the cave asleep. I didn't think anybody would be following me, for a while, anyhow. I started off, slipping from tree to tree, and I got quite a way up the hollow. I knew nobody was following me, but I would keep looking back over my shoulder all the time. I got to thinking. I didn't have any way to kill game, and nothing to eat but two strings of jerked meat. I didn't even know how far I'd have to go before I came to any settlement. Worst of all, I didn't even know which way to take. Likely as not I'd starve to death in the woods, or freeze if the weather turned. I'd better stay with the Indians, where at least I could sleep warm and eat, if it wasn't anything but parched corn. I picked up my load of wood and got back to camp quick as I could, and didn't none of them ever know I'd been away.

I never tried it again, but sometimes I'd sit there on the edge of the cliff and pick out the way I'd take if I did go. There was a ridge covered with black pines rose up right in front of the rockhouse. I thought if I could once get up there I could get down into the valley easy. I hadn't ever been over there, but I knew what the country would be like. I saw myself slipping along through that divide, around the foot of the mountain and over some more mountains till I'd come out on a clearing. I'd slip up to some cabin, toward dark. They'd think I was an Indian at first, maybe, and then they'd see my eyes was light and they'd take me in and keep me till I could get back to my own folks again.

We stayed in that rockhouse a long time. The leaves all fell off the trees, and one or two light snows fell, but the real cold weather was late coming. The Indians hunted just enough to keep us in meat. They said the pelts were thin that year and not worth taking. Sometimes they would take me along to bring in the game, but mostly they left me to work by myself. When cold weather set in we built big fires in the cave and it was warm inside like a house. When the Indians weren't hunting they would lie around on buffalo skins and sleep. The smoke was terrible and the smell of Indians was all over everything. At first it bothered me, but after a while I got so I didn't notice it.

I wasn't in the cave much, even in bad weather. I had to gather all the firewood. The Indians didn't have an axe and I couldn't get anything but dead branches. There wasn't much down timber on the cliffside; so I'd mostly go up over the cliffs when I was hunting wood. There was a barren there, flat as the palm of your hand and covered with a thin kind of grass. It had plenty of trees on it but they were all twisty and stunted by the wind. The only sizable tree was a big elm. It was peeled for thirty or forty feet and had a rattlesnake painted on it—a monster snake coiling up around the trunk. You could see that snake from everywhere on the barren. I was feared to look at it. The Indians seemed to think a lot of it. Sometimes they would go up there at night and I would hear them singing and dancing and calling to the snake.

Somewhere on the barren there were lead mines. The Indians never let me go to them, but they would go off and stay two, three hours and come back with big balls of lead. They made me smelt it out for bullets. I had to have a mighty fire. It would take me days and days to get up enough wood. I would heap it up in a big pile and then I would kindle the fire and keep it going for hours. When the lead melted, it ran down through little ditches into holes that I had dug to form the bullets. It would take the lead a long time to melt. Sometimes I would be up on the barren from sunup to sundown.

I would sit there and think about my husband and my children. I would wonder whether Tom went out in the woods hunting ginseng the way he used to do, and was he still looking for me or had give me up for dead. When I thought of Tom the house would be there, too, not burning down the way it was last time I saw it, but standing with the rooms just the way they always were. I could see both rooms plain, even to the hole that was burnt in the floor when a big log fell out one night. The children would be playing in and out of the house like they did. It was like they were all living; it was only me that was gone away.

I would think back, too, over things that happened long before ever I was grown and married to Tom Wiley. There was a man named Rayburn stayed at the settlement one winter. Lance Rayburn. A big, strong man and a mighty hunter. We ate bear of his shooting all that fall. He was handy with snares too, and took over a hundred beaver down in the bottom. He courted me some that winter, sitting in front of the fire after the old folks were in bed. I laughed and went on with him, but Tom Wiley had just started a-courting me and all the time my mind was on him more'n it was on the stranger.

Come time for Rayburn to pack up his pelts to take to the station, he saved one out for me. Beaver, and extra fine and soft. He give it to my sister, Sarah, and told her to hand it to me when I come to the house. She made one of the children bring it down to the creek where I was boiling clothes. I laid it there on the grass and I would stop and look at it as I went back and forth with my clothes, and sometimes I would wipe my hands dry and lay them on the soft fur for pleasure in the feel. But all the time I knew I wasn't going to keep it. When Rayburn come toward me through the willows I went to meet him with the pelt in my hands.

"Keep this," I said, "and give it to some girl where you're going."

"Don't you want it?" he asked.

"I ain't taking nothing from you."

He stood up there looking at me and all of a sudden his eyes narrowed up like a cat's. "You're full young to be marrying," he said.

"I ain't too young to know my own mind," I told him, and before I thought, I laughed.

He come toward me, and before I knowed what he was up to he was on me and trying to bear me to the ground. He was a strong man but I was stout, too, and I stood up to him. We was rassling around in the bushes quite some time before he got me down, and then he had to keep both his hands on my chest. I laid there right still, looking up at him.

"What you reckon my pappy'll say when I tell him about this?" I asked.

He laughed, "I ain't a-feared of no Sellardses that ever walked," he said, "but that Tom Wiley ain't no manner of man for you," he said.

"You can talk against Tom Wiley and you can hold me here till Doomsday," I told him, "but it ain't going to do you no good. I ain't going to have none of you no matter what happens."

His face kind of changed. Looked like it hurt him to hear me say it. He got up off me right away and he picked the beaver pelt up from where it lay in the grass and he throwed it hard as he could into the creek.

"It'll git to my girl that way fast as any other," he said.

I watched the pelt floating down the water and onto a rock and then off again. When I turned around he was out of sight and he was gone when I got back to the house. He stayed at the station a while and then he went off in the mountains hunting bear and wasn't ever heard of again. Some said he was killed by wild beasts. A rifle and a cap that they said was his was found up in the hills. The man that found the rifle kept it, but they give the cap to the Borderses. Wouldn't anybody wear it, and Sally hung it up in the dog alley. I used to look at it every time I passed and wonder whether it had ever been on Lance Rayburn's head and was he dead or still living. And sometimes I'd wonder how it'd been if I'd married him instead of Tom, but I knew all the time I wouldn't ever have married anybody but Tom because he was the one I fancied from the time I was a chap, living neighbor to the Wileys, back in the Roanoke country.

I thought about Lance Rayburn and I thought about a lot of other folks that had come to the settlement and stayed and then gone on and wouldn't anybody know whether they were living still or dead. And I thought about people dead long ago, my old granny back in Carolina, ninety-eight years old and turned simple. She'd sit in the chimney corner all day long, singing the likeliest tunes!

"Pa'tridge in the pea patch," she'd sing, and call me to her and fondle me, liking gals, she said, always better than boys.

> "Pa'tridge in the pea patch
> Pickin' up the peas.
> 'Long comes the bell cow
> Kickin' up her heels . . ."

"Oh . . . h, the bell cow," she'd sing, and catch me by my little shimmy tail. "O . . . O . . . hh, the bell cow . . ." and hist me up over the arm of her chair. "O . . . O . . . hh, the bell cow, kickin' up her heels. Call the little gal to milk her in the pail."

I used to call those songs to mind when I had to go down to the lick for salt. It was a place I didn't like to go. A deep hollow with three sulphur springs and a lick that covered nigh an acre of ground. The biggest lick ever I saw in my life. The way was white with the bones of beasts, and in between the piled-up bones the long furrows that the buffalo made licking the ground for salt. I would walk down those furrows to the spring and fill my bucket with the salty water and go back up the hill to where my kettle was slung between two little birches. Sitting there waiting for the water to boil, I couldn't keep my eyes off the bones. I would take them up in my hand and turn them over and over, wondering what manner of beasts they had belonged to.

Once I made myself a little beast, laying all the bones out on some lacy moss, the front feet stiff like it was galloping off in the woods, the hind legs drawn up under him. A hare it might have been or a little fawn. Or maybe a beast that nobody ever heard of before.

There were beasts come to that lick one time or another not known to man. Bigger'n buffalo they must have been. One thigh-bone, I mind, longer'n I was and twice as big around as two good-sized men.

I thought of a man used to be around the station, Vard Wiley, second cousin to Tom. Folks said he was the biggest liar in the settlements. He would stay off in the woods hunting day after day and never bring in any game except maybe a brace of wild turkeys. And he told tall tales about a lick bigger'n any lick around those parts, where the beasts come up in tens of thousands. He would lay up in a tree all day and watch 'em, he said, and not take a shot for wonder. There were beasts used there, he said, ten times the size of buffalo. He offered to take anybody there and show them the bones, and when they asked him why he didn't bring them back to the settlement he said couldn't no man carry them, nor no two horses.

Folks laughed at him, and the children round the settlement used to sing a song:

> "Vard Wiley's gone west, Vard Wiley's gone east,
> A-huntin' the woods for a monster beast.

> "He'll make him a tent out of the wild beast's hide
> And all the king's horses can stable inside.

> "He'll make him a wagon out of solid bone
> And it'll take ten oxen to draw it home."

I called that song to mind and I thought how if I ever saw Vard Wiley again I'd go up to him and say I knew him to be a truth-teller, and all the people would laugh at me maybe, the way they did Vard Wiley, but all the time I would be knowing it was the truth.

I thought, too, of other tales he told and of jokes he played. Of the time he borrowed my dress and sunbonnet and shawl and went and sat on the creek bank when the schoolmaster was in swimming. He sat there all evening with the sunbonnet hiding his face and old Mister Daugherty shaking his fist at him. "You hussy! You brazen hussy! Don't you know I'm naked?" and finally when he come up out of the water naked as the day he was born Vard took out after him and run him clean to the house. Old Mister Daugherty went around saying there was a woman ought to be run out of the settlements, and Vard would talk to him and make out it was me. But old man Daugherty knew wouldn't none of Hezekiah Sellards's daughters be carrying on like that. He was bound it was a woman from Ab's Valley.

I would think about 'em sitting there and arguing about how the hussy ought to be run out of the settlements, and I would laugh all by myself there in the woods. Throw back my head and laugh and then feel silly when the woods give back the echo.

I did a lot of work while I was with the Indians. It was hard on me at first but I got used to it. It was better after Mad Dog left us. The old chief was like a father to me, and the young ones knew I belonged to him and didn't bother me. I slept off by myself in a far corner of the cave and he would wake me up at daybreak and tell me what there was to do that day. He took pains to show me how to flesh pelts and cure them, and he showed me how to split a deer sinew for thread and how to make a whistle to call deer out of birch bark and sticks. And after I got so I could sew skins good he had me make him a pair of leggings and trim them with porcupine quills— porcupine quills colored with some roots he got out of the woods.

It bothered him the way I looked and he made me paint my face the way the Indians did. Fixed me up some of the red root mixed with bear's grease, and after I'd been putting it on my face for a while you couldn't told me from an Indian woman, except for my light eyes.

He'd stay in the cave with me sometimes all day, his buffalo hide wrapped around him so tight that his knees were up against him like a chair. He'd sit there and rock back and forth on his heels and talk while I worked. Down in the hollow the young braves would be practicing their war whoops. He would listen to them and laugh.

"Our young men give the war whoop loudly to cover up their fear of the enemy. It was not so when I was young. There was joy in the war whoop then."

He said he was a chief but he might have been something better. He might have been a medicine man. He had the gift of it from his grandmother. His own mother died when he was born, he said, and his old granny raised him. He told me about how she would take him into the woods with her looking for yarbs and roots, and how she knew where everything grew and which roots would be good to take and which had no strength in them. He said that after I was adopted into the tribe he would tell some of her secrets to me, but the Spirit would be angry if a white woman knew them.

I asked him wouldn't I still be a white woman after I was adopted into the tribe but he said no, the white blood would go out of me and the Spirit would send Indian blood to take its place, and then I would feel like an Indian and know all the Indian ways and maybe get to be a wise woman like his old granny.

He told me about his youngest daughter and how she come by her death, following what she thought was a fawn bleating. They found her days afterward, three enemy arrows in her. Her death had been paid for with three scalps of warriors, and he would say that he didn't grieve over her, but I knew he did. I got to feeling sorry for him sometimes to have lost his daughter that meant so much to him, and then I would think how I had lost all my children and my husband and I would cry, dropping tears on the skin I was sewing.

I got so after a while that the Indian way of doing things seemed natural to me. I thought nothing of seeing dark faces around me all the time, but in the night sometimes I would dream of white faces. White faces coming toward me through the trees. Or sometimes I would be in a house again and look up all of a sudden and all the faces in the room would be white.

One white face was always coming to me in my dreams: Tice Harman, the man whose house the Indians thought they were burning the day they burned ours. I always thought that if anybody came to save me it would be Tice Harman. I could see him plain in my dreams. A little man, wouldn't weigh more'n a hundred and twenty pounds, but he had a big head. A big head and a big beak of a nose and long yellow hair down to his shoulders. His eyes were blue and in my dreams they glittered like ice. I would dream about

Tice Harman and when I waked I would think what I'd heard said of him—how he could go further and stand more than any man in the settlements, and how he loved to fight Indians better'n eat when he was hungry. I would think, too, of how folks said he would bring trouble on the settlements shooting that Indian down when there warn't really any use in it; and I would think that since it was him that brought all my trouble on me, maybe it would be him that would get me away from the Indians. But time went on and nobody came, and after a while I got so I didn't think much about it.

One evening I was gathering wood on the cliffside and I heard a lot of whooping and hollering down near the mouth of the creek. The Indians come out from where they were sleeping back in the cave and stood looking over the falls. A long whoop came and the old chief put his hands to his mouth and answered it. There was more whooping back and forth, and then Mad Dog came up the trail by the falls with about twenty Indians following him. They were painted for war and marched single file, all except the last six or eight. They were in pairs and in the middle of them a white man, walking with his hands tied behind him. A white man? A boy. Couldn't have been more than eighteen years old.

I had to step out of the path to let them by. The dead branches rustled in my hands. The prisoner turned his head. He looked straight into my eyes. It was like he didn't know I was there. I spoke to him.

"I can't do nothing," I said. "I'm a white woman, but I can't do nothing. Christ!" I said. "There ain't nothing I can do."

He kept on looking at me but he didn't speak. They were hurrying him past. I dropped the branches and run after them. Mad Dog called to one of the young bucks and he caught me and held me. I fought him, but he held me till they had all gone up the path.

I went on to the rockhouse and kindled up the fire. After a while Mad Dog come down and told me to cook up some meat quick as I could. There would be singing and dancing, he said; they would want meat all night long.

I looked at him. "A present," I said. "A present for Kagahye-liske's daughter. Give me this boy. He is not good for anything but to gather wood."

His eyes were fierce. "Boy?" he said. "He has this day killed my brother." Then he laughed and smoothed my hair. "Jinny," he said, "pretty Jinny."

I made out I had to see to the fire and walked away. I put some bear meat on to boil and I told him I would call him when it was done, and he went on back up the path.

There was a moon coming. I sat there waiting for the meat to boil and watched it rise over the pines. Up on the barren the Indians were dragging up all the dead branches they could find into one pile. After a while I looked up over the rockhouse and saw the sky all light and knew they had kindled the fire.

The stamping and yelling went on, and every now and then a gun would go off. Then there was running around the tree. You could hear the feet pounding and the long calls. "Ai . . . yi . . . Ai . . . yi . . . Ai . . . yi . . ." One for each man that had died that day. And the sharp cry for the scalp taking. They would act it all out and the boy standing there watching. He was dazed, though; he wouldn't see it for what it was. He wouldn't know what they were doing, might not know what they were going to do. There on the path he looked at me and didn't know me for a white woman. I ought to have found out his name and where he come from. I ought to have done that much. But he wouldn't have answered. And what good would it do his folks . . . if I ever saw white folks again. Then Mad Dog's hand on my hair. "Pretty Jinny . . . pretty Jinny . . ."

The flames shot up and lit the whole valley. The moon looked cold where it hung over the pines. I kept the fire up under the kettle but I couldn't sit still. I walked back and forth in the rockhouse, back and forth, back and forth, waiting for the shrieks to start.

They were a long time coming. I thought maybe it was already going on. Indians can stand there burning and not make a sound, and there have been white men that could. But this was just a boy . . .

The first shriek was long and then they come short and quick, one right after the other. I got over in a corner of the rockhouse and held on tight to a big rock. After a while I let go of the rock and put both fingers in my ears and then I was feared to take them out, thinking it might not be over yet. The Indians were still yelling and stamping. The young ones kept running down and grabbing up chunks of meat from the boiling pot and carrying them up to the barren. I could see the old chief's shadow where he stood on the edge of the cliff calling to the new moon.

When he came down to the rockhouse Mad Dog was with him. They stood there dipping meat up out of the kettle. Mad Dog talked.

"It is too much. For five hundred brooches I could buy a girl of the Wild Cats, young and swift, a fine worker in beads. A girl like a moonbeam, daughter of a mighty warrior."

His eyes were black in the circles of paint. His tongue showed bright between his painted lips. The red lines ran from his forehead down the sides of his cheeks to make gouts of blood on his chin.

A devil. A devil come straight from hell to burn and murder. Three white men killed that day and the boy brought back to torture. It was him that killed them, him that yelled loudest when the boy was burning. Him that set fire to my house and burned my children . . .

I saw him running through the woods, white men after him. I saw him fall, a dozen bullets in him. But he wouldn't be dead. He would lie there bleeding and look at me out of his painted eyes, and I would go up and stomp on him, stomp him into the dirt . . .

My hands shook so I dropped the sticks I was carrying. I was near enough now to hear all they were saying. Mad Dog was taking little silver brooches out of a buckskin. He poured them out in a pile on a rock and then counted them. The old chief stood there till he got through counting; then he swept them all up into a bag he took from around his neck.

"Brother," he said, "the woman is yours."

Mad Dog had left the fire and was coming toward me. I ran over and caught hold of the old chief's arm. I called him by his Indian name.

"Kagahye-liske, do not give me to this man. He has killed my children and burned my house."

He looked down at me and it was like he'd never seen me before. His face, not painted, was as cruel as the Cherokee's, the eyes blood-shot and the whole face swollen from the meat he had eaten.

"The war whoop drowns sorrow," he said. "This chief is my brother and a mighty warrior. He has this day killed three white men."

I hung on to his arm. "Keep me for one of the young men of your village," I said. "The Cherokee are old women. You have said so and you have promised. You have promised to take me with you wherever you go."

He shook my hands off. "A promise," he said, "to a white coward! Go to your work."

He turned around like he was going to leave the cave. I run after him and caught hold of his knees, but he broke away. Mad Dog come and tied me up tight with thongs that he cut from buffalo hide, and then they both went on up to the barren where the other Indians was still screeching and stamping.

The screeching and stamping went on far into the night. The fire under the kettle went out and it was dark except for a little light from the moon. I laid there on the floor, listening to the Indians and thinking about how it would be when Mad Dog came down to take me for his wife. I laid there, expecting him to come any minute, but the singing and dancing went on and he didn't come, and after a while I went to sleep.

v

The white boy that they had burned came to me while I was asleep. He came carrying a lamp that was made from the bleached skull of a sheep. The brain hollow was filled with buffalo fat and there was a wick in it burning bright. He came walking between the trees like he didn't have need to look where he was going. His hair was light like I had seen it when he passed me there on the path, but it was long, too, like Tice Harman's. His eyes were the same eyes that had looked at me there on the path.

I said to him what I had said there. "I couldn't do nothing," I said. "There wasn't nothing I could do."

He didn't speak—only made signs for me to follow him. I got up and walked after him. The rawhide thongs were still on me but they didn't bind anymore and I moved as easy and as light as he did. He went down by the falls and clomb up over the hill to where the elm tree stood that had the big rattlesnake painted on it. He walked past the elm tree and struck out through the black pines that were all over that ridge. Sometimes he would go so fast that I couldn't keep up with him, and then I would stand still and after a while I would see the light flickering through the trees and I would go on to where he was waiting for me. We went on through the pine woods and started down the side of the ridge. I heard water running somewhere far down below. I thought that would be Mudlick Creek, but when I got to it it was a branch I'd never seen before. We crossed it and went on up a path through a clearing. There were little shrubs all around like the ones up on the barren, and in the middle of them was a house. It was my house and yet it wasn't. White all over and the walls so thin you could see the light from the lamp shining through the logs.

People were walking around in the yard and sitting on the doorstep. They moved to let me go through the door, but they didn't speak to me and I didn't speak to them.

The men that were sitting in front of the fire playing draughts didn't even look up when I came in. I went over to the hearth and tried to dry out my clothes. I stood there holding out my hands but no heat came. I looked at the logs and they were white like the timbers of the house, and the same light came from them. I saw that the men playing didn't have a lamp and yet there was light all around them.

People kept walking in and out of the cabin, men and women and little children. I would go up to them and look in their faces, but there wasn't anybody there I knew. I walked round and round the room. Every now and then the people would move out of the way and I would catch sight of the walls. White, with patches of green on them. I put my hand up and felt one of the logs. It was round and cold to the touch. No log at all, but bleached bone. I knew then that all the house was bone, the floor and the walls and the chimney, even the table that the men were playing on, all made from the big bones down at the lick.

One of the men at the table stretched his arm out and pulled me over to him. He had on a beaver cap and his face under it was pale like he'd been in the woods a long time. He looked at me and I saw it was Lance Rayburn. He sang, pulling me up over the arm of his chair:

> "Oh . . . the bell cow, kicking up her heels,
> Call the little gal to milk her in the pail . . ."

Fiddling started up somewhere and all fell to dancing. They danced to one of my old granny's tunes:

> "There was an old lord lived in a northern countree,
> Bowee down, bowee down . . ."

There was bowing back and forth and balancing, and there were figures called, but wasn't any women dancing. I would see something going by and think it was a woman's skirt, but when I got up to it it would be fur or feathers dangling from a belt and all the faces around were dark, not like they were at first.

The great flames went leaping up the chimney, and all of a sudden I knew that they had built that fire to burn somebody by. I looked around for the one they were going to burn but he wasn't there. I said, "They will burn me next," and I saw what they would tie me to—the rattlesnake tree, going straight up from the table through the roof.

I went to the door and I saw through the black trunks a light flickering. I run and Mad Dog and the old chief were after me the way they were that day in the hollow. I thought, "They will kill me now when I go down," and I run faster and then they were both gone away and I was walking through pine woods, the light flickering on ahead of me.

I walked on and come to a creek that run along between wide banks of cane. The light shone on the water and made it light as mist. I stepped in, not knowing whether it was water or mist, and I could feel it coming up around my knees, water and yet not water. I moved along through it light as the wind till I come to where the creek forked. I could see the two forks and the white trunks of the sycamores along the bank, but I didn't know which way to go.

The light was all around me. I could see it shining on the reeds and on the little leaves of the cane and on the water where it broke on the rocks. Behind me there were voices talking.

"Jinny Wiley . . . Jinny Wiley, that was stolen and lived with the Indians . . ."

And then it was the old chief talking to the new moon:

"The white people . . . The white people are all over the land. The beaver makes no more dams and the buffalo does not come to the lick. And bees swarm here in the ancient village. Bees swarm on the graves of our fathers . . ."

The light that had been around me was gone. It was shining now through the tree trunks down a fork of the creek. I waded toward it through the light water, the voices following, and then they were gone and I was standing at the foot of a high mountain. I looked up and saw the light flickering at the top and I clomb toward it, pulling myself up by the scrubs and holly bushes.

I got up on the mountaintop but the young man wasn't there. I walked out onto the edge of a cliff and he was by my side. He said,

"Look, Jinny!" and the flame of his lamp leaped up and lighted the whole valley and I looked across a river and saw a fort. I saw the roofs of the houses and the stockade and the timber burned back over the rifle range, and I saw men and women walking around inside the stockade.

I said, "I'm a-going over there," but the young man wasn't with me anymore, and the dark that was all around was the inside of the rockhouse.

VI

When I woke up the next morning the Indians had a big fire going and were all sitting around eating. I laid there and made out I was still asleep. They had found trace of buffalo down at the lick and were making ready for a big hunt. I thought maybe they would take me along to bring in the game the way they did sometimes, and then I heard Mad Dog say they would leave me tied up in the cave till they got ready to start for their town.

I was laying with my face turned up and I was feared they could tell by my eyes that I wasn't asleep. I give a kind of groan and rolled over on my side. I laid there not moving while the talking went on all around me. Once footsteps come over to the corner where I was laying and I heard something slap down on the ground right by me but I didn't give any sign and the footsteps went away.

I laid there so still that I went to sleep again with the talking and the making ready for the hunt still going on. I was waked up by a kind of roaring sound. At first I thought it was the falls and then I knew the falls wouldn't sound that loud. I opened my eyes. The Indians were all gone and there was a big storm blowing up.

I laid there watching the pine tops lash back and forth in the wind, and the dream I'd had come back into my mind as plain as if it was something that had happened. I thought it was sent to me on purpose to tell me that now was the chance to get away. I knew that if the Indians come back with any game that night they'd feast high again and were more than likely to take me up on the barren and burn me like they done that boy.

I sat up. A piece of meat was lying on the floor right by me. That meant that the Indians would be all gone all day and maybe another day. If I could only get free of the thongs I might get a long way off before they knew I was gone.

There was a knife stuck in a crack of the rock where they laid the meat. If I could only get hold of that! I rolled over and over till I got to the rock and managed to get up on my knees, though the thongs cut into me bad. I could see the handle of the knife sticking up out of the crack and I laid my face down flat on the rock and tried to catch hold of it with my teeth. But it was too far down and all I did was get my mouth full of grit and sand. I gave up and laid down again. The wind wasn't as high as it had been, but the rain was coming down hard. It blew way back into the cave. I laid there with the big drops spattering in my face and a thought came to me. I rolled over to where the rain was pouring down off the roof and I laid there till I was soaked through. All the time I kept straining at the thongs and I could feel them giving a little, the way leather does when it's wet. I kept on, getting them looser and looser till finally I worked my way out of them and stood up free.

I listened and I couldn't hear anything but the roaring of the wind and the beating of the rain on the ledge. I tiptoed to the end of the cave and looked down the path. But I couldn't see any sign of living creature. I dug the knife out from between the rocks and I took the piece of cooked meat and a little kettle that the old chief had left laying around, and went off out of the other end of the cave and along the cliffside.

I kept to the path a little way and then I struck off through the trees down the hillside. The ground was wet and slid from under my feet in big chunks. I caught on to the trees all the way to keep myself from falling. When I got to the bottom I could look back and see where I'd come, as plain as if I'd blazed a trail. I knew I'd have to strike water. I run in among some pines and come to a wet-weather branch. I waded right in. It was swift water and full of holes. I would step in one every now and then and go down, but I kept on as fast as I could. I felt all the time like the Indians were after me. I knew they had gone south toward the salt lick and I knew the whole cliffside and the barren was between me and them, but all the time I felt like they were right behind me. When I looked over my shoulder the top boughs of the rattlesnake tree showed from the barren. I was glad when I rounded a bend and it was out of sight.

When I come out to where the branch flowed into the creek I didn't know which way to go, and then I thought that in my dream

I was following water and I struck right down the stream. It was harder going here than it was in the branch. The snows melting had filled all the dry-weather branches, and muddy water kept running in till you couldn't tell anything about the depth. It was well I was going downstream, but even then the current was a hindrance to me, reaching in and sweeping me off my feet sometimes into a hole that I would have a time getting out of. More than once I was in danger of drowning.

I kept on like this all day. When it was drawing toward dark I crawled up on the bank under some cedars and I laid there and I ate a good-sized piece of the cooked meat I had brought with me. The rain had fallen off to a light drizzle and there was some color in the sky, sign of a clear day tomorrow. There was a flight of little birds over the water and then round and round the tops of the cedars. Some of them lit in the boughs of the tree I was laying under. I could hear them flying in and out and the quick cries and then the twittering as they settled down to roost. It was dark under the trees but the streak of light stayed on the water. I laid here and watched it fade and I wished I could stay there where the cedar boughs were like a little house. I wished I could stay there and not run any more. I thought I would maybe sleep a few minutes and then I could go on faster. But when I shut my eyes I would think I heard the Indians coming through the trees and after a little I got up and went on again.

I tried wading some more but I couldn't make it in the pitch dark. I got up on the bank of the creek and pushed my way through the bushes as best I could. Sometimes the undergrowth would be so thick I couldn't make it, and then I would have to get down in the water again. All the way I was worrying about losing time following the bending and twisting of the creek, and then I would think that was the only sure way to get out of the hill country and I had best stick to water, spite of all the bending.

Sometime during the night I lost my way from the creek and wandered in the pitch dark into a marsh that was all along the creek bottom. More like a bog it was. I couldn't seem to get out of it no matter what I did. I stood there bogged to the knees and couldn't even hear the creek running—nothing but the wind soughing in the trees. And I thought what a lone place it was and if I came on quicksand, as was more than likely, I could go down and even my bones never be found. And I thought of how Lance Rayburn's bones might have been laying all this time in some hollow of the mountain and nothing maybe but squirrels or deer ever going near the place, and it seemed to me I might better have stayed with the Indians. But I knew it wouldn't be any use going back now. They would put the fire to me sure.

I stood there and I heard some wild thing passing. *Pit pat pit pat* it went; feet falling on dry ground. I pulled out of the muck and made toward the sound, and a deer or something broke through the thicket and went off through the woods.

I followed and come out on high ground, a slope covered with pine needles. I threw myself down flat on my face. I must have gone off to sleep. When I come to myself light was growing through the trees, and all around me I could hear twigs snapping and little rustlings. I got up quick, thinking it was the Indians coming, and then I felt foolish, knowing it was only game stirring at break of day. I saw two deer go by, moving slow over the brown pine needles. The air was so still they didn't get a whiff of me until they were out of the thicket. The buck wheeled so quick he almost knocked the doe over, and then they were both clattering off over the hill.

I went down to the creek bank and washed my face and let the water run over my wrists where they were scratched by the branches. I ate the last of my meat sitting there on a rock. When I got ready to go I found out that one of my strings of jerked meat had slipped off during the night. I couldn't hardly believe it at first. I stood up and felt all over my clothes time and again but it warn't there.

"Well," I said, "it's gone and they ain't no use crying over it, but I wish to God it'd a been the little piece."

I got in the water and started wading again. The creek was shallow for about half a mile and then it run into a bigger creek. The two of them run on before me and I didn't know which way to go. I stood there looking. The sun was up and it shone on the water. I watched the riffles break on the black rocks where the sun caught them, and the place was not the same place I had seen in the dream and yet it was the same because of the light that was over everything.

I remembered the way I took in the dream. "Left I'll go," I said, "like it was in the dream, and if it don't turn out right it's no fault of mine."

I went on, wading half the time. All that day I was thinking about something to eat. Seems like everything good I ever had to eat in my life come back to torment me that day. The smell of herring, cooking, bothered me most. I would see myself, a chap, back in the Roanoke country, broiling herrings over the coals the way children did when their mammy wouldn't give them anything else to eat between meals. I would go over it all, time and again, the herrings hanging in rows in the smokehouse, like tobacco in a barn, and us climbing up on a slab of wood to get at them.

"Three," Dinny, that's my eldest brother, 'd say every time. "Three. You might as well get one apiece while you're at it."

I thought, too, about people wasting things, of a woman I knew used to give all her buttermilk to her pig, and I thought how it was shameful to have no mind for them that might be starving. And I thought how if I could have that pig's dinner one time, or even a moldy piece of bread, the kind I'd thrown away many a time as not good enough for the dogs. And yet I'd been as wasteful as any of them in my day—worse, even, with game. I used to go hunting just for the fun of it. Seemed like there warn't nothing I liked better than sighting down a rifle. Warn't none of the Sellards or Damron boys a better shot than I was, and I could throw a knife with the best of them. That time John and Dick and me and the two Damrons went to Sinking Fork on a big hunt I shot eighteen wild gobblers, and when we loaded up and there were more'n we could carry it was me that said to leave them laying, that there warn't no use in breaking yourself down and the woods full of gobblers. I thought about them gobblers more'n once that day and, Lord, how I wished I could git my hands on a rifle butt just one more time.

I threw my knife once or twice at some small game, mostly rabbits, but it was a rusty old thing and not fitted to the hand the way a knife has to be to turn proper. One rabbit that I hit square in the middle got up and skittered off like nothing had happened, and I saw then it was a waste of time to throw at them.

Late that evening I come on some forward wild greens in a sheltered place on the creek bank. I went down on my knees and gathered every shoot. I found some punk and went up to a rockhouse on the side of the hill and built a little fire way in under the ledge the way I'd seen the Indians do. I knew it was craziness to build a fire, but it might be days before I'd come on any wild greens again. "I'll eat," I said, "varmints or no varmints."

I put my greens on to boil in the little kettle with a piece of the jerked meat and sat there, thinking about how Indians would go up on a cliff to sight over the country and how the least little smoke curling up would be a sign to them. Once I was on the point of putting the fire out but I couldn't bring myself to do it. I feared to feed it much and yet I'd catch myself putting dead twigs to it. It was a long time before the bubbles started rising up in that little old kettle. I sat there rocking on my heels and talking to them.

"Boil," I said, "boil. God's sake, can't you boil no faster'n that? And me setting here starving."

I ate up every mite of the greens and drank the pot liquor and licked the kettle and then I put out down the hill as fast as I could. I could feel my stomach tight under my waistband and strength coming up in me from the vittles and I run faster than I'd ever run before. It was dark under the trees but there was still light down the watercourses. I thought how in some cleared place or in a town it wouldn't be dark for two or three hours yet and I saw myself in such a place, moving around and talking to people but staying always in the light. And I said to myself, if I ever got into such a cleared place again it'd be hard to get me to set foot in the woods.

The creek I was following was a master tumbler. Straight down it went over big rocks and the water white everywhere with its dashing. Once I thought I would leave it and strike out through the woods again, and then I thought falling water'd take me out of the hills quicker'n anything else and I'd best stick to it long as I could.

I went on and then all of a sudden I come upon something that froze my guts cold: the print of a foot by the water. I knew it would be a moccasin but I stooped down and looked at it good. I told myself it might be a white man—might be a hunter wearing moccasins like most of 'em did; but I went on a little way and there were three, four footprints in some wet sand and all of them were moccasins. I thought then the game was up or would be directly, but I run on. I run on. I couldn't think of anything else to do.

It was still light when I come out on a big rock by some little falls. I stood there looking and I couldn't believe my eyes. A broad river ran there before me with clearings here and there on the bank and, right across from the rock I was standing on, a fort: a blockhouse with a stockade fence around it and the timber burned back over the rifle range.

I got off the rock and run down toward the water. A woman and some children were walking along outside the stockade. I called to the woman. She give one look at me and turned and run inside the fort, the children after her. I saw the gate swing to behind them and I knew they had shot the bolt.

I tore off my petticoat and waved it over my head and yelled loud as I could:

"Let me in! Let me in, I tell you!"

I could see heads at the upper story and one somebody standing up on a stump to look over the stockade. But nobody answered and there wasn't no sign of the gate opening.

I looked over my shoulder. The woods were dark behind me and there wasn't any signs of Indians, but I knew they'd be coming any minute. I felt like I knew the place in the woods they were at now. I saw them trotting, trotting through the trees, one after another, the way they went.

I thought, "I'll have to do something quick or they'll get me sure, after all my trouble." I started in to swim it but I couldn't make headway against that current. I saw I would be drowning in a minute, and I swum hard and got back to shallow water. It come to me then that the folks in the fort didn't know who I was. I stood up in the water and yelled, loud as I could:

"I'm Jinny Wiley . . . Jinny Wiley that the Indians stole."

The echo came back to me from the woods, but there wasn't any sound from the fort. Then the gate opened a little way and an old man come out with a gun in his hand. He stood there looking at me and he turned around and said something to the folks in the fort and then he started down the path. I watched him coming down over the rifle range, an old man, gray-haired and feeble enough to a been my grandsire. I shouted at him.

"You can't do it. Send some young body over."

He stood on the bank and shouted back at me, his old voice quavering across the water:

"Where'd you come from?"

I jumped up and down and shrieked, top of my voice:

"God's sake, man, you going to let me die right here before your eyes? I'm white! White, I tell you!"

"All of 'em's gone but me," he said, "and they ain't no canoe."

"Make a raft," I told him.

He nodded his head up and down. I could see his old gray beard a-shaking. "You better be ready to swim for it," he said. "I don't know as I can git across."

He called to the women in the fort and they come and brought an axe. There was a dead mulberry tree on the bank and they went to work felling it. The old man went off in the woods and come back with some grapevine. When the tree fell it split into three logs and he tied them together with a grapevine and then he and the women rolled them down to the water. They handed him two rifles and he laid them on the raft and started poling. The current caught him and he was going downstream. Yelling had started behind me somewhere in the woods. The Indians were coming.

I run down the bank till I got even with the raft and I swum out and clomb aboard. The old man poled hard. We got halfway out in the river and then the vines begun to come loose and the raft was spreading apart. I knelt down and held the logs together with my hands the best I could. The old man fell down on his knees and started praying.

" 'Tain't no use," he said; "we can't make it."

I looked over my shoulder. The Indians were swarming down to the water. I knew they'd be swimming directly. The old man was still praying. I took the pole away from him.

"Go on and pray, you old fool," I said. "I'm a-going to git across this river."

I put all the strength I had into it and we made some headway. The yelling was closer now. The Indians were in the water. A shot rung out. I hoped to God one of 'em was hit. I poled harder and I saw some willow boughs ahead of me. I reached out and grabbed hold of 'em and we pulled ourselves to shore.

We went up over the rifle range fast as we could. I looked back once. The Indians had left the water and were standing on the bank. I heard Mad Dog calling:

"Whoopee! . . . whoopee! . . . pretty Jinny!"

We went through the gate. I heard the bolt shoot home and I knew I was inside the fort. I fell down on the ground and the women and children come crowding. The Indians were still yelling. I sat up and the high stockade fence was all around me.

"Lord God," I said, "I was lucky to git away from them Indians!"

Three

The Brilliant Leaves

At three o'clock he came out on the gallery. His mother and his aunt were at the far end, knitting. He had half an hour to kill and he stood, leaning against a post and listening to their talk. They liked to sit there in the afternoons and gossip about all the people who had come to this summer resort in the last thirty years. The Holloways—he was the grandson of a South Carolina bishop and she allowed her children to go barefooted and never attended vesper services; that Mrs. Paty who had had a fit one day in the post office; the mysterious boarder who came every summer to the Robinsons. They knew them all. They were talking now about something that had happened a long time ago. A girl named Sally Mainwaring had climbed down a rope ladder to meet her sweetheart while her father stood at another window, shotgun in hand. When she got to the ground the lover had scuttled off into the bushes, "and so," his aunt concluded dramatically, "she came back into the house through the front door and was an old maid the rest of her life."

"Those Mainwaring girls were all fast," his mother said reflectively.

"Not fast, Jenny, wild."

"High-spirited," his mother conceded. "Come to think of it, Sally Mainwaring was the first woman I ever saw ride astride. I remember. I was about ten years old and she came by the house on a big black horse. I thought about Queen Elizabeth reviewing the troops at Banbury."

"Tilbury, Jenny. You always get things wrong."

213

"Tilbury or Banbury," his mother said. "It's all one. Kate, do you throw over a stitch here or just keep on purling?"

He had his watch open in his hand and now he snapped it shut and stepped off the gallery onto the ground. His mother looked up quickly. "Aren't you going to play tennis this afternoon, Jimmy?"

"No," he said. "I thought I'd just take a turn in the woods," and he was gone up the path before she could speak again.

The path took him quickly into the woods. The mountain arched up its western brow here and it was all wooded, but the cottage—the cottage to which his family had come every summer since he was born—was on an open slope facing north. When you stood on the gallery and looked out, you had the roofs of all those little white houses spread below you. He halted once imperceptibly and glanced back. They always looked just alike, those houses. He wondered how his mother and his aunt could sit there every afternoon talking about the people who lived in them.

He took his watch out again. "Meet me at half past three," Evelyn had said. It was only ten minutes past now. He didn't want to get there first and just stand waiting. He slowed his pace. This part of the woods he was in now was full of black gums. The ground under his feet was red with the brilliant, fallen leaves. "Spectacular," his aunt called it. He had come here yesterday on a duty walk with her and with his mother. His aunt kept commenting on the colors of the leaves, and every now and then she would make him pick one up for her. "The entrance to the woods is positively spectacular," she told everybody when she got home.

All the time he had been wondering when Evelyn would get there. And then this morning her letter had come. ". . . We're leaving Friday morning. I've got to get up in a minute and start packing. . . ."

He said over to himself the part about the train. "I'm telling you which one it is, but don't come to meet it. Don't even come to the house—first. I'll meet you at our tree. I can be there by half past . . ."

He came to a log and, standing flat-footed, jumped over it. When he landed on the other side he broke into a run, hands held chest high, feet beating the ground in a heavy rhythm, the kind of stride you used in track. He ran four or five hundred yards, then stopped, grinning and looking about him as if there might have been somebody there to see.

Another five hundred yards carried him to the tree. Evelyn was already there, walking up and down, her hands in the pockets of her brown sweater. She heard him, turned, and came running, so fast that they bumped into each other. She recoiled but he caught her to him and held her awkwardly until he had pressed his mouth on hers. Her lips, parting beneath his, felt firm and cool, not warm and soft as they had been when they kissed goodbye in June under this same tree.

His arm was still about her, but she was pulling away to look up into his face. "Dimmy!" she said.

They both laughed because that was what his aunt called him sometimes and it made him mad. Then they drew apart and started walking down the road. Her brown hair was long, now, and done up in a knot, and she had on Girl Scout shoes and bright red socks and she kept scuffling the leaves up as she went. He walked beside her, his hands in his pockets. Now that he didn't have his arms around her he felt awkward. That was because she was silent, like the picture he had at home on his dresser, not laughing and talking or turning her head the way she really did.

She looked up at him, sidewise. "It's different, isn't it?" she said.

His impulse was to stop short but he made himself walk on. He spoke and was surprised to find his voice so deep. "Why is it different, Evelyn?"

Color burned in her smooth cheeks. She fixed bright, shy eyes on his. "*Silly!*" she said.

He thought that he must have sounded silly. Still she didn't have any business to say what she had. His face hardened. "Why is it different?" he persisted in the same controlled voice.

She jumped up, high enough to snatch a wine-colored leaf from the bough over her head. "Everything was green, then," she said. "Last time we were here the woods were just turning green."

He remembered the June woods. His face, which some people thought too heavy, lightened. "I know a place where it's still green," he said. "I was there the other day. There's some yellow leaves but it's mostly green. Like summer."

"Come on," she said, and caught his extended hand. They raced down the road, scattering the brilliant leaves from under their feet. After a little they came out on the brow of the mountain. There was no red carpet there. What trees could be seen, stunted hackberries mostly, grew in crevices of the rock. They went forward and stood on the great ledge that was called Sunset Point. Below them the valley shimmered in autumn haze. They could see the Murfreesboro road cutting its way through fields of russet sedge, or suddenly white against a patch of winter oats. They watched a black car spin along past the field and disappear into the tunnel of woods that marked the base of the mountain. Suddenly she stretched her arms out and tilted her head back so that she was looking straight into the sky. "The sky's on fire," she cried, and laughed out loud like a child.

He touched her arm. "Let's go down there," he said, and pointed to the road which wound along the side of the ledge.

They stepped over the drift of dead leaves which choked the entrance and started down. The road slanted steeply along the mountainside. The boughs of the trees met over it in some places. Frail grass grew in the ruts and there were ferns along the edge. What sun got through lay in bright coins on the frail grass and the ferns. The air was cool, not with autumn chill but with the coolness of the deep shade.

The rock they sat down on was tufted with moss. She laid her hand on it, fingers outspread and curving downward. "Look," she said, "every one's like a little pine tree."

"Sometimes they have little flowers on them," he said.

He watched the slim, tanned fingers sink deeper among the little green sprays. "I thought you might not come today," he said. "I heard the train and I thought maybe you didn't come."

"We almost didn't," she said. "Mother got a telegram at the last minute."

"Who from?"

"Aunt Sally Mainwaring. She's always coming to see us."

"Is that the old lady that stays at the Porters'?"

She nodded indifferently. "She's awful crabby."

"I heard Mother and my aunt talking about her. They said she climbed out of a window to elope."

She nodded again. "But he was gone when she got down there, so she was an old maid. That's what makes her so crabby."

They both laughed. Off in the woods a bird called, an unbearably sweet note that seemed to belong to summer rather than autumn. She was looking at the road where it disappeared around a great boulder whose base was thick with ferns. "Where does it go?"

"To Cowan. They call it the old Confederate road. My grandfather came along here once."

"What for?"

"I don't know," he answered vaguely. "He said it was a night attack."

She had got up and was moving over to the place where the ferns drew most luxuriantly. She stood and looked down at them. "Just like summer," she said. "It's just like summer in here, isn't it, Jimmy?"

"Yes, it is," he said.

She walked on. He followed her around the corner of the great boulder. "Have you been playing much tennis?" she asked.

"There wasn't anything else to do," he said.

"How's your backhand?"

"Pretty good. There was a new fellow here this summer could beat me two out of three."

"That Jerrold boy from Atlanta?"

"How'd you know about him?"

"Pinky Thomas wrote me."

He was silent. He had not known that she corresponded with Pinky Thomas. "I don't reckon I'll be playing so much tennis from now on," he said at length.

She made no comment. He leaned down and pulled some beggar's-lice from his trouser leg. "I don't reckon I'll be up here much next summer. Not more'n two weeks anyhow. You lay off all summer and it shows on you all right. But I don't reckon that makes much difference."

"Why won't you be up here next summer?" she asked in a low voice.

"Dad wants me to go in his office," he said. "I reckon I better start. I suppose—I suppose if you're ever going to make a living you better get started at it."

She did not answer, then suddenly she stepped up on the edge of the rock. He jumped up beside her. "Evelyn," he said, "would you marry me?"

She was looking off through the woods. "They wouldn't let us," she said; "we're too young."

"I know," he said, "but if I go in Dad's office. I mean . . . pretty soon I'd get a raise. I mean . . . you would, wouldn't you?"

She turned her head. Their eyes met. Hers were a light, clear brown like the leaves that lie sometimes in the bed of a brook. "I'm perfectly *crazy* about you," she said.

He lifted her in his arms and jumped from the rock. They sank down in the bed of ferns. When he kissed her she kissed him back. She put her arms around his neck and laid her cheek against his, but when he slipped his hand inside the V of her sweater to curve it into the soft hollow under her arm she drew away. "Don't," she said, "please, Jimmy."

"I won't," he said.

She let him kiss her again, then she got to her knees. He sat up straight beside her and caught her hand and held it tight. Her hand fluttered in his, then broke away. "It's still in here," she said. "No, it isn't, either. I hear running water."

"It's the falls," he said. "Bridal Veil Falls is round the corner of that big ledge."

"I never have seen it," she said.

"It's not very pretty around there," he said.

She was laughing and her eyes had more than ever that look of leaves in a running brook. "I bet it's prettier than it is here," she said.

He stood up, straightened his tie and passed a hand over his hair, then stretched a hand out to her. She jumped up beside him lightly. "It's this way," he said, and struck off on a path through the ferns. She followed close. Sometimes they could walk side by side. Sometimes when he had to go in front he put his hand back and she held on to it.

He stopped abruptly beside a big sycamore. She was walking fast and ran into him. He embraced her and kissed her, hard. "You're so sweet," he whispered.

She said again, "I'm *crazy* about you," and then she pulled away to look up at him. "Don't you—don't you like doing things together, Jimmy?"

"Some things," he said, and they laughed and after that stepped side by side for a while.

They came out of the hollow and were on the brow of the mountain again. In front of them was a series of limestone ledges that came down one after another like steps. Gushing out from one of them, filling the whole air with the sound of its rushing, was the white waterfall they called the Bridal Veil.

She drew her breath in sharply. "I never was here before," she cried.

He led her past one of the great boulders which were all about them. They set their feet on the ledge from which the water sprang.

"Look," he said, "you can see where it comes out." She leaned forward in the curve of his arm. The water came down out of a fissure in the highest ledge. It was pure and colorless at first, but it whitened as it struck the first rock step. She leaned farther forward, still with his arm curving about her. Far below were a few pools of still water, fringed with ferns, but most of the water kept white with its dashing from ledge to ledge. She turned quickly, and he felt the cold drops of moisture as her cheek brushed his. "It is like a bridal veil," she said.

He was eyeing the great shelf that made the first falls. "There's a place in there where you can stand and be dry as a bone," he said.

"Have you been there?"

He nodded. "Bill Thompson and I climbed through once. Long time ago. We must have been about ten years old."

She was still turned away from the water, facing him. Her eyes brightened. "Would you do it again?" she asked.

He hesitated, conscious of his body that seemed now to belong more to the ground that it had eight years ago. "I reckon I could if I had to," he said.

Her fingers closed on his arm. "Let's do it now."

He stared at her. "Are you crazy?" he asked.

She did not answer. Her face was bent down. He could see that her eyes were traveling along the main ledge. "How did you go?" she asked.

He pointed to a round rock that rose in the middle of the shelf. "We climbed up over that and then when you get back in there it's like a little path."

Her fingers were softly opening and closing on his arm. She reached up suddenly and gave his cheek a feather-light touch. "I *like* doing things together," she said.

He was looking at her steadily. The color had risen in his cheeks. Suddenly he bent and began untying her shoelaces. "You'll have to take these off if you're going along here," he said.

She stood on one foot and drew off, one after another, shoes and socks. He took his own shoes off and tied them around his neck, then slung hers around, too. "You're the doctor," he said. "Come on."

They climbed to the top of the round rock. He jumped down, then stood braced while she jumped beside him. They stood there and looked down the great black staircase. She squeezed his arm and then she leaned out a little way over the ledge. "Look how the ferns follow the water all the way down," she said.

"Don't try to see too much," he told her, and made her straighten up. They stepped carefully along the ledge over the place that he had said was like a little path. The falls were not three feet away, now. He could feel the cold spray on his cheek, could see the place under the water where you could stand and be dry. "Come on," he said. "One more rock to get around."

The second rock did not jut out as far as the other, but the rock under their feet was wet and a little slippery in places. He thought he would go first and then he decided he could help her better from his side. "Go easy," he said.

She stepped lightly past him. He saw her foot go out and her body swing around the rock and then—he never knew. She might have slipped or she might have got scared, but her foot went down, sickeningly, and she was falling backward from the rock. He clutched at her and touched only the smooth top of her head. Her face was before him, thrown sharply backward, white, with staring eyes—and then he had to lean out to see, lying far below among the ferns—the brown heap.

He got down there—he never could tell them afterward what way he took—but he got down there, slipping, sliding, over the wet rocks. She was lying by one of those little pools on her back, her brown hair tangled in the ferns. He knelt beside her. "Evelyn," he said, "are you hurt? Are you hurt very badly?" Her eyes were open but she did not answer except for a moan. He bent over farther, put his hand on her shoulder. "Could you stand up?" he asked. "Oh, darling, couldn't you just stand up?" The moaning sound went on and now he knew that she did not see him and he started up, his hands swinging at his sides. Then he knelt down again and tried to lift her up. She screamed twice horribly. He laid her back. The screaming had stopped. He could hear the water rushing down onto the rocks. He passed his hand over his trembling lips. "I got to get some help," he said.

He said that but he took another step toward her before he turned away. His hands, still hanging at his sides, danced as though he were controlling invisible marionettes. He stared at the gray mountain ledge. "I reckon this is the way," he said, and started upward, stumbling over the wet rocks.

Fifteen minutes later he came up over the top of the ledge onto the western brow. One of his trouser legs was torn off and blood showed through the fluttering rags of his shirt. He stood on the ledge and put his hand up and wiped the sweat from his forehead and shut his eyes for a second. Then he plunged into the underbrush. A few more minutes and he came out onto the woods road. He ran slower now, lurching sometimes from side to side, but he ran on. He ran and the brilliant, the wine-colored leaves crackled and broke under his feet. His mouth, a taut square, drew in, released whining breaths. His staring eyes fixed the ground, but he did not see the leaves that he ran over. He saw only the white houses that no matter how fast he ran kept always just ahead of him. If he did not hurry they would slide off the hill, slide off and leave him running forever through these woods, over these dead leaves.

Her Quaint Honor

The first year I was at Taylor's Grove I raised ten thousand pounds of tobacco. Five thousand pounds of lugs and seconds and five thousand pounds of prime leaf. And, boy, was it prime! I ought to have got thirty cents for that leaf, the way it was selling that year. But I didn't get but fifteen. That yellow wife of Tom Doty's was the cause of that.

I was raised at the Grove but I had a fuss with my folks one fall and went off to Louisville and worked in a garage. I got to be a pretty good mechanic but they kept me at it eighteen hours a day. I figured there was no percentage in that so I saved up some money and started me a combined garage and filling station. I made money on the service end, or would have if it hadn't been for my friends. They came from all over town and were all slow pay. Then the Depression hit us. I started lying awake nights worrying about the payroll. One night I got to thinking about all that land at the Grove. It don't belong to me or to any of us—yet. It belongs to my grandmother. She is seventy-five years old and hell on wheels. Always has been, they tell me. Still, I knew that if I could stand the old lady I was welcome to go there and farm.

I got up the next morning and went to see a man I know. By afternoon I'd sold the shop, including some high-priced accessories, and was heading for South Todd.

But I didn't go straight to the old place. I went by to see a nigger I know. Tom Doty was the house boy at the Grove when I was a kid. Then later he got to be a hand and finally foreman and he stayed there till he had some trouble with my grandmother and had to leave. I reckon I'd better stop now and tell you about my grandmother. She is the only woman in South Todd old enough to have owned slaves—her parents died when she was little—and she has never got over it. The niggers say can't anybody get along with her and don't any of them try it. The poor white people don't know her as well as the niggers do, and two or three families move on the place every year. But they never make more than one crop there. As the old lady says, "They don't suit the place."

But this Tom Doty I was telling you about always could get along with her when he wanted to. And, besides that, he is the smartest nigger and the fastest worker I ever knew. I always said that if I ever went to farming I'd try to get hold of Tom, so I stopped at Price's Station and found he was cropping at a Mr. Bannerman's and went right on over there.

It was just before Christmas but it was a warm day. Tom was sitting on the doorstep, sunning. I thought he must be doing right well at Mr. Bannerman's, for everything he had on was new— leather coat and tan shoes and a pair of those purple corduroy pants the niggers like so much. He looked good in 'em too. Tom is a tall, handsome nigger, with a very black face and a big, real nigger mouth. My grandmother always said he had Coromantee blood in him.

I drove up to the door. "Hello, Tom," I said. "Have you traded for next year?"

He jumped right up. "God help me! If it ain't Mister Jim!"

"It ain't anybody else," I told him. "Have you traded yet?"

"I ain't named it to Mr. Bannerman," he said, "but I reckon he'll let me stay here long as I want to."

"How'd you like to make a crop with me?"

Tom kind of grins. "Whereabouts?"

"Well," I said, "there's a lot of land over at the old place ain't in use."

Tom grins again. "Hi yi! You reckon Miss Jinny'd let us stay on the place long enough to make a crop?"

"I was thinking about trying it."

He stood there looking at me a minute. "Mister Jim, I got a wife in there I believe can git along with Miss Jinny."

"You *got* something then," I said. "Let me see her."

He called, "Frankie!" A girl came to the door. I didn't like her looks much. For one thing she had on lipstick and rouge. She was almost as tall as Tom and plump. And she had gray eyes and a bright skin. I never did like to see gray eyes in a nigger's head, and a light-skin nigger always looks sassy to me. Still, she had a good-natured smile and good nature was what I was after.

"Howdy, Frankie," I said. "Whose girl are you?"

"I'm old man Gus Byars's daughter."

I was glad to hear that. Those Byars niggers are as respectable niggers as we've got in our county. Old Gus is the grandson of a white man, Mr. Jim Parlow, who died right after the Civil War. He had four hundred acres of land and in his will he divided it up among his four mulatto sons, said, "They may be niggers but they're damn fine boys." The rest of them had lost their land long ago but old Gus still had fifty acres of his.

"Frankie," I said, "you know Miss Jinny Taylor?"

"Naw, suh, but Papa say he been knowin' her all his life."

"Can your papa get along with her?"

"Naw, suh, he say cain't nobody git along with her, black or white."

"Well, Frankie, Tom here says you can get along with her."

She laughed and ducked her head. "Folks generally likes me," she said.

Tom had sat down and was whittling on a stick. He'd been eyeing Frankie like he'd never seen her before and was trying to make up his mind about her. "Mister Jim, I believe she kin do it," he says finally in that soft voice of his.

"Well, what about it, Frankie?"

She was looking at Tom. I could tell from that look that they were a mighty loving pair. "Whatever Tom say," she told me.

"All right," I said, "we've done traded. Tom, you got a wagon?"

"Yes, sir."

"Well, you be ready to move your stuff around New Year's."

"How you know Miss Jinny got an empty cabin?"

"I'll empty one."

He laughed. "Miss Jinny gwine have something to say to that."

I drove on over to Taylor's Grove. Got there about four o'clock.

The front door was locked. I knocked on it a long while. Nobody came but I could hear a radio going full tilt inside. Finally I shouted: "Mama! Mama!" (My mother died when I was little so I always call my grandmother "Mama.") There was a lull in the music. The old lady came to the door. She is a small old lady with white hair and real pretty blue eyes. She wears gray gingham dresses and if it's cold a little shawl. She stuck her face up against the screen. "Who is it? What do you want?"

"It's Jim," I told her. "Looks like you'd let me in after I drove all the way from Louisville to see you."

She opened the door mighty quick then. That old lady likes her own flesh and blood. She just can't stand to have them around long at a time.

"Jim!" she said. "Jim, I'm glad to see you."

"Why'n't you let me in, then?" I asked, kidding her like I always did.

She said: "I heard somebody calling 'Mama' but I thought it was the music. So many of these new songs have 'Mama' in them."

We went in and sat down and she told me all the news, mostly about a polecat had got in the hen house and how the tenants were drying up her cows. After a while she asked me if I didn't want supper the way people do when they expect you to say "No." I told her I could eat a house. She looked kind of worried and then she said she wasn't figuring on eating any supper and had let the fire go out but she could scramble me some eggs.

I kindled a fire in the stove and she fixed the eggs. But it took her a long time. I could see that she had broken a lot since the last time I was here. I thought it was time some of her own folks came to live with her.

After supper we went and sat in her room some more and listened to the radio. She is hell on politics and likes to know what is going on in Soviet Russia and China. I sat there looking at her and thinking how she'd kept us all in a stew for twenty or thirty years and would keep it up too till she died.

The way I figure it she isn't mean. She just has more curiosity than most folks. When she has anybody around her she just has to take 'em to pieces to see what makes 'em tick. And when she finds the weak spot she can't help probing it. I decided that if I was going to make a crop there I'd try to stay away from the house as much as possible. I wasn't thinking much about the future in those days. Just to make one crop was all I figured on.

It was ten o'clock. She got up and said it was time to go to bed. I knew it was time to strike.

"Mama," I said, "how'd you like to have me come here and make a crop?"

She blinked. Her face worked like she was going to cry. But that old lady is game from the word "go." "Well," she says, offhand, "I'll have to see what Phil says about it."

Uncle Phil is her brother, lives on the next farm. He is seventy years old and weighs two hundred pounds. He manages her business like he manages his own by sitting on the front porch and hollering at the hands.

"That's right," I told her, "we'll have to see what Uncle Phil says," and I went on upstairs to my old room and went to bed.

In the morning the old lady called Uncle Phil up and had a long talk with him. When she got through she said that Uncle Phil thought it was a good idea but I'd have to talk over the details of the trade with him. I told her that was all right. I'd go over to see Uncle Phil that morning. Then I asked her if there was an empty cabin on the place and when she said there was I told her I thought I'd try to get Tom Doty for a cropper. She said that was fine. She always liked Tom.

I thought it was about time to hit the big road so I said I'd go on over and have my talk with Uncle Phil. I stopped at a country store and telephoned him. He must have heard I was there. "What's the matter?" he sings out. "City got you down?"

I said that that was the size of it and told him I'd decided to make a crop at the Grove if he was agreeable.

He didn't say anything for a minute. Finally he said: "What you want to make a crop for? Why'n't you just go there and stay as long as you want to?"

"Listen," I told him, "I've been working eighteen hours a day in that garage but I'm not ready for a nursemaid's job yet. And if I was I wouldn't start on Mama because she is hell on wheels and always has been."

"She don't mellow much," he said and then he gave a sigh. "I reckon you got to get experience. . . . Come on over in a few days and let me know how you make out."

I told him I would, and then I drove over to Bannerman's. Tom was sitting there on the doorstep. "Well, Tom," I said, "you can move in any time you want to."

Tom looked at me kind of funny. "How Miss Jinny gettin' along?" he asked in that polite voice of his.

"She says it's fine for you to be my cropper. I think Frankie could handle her."

Frankie smiled, and Tom laughed too. "That's right," he says.

They moved in three days later. Right then I came near making a big mistake. I went on down to the cabin that first morning and told Tom I reckoned Frankie'd better go up and see about working for Miss Jinny.

Tom looked upset like he always does when he has to go against white folks. Finally he says, "Mister Jim, it ain't *time* for Frankie to go to the house yit."

I told him all right. I was pretty busy for the next week or so and I didn't have time to think about those niggers. All this time the old lady and I'd been having snacks off the kitchen table because it was too much trouble to light a fire in the dining room. Then one night when I rolled in for my scrambled eggs there was a fire going in the dining room and the table was all set. Frankie was in the kitchen standing over the stove and the old lady was ambling around telling her to do this and that. I beat it across the hall and waited till they rang the bell.

There was fried chicken and mashed potatoes and mustard greens. The chicken was fine and the greens were cooked down like I like them but I was waiting for the biscuits. Those old-fashioned house-keepers judge a cook by her bread. I picked one up looking kind of sour as if I expected the worst. It was light as a feather. I ate seven and I could have eaten more but I was afraid the old lady would think I was dissatisfied with her cooking. We had some kind of pudding after that and I had a cup of good coffee. The old lady just picked at a chicken wing and she wouldn't drink any coffee for fear it would keep her awake. I went on across the hall and after the old lady had shown Frankie where to put things and bossed her about the dishwashing she came too. The old lady can't read much at night on account of her eyes so she usually keeps the radio going till ten or eleven o'clock. She turned it on tonight same as usual. It was a talk on Soviet Russia but it didn't seem to hold her. She turned it off and came over to the fire.

"That wife of Tom's came up today," she says, "and wanted to know if I wouldn't give her some milk. I told her I'd give her a gallon if she'd churn every day."

I put my paper down. "A gallon of milk! You know what that would cost you in town?"

"I ain't in town," the old lady says, "and ain't going to be if I keep my reason. The milk don't cost me anything and I'm glad for 'em to have it. I'm going to have Frankie get supper every night too. Of course I'll pay her extra for that."

"You don't really need her, do you?" I asked.

"No, I don't need her," the old lady says, "but when I find one that's willing to work I like to encourage 'em. So many of 'em won't do a hand's turn these days."

"Tom's a good man," I says, "but that Frankie don't look like much of a worker to me."

"She ain't overly strong," the old lady says, "but she's a good cook. All those Byars girls are good cooks."

Well, it went on like that. The way I figured it Frankie got paid for everything she did but every day she'd do a little something extra that she hadn't been paid for and that kept the old lady feeling good. It was like they were running a race, with Frankie lagging on the turns so the old lady'd always keep in the lead. I got to worrying for fear they'd get all the chores done someday and Frankie'd have to pass the old lady.

There was one other thing worried me. Frankie was well named. She and Tom were just like the niggers in the song. They were willing to work but loving came first. Every day after dinner Frankie would leave the dishes there on the table and she and Tom would head for the cabin. I was afraid the old lady'd notice and one day I took the bull by the horns. "Don't Frankie do any work in the afternoons?" I asked. "I came through the kitchen at one o'clock the other day and she'd left all her dinner dishes."

The old lady bridled up. "She goes to the cabin to rest a few minutes right after dinner. Good cooks are all like that. They get nervous, cooking. They have to cool off before they can eat anything."

I thought that as long as the old lady thought Frankie went to the cabin to cool off it was all right. I was pretty busy about that time. I don't know whether you ever raised any dark tobacco. A man ought not to go into it unless he wants to keep on the move.

There's something to do every month in the year. We start burning our plant beds in February. In April it's time to take the canvas off and let the plants toughen up. Then from the middle of April on through May and sometimes up to the first of June you're on pins and needles waiting for a good season to set your tobacco. In our country we have some of the worst droughts in the spring. It's a hard proposition, setting tobacco when the ground isn't wet. You have to water every plant by hand and at that you're lucky if you get a stand.

We had some good rains in May, though, that year. I got my whole crop set on two rains. It was a fine stand and grew off pretty. By July my tobacco was waist-high, good, broad, spreading leaves too. She was ready to cut by the first of August. And I got the whole crop—ten thousand pounds of tobacco—cut and into the barn by August 15. I felt pretty good about that but I knew the hardest job was still ahead. It's the curing that tells the tale. You've got to put the smoke to her just right.

I'd been around tobacco barns a lot when I was a kid. I knew it was the devil of a job to get the right color and finish on a leaf but I wasn't worrying. Uncle Phil, for all he is so lazy, knows a lot about farming. I thought I only had to ask him when the time came.

I let my tobacco yellow for about a week before I started the fires: good chunks of hickory going in all four corners of the barn. I fired off and on, according to the season, for two weeks and then I called the old man up and asked him how much longer I ought to let the fires go.

"Hell," he says, "how do I know?"

"You been raising dark tobacco for fifty years," I told him. "You ought to know something about it."

"I know one thing," he says, "you'll houseburn it, sure as God made little apples, if you're let alone."

"Why'n't you come on over and show me how to fire it then?" I asked, knowing he wouldn't stir out of his house if half the barns in the country were burning down.

"I haven't cured a crop of tobacco in thirty years," he says.

"What do you do when firing time comes?"

"I get somebody that knows more about it than I do. Go on over and get Bud Asbury. He's a genius at it."

I drove over to the Asbury place. The first thing I saw was old man Asbury coming around the corner of the barn. He hadn't changed since I was a child: little old dried-up pea of a man rattling around in his overalls. I had to go in and howdy with old Mrs. Asbury before I could tell him what I wanted. He said Bud wasn't home right now but he knew he'd be glad to help me. "All right, then," I said, "tell him to drop around tomorrow morning."

The old man looked kind of worried. He began all over again, saying Bud would be proud to help me—if he was home when the time came.

"Has he got a job somewhere?" I asked.

The old man said no, he didn't have any job.

"Well, don't he come home to sleep?"

The old man said the fact was he hadn't seen Bud for three, four days. "You know he always was a rambling sort of a boy," he said.

"Well, I hope he'll ramble in here tomorrow morning," I told him, "or I'll have to get somebody else to cure that tobacco."

I went on home. Fifteen minutes after I got there Uncle Phil called up. "Have you read today's *Tobacco-Leaf*?" he asked.

I told him I'd been too busy to even take the paper out of the box.

"It's a good thing for you I read the paper," he said. "You better go on into town and get Bud Asbury out of jail."

"What's he in jail for?"

"For taking a man's car."

"Maybe he'd better stay in jail," I said.

The old man laughed. "Bud wouldn't steal a pin. You go on in there and tell the judge to turn Bud loose, that you need him to fire your tobacco. No, tell him I said I needed him to fire *my* tobacco. You better take some money. There's a drunk-and-disorderly charge too."

I went on in. The judge is a mighty pleasant old man. We howdied about the healths of both our families and then I told him what Uncle Phil said. "Well, now," he said, "I'm glad Phil can use him. That charge they've laid against Bud is just a piece of Bill Cain's foolishness."

Bill Cain is our prosecuting attorney. "Has he got it in for Bud?" I asked.

The judge explained that Bill Cain and Chief Patterson didn't exactly have it in for Bud. They were just worn out with him. It seems that Bud is a spree drinker, goes on a bat regularly every two or three months. He's also one of these blind drunks that never lose the use of their legs. This time he'd come out of a speakeasy and got in somebody else's car and drove off. The man who lost the car figured that Bud had it because Bud's car was still sitting there in the square next morning. But he goes ahead just the same and swears out a warrant for Bud's arrest.

"And Bill Cain," the judge said testily, "was fool enough to serve it."

I told the judge I thought Uncle Phil would go on Bud's bond and in the meantime I'd take him home and sober him up with a little work. Tom said he'd drive Bud's car over to the Asburys'. I went by police court and paid his fine and then went on over to the county jail.

Mr. Cleaver, the sheriff, and Bud and two niggers were sitting in the hall playing checkers. I told Mr. Cleaver what I wanted and he said all right but he'd be obliged if I'd wait a few minutes: he and Bud were having a tournament with the niggers. "This boy, Billy," he says, pointing over his shoulder, "is the champion of Dunham's warehouse but Bud and me are going to beat him if you'll give us time to finish this game."

I said all right and came in and watched them. Bud looked like he was still drunk or else he had a whale of a hangover. He sat up there stiff as a dead man, pushing those checkers around. He's a tall, lean fellow, about forty years old, one of the handsomest men I ever saw in my life but with a kind of shattered look to him. It wasn't his features or the fact that he'd slept in his clothes. It was his eyes: he had that cold-looking blue eye you see sometimes in steady drinkers or sometimes in men that just don't give a damn. I decided I'd as soon not meet him when he was on one of his sprees.

They finished their game—the niggers beat 'em four out of six. The sheriff went in his office and telephoned Uncle Bill, then came back and told Bud goodbye. "Don't stay away so long next time, Bud," he says, winking at me.

"They ain't goin' to be no next time, Mister Cleaver," Bud tells him.

As we drove home he gave me quite a lecture on drinking. The trouble, he said, was the liquor they sold you nowadays. It had got so that he was almost a teetotaler, never knowing how the liquor would take him. Once he wanted me to stop the car. He was a mind to go back and beat up Lonny Cross, who'd sold him the liquor. You'd think, he said, that you could go in a man's bar and have a drink, friendly like, without him poisoning you. I told him he'd better leave Lonny Cross alone. He wasn't out of the woods yet on that larceny charge. He didn't seem worried about that. His idea was that the prosecutor must have been drunk when he let the man swear out the warrant. "Must have been. Mister Cain knows I wouldn't steal anybody's car. Why, a man needs his car to get around in."

We drove into the Grove about five o'clock. Tom had just got back from the Asburys'. I stopped by the barn a minute and then I took Bud on up to the house. I went in the back way like I always do when I've got mud on my boots. Frankie was frying some fish one of the boys had caught in Grinstead's pond. She said the old lady hadn't been feeling so well and was lying down.

The kitchen smelled mighty good with fish frying and coffee making. There was a table in the corner that Frankie always kept covered with a fresh cloth. I thought that as long as the old lady wasn't coming in Bud and I might as well eat at that table so I told Frankie not to bother making a fire in the dining room and then I went on in to see the old lady.

She was lying down, listening to the radio. I stayed with her awhile and then I left her with the radio turned low and went back to the kitchen.

Tom had come in from the barn and was sitting on his bench back of the stove. Frankie had put a chair up to the table for Bud and he was sitting there, smoking. I thought he must be needing a drink bad by this time so I stepped into the dining room and found a pint bottle that was three-quarters full of whiskey. I divided it between the four of us, giving Bud a little the best of the deal.

He turned his glass up and downed her at one smack. "You ain't got any more of that?" he says.

I told him that as far as I knew it was the last in the house. "Miss Jinny and Frankie are teetotalers," I said.

Tom lets out a laugh. That was a joke we had. The old lady doesn't believe in using liquor except for medicine and cooking. "I just take it to ease the pain," she says, but one way or another she and Frankie get through with about a quart a week.

Frankie laughs too. "You can leave it around here all you want, Mister Jim. I ain't gwine tech it."

"I'll drink your share, Frankie," Bud says.

He was looking different from what he had when he came in. Those funny blue eyes were shining and he had color in his cheeks.

If I hadn't known there wasn't any liquor in the house I'd have thought he was starting on another drunk.

Frankie was taking her fish off the stove. We drew up our chairs. Her coffee was good that night and we had a dozen of those little pond perch fried a golden brown. And every time we turned around Frankie was there with more batter bread. I told her I believed it was the best she'd ever made.

She had just handed me a piece and was going on to Bud. He looked up at her. "Yeah," he said, "and them's mighty pretty little yellow hands that made it."

Nobody said anything for a minute. Before I knew it I'd looked over at Tom. He was sitting on a bench by the stove and he slewed around as sudden as if he'd been pulled by a string. His eyes popped open and fastened on Bud's face. Then he realized that I was looking at him and he ducked his head and began eating again, real slow.

I looked back at Bud. He looked back as unconcerned as you please. I kept on looking at him. I made my voice real hard. "Eat up, Bud," I said. "It's time we were getting to the barn."

"That tobacco ain't goin' to walk off," he says and laughs and looks up at Frankie, who was still standing there by the table.

I pushed my chair back. "I'm ready now," I said. "I'll be obliged if you'd come with me."

He put one last piece of corn bread in his mouth and reached for his hat. We went out the back way and started down to the barn. We hadn't gone far before Bud said he'd have to stop a minute. I thought he had to see a man about a dog and walked on. I hadn't been in the barn more than ten minutes before he came in. And in a little while Tom came too.

We set to work building up the fires. You can't have flames going any length of time. You've got to have red-hot embers and keeping a hickory log at that stage takes doing. But Tom was good at it, as Bud remarked.

Bud seemed to be feeling better and better. He went over the barn, pinching a leaf here and there. He said the tobacco was in exactly the right order. Seems it's all a matter of draft. If you have too much draft the lighter edges of the leaf'll dry out too quick and set in whatever color they happen to have at the time, instead of making the nice brown everybody wants.

He talked a lot about houseburning. Said there wasn't any use of anybody houseburning their tobacco if they kept their minds on it. Said it comes from letting your fires die out too sudden. That vapor'll stop right in the middle of the barn and condense into sweat. She's gone then, he said, and can't anything bring her back. But the nearer you can bring her to houseburning without burning her the prettier she'll be.

About twelve o'clock we got up to go up to the house for more coffee. Tom got up too. I'd intended to leave him there to watch the fires but something about the way he looked made me change my mind.

The three of us started back to the house but Bud dropped off as we were crossing the yard. Seemed to me he was having a lot of sudden calls that night and I so remarked to Tom.

Tom laughed, kind of surly. "He done gone to git him some more of that wine. Whilst you in talking to old Miss he went in the dining room and got him a whole jug of blackberry wine."

"Why'n't you stop him, Tom?"

Tom laughed again. "Mister Jim, you know I couldn't head Mister Bud Asbury off when he wants to do anything."

"Is he mean?" I asked. "Has he got the reputation of being mean?"

"He's hard to head," Tom said. "The jedge or anybody that has the handlin' of him'll tell you that."

Bud was already sitting up to the table when we came in. "Come on," he called, like it was his house and not mine. "Come on and git some of these good sandwiches Frankie made us."

I could see he'd taken on another load of the old lady's wine. He kept laughing most of the time and once when Frankie was passing something he made a swipe low with his hand and caught hold of her ankle.

Frankie was quick. She flopped over against the table, spilling half the sandwiches. " 'Scuse *me*, Mister Bud," she says, "I mighty nigh fell on you."

"It don't make a bit of difference," Bud says genially. "You fall all over me if you want to."

I was stumped. I've been around a good bit. I know plenty of men that think nothing of sleeping with nigger women but I never saw one in the act of going after a nigger woman before. It gave me a funny feeling. And I was worried about Tom. Tom is a boy that thinks a lot of his raising. I don't reckon he'd ever spoken an out-of-the-way word to a white person in his life—until that night.

Bud finished eating and got up and went out on the porch, to get a drink of water, he said. He was out there a few minutes and then he came to the door. "Frankie," he called, "step here a minute."

Frankie jumped up quick like she always does when there's any waiting on to do and then she must have realized what he wanted, for she stopped short and just stood there, staring at him.

Tom was getting up from his bench behind the stove. He kept on coming till he was right in the middle of the floor and then he stopped. "Mister Bud," he said, "that's my woman."

I saw his hand go up, slow, over his jumper. He wears one of these old-fashioned cutting razors slung around his neck on a piece of string.

I stepped out between them. I looked him straight in the eye. "Tom!" I said, "*Tom!* You sit down there behind that stove."

That nigger looked at me like he'd never seen me before. Then his eyes changed. "Yas, sir," he said, kind of dazed. "Yas, sir, that's what I was going to do."

I looked at Frankie. I was mad through by that time and it seemed to me that more'n half of it was her fault. Those high yellows just can't help bridling if a man looks at 'em. "Frankie," I said, "do you want to go out on that porch with Mister Asbury?"

She was crying. "Naw, suh, I don't want to go out there with no white man."

"Well, go on over there and sit down by Tom and try behaving yourself for a change."

She went off sniffling and I walked over and stood in front of Tom. "Tom," I told him, "I'm going out there to see Mister Asbury and I don't want any niggers mixing in. You understand?"

"Yas, sir," he said, keeping his eyes on the floor.

I stepped outside. Bud was walking around in the yard. It was dark out there when you stood away from the window. The fool thought I was Frankie. He made a dive at me. "Come on, honey," he says, "let's you and me take a walk."

I caught him by the arm. "You're going to take a walk," I says, "but you ain't going with Frankie. Now, Bud, when you get through that gate you hit the big road and you keep going till you strike your old man's house."

We were passing the window. I could see the surprised look on his face. "Now, Jim," he says, "what have I done to get you down on me like that?"

"You been making passes at Frankie right in my kitchen," I told him. "I ain't going to have it."

"All right," he says sadly, "if that's the way you feel," and he goes off across the yard. He hadn't gone but a few steps before he stopped. "I ain't goin'," he says, sullen like a child. "I ain't ever started curing a crop of tobacco that I didn't finish it. I'm goin' right back to the barn."

I saw there was nothing else for it so I tackled him. I caught him around the knees and we both went down together in the mud. He tried to get up but I shifted my hold and got him around the chest. He broke my hold without half trying and the next thing I knew he had me flat on my back in the mud. "I hate to do this," he says, "but you don't seem to have no sense tonight."

I didn't say anything and after a minute he let me go and got up. I jumped to my feet and went at him again. This time I knocked him over backwards, but he turned, quick as a cat, and had me with a leg hold.

We clinched two or three times after that. I never could break his hold but he'd let me go just so I could come at him again. His blood was up now and he was enjoying himself. As for me I was beginning to think that if anybody hit the big road that night it'd be me.

The last time he threw me plumb over his head. I landed so hard I thought my neck was snapped in two. I lay there a second trying to get my breath. Then I realized that my left hand was hurting like blazes. I moved it. Something rattled. I'd landed against a pile of tobacco sticks. I took another good breath and got up with one of those oak sticks in my hand.

The kitchen door opened, real soft. Tom came out. "Mister Jim," he called, "you want me come out there and help you tie up Mister Bud?"

"You come out here," I said, "and you'll get the worst beating you ever got in your life."

I walked over and let Bud have that solid oak, whang, on the side of his head. He rocked a little like cattle do when you fell them and then he started toward me. But my legs were still good. I jumped to the side, quick. "Bud," I said, "I'm going to raise knots on the other side of your head if you don't hit the big road."

I don't believe he knew what had hit him till that minute. He stopped and fingered his head and then came at me. I let him have it again, a harder lick this time. It knocked him down but not out. That boy's head was hard as bow-dock. After a bit he got on his feet. He stood there, staggering, then he says, real polite, "All right, if that's the way you feel," and starts for the gate.

I went on in the house. "Come on, Tom," I said, "we better get back to the barn."

We took turns the rest of the night, sleeping and firing. But we had let the fires go plumb out while we were having the ruckus and the barn had got cold. We got the fires going good again and kept a steady fire the rest of the night and the wind had changed so it was making the draft just the way you want it. But before I left the barn, toward daybreak, I pulled down a leaf and felt it. It wasn't what you'd call dry but it had lost that kid-glove feeling. Tobacco has a skin just like a woman. Once that stretchiness is gone out of a leaf it's gone and there ain't anything can bring it back.

Daylight was coming in through the open doors. I looked at the tiers of tobacco hanging all the way up to the roof. Ten thousand pounds and if it had been cured right we'd have got thirty cents for every pound of the prime leaf but now we'd do well to get fifteen.

Tom was just getting up from a pile of sacks, feeling his leg that had gone to sleep. "Tom," I said, "take a look up there."

"What is it," he says, "old possum or something on the rafters?"

"It ain't any possum," I said, "but last night we had nineteen hundred and sixty dollars hanging up over us and now we ain't got but nine hundred and thirty."

Tom looked at the tobacco and then he looked at me. He poked his lip out. "That Mister Bud Asbury," he said, "I don't care how good he can cure tobacco. He better stay away from my woman."

I didn't say anything. A man has to fight if somebody tries to take his woman. It struck me as a funny business. Always has.

Mr. Powers

Jack and Ellen had been living at the hill farm a little over a year when a strange man came up the path one morning, a well-set-up young man with blue eyes in a wind-burned country face. He and Jack talked together a few minutes on the porch, then they stepped down on the path and walked slowly over the lawn and out to the brow of the hill. They stood there a while, talking, gesticulating occasionally toward the green wooded hill that rose up sharply from the river bottom just opposite the Cromlie house. Ellen watched the two figures poised there against the bright sky and thought that they seemed to belong to the landscape: Jack, slouching and relaxed in his old corduroys and the sweater that was already weathering to the color of the hillside; the young countryman, more composed, erect except for the stoop of the shoulders that she had come to recognize as the mark of a teamster.

When Jack came back he said that the man had made him a proposition: he wanted to go through the woods and get the fallen trees and the trees that were dying out "on shares." He would saw them up into the right lengths for stove and fireplace, giving the Cromlies a half of all the wood he handled and selling his own share in Gloversville.

"He wants to rent the old cabin too," Jack said. "He's going to give me five dollars a month for it."

"Hadn't you better find out something about him first?" Ellen asked, and then pretended that she hadn't spoken, seeing by Jack's face that the trade was already made.

"Powers," she said, musing, "Powers. That's a good country name. I reckon he's all right."

At lunch they were very gay, saying that now they had a settled income from the place. "Sixty dollars a year for that old cabin," Jack said, "and without turning your hand over to get it. That's not bad."

"It'll pay the milk bill," Ellen said.

Early in the afternoon Mr. Powers's little dun-colored mules drew up before the cabin that was set in the hollow just below the Cromlie house. Mrs. Powers sat beside Mr. Powers on the driver's seat, holding a child in her lap. Their household goods were stacked behind them in the rickety wagon. Ellen, in the swing with Lucy, watched them unloading. There was not much to carry into the house. A little rusty stove, a bed, a roll of quilts and blankets, and a bushel basket heaped with pots and pans and skillets.

Lucy pulled at her mother's arm. "Where does the baby sleep?" she asked. "Mama, where does the *baby* sleep?"

Ellen was thinking of some plates, flowered plates with gold rims that she never used. There were two or three tablecloths, too, that didn't fit either the dining table or the small table in the window nook. "I have no idea," she said absently.

She decided that she would not offer the plates or the tablecloths to Mrs. Powers, not just yet anyhow. They all said it was better not to start off being too intimate with your tenants. Aunt Molly was always having trouble with hers. Tom Potter had actually stolen three loads of tobacco out of her barn. Took them to a loose floor in Springfield and sold them as his own crop and never gave her any account of them. Cousin Sarah thought that Aunt Molly had started Potter off on the wrong track by being too kind to him. "I'm going to be Christian. I hope I'll always be Christian to people, but I'm going to stand on my dignity. I believe it pays, with tenants."

At three o'clock Ellen and Lucy took a basket of butter beans out under the trees to shell. They had not been sitting there long before Mrs. Foster came toiling up the path, leaning on her blackthorn stick. Ellen brought a chair for her and then went into the kitchen and fixed a tray with a plate of ginger cookies for Lucy and a decanter of blackberry wine for Mrs. Foster and herself. They sat there all afternoon talking and drinking their wine and looking out over the valley that was already beginning to shimmer with blue haze. It was five o'clock when Mrs. Foster moved nearer to Ellen and laid her hand on her knee. Her eyes were sparkling and her mouth made a straight line across her tanned face. "I told Ed I was just coming up here and see you myself," she said. "I told him you was new people here and it wasn't reasonable to expect you to know everybody in the country . . ."

Ellen had been looking at the fields on the other side of the river, thinking that it was strange that one patch of ground should be in deep shade and the one adjoining it in brilliant sunshine. She raised her eyes to the horizon now and saw that it was filled with thick, scudding white clouds.

"It's something about our new tenant," she said.

She was waiting at the gate when Jack came home that night.

"Do you know who our new tenant is?" she cried. "Do you *know* who he is?"

Jack waited until he had put the car in the garage before he answered. "He's Bill Powers's brother," he said then. "They're both sons of that old Albert Powers who used to be miller."

"If you'd read the paper once in a while you wouldn't be so ignorant," Ellen told him. "Everybody in the whole country read about it except us."

She gave him Mrs. Foster's account of Mr. Powers. He was the Powers—the Jim Powers—that had killed his little boy over in the Brush Run community in a fight with the hired man over his wife. They had had a new hired man all summer, "a mean feller named Shell, from over in Trigg County." Jim had been down guarding his watermelon patch and had come back to the house around midnight to find his wife out in the grape arbor with the hired man. There had been a good deal of shouting back and forth and calling of names. Jim's sister and his six-year-old son had come downstairs in their nightclothes to find out what it was all about. Jim finally picked up an axe and went after the feller with that. Shell had dodged in time, but the double-bladed axe, swinging backward, had caught the little boy in the side of the head and felled him to the ground. Shell had run off down the road while they were all going on over the child, who had never regained consciousness and had died in a few minutes. Jim had stayed right with him, holding his hand.

Ellen was laughing hysterically when she finished.

"I asked him yesterday if he had any children and he said, 'Just one. She's mighty spoiled!'"

"Cool feller, isn't he?" Jack said. He had been standing looking straight ahead while she talked. He started up the walk now. Ellen hurried to catch up with him.

"Mrs. Foster couldn't understand why we hadn't heard about it." She imitated Mrs. Foster's high-pitched country drawl: "I told Ed I didn't see why they didn't know about it. They git the paper every day and both of 'em can read . . ."

"Can't Mrs. Foster read?" Jack asked.

"No. She has to wait for things like this to happen. She seemed to think Mr. Powers had taken an unfair advantage of our innocence. She kept saying, 'An' him coming and settin' down on y'all just 'cause you was new here!' "

"I reckon the poor devil was up against it," Jack said. "I reckon we were the only people in the country who would take him in."

"We are going to let him stay," Ellen said. "Jack, we *are* going to let him stay, aren't we?"

Jack laughed. "*You* put him out," he said.

The Cromlies could look down from their high porch almost into the back windows of the Powerses' cabin. When the white curtains were pushed aside they could see Mrs. Powers preparing the meals in the small room that was used as a kitchen. A small woman, with an untidy mass of blond hair, she moved slowly about from kitchen to porch and back again, wearing always a faint, excited smile.

"It's the most extraordinary expression," Ellen said, "a sort of smirk. You know, the way people look when they're so pleased with themselves that they simply can't hide it! What *I* can't understand, though, is why she's stuck to him through all this."

Jack said that he thought Mrs. Powers's situation must be in some ways highly satisfactory. "Probably the first time in her life she's ever had the upper hand of him, morally, I mean. They've changed places at one fell swoop. Whatever her sins have been in the past, his are greater . . . since this killing. Must leave 'em both a little dazed."

"It's terrible," Ellen said. "It's terrible to think of them being there together. What do you suppose they can find to say to each other?"

"Well, talking things over is hardly in Powers's line," Jack observed. "He's a man of deeds. I was talking to Judge Pryor about him the other day. He lived on his place five years. The judge thinks a lot of him. Says he's always had this quick temper, like all the Powerses, but he's all right if you handle him properly. He's a hustler, too. Got nine hundred dollars for his share of the tobacco crop the last year he lived on the judge's place."

"Does the judge think he's got any chance to get off?" Ellen asked.

"Oh, they all think Scott'll get him off with a light sentence. Ten to twenty years. He could hardly expect to get off with less than that."

"Twenty years is a long time," Ellen said. "Ten years is a long time."

"It's a hell of a long time," Jack said.

People who came out from town were very much interested in the Powers family. They peered fearfully over the balcony railings, speculating on what sort of mood Mr. Powers was likely to be in that day and discussed his chances for escaping the pen. Tom Eliott suggested that he and Jack fight a duel, with hatchets, at twenty paces. Jack said that he was thinking of putting a machine gun in the crape myrtle bushes.

"You could do a lot of damage from this hill with a machine gun," he said.

Nobody at the Cromlie house was ever up in time to see Mr. Powers go off to work in the morning. They could hear the sound of his axe ringing out in the woods, though, all during the day, and occasionally the great crash of a falling tree shook the whole valley. When this happened Ellen stopped whatever she was doing and a little chill went over her as she thought of Mr. Powers moving about in the dim light among the fallen green boughs. She thought, too, of what Jack had said, that he would certainly go to the penitentiary, and tried to imagine the tall, red-faced countryman in prison.

"I hope they let him drive a team or something like that," she told Jack. "They do have wagons and teams at the penitentiary, don't they?"

"No," Jack said. "They're progressive up there. Use trucks."

One afternoon when they came back from town they saw Mr. Powers's wagon standing beside the drive, filled with logs. Mr. Powers was stooping beside the off mule, mending a trace chain with a length of wire.

Jack came to a halt opposite the wagon. "You got some nice logs there," he said.

Mr. Powers straightened up. Standing with his arm lying along the mule's back, he pointed to the strip of woods that lay next to the cornfield. "I aim to get down in the bottom tomorrow," he said. "Thar's some timber in thar needs takin' out."

"What kind of wood is it?" Ellen asked.

He pushed aside the black lock that overhung his forehead. His eyes—very blue eyes with wrinkles raying out from the corners— rested on her face for a moment. "Hickory, mostly," he said. His gaze shifted to Jack. "You don't want to burn up all your barn wood, but them saplings is too thick in thar. Won't hurt to clean 'em out a little."

"Well, hickory's fine to burn," Jack said.

Mr. Powers nodded. "Ain't nothin' better than a hickory fire," he said.

They did not see Mr. Powers again for several days. When he appeared then he said that he and his wife found that the cabin was too small, after all. They were moving back to his father-in-law's that afternoon. He would be glad, though, if Mr. Cromlie would let him keep his mules in the stable that was across the road from the cabin a few days longer. His father-in-law didn't have any more stable room than he needed himself.

Ellen was waiting in the living room when Jack came back into the house. "Did he say anything about the wood?" she demanded.

Jack lit a cigarette. "We didn't get around to that," he said.

"Then I wouldn't let him keep his mules in our stable," Ellen said. "I wouldn't let him get away with it. I just would not do it."

"Oh, he'll be all right," Jack said. "That first load was his, anyhow, according to the trade. He probably took it off to town and sold it on the spot. Needs cash, I expect." He grinned. "You have to excuse him for being a little absent-minded. He has important business on his hands."

Ellen reflected that Mr. Powers's hearing was set for Monday week and said no more about the wood.

At the preliminary hearing Jim Powers was charged with murder and released after he had executed bond for a thousand dollars. Ellen was aghast when she heard the news.

"But they *can't* accuse him of murder," she said. "The most they can accuse him of is involuntary manslaughter."

"Manslaughter and assault and battery with intent to kill," Jack said. "He could get life for that."

They saw Mr. Powers occasionally at a distance, taking his mules in or out of the old stable, but they had no conversation with him. He was reported by Mrs. Foster to be living in a cabin that belonged to his father-in-law, Nate Dockery. The Dockery place joined the hill farm. Ellen speculated as to whether the trees that were heard to fall occasionally in the woods belonged to Mr. Dockery or to the hill farm.

Jack was irritable when she suggested that he walk over in the woods and see if the cutting was being done on their line.

"There are fully ten thousand trees in that piece of woods," he said, "and not more than twenty of them are worth a damn. And those twenty are red oaks, worth, say, four dollars apiece, board measure. Well, I hotfoot it over there this afternoon and save two trees. What do I get for my afternoon's work? Eight dollars. I can make two hundred if I get on in the house and finish that article. Miller's wired for it twice now."

"Oh, all right if you feel that way about it," Ellen said. "I just hate for him to think we're soft. Everybody in this country thinks we're soft because we're city people."

She did not mention the matter to Jack again, however, seeing that he so disliked the idea of talking to Powers about the wood. It was not long after that that Mr. Powers took his mules out of the old stable. Shortly afterward the axe strokes ceased to ring out in the woods. Mr. Powers, Mrs. Foster said, had moved again. He and his father-in-law had never gotten on any too well and it stood to reason that they wouldn't get on no better after what had happened. He was working now for a Mr. Mason out on the Jasper road. He and Mrs. Powers were still living together. Ellen was curious about the character of the woman who had been the cause of the affray.

"Has she had a bad character before this, Mrs. Foster?" she asked.

Mrs. Foster compressed her lips. "Ever since she was big enough, Miz Cromlie," she said. "But you can't tell Jim nothin'. All them Powerses is hardheaded and he's the hardheadedest of all of 'em."

Mrs. Powers's name was mentioned less and less often in the Cromlie household from that time forward. Ellen remarked once that he had to pass their house every time he went to town. "If I ever meet him in the big road I'm going to ask him about that wood," she said. "I swear I am!"

" 'Twon't do you any good," Jack said. "He'll just tell you what he told me."

"Well, what *did* he tell you?" Ellen asked.

"Just smiled and said he'd been aimin' to get at it now for two, three days. He means it too. He'll get us up a load one day."

"Unless he goes to the pen first," Ellen said.

The season turned slowly toward fall. The trees on the hill had not begun to turn, but their green was softened, verging already toward yellow. And yellow leaves from the willows fell occasionally into the green water of the swimming hole. The air was clear and bright, touched faintly with cold in the early morning.

The Negro boy, Chap, spaded up wide beds of earth in front of the house and on either side of the brick walk and set out iris and tulip and jonquil bulbs and scattered larkspur and delphinium seed among them. The Cromlies walked around in the yard or out from the shade of the beech trees and down the slope. Sometimes Ellen, standing on the walk, would look back into the hall and think how the house that was spread out now, with all its doors and windows open to the sunshine, would contract and darken soon with winter.

One evening at sunset she and Lucy walked out on the brow of the hill and sat down on the bench that was fixed around the big beech tree. Sitting there they had the whole valley spread out before them, the wooded hill that rose steeply on the right, with the Jasper road curving between it and the river, and stretching away on the other side of the river beyond the old covered bridge the flat fields that were still covered with late corn and tobacco. Some of the blue haze that had been over the whole country all day still lingered in these far fields, but the rest of the valley was bathed in bright, flickering light.

A wagon drawn by two mules came up over the hill and began the long descent to the bridge. Ellen watched the mules hold back at first and then put their feet down faster and faster as the driver eased his brake on. A tall young man in blue shirt and pants, he sat sidewise on the high driver's seat with his face turned toward the river.

Ellen looked away and then back again, trying to fix the scene in her memory. The broad valley, the turning green river, and the long line of the old covered bridge would stay, she knew, in her memory, but the bright, flickering light that was so much a part of it all would grow dimmer and more unreal until finally it would vanish entirely. You could not prison light in the memory.

The team of mules and the wagon were directly beneath the bench now. The driver had taken his hat off and flung it in the bottom of the wagon. His head bared to the evening air, he sat whistling, breaking off occasionally to call to his mules in a loud, clear voice.

Lucy had got up and was standing on the brow of the hill looking down at him.

"Mama," she cried out suddenly, "it's Mr. Powers! It's Mr. Powers, Mama!"

"Hush!" Ellen said. "He'll hear you."

She watched the mules round the curve and approach the bridge. Mr. Powers's figure was bright for a moment against the black shed, then it disappeared into the dark. His whistle could be heard for a little while, mixed with the rattling of the mules' feet on the wooden flooring; then that too died away. Ellen stood up. Most of the color was gone from the west by this time, but the east still held a reflected glow, soft lavenders and pinks and here and there a streak of azure.

Lucy was tugging at her mother's hand.

"Didn't you want to speak to him, Mama? You said you wanted to speak to him."

Ellen shook her head. "No," she said, "I don't want to speak to him."

All Lovers Love the Spring

My third cousin, Roger Tredwell, is the president of the First National Bank in our town, Fuqua, Kentucky. He is also president of the Chamber of Commerce and permanent treasurer of the Community Chest and chairman of the board of directors of the hospital. People say that if you want anything done for the community you turn it over to the busiest man in town. I imagine Roger serves on a lot of other committees I never even heard of. I don't belong to any more organizations than I can help, but, after all, my family has lived here ever since there was a town and there are some things you can't get out of. I won't have anything to do with Kiwanis or Rotary but I serve on the women's auxiliary to the hospital and I'm a member of the Y.W.C.A. board and chairman of the board of the Florence Crittenden Home. Some people think they ought to have a married woman for that and I always say that anybody that wants the job can have it but I notice nobody ever takes me up on it.

Nowadays if as many as six women—or men—form an organization they have got to have a dinner at least once a year. Minnie Mayhew, who runs the Women's Club, caters for ours and always serves green peas, no matter what time of year it is. I often sit next to Roger at these dinners. He is the most prominent man in town and, after all, I am a Fuqua—have been one for forty-two years. There are some of my stocks never came back after the Depression; I always wear the same dress to these dinners: a black crepe de chine, with narrow white piping on neck and sleeves. It was a good dress when I bought it and it still fits perfectly but I never looked well in black.

Roger's wife says she is sure he wears out more white shirts and black ties than any man in town. He has taken on weight since he got middle-aged, and the Tredwells turn bald early. When a man gets those little red veins in his cheeks and his neck gets thick, so that it spreads out over his collar, there is something about a dinner jacket that makes him look like a carp. Or, as my father used to say, a grinnell. He was quite a learned man but always preferred to use the local name for a thing instead of the one you get out of the encyclopedia.

When I was thirteen years old my father got tired of living in town and moved back to the old Fuqua homestead on the Mercersville pike. The government set fire to the house the other day, after it bought a hundred and thirty thousand acres of land on the Mercersville pike for an army camp. But in those days it was still standing. Rather a handsome old brick house, set back from the road in a grove of silver poplars. When we went there to live tenants had been farming the place for twenty years. The yard was grown up in dog fennel as high as your waist and silver poplars had sprung up everywhere. They are like banyan trees; you have one poplar and a hundred shoots will spring up around it. The underside of the poplar leaf is white, like cotton, and shines. In the least little breeze all those leaves will turn and show their undersides. It's easy to see why you call them "silver poplars."

A perfect thicket of silver poplars had come up right back of the house but in amongst them were trees that had been grown when my father was a boy. There was one big tree that we children called "ours." It had four branches sticking up like the fingers on a hand, and one stout branch that had been half lopped off was the thumb. Each of us Fuquas claimed a finger for our special seat; Roger Tredwell, who was fifteen years old then and used to come out from town and spend every weekend with us, claimed the thumb.

The boys got hold of some old planks and built a platform high up in the branches of that tree. Then they made walls to it and we called it our "tree house." We used to haul up "supplies" in a bucket tied on to a rope. Joe—he was eight years old—was the one that had to sneak ginger cakes and cold biscuits and ham away from the cook to put in the bucket. The older boys, Tom and Ed, did most of the carpentering for the house but it was Roger's idea. He got tired of it, though, as soon as it was finished and never wanted to just play in it but was always adding something. Like the pulleys that went from that tree to a big maple. There were four wires stretched tight, and five things that looked like saddles slipped along on them, pads made out of tow sacks. You were supposed to hold on to them and swing over to the sugar tree. But the wires were stretched too tight or something and the whole thing broke the first time we tried it.

Roger was never disappointed or upset when anything like that happened but just went on to some other idea he had had in the back of his mind all the time. I don't believe he came out a single time that year that he didn't have some perfectly splendid idea, like nailing tobacco sticks onto mallets and playing croquet from horse-back—I couldn't help laughing the first time I saw a polo game, thinking about me up on Old Eagle, trying to send the blue ball through the wicket!

Tom was fifteen that summer and Roger was almost sixteen, that tall, lean kind of boy; it was hard to imagine that he could ever get fat. They never paid much attention to me unless they needed me, for something like starter in the chariot races or, when we were younger, to help make up Robin Hood's band. Roger was always Robin, of course, and Tom was Little John. I had to be Allan-a-Dale. I remember their telling me he was the only one of the band that knew how to write his name. I had to be Chingachgook, too. I forget what excuse they gave for foisting him off on me.

But unless they needed me real bad they didn't want me along and when they started out for the stable would pretend they were going to see a man about a dog or even that some animal was being bred out in the stable lot, to keep me in the house. Every Friday night before I went to sleep I used to make up my mind that I wouldn't have anything to do with them, but when Saturday morning came I'd get out and follow them, far enough behind so that they wouldn't notice, pretending I was playing something by myself. Do you remember that when you were a child there were some people you couldn't stay away from because it seemed like there wasn't any use in being anywhere else?

I went off to school when I was sixteen, to Bardstown Academy, where Mama went. Roger went to Webb. He asked me for a date the first night he got home. It was a lawn party at the Harpers'. Mrs. Harper was the kind that like to play charades and was always asking the young people why they didn't get up a play. That night they had Japanese lanterns strung between the trees, and in the back yard

Eleanor Harper was a witch, telling fortunes in a little hut made all of green boughs. But there weren't very many young people there. For some reason they didn't much like to go to the Harpers'. Maybe they were afraid Mrs. Harper would make them get up and dance the Virginia reel. I had on a blue dress that had white eyelets worked in the ruffles and I had had a big fuss with Mama before I left home. She thought that I ought to get in by eleven o'clock at the latest. But we got home by ten-thirty. Roger was the one who suggested going, said he didn't like peach ice cream and we could stop by Shorty Raymond's and get a sandwich and a Coke on the way home. I knew I ought not to go inside a place like Shorty Raymond's at that time of night, but the Negro boy brought a tray out and we had a sandwich apiece and Roger had a Coke and I had an orangeade.

The next night Esther Morrison had a party for a girl that was visiting her from Paducah. . . . I was never specially pretty when I was young, but there were two or three men wanted to marry me. I see them around town now, and I can't say I ever passed one of them on the street and felt I'd made a mistake when I didn't take him. . . . Mamie Tredwell—Mamie Reynolds she was when she came to visit Esther—was a heap prettier at seventeen than she is at forty-three. She had the prettiest skin I ever saw on anybody except a baby, and that soft, brown hair that has a natural wave in it and can't fall any way that isn't graceful. But her eyes were always too wide apart and had that tiresome look in them, and she had that habit then that she has now of starting out to tell you something and taking in the whole universe. I have to go to dinner there once or twice a year and I always dread it. The other night I was there and she was telling me about old Mr. Wainwright falling off the roof when he was trying to fix his gutter and she got off on the guttering that new tinsmith did for them—it wasn't satisfactory and they had to have Roberts and Maxwell rip it all off and put it up again. "What was I saying?" she asked me when she got to how much it cost them; money's one thing that'll always bring her up short. "I don't know," I said, "but I've already heard what Mr. Wainwright said when he hit the ground: 'Ain't it just my luck? To fall off the roof and not break but one leg!'" He's a happy old soul. I always liked him.

Mama will be eighty-three this March. She's not as independent as she was a few years ago. Breaking her hip seemed to take all the spirit out of her. She wants to be read to a lot and she's crazy to know everything that's going on. I went to the post office the other day and when I got back I told her that I hadn't passed a soul but three boys shooting craps, and didn't talk to anybody but a bullfrog that was sitting in a puddle, and all he had to say was that things had come to a pretty pass. . . . Mama says that I don't take after her people, that I'm all Fuqua.

They say a person ought to have a hobby. I always thought that was all foolishness, until last fall, when my niece, Cora, came to visit and left that mushroom book behind. It cost twenty dollars—and no wonder. The illustrations are something to look at, in beautiful colors, and some of the mushrooms have the most extraordinary shapes. Like one that's called a Bear's Head Mushroom that grows out of the trunk of a tree and has white, spiny hairs that look like a polar bear's fur hanging down, and inside is all white and soft, like marshmallow. I started hunting for that one first because Cora told me it was good to eat.

The folks in town all say that I'm going to poison myself, of course, but I don't pay any attention. In our climate there's some mushroom that you can hunt almost every day of the year. But, of course, when the earth gets steamy and hot in the spring is the best time. I start in April—you can find the sponge mushroom then —and go every day I can get a little Negro girl to sit with Mama.

Yesterday I was out in the Hickman woods, about three miles from town. There is a swampy place in those woods where things come out earlier than anywhere else. The honeysuckle vines go up to the tops of the trees. Sometimes a vine will climb out to the end of a limb and then hang down in a great spray. I had to push a lot of those sprays aside before I got in there. But I was glad I went. On a mound of earth, in that black, swampy water, a tame pear tree was in bloom. An apple tree will bend to one side or fall if you don't prop it up, and peach trees don't care which way their boughs go, but pear branches rise up like wands. Most of the blossoms hadn't unfolded yet; the petals looked like seashells. I stood under the tree and watched all those festoons of little shells floating up over my head, up, up, up into the bluest sky I've ever seen, and wished that I didn't have to go home. Mama's room always smells of camphor. You notice it after you've been out in the fresh air.

The Waterfall

Lucy Allen was sitting in the window seat in the dining room, reading "Undine," when she saw the car come through the gate and start slowly up the drive: a dark blue convertible, its top lowered; a big red-headed man was bent over the wheel.

It was three o'clock in the afternoon. Lucy had that morning returned from a two-day visit to her friend Evelyn Chase, who lived in the nearby town of Gloversville. They had gone to the movies on both Wednesday and Thursday afternoons and at the end of each matinee had gone to Grimstead's Drug Store to eat banana splits. Evelyn's sister, Margery, had been invited to a dance at the Country Club on Thursday night. They had stayed in her room to watch the long, ice-blue satin frock that her mother had just finished sewing slide over her blond head, and after she departed for the dance had lain in her bed and talked far into the night. Evelyn thought that if a boy ever wanted to kiss her she would let him do it. Lucy said that there were boys in their class at school whom she would not allow to kiss her big toe. Evelyn maintained that Lucy was in reality of the same mind as she was and only pretended to think differently. That was because Lucy was "around grown people" so much, she observed. Her own mother had said that she was surprised that Lucy wasn't queerer than she was. As for Lucy's pretense of being reluctant to be kissed, it deceived nobody and only spoiled the fun. There was no use in "talking" unless you told everything. . . . When Lucy came at noon into her own, cool, high-ceilinged brick house she had carried a book to the luncheon table and had read surreptitiously throughout the meal.

It was three o'clock now, and she was halfway through "Undine." The sun blazed on the graveled drive, the leaves on the maple trees hung furled. The cook, who was ordinarily her companion at this hour of the day, had gone to her cabin right after lunch, announcing that she had a toothache and was going to sleep it off. In their bedroom on the second floor Lucy's father and mother were asleep, too. "Time to take a nap . . . just time . . ." they had said as they rose from the table. Her father, as usual, looked abstracted. Her mother had seemed excited. One of them had uttered the name of the guest who was expected—there had evidently been a long-distance telephone call just before she arrived—but she had been busy, concealing her book under the tablecloth and had not listened to what they were saying.

She frowned and shook her long, light hair back from her face before she put her book down and went out onto the front porch. The car had halted beside the crape myrtle bush. The red-headed man sat staring at the river.

The screen door creaked as it went shut behind her. He turned his head and gazed at her calmly for a second. A delighted smile came over his face. He sprang out of the car and up the steps and, seizing her in his arms, swung her high above his head.

A thin scream burst from Lucy. Horror-struck, she compressed her lips and looked down stoically into his upturned face. His brows were shaggy and rufous. His light brown eyes were flecked with green. She shut her own eyes and did not open them until she felt herself being set down gently on the floor.

He was kneeling on the floor beside her, putting out a big hand to give her shoulder a quick pressure. His green-brown eyes darted merry glances at her. He said, "Two—weeks—ago—today—*where* do you suppose I was?"

She resisted the impulse to draw away. "I don't know," she said faintly.

"At Rumpelmeyer's!" he said.

She did not answer.

"At *Rumpelmeyer's*," he repeated. "There was a fat man sitting at *our* table. A fat man in a fez. . . . What do you suppose that old devil was eating?"

To look into his eyes long was like falling into tumbling water.

She lowered her own gaze to the porch railings. "I don't know," she said again.

He released her shoulder and, straightening himself to his full height, shook his head slowly from side to side. "A *Monte Carlo*," he said, "I'm damned if he wasn't eating a Monte Carlo! As I went past I just upended it. 'Sir,' I said, 'do you mind if I turn down this empty glass?' "

There were hurried steps in the hall. Her father and mother came tumultuously through the front door. Her father was dressed, but her mother's dark hair hung over her shoulders in two long braids and she wore only a thin green robe drawn over her nightgown. She shrieked and stood on tiptoe to throw her arms about the visitor's neck. "It's so divine you've come, Tubby," she said, "so divine. . . ." As she stepped aside to let the two men shake hands—only Tubby put his arm around Daddy's neck and hugged him, too—Sarah Allen bent on Lucy the candid, radiant smile she usually reserved for adults. "Isn't it wonderful Uncle Tubby's here?" she asked.

Lucy did not answer. The four of them entered the hall, which at this time of day was darkened for the sake of coolness. The visitor carried his head high and took long steps. It seemed that he might stride right through the hall and off the hill before her father opened the east door and they walked out onto the river gallery.

He stood and gazed at the river, glinting green through the willows, and then at the far meadow and the cornfields that stretched on to the bend in the river before he turned and gazed at Stephen Allen.

"You didn't tell me you were in the money!" he said.

Stephen Allen's lean face flushed. "Not exactly," he said.

His wife went quickly up to him and hung on his arm, swaying a little and laughing. "We're 'way above our raising!" she said.

Uncle Tubby looked at Lucy. "*That's* why she's so cold to me! An heiress, hunh?" He again bent his shaggy head over her. "*Je demande une lawleepawp!*" he uttered in a finicking tone. "You may laugh off Rumpelmeyer's but what about that *Tabac* on the Place de l'Odéon? Heavens, woman, I have witnesses! We were seen entering it practically every Thursday—when Madame Combet was at Confession. . . . I suppose next thing you'll be telling me that you don't remember *her?*"

"I don't remember her very much," Lucy muttered.

He made with his huge, outstretched hands a gesture that indi-

cated that he had heard enough. "A regular *belle dame sans merci!*"
he exclaimed.

Sarah Allen let go of her husband's arm and, slipping her arm
around Lucy's shoulder, drew her toward her. "The poor child's
been dragged around so, from pillar to post. . . . And you know,
they forget it on the boat. Really, they do."

Uncle Tubby was looking at the columns made of rose-colored
brick that supported the gallery. "Damn creditable pillars!" he said.
"And what a *pleasure*—to me, who was with you in the ships at
Mylae!—to see you provided with an establishment suited to persons of your quality. . . ." He broke off, shouting: "Pompey! You
black rascal!"

"It was Steve's rich brother," Sarah said, "gave us the house and
a hundred acres of land. Wasn't it darling of him?"

"I long to know that fellow," Uncle Tubby said. "I long to shake
him by the hand. Everybody ought to have a brother like that."

Her father laughed. "Well, you've got one now. Brother Warren
B. Zaalberg."

Uncle Tubby laughed, too, and threw his head back so sharply
that a tendril of trumpet vine was jarred from its place on the pillar.
The green spray, curving back upon itself, its first and last leaves
actually intertwined, gave Lucy for a second the impression of a
wreath set upon the coarse, clotted curls that were the exact color
and consistency of the hairs in the tail of her grandmother's buggy
horse. He *was* more the color of a horse than a man. All sorrel.
Wreaths were put upon horses' necks when they won a race. You
could imagine him winning all the races, the Derby, even. . . . He
was still laughing about Warren B. Zaalberg.

"I've given him of my blood and he's given me a modicum of
his'n. But I can't look on him as a blood brother. Still, we'll drink
to him. . . . Brother Ben Allen! Brother Warren B. Zaalberg!" He
batted his eyes and roared: *"Pompey . . . Pompey!"*

"We'll get your bags in, first," her father said, and had started
through the door when Uncle Tubby roared *"Pompey!"* again and,
pushing past him, ran through the hall and down the front steps to
where his car was parked.

"I've got to get something on," Sarah Allen said, and went into
her bedroom and shut the door. She opened it immediately to say,
"Lucy, will you tell Uncle Tubby where to go?"

"Well, *where?*" Lucy demanded.

"In the room across from you," her mother said, and shut her door.

Lucy stood in the hall and watched Uncle Tubby coming up the steps, carrying a big pigskin bag easily in each hand. Her father had disappeared down the steep flight of stairs that led to the lower floor. She could hear the refrigerator door slam and the sound of water running over the ice cubes that her father would by this time have taken out of the refrigerator. Uncle Tubby came abreast of her. She motioned to him to ascend the stairs to the third floor, where there was a little guest room, across the hall from her own bedroom. He thanked her with a low bow, even while with a wave of his hand he dismissed his imaginary companion. "Be off, sir. To the quarters!"

Lucy could see the colored man—he was not more than eighteen years old and wore a red swallow-tailed coat over a pair of pink and white striped trousers—running down the stairs. Involuntarily she pressed back against the wall while a ripple of laughter went through her. Uncle Tubby, halfway up the stairs, heard the minute sound and turned and smiled at her.

"Where'd you get him?" she asked before she realized what she was doing.

He had come to the landing. He set both bags down and grasped the brown railing with both hands. For a moment he looked as if he might spring over it and land in the hall beside her, but he only leaned far over, to say in a hoarse whisper, "In a poker game. From General Nathan Bedford Forrest."

"*General Forrest!*" she said scornfully. "He don't ever play no cards."

He leaned still farther over, to look through the open door to where beyond the river, on the white highway, the cars kept spinning all day long.

"You never saw him in Paris?" he said. In the *spring.* . . . You'd be *surprised!*"

Her mother came out of her room, in blue jeans, but with her face made up and her hair freshly braided. "Don't you want to go downstairs and help Daddy?" she asked.

"No, I don't," Lucy said, and walked out on the gallery and sat down in the swing. The dachshund who slept there in a nest of pillows groaned softly and rolled over on his back, all four paws extended in the air. She bent and laid her face against his warm muzzle, and said in the high, thin tone both she and her mother used when addressing him, "Borcke . . . Borcke . . . *Borcke Dog!*" thinking how, when she got her pony and rode him along the lanes, he could run beside them. . . . But they couldn't buy the pony till another check came in, Daddy said. . . . If they bought it then. . . . *Couldn't you wait till next summer? You've got Borcke and the cats. Couldn't you just wait till next summer? You'll be nine years old then. . . . Yes, if I'm not dead with all y'all's goings-on. . . .*

Her father came through the door, holding a tray full of bottles and glasses. Her mother came after him, bearing a bowl full of ice cubes. "Lucy," she said crisply, "will you run downstairs and get me some limes—*three limes*—out of the refrigerator?"

When Lucy came back with the limes Sarah was lying in the hammock and Uncle Tubby was sitting in the swing beside Borcke, a glass in his hand. He had taken off his coat. His shirt, which was almost the color of his hair, was open at the throat. He said to her father, "Where're you operating now?"

Her father smiled absently and looked off over the fields for a second before he answered. "I'm still in the Wilderness. . . . Grant has just made his first move by the left flank. Toward Spotsylvania."

"Then Longstreet has just rolled up his left flank," Uncle Tubby said. "If Lee hadn't waited to re-form his troops he might have routed Grant. I make something of that in the poem, you remember."

"I don't know . . ." Stephen Allen said. "There weren't sufficient reserves, as a matter of fact. The half of Grant's army that he had left was as big as Lee's whole army. . . ."

Sarah Allen, swaying forward in the hammock, fixed the visitor's face with her dark eyes. "But where would *If It Takes All Summer* be if Lee had won? . . . Honest, Tubby, did they really pay you sixty thousand dollars for that poem?"

"Did it really take you all summer to write it?" Lucy asked, and bit her lip as she realized that she was speaking at the same time as her mother.

Sarah clapped her hand over her mouth. Lines in her cheek went taut, then smoothed out again as she let her hand fall into her lap. "It took him all winter, too," she said severely. "You don't just dash off a poem of five thousand lines, Lucy. . . . Tubby, how much *was* your take?"

"It was the damnedest thing you ever heard of," Tubby said. "You know they'd already paid twenty thousand for the title?"

"Yes," Sarah said, "we read that in the *Times*."

"It was just after I'd got the *NOW* job," Tubby said, "but I had four weeks to kill. Wimscott has been out there three years, you know. He'd been so darned nice about the whole thing, I thought this was a good time to make him a visit. . . . Of course, after I got there he had to take me around some. . . ."

"So you met all the producers?"

"Hell, no. I met Zaalberg." He threw his head back and emitted his raucous laugh. "But I was drunk as a coot. Have to take Wimsy's word for what happened."

"Well, what *did* happen?"

"Zaalberg was coming to dinner. But I didn't have any illusions about that. I knew they'd just bought the title because they were scared to leave any Civil War stuff lying around loose, after *Gone With the Wind*. So I didn't think anything about Zaalberg. We were going on to some gambling place after dinner—Wimscott has to lose a thousand dollars every night or so or he gets restless. But Zaalberg got to brooding and Wimsy didn't seem to like to disturb him. We just sat in the patio while Zaalberg went on brooding. Seems he's been low lately, on account of *Gone*. It *is* hard on the fellow. . . ."

"Simply damnable," Sarah said. "I don't see how he stands it."

Uncle Tubby made a sudden movement. Lucy felt that if he had got out of the swing he would have caught her mother up and swung her high over his head, the way he had swung her; but he sank back, saying only, "Oh, *you* . . . ! Want to hear what really happened?"

"That's exactly what I want to hear," Sarah said.

"Well, there was a pool in the patio. I went to sleep on the springboard. Seems I kept diving in, trying to sober up, but couldn't make it. Zaalberg kept on brooding over how much money MGM was making and finally Wimsy told him he was the feeb of the world, had a property worth just as much as *Gone* all the time and didn't know it. . . . Zaalberg comes out of his trance enough to ask, 'Where?' and Wimscott—so he *says*—sat down and read him *If It Takes*. . . . And there I was, snoring away on the springboard and didn't hear a word of it!"

"*Figuerez-vous!*" Sarah said. "I don't suppose Zaalberg did, either."

"He called me up at ten o'clock the next morning! Says, 'Is this

Mr. Madden, the poet?' 'Yes,' I says. 'Mr. Madden,' says he, 'I very much admire your long poem, *If It Takes All Summer*. I particularly admire the fiftieth stanza. . . .' " He had been looking at Sarah as he spoke but his gaze went now to Stephen Allen. "The *fiftieth*," he said.

Stephen Allen's head tilted slowly to one side. "Well, I'm damned," he said. "That's the best stanza."

"That was what he told me. Then he said that their Mr. Forman would like to talk to my agent sometime during the week and when I said I didn't have an agent he laughed and said that in that case Mr. Forman would like to talk to me sometime during the day and was six o'clock all right? And I said it was. And Forman came around at six. . . . In addition to the twenty thousand they'd already paid for the title they paid another sixty thousand."

"Eighty thousand dollars for a poem," Stephen Allen said. "Yea, Bo! That calls for a drink." He rose and went over to the table where he had set the tray.

"*Don't* put any sugar in mine," his wife said. "My God, Tubby! I just simply can't take it all in. . . . Then you went on to India and interviewed the Mahatma. . . . What made you come back to Paris so soon?"

"There was a damsel there in distress," Uncle Tubby said. He glanced at Lucy and then back at her mother. "All General Forrest's fault. You know how chivalrous he is. Nothing would do him but we must go over and help her out."

"Was it a damsel we know?" Sarah asked.

"Sure," he said. "Isabel."

"Isabel . . . ?"

"Isabel Reardon."

"I don't believe I know her," Sarah said.

"Oh, yes, you do. She thinks Steve is the greatest poet ever lived. . . . Isabel Shaw she was."

"Isabel Shaw!" Sarah said. "The one who wrote 'The Water Bearer'? Oh, come, Tubby!"

"She's pretty good," Tubby said, "at least she used to be. She hasn't written anything for a long time now."

"I suppose she has an unsympathetic husband . . ." Sarah said.

"Well, it never was anything but watered-down Millay."

"Oh, I don't know," Stephen Allen said, "more like Katherine Philips."

There was a silence till Sarah said, "Well, who is she married to now?"

"Same person. Dan Reardon."

"Dan Reardon!" Sarah said. "We went to a party there once. The bar was full of tuberoses. There was a Papal countess made passes at Steve. . . . And three or four of the Guinness girls."

"I thought they were dead," Stephen Allen said.

"The Guinness girls?"

"No. Isabel and Dan Reardon."

"They were in the hospital for months. Isabel had to learn to walk all over again."

"I remember," Sarah Allen said, "they'd been at the Weavers' and they all got drunk and drove up that mountain and it's a one-way road and they met a car. . . . Weren't there a lot of other people with them?"

"Two. A movie actor and his girl. They were both killed. . . . Isabel and Dan lay out in the woods all night. . . ."

"What's *he* like, really?" Sarah asked. "I can't remember him that night, except just walking around and smiling at people. I suppose he was dreadfully drunk. I do remember now! He sat down in an old lady's lap. Steve was frightfully annoyed. She was a cousin of the Duc de Guise and Steve was having a heavy conversation with her about her great-uncle who was over here as an observer during the war. . . ."

"The Civil War, I take it?" Tubby said.

She smiled at him. "*Your* war," she said.

"*Touché!*" Tubby said. "Well, he doesn't drink now."

"What's the matter? Can't he? I knew a man in Paris once had a silver plate in his head and every time he took a drink he . . ."

"I wouldn't know what's the matter with Dan Reardon," Tubby said, "I can't figure him. . . ."

"What does he do that's so funny?" Sarah asked.

Tubby shook his head. "Art Pearce knew him at Harvard. Says he's been a different fellow ever since he got hit on the head in that wreck. . . ."

"Like Hans's father, in *The Silver Skates*," Lucy said. "They thought he was loony and then they operated on him and he had just as much sense as anybody else, and Hans and his sister. . . ."

"They'll probably have to lock him up," Mama said, and laughed. "Isabel can latch on to somebody else then."

Uncle Tubby looked at Mama thoughtfully. "That's what I tell her," he said, "but life is fell strange, you know. There are complications."

"What kind of complications?"

"Well, we needn't go into them now." He glanced at Lucy again. "How's Lady Souse?" he asked. "How's Stutts Watts, the poet?"

Lucy smothered a yawn. "I don't know," she said, "I don't know anything about those old people," and it was true that they were now nothing to her but names, imaginary companions, who, her father and mother told her, had traveled all over Europe with them. But he had been five years old then. Uncle Tubby was thirty-two and still had "that black rascal Pompey" and General Forrest. Perhaps it took boys longer to grow up than girls.

She leaned back in her deep chair and thought of all the far places Uncle Tubby had been in. To Hollywood, to see about his long poem that was being made into a movie, and after that to India, to interview the Mahatma Gandhi for a magazine he worked on called *NOW*, and then from India he had gone to Paris. In an airplane.

He was talking now about what he and she had done in Paris. Every morning, he said, he had walked with her and her nurse, Madame Combet, to the Gardens. On their way they had stopped at the church of Saint Sulpice for Mass. He said that he still had callouses on his knees—he would show them to her as soon as he got into shorts—from kneeling on those cold, stone floors. He was surprised when she said that she did not remember Monsieur l'Abbé. He well remembered being presented to that worthy by Lucy herself, at the corner of Férou and Vaugirard, right under the windows, it happened, of Monsieur l'Abbé's parishioner, Monsieur Hemingway. After that, under Lucy's direction, he had saved all his stamps for Monsieur l'Abbé—until Lucy bestowed her affections elsewhere, on one Ramon, the patron's son, after which he had ceased saving stamps for Monsieur l'Abbé and had even given him the cut direct when they met in the formerly sacred purlieus.

"The purlieus" were the streets around the church of Saint Sulpice. Every time he said "Saint Sulpice" it was as if a great bell started tolling somewhere and she was moving, with many other people, into a vast, chill place where candlelight flickered on stone. But she could not really remember the church, or even call Madame Combet to mind, though she had been told often how much the old lady had loved her and there was in her room at this moment a little New Testament in French, with a bookmark, a picture showing Jesus on one end of a crosscut saw, a little child on the other, with the motto: "*Tout est facile quand Jésus aide*," that Madame Combet had said she must keep always. She would look at it sometimes and say to herself: "Madame Combet . . . Madame Combet . . ." but nothing came back, except running fast on the street to keep hold of a warm, dry hand, or stopping sometimes beside something black that was higher than her head, while a hand—paper-white now— disappeared into a black bag and came up holding something—the stamps, probably, for Monsieur l'Abbé. She thought all at once that if it had been winter and Uncle Tubby wearing a heavy woolen suit and she sitting beside him on a sofa she might have remembered him better. For she had sat on a sofa, in front of a fire, close up against somebody who bent over her, to read from a book that lay open on her knee:

> "So now you know why Henry sleeps
> And why his mourning mother weeps
> And why his weeping mother mourns
> He was not kind to unicorns. . . ."

A unicorn was an animal you read about in books, white, usually with a horn in the middle of its forehead. . . . A little horse. . . . If they would only quit talking—and drinking, for the more they drank, the more they talked—there would still be time to drive out to Mr. Warfleet's and look at the pony that he had said would do so nicely for her. . . . *You got only one child? Then I'd advise against a Shetland. Rather bite than eat. . . . Now this pony is part Morgan and part Arabian. See the deer look to her head?"*

Her father was trying to catch her eye. He wanted her to go downstairs and get some more ice. She stared past him. He sighed and fished three slim cubes out of the water and dropped them into Uncle Tubby's third drink. Uncle Tubby pretended that Pompey had handed it to him and with a "Thank you, my lad," rose and began pacing up and down the gallery, talking on and on about people they had known in Paris.

. . . Thirteen hands high. Brown, with white spots. A star on the forehead, a white stocking and one white splotch on the barrel. The mane was half white, half brown, but the tail . . . the tail was pure white and rippled. . . .

She opened her mouth too suddenly. Air, rushing into her wind-pipe, made her gulp. Her mother started and set her glass down on the floor beside the hammock. "Lucy," she said vaguely, "Lucy, why don't you go and comb your hair?"

"*You've* got to dress from the skin out," Lucy said.

Her mother looked down at her jeans-clad legs. "Tubby," she said, "how would you like to drive out in the country and look at a pony? We can't buy it yet," she added hastily, "but we *could* just look at it."

Uncle Tubby brought up short in his pacing. "What's the matter with it here?" he said. "Thish admirable porch!" He looked about him, at the far fields and then at her father's and mother's flushed faces, and suddenly let his hand drop on her father's shoulder. "Why, it's as good as Cassis!" he said.

It was at Cassis that Uncle Tubby had written the long poem that was going to be made into a movie. The poem was in a black book, on the top shelf by Daddy's desk; gilt letters went in a column straight up one side of it: *If It Takes All Summer.* Her father had read out loud from the letter that said Uncle Tubby was going to get eighty thousand dollars for the poem. "That's a hell of a lot of money for a poem," he had said. Her mother had frowned and looked out of the window. "Do you think he can take it?" she asked. "He can take it if anybody can," her father said, but he was frowning when he got up from his desk. . . .

They were talking now about a picnic they had gone to at Cassis. It had lasted three days. The man who made the bouillabaisse sang a different opera every day. Her father and Uncle Tubby had recited their own poems, and an old gentleman named Monsieur l'Ermite had recited Racine. He had walked over the mountains, bringing seven different vintages of wine in a hamper. Four of his hounds had come with him. She had been in Paris, then, with her nurse, but when they talked about how, after supper, they would go out in the bay and, wearing special glasses, dive to look at the flowers that grew on the bottom of the sea, she could see the flowers, too: pink and blue and purple, star-shaped, some of them, others round, like little Banksia roses.

The town clock struck four. It was coming across all those fields and the water that made the sound so mellow. She got up and walked to the banister. Patterson's barn, which all afternoon had glowed silver in the sun, turned lavender as a ragged cloud drifted over it.

The sumac bushes that fringed the lawn were shaking. Two heads appeared, surrounded by foliage of a lighter green than the sumac leaves.

"Mr. MacDonogh has got Mr. Lancaster to help him," she said.

Uncle Tubby stopped pacing and came and stood beside her, looking down at the two men who walked slowly across the lawn, each bearing on his back a great, rope-tied bundle of fresh-cut boughs.

"What are they going to do with those branches?" he asked.

"It's for the bush arbor meeting," she told him.

Her father had come over and was standing beside them. "The Holy Roller meeting," he said, "starts tonight."

Uncle Tubby's glass swung out in an arc so wide that a few bright drops fell in the wake of the men passing just then beneath the gallery. "Why do these holy men gather in your back yard?" he asked. "Is it your fame—or your impiety—that attracts them?"

"They set fire to Judge Rives's woods last summer," Stephen said. "Had to find a new place. . . . You better attend, Tubby. You might get converted."

Lucy stared at her father. His eyes were clear and as yet no little veins showed in his lean cheeks. It was when he spoke that you realized that he had had three Tom Collinses since lunchtime. He was leaning over the rail, shouting, as if Mr. MacDonogh were a mile away and not right there under the porch. "Better hurry! You won't get 'em up in time."

One of the men gave no sign that he had heard. The other turned up a thin face, encircled by a ragged auburn beard. He laughed. "Yes, sir," he said, and laughed again, revealing in the wider rictus sharp, stunted teeth that might have been a child's. "You better come on and help us," he added, and, ducking as if he were afraid of what the sally might bring forth, followed his companion around the corner of the house.

"That's Mr. MacDonogh," Lucy said. "He don't eat mutton . . . or lamb."

Uncle Tubby was looking at her father. "She's kidding me."

Stephen Allen shook his head. "*Agnus Dei . . . qui tollis peccata mundi.* . . . His life is one long Eucharist."

"Aren't any of the children saved except Ruby," Lucy said, "but Mr. and Mrs. MacDonogh are . . ."

"And Sanctified," her mother said from the hammock.

Lucy turned around. Her voice sounded shrill in her own ears after its long disuse. "That's what *you* think! Mrs. MacDonogh's Sanctified, but Mr. MacDonogh isn't."

Sarah Allen sat up in the hammock. One of her dark braids had slipped from its pins and hung rakishly over her shoulder. She held her hairpins in her mouth and spoke through them quickly. "Lucy, Mr. MacDonogh is a great deal more religious than Mrs. MacDonogh. . . . Mrs. MacDonogh chews tobacco." She hesitated a moment and added, "And she had a child before she was married."

"She's seen Jesus flying through the air on wings!" Lucy said.

Her father and mother were looking at each other. Uncle Tubby's eyes were bright on her face. "How do you know, Lucy?" he asked.

"Ruby told me, and so did Mary Magdalene."

The hammock creaked as her mother lay back among the pillows. "If she said she saw Jesus flying through the air on wings, she saw him, as far as I'm concerned," she said. "She wouldn't steal a pin."

Uncle Tubby laughed. "Why should she go around stealing pins?"

Sarah Allen turned her head and looked at him reflectively. "I expect they're hard put to it to find a safety pin sometimes. With all those babies."

"Who's the other fellow?" Madden asked, looking at her husband.

"Mr. Lancaster. He's quite a worldly fellow. An agnostic, in fact."

"But he's got a magnificent tenor voice," Sarah said.

"Do you go to the meetings?" Uncle Tubby asked Lucy.

"I am this time." She looked at her mother, who just then extended an empty glass to her husband. "That's your third drink," she said. "If you take three drinks you can't drive. Can she, Daddy?"

But her father was looking past her into the hall.

"Somebody's coming," he said.

"Oh, God!" Sarah said. She got up hastily out of the hammock and, standing on one foot, shook down first one and then the other pant leg. "Go peep and see who it is," she said to Lucy.

Lucy tiptoed through the hall and, sliding behind the half-open door, peered out onto the circular driveway. A car had been parked on the other side of the lilac bush. Two women were coming up the brick walk. A young woman wore a green flowered print dress and a big hat and walked slowly, supporting a smaller, older woman, dressed all in gray. Lucy ran back to the porch.

"It's club women," she said.

Stephen Allen picked up a tray from the table and, beckoning to Madden, silently retreated through the hall and down the back stairs. Sarah, too, ran through the hall. Lucy was alone on the porch. She heard quick footsteps and then the sound of a dresser opening. Her mother would be putting on fresh lipstick or perhaps changing from the jeans to a dress. But she couldn't do anything about the way she smelled. She looked down at the skirt of her dark blue gingham. There was a grass stain on the hem. She had wanted to change her dress right after lunch, but her mother had told her to wait until they went out to Mr. Warfleet's. If these ladies stayed a long time it would be too late to go to Mr. Warfleet's. . . .

The knocker sounded. Lucy advanced slowly to the door. Her mother was ushering two ladies into the hall. She hadn't changed to a dress, after all, and she couldn't have had time to braid her hair, either, but it was pinned up neatly and her sun-burned skin glowed smooth through fresh make-up.

The young lady had eyes as dark as Mama's. The eye shadow she used made her lids shine. She looked about the square hall, with the Confederate flag draped over the mirror, and then at the river and the fields framed in the doorway. "I love this house," she said. "Miss Grace, did you know that Jim and I almost bought this house?"

The old lady was smiling at Lucy. Sarah drew Lucy forward. The gin smell rose sharply above the mingled fresh odors of power and the rose perfume Sarah had brought from France. She ought not to use that when she's drinking, Lucy thought, and was about to curtsey—disregarding her mother's commands, she did it only on impulse—when the young lady put out a hand and gave her a friendly jab on the shoulder. Lucy arrested the bending of her knee and, muttering "How-do?" slipped ahead of them into the parlor and seated herself on the haircloth-covered sofa that occupied the center of the room, then, as they entered, was about to get to her feet again when she realized that her mother, sitting forward on the chair, her hands clasped between her denim-clad legs, was giving her whole attention to the young lady, Mrs. Eglinton.

". . . stopped the car there on the other side of the river. 'It's up to you,' Jim said. He can make up his mind just like that. . . ." Diamonds to the size of your thumb were clustered on Mrs. Eglinton's ring finger; her wedding ring was platinum, inset with diamonds. "I said, 'Jim, you just bring me out here to torture me.' . . .

No *place* to put another bedroom. . . . Without spoiling it, I mean. And then Daddy gave us that lot in Englewood. . . ." Her cheeks were as softly grained as rose petals. Her hat was of dark brown straw, looped with narrow black velvet ribbon. In the delicate gloom of its brim her face took on a flowery pallor. Her lips opened wider until her whole face swayed at you, like a flower on its stalk. "I *told* Daddy he did it just for meanness. . . ."

". . . bathrooms, either," Sarah said. "That one downstairs, they were using it for a hen house. A hen roost going up to it from outside and a row of nests along the way. A setting of eggs in one of them. . . ."

"Did you put one on this floor?"

"Eggs? . . . Oh! Bathrooms? No, you always have to go upstairs or downstairs when you want to go to the bathroom. It's dreadful. . . ." She was looking at the old lady. "You're Mrs. *Merritt*," she said. "You live in the house with the iron balconies."

The old lady's laugh ran through the room like a breeze. "They've fallen to ruin. I told Tom the other day that we ought to rip them off."

Her hair had a deep, soft wave in it and shone like silver. Her skin was as fine as tissue paper that somebody had squeezed into a ball and then smoothed out again. She sat down slowly in the red armchair. There were long ruffles sewed to the sides of her gray voile dress. One of them fell to the floor. She lifted it and folded it carefully across her knee. "Outmoded elegance," she said, "I don't know why people in Gloversville had all that ironwork shipped up here from New Orleans. It served no purpose whatsoever."

The young lady, Mrs. Eglinton, still stood, looking first at the yellow curtains and then at the white mantel, whose wide shelf and fluted columns had been carved, Lucy knew, "by slave labor." She saw Lucy looking at her and winked. All the time she was talking she stood a little way off and looked at herself and every now and then she realized that you might not like what she was saying; it was then that she turned her prettiness off so you would have a chance to see what she was really like. Her hips were as trim as a quail's under the green silk as she crossed the room to stand before a picture that hung on the west wall. Lucy turned her head and stared, too. There was something in the center of the canvas that was intended, she knew, for a patchwork quilt. A figure lay upon it, arms and legs wide spread, while around it other figures revolved:

Daddy, in a big straw hat, mowing the lawn, she and Wigwam, the dog she had had before he was run over, skipping in front of him, Electra, the cook they had had before Jenny, standing, in a blue dress, before the block rolling out biscuits, a young poet swimming in the river, which, in the picture, was blue and not muddy, the way it was at this time of the year, her hens, Red Lily and Leaf Flower, with the red rooster Mammy had given her, the pony that she had had only one night—he bit her leg so badly that they had to take him back to the man they had bought him from—some visitor going down the brick walk, with his wife, and she herself and the four MacDonogh children crouched beside one of the columns of the gallery. She wondered whether Mrs. Eglinton would know that the rose-colored blob there beside the column was Lucy Allen. She hadn't recognized herself till they told her who it was, but ever since she had liked to come in here from time to time and seem to see herself walking about in the picture.

Sarah had risen to stand beside the guest. "It's called 'Life at Benfolly,' " she said.

The old lady laughed. "It looks like a merry-go-round."

"That's what it's intended for," Sarah said.

Mrs. Eglinton winked at her. "Did you paint it?"

"Heavens, no! It's a Biala. She visited here one summer. I suppose that's the way life here impressed her. It *was* a hectic summer. . . ." She sketched a circle in the air with a thin, nervous hand.

"Do you know Melvin Archambault?" Mrs. Eglinton asked.

Sarah shook her head.

"He's from Chicago," Mrs. Eglinton said, "but he had a show last year at Palm Beach. The most livid greens! Jim says, 'Louise, you can't possibly like that stuff,' but I said, 'Jim, I really do. . . .' We bought one watercolor. . . . Miss Grace, I'm going to hang it in that little place between the dining room and the living room. . . . Have you ever made any talks on art?"

"No," Sarah said, "I don't know anything about it."

"She's always painting, though," Lucy said, "but they aren't any good, and she has to tear 'em up."

The old lady smiled at her, folding her hands. They were swollen at the knuckles, like Mammy's. "When I was twelve years old I used to come out here to take china-painting lessons from Miss Clara Swanton. . . . Sarah, does this room still sway when you get enough people dancing in it?"

"We haven't done much dancing," Sarah said. "Really, we don't have much company."

"One night we danced so hard that old Mr. Swanton made us stop," Mrs. Merritt said. "Around four o'clock in the morning, I must say, in justice to him. And the next day he had those iron bars driven through the walls. He said the house might last then till Belle got married. . . . But poor Belle. . . ."

"She was the one went crazy, wasn't she?" Mrs. Eglinton asked. "But, Miss Grace, I've always heard that she was so attractive."

"All the Swanton girls were attractive," Mrs. Merritt said. ". . . Sarah, how does your grandmother like your house?"

"She never has seen it," Sarah said. "She stays out there and sometimes six weeks goes by and she doesn't see a white face." She laughed. "But she sent one of her niggers over here the other day, with an old bed she was giving me, and when he got back she said, 'Well, Morris, how do you like Miss Sally's house?' and he says, 'Miss Sally, I sure do hate to think of little Miss Sally living in a place like that.' "

"Why, it's a perfectly beautiful house!" Mrs. Eglinton said.

"I know, but he didn't look at the house, just saw how poor the land is. The hogs have rooted the foundation out from under Ma's house, but he never has noticed that. . . ."

"It's the roof's the worst," Lucy said. "She has to put spittoons on the stairs to catch the rain."

"I haven't been out there in years," Mrs. Merritt said. ". . . Twenty years. . . ." She straightened her shoulders and looked first at Mrs. Eglinton and then at Sarah. "Sarah, Louise Eglinton here is just as smart as she can be. . . ."

"It's modern poetry this year," Mrs. Eglinton said. "We had T. S. Eliot the last meeting in April. . . ." Her beautiful eyes rolled sidewise in her head. "You ought to hear me read 'Sweeney Agonistes'! . . . They want me to read Mr. Allen for the first meeting in the fall. But I said, 'Y'all are crazy,' I said. 'The man's right out there on the hill. I'm going to make him come in and read them himself. . . . The first meeting is in September. Will the seventeenth be all right?"

"Steve's just up to his ears," Sarah said, moving her shoulders nervously.

"Well, he can spare one little old afternoon," Mrs. Eglinton said. "Do either of you play Contract? . . . There are eight of us. Meet

Friday night. But Marie Evans has got to go to Birmingham to live. . . ."

". . . You wouldn't play with me . . ." Sarah said. "I tell you now he's not going to do it! He's one of the meanest white men ever lived."

Mrs. Eglinton's flower lips opened. She swayed forward on her green stalk. "Let me ask him."

Sarah's eyes dodged aside, like somebody coming around the corner of the house on something they mustn't look at. She drove them back to the lady's face. "He's in Nashville," she said. "I'll make him write you a letter. As soon as he gets back I'll make him write you a letter."

Mrs. Eglinton winked bravely. "Or call me up," she said. "Tell him I'd at least like to hear his voice on the phone."

Mrs. Merritt stood up in a flutter of voile. "Louise, I told Tom I'd be back by four o'clock." Sarah and Lucy both stood up. Mrs. Merritt laid her hand on Lucy's shoulder. "This child isn't a Fayerlee, and she doesn't look like Professor Maury, either. Is she like her father's people?"

"She's got his coloring," Sarah said, "but not his features, or mine, either, thank Heaven. She's sort of a changeling. Aren't you, darling?" Her hand, too, rested on Lucy's shoulder. Lucy could feel the fingers trembling.

They were in the hall. Through the door which had been flung wide open when they came in you could see the willow tree. Under its drooping boughs Daddy and Uncle Tubby stood facing each other. Uncle Tubby had taken off his coat; his shirt sleeves were rolled up; he held a glass in his hand. Daddy still had on his checked shirt and those old blue fisherman's pants that he had brought from Concarneau and on his bare feet sandals that were held on by two crossed leather thongs. The fisherman's pants had two big patches on them that Lucy had never noticed before.

He heard them coming and turned so that his back was toward them. Uncle Tubby glanced up at the porch and went on talking. He was asking Daddy something. Little points suddenly showed in his eyes, he thrust his face closer to Daddy's. Daddy's back stayed stiff and still. Lucy knew what his eyes would be like if you were around there where you could see into them, the fair brows drawn straight across and the eyes a cold blue, like a pond frozen over in the night.

Uncle Tubby looked at Mrs. Eglinton and bowed as the ladies went past, but Daddy didn't turn around or make any sign. They were past them and at the lilac bush. Mrs. Eglinton helped Mrs. Merritt into the car and then got in herself. She put on fawn-colored gloves. Her face shone pink as a camellia as she tossed her head back under the big hat. Her hands took hold of the wheel. The car started moving. Mrs. Merritt sat hunched in the seat, looking straight ahead until it started, then she straightened up and smiled and waved her hand.

Sarah took two steps beside the car. "Goodbye . . . Goodbye . . . Miss Grace, I'm so glad y'all came."

They stood there, watching, until the car had passed through the gate and was headed back toward town, then Mama drew a deep breath and started up the brick walk.

Lucy followed her. "You told a lie," she said.

Mama didn't answer. She went on around the corner of the house. Daddy and Uncle Tubby were on the lower gallery, Daddy sitting on the chicken feed box, Uncle Tubby standing in front of him, talking. Mama stood there and looked at them and then she fell down on her back on the ground and kicked her legs in the air.

"My God!" she said.

Daddy sat where he was on the feed box, but Uncle Tubby came and stood over her. "That was quite a boner we pulled, wasn't it?" he asked.

Mama stopped kicking and sat up. She put her hands up to her face, first, and then she clasped her stomach in, tight. "I make the supreme sacrifice," she said, "and you two louts won't even stay out of sight!"

Daddy looked sulky, the way he always did when anybody said there was anything wrong with him. "They thought I was Mr. Mac-Donogh," he said. "That was why I didn't turn around."

"Mr. MacDonogh wouldn't be caught dead in those pants!" Mama shrieked.

Uncle Tubby was looking at Mama. "Did you know those ladies?" he asked.

"Oh God," Mama said, "I don't know them but I know who they are. And they know who I am. . . ."

"Who are you?" Uncle Tubby asked.

"I'm Professor Maury's daughter fallen among thieves," she said. "Oh God, you louts!"

"She had to go to school with the boys. That's what makes her so peculiar," Lucy said, and was afraid Mama would be angry, but Mama said only, "One of the things . . ." and looked at Daddy. "I didn't care about that Lassiter girl, but Mrs. Merritt is a friend of my mother's. . . ."

Daddy still looked sulky. "Old bitches" he said, "I'm not going to have them hounding me."

"Mrs. Merritt is not a bitch," Mama said. "She's a lovely lady of the old school."

"Was Mrs. Lassiter the one who served her face up to you on a platter?" Uncle Tubby asked. "I thought she had a lot of stuff."

"She was born a Lassiter. Married Jim Eglinton. All those Lassiter girls are perfectly beautiful," Mama said. She looked at Daddy. "She's going to interpret your works for the dilettante club—unless you do it yourself."

"Why don't you do it?" Uncle Tubby asked. "Tell 'em what's what."

"Did you tell her to go jump in the river?" Daddy asked.

"I told her a lie. Told her you were in Nashville." She clasped her stomach again. "My God! Sometimes I feel like we're criminals in hiding. Having to skulk through town, scared all the time we'll run into somebody we know. . . ."

"You *have* committed a crime," Uncle Tubby said. "Every time Steve sits down at his desk he challenges the existing order."

Daddy grinned. "They'd ride *you* out of town on a rail," he said, "if they knew that you didn't believe in the existence of private property."

"I haven't got any immediate designs on their property," Uncle Tubby said. "What do they think of you?"

"They think we're nuts," Lucy said, and was a little taken aback to hear her voice sound so loud and clear.

"They think we're nudists!" Mama said. "When we bought the place word went around that we were going to found a nudist camp. . . . Poor things! I reckon they hoped we would."

"Had you been guilty of any indecent exposures?" Uncle Tubby asked.

"Not any more than usual. . . . Well, those sandals of Steve's. I heard that Miss Minnie Wellfleet doesn't like them."

"He wears them to town," Lucy said.

"Whereas I go dowdy," Mama said, "and he can't get it into his head where the center of town is. Made a U-turn right by the bank the other day, with Mr. Tom Davis standing there looking at him."

"Who's Mr. Tom Davis?"

You would have thought from the way Mama looked at Uncle Tubby that he was the one she was angry with. She said in a rasping voice, "He's a man that the Yankee newspapers are always writing up for being a benefactor of the Southern farmer. . . ."

"He's the president of the bank," Daddy said. He walked over and handed her a cigarette. He was still not in a good humor but he was afraid she would say something else about Yankees. She took it without thanking him and stood, holding it in her hand and looking off over the river. "He's the great-grandson of our old slave trader," she said.

Uncle Tubby slapped his thigh. "Gad, that's symbolic!"

"It's going to be mighty symbolic when we have to try to borrow money from him," Mama said.

"Well, we've still got four hundred of the advance left," Daddy said. "Let's cross that bridge when we get to it."

Lucy went over and stood beside Mama. "Shall I wear my blue linen?" she asked.

Mama started. "What?" she said. Lucy thought that she was talking to her and repeated, "Shall I wear my blue linen?" but Mama was looking past her at Uncle Tubby. "*What* did you say?" she asked again.

Uncle Tubby laughed and looked across the river to the long white road. "I said the Reardons ought to be rolling in pretty soon."

"The *Reardons?*" Mama said.

Uncle Tubby looked at her and then he looked away quickly. "The Daniel B. Reardons," he said, "of New York and Paris and the Villa Marthe. They were visiting in the neighborhood, so I told 'em to come down here. I thought you wouldn't mind. . . . As long as they were this near. . . ."

"No," Mama said, "of course not. . . ." She looked as if she were about to say something else but Daddy went over and took hold of her arm. "If you're going out to Warfleet's you'd better start," he said. "It's nearly five o'clock."

Mama looked at him. "*Warfleet's?*" she said.

Lucy felt the bottom drop out of her stomach. She cried out, "You said you'd go this afternoon. To look at the pony. You said . . ." but Mama was walking toward the house.

Daddy looked after her and then he looked at Uncle Tubby. "Tubby, you want a drink?" he asked.

"I don't mind," Uncle Tubby said, and they, too, went toward the house.

Lucy stood there and looked down at the river. You could see the near bank only through the gaps in the willows but on the other bank, where it overflowed every year into Patterson's bottoms, there was a long stretch where there weren't any trees, just a shelf of yellow, blistered mud. Daddy said that copperheads sunned themselves there on the flat rocks. . . . She had known all along (she always knew when they weren't going to do what they had said they would do), she had known when Uncle Tubby stepped out of his car that they would forget all about the pony, but all afternoon, sitting up there on the gallery, listening to them drinking and talking, she had kept hoping. It was no use now.

She walked slowly over the grass and, crossing the porch, stepped into the kitchen. Uncle Tubby must be drinking all by himself upstairs, for Daddy was in there, with Mama. He was leaning against the sink. She stood in the middle of the floor, looking as wild as a buck.

As Lucy came in she put her hand to her forehead. "I could take some of that chicken and cream it," she said. "And Mrs. Mac-Donogh would lend me some tomatoes. . . ."

"And there's plenty of gin," Daddy said. He laughed. "Old Tubby is sure in fine spirits."

"He makes me nervous with all that schizoid talk," Mama said.

"He's not any worse than you are, talking for Borcke," Lucy said. "Half the time that isn't what he thinks, either."

Mama glanced at her absent-mindedly. "That's different, Lucy," she said. ". . . I wish he wouldn't get fat."

"He's not fat," Daddy said.

"He's lost that *quattrocento* look. One trouble with the fleshpots is they always make people fleshy. . . . Come on, honey!"

"What do you want?" Daddy asked.

"We've got to get everything out of Tubby's room and the beds all changed before they come."

Daddy looked stubborn. "I don't see any point in that."

Mama flipped her cigarette, still burning, into the open garbage can, where, for a second, it hissed softly against a fresh-cut orange peel.

"I can't put Isabel and her husband in the same room," she said.

"Why not?"

Mama shut her eyes for a second, the way you do when you think somebody else is the biggest fool in the world. "Honey, I couldn't do that to Tubby."

"Tubby!" Daddy said. "What in the hell has he got to do with it?"

Mama batted her eyes again. "Darling, didn't you hear what he said about that damsel in distress?"

"You mean that Isabel is the damsel?"

"Who else?"

"Well, suppose he is having a flirtation with Isabel Shaw? That doesn't mean that he's got to sleep in the same room with her."

"It's none of my business, of course," Mama said.

"It certainly isn't."

"That's why I'm putting everybody in separate rooms," Mama said.

"Without any consideration of how much trouble it makes."

Mama screwed her face up. "Don't worry me!" she said. "For God's sake, don't worry me now. . . . *Chicken* . . . and *salad* . . . and we *could* have some black-bean soup. . . ."

"Where's Jenny?"

"Down in her house. With a toothache. . . . Wouldn't you know that he'd go for a man-eating tigress?"

"She's probably not any worse than any other lady poet," Daddy said.

"Good God!" Mama said. "Why, the sands are white with bones!" Her eyes suddenly grew very bright. "And she thinks *you're* the greatest poet ever lived . . . !"

"Oh, for God's sake," Daddy said, "don't start that!"

Lucy looked hard at Mama, hoping that Mama would know what she was thinking, but Mama didn't seem to know that she was in the room. "I knew all along," Lucy said slowly, "I knew all along we wouldn't go."

"*Lucy!*" Mama said. "I've got to get dinner for five people."

"You needn't get me no damn dinner," Lucy said.

Mama shut her lips so tight for a second that none of the red showed. "*Lucy,*" she said, "Daddy and I have got to move Uncle Tubby. Now you take him for a walk or something."

"I'm tired of him," Lucy said.

Daddy set his glass down on the table. "Go on," he said, "I'll come out after a while and we'll look at the stars."

"My God!" Lucy said. "There won't be any for hours."

Daddy took a step toward her. "What did you say?"

"I said there wouldn't be any for a long time yet."

"Well, we'll look at them when they do come out. . . . Go on. . . . *You hear me?*"

Lucy walked out of the kitchen and around to the front of the house. Borcke had come out and sat on the top step, slowly slanting his nose this way and that, to catch the wind. She sat down beside him. A faint smell of horse manure came up to her—he *would* roll in it. She pulled him up into her lap. He struggled for a second, then, when he found that she would not let him go, sank back but kept turning his head as the breeze shifted.

Uncle Tubby came down the steps. "Where are the slave quarters?" he asked.

Lucy pointed to a plantation of locusts on their right. "They used to be over there but they blew off the hill. A long time ago."

He sat down on the step below her and took out his pipe. "All wreathed in trumpet vine," he said, "just like the big house. . . . I intend that Pompey shall sleep there tonight."

"Does he sleep in the bed with you?" Lucy asked.

"God forbid! He sleeps on the floor. On a pallet on the floor. But he snores like the devil."

"So does Borcke," Lucy said.

Uncle Tubby turned around and bent his head to sniff Borcke's back. "Horse . . ." he said. "You know, the minute I laid eyes on that dog I knew he slept in the bed with you."

"Mama's got to take more care of him when I get the pony," Lucy said.

Uncle Tubby turned around again and clasped her ankle in his big, warm hand and shook it. "Ah, sweet melody of love!" he said. "The exercising, the currying, the deliberation as to whether it ought to be eight ears of corn or six. . . ."

"Four is about right for a pony," Lucy said, "unless they're nubbins. . . . But nubbins," she added dreamily, "are often wormy. I wouldn't give 'em to *my* horse."

They were silent. Uncle Tubby sat hunched over, smoking. At the foot of the long slope the sun was setting behind the woods. In its red glow the beech trees stood out black, like twigs somebody had thrown into a giant grate. Lucy stopped thinking about the pony in order to savor her bitterness. *The witch . . . the witch that lives in the woods. She will roast us in her great red oven and tear us limb from limb. But what difference does it make? I am not anybody to save. I am just a changeling. My mother said I was a changeling. . . .*

Uncle Tubby stood up and knocked out his pipe and reached a hand to her. "How long will it be before dinner?" he asked.

"A long time," she said, "Mama's got to get it."

"What say we take a short run in the woods, then?"

She rose and laid her hand in his for a moment before she let it drop at her side. They went through the garden gate and took the shortcut down the hill, past the MacDonoghs' cabin. Through the open window they could see the MacDonoghs still gathered around the table.

"What are they doing?" Uncle Tubby asked.

Lucy laughed. "They're eating dinner."

"Isn't it rather early?"

"They eat breakfast at four o'clock in the morning," Lucy said.

"And when do they eat lunch?"

"They don't have any lunch."

He shook his head. "Such odd hours they keep! Do you suppose it's to get an early start on their matins?"

"I don't know," Lucy said, "it's just the way they do."

"Strange country," he said, "strange, magical country!" He threw his head back and laughed. "Why, I never saw such a country! But they do have some good ideas, those MacDonoghs. Now that bush arbor. . . ." He walked closer to her and, catching hold of her hand, swung it between them as they walked. "*Il y avait un vieil ermite qui s'appellait St. Brendan. Il quitta son pays et traversa l'océan jusqu'en Bretagne. Lorsqu'il y arriva il traina son bateau sur la plage et il était si fatigué qu'il partit dans les bois et s'étendit par terre. Mais avant de s'endormir il regarda le ciel et il lui sembla qu'il pourrait pleuvoir avant le jour. Il prit donc deux arbustes et les lia l'un à l'autre avec un rameau de saule. Alors il considéra son ouvrage et il pensa que la pluie pourrait pénétrer; il inclina deux arbustes de plus, les lia l'un a l'autre . . .*"

Borcke was digging in the loose dirt between two spreading roots. Lucy stopped and picked him up and shook him and set him back on the path.

Uncle Tubby had stopped, too, and was drawing two intersecting arcs in the dirt with a stick. *"Et lorsqu'il se réveilla le lendemain matin, il avait une église. Comprends-tu?"*

"I don't speak it," Lucy said.

"Tu le parlais le temps lorsque tu étais en France. Pourquoi ne veux tu pas le parler maintenant?"

"I forgot it coming over on the boat," Lucy said.

They had passed through the plum thicket and were in the woods. The crimson glow was just sunlight washing the trunks of the trees now. Uncle Tubby was still looking at her. *"Je pense que tu es la plus belle petite fille que j'ai vu depuis longtemps,"* he said.

"Magdalene MacDonogh is a heap prettier'n I am," Lucy said.

"I bet she hasn't got that look in her eye. . . . What do you suppose gives it to you?"

"Tending to my own business," Lucy said.

If he had had dark hair and long ears he would have looked like Borcke then, his head on one side, his eyes in the leafy light dark and as soft and as sad as Borcke's eyes. "All right, young lady," he said after a little.

They walked on. It was the first time he had called her "young lady." He wouldn't have done it if she hadn't spoken sharply to him. She told herself that she was not sorry. Grown people didn't expect you to answer what they said to you. Half the time when they said anything they were not talking to you but to themselves. She had found that out long ago.

The path wound downhill, between beeches whose huge boles were roughened by carvings, initials, dates, the inscriptions often enclosed in hearts or winged with arrows. Uncle Tubby walked with his head thrown back, gazing up into the leaves which would not turn yellow for months. Suddenly he stopped, lifted his foot, examined the sole of his shoe, and put his foot down again. He did not know that he was walking on top of a branch. Everywhere around here the earth was soggy because a branch flowed under it. It went underground a little below the waterfall and flowed under the cornfield to emerge again as a spring in a wild chasm on the riverbank.

He stopped. "I'm damned if I don't carve my name," he said. "Yours, too."

He took a penknife out of his pocket and wandered off among the trees. Lucy sat down on a rock. A clump of sweet fern came up beside it. She plucked a frond and crushed it in her fist and thought of the stream flowing secretly under the rock, under the dead leaves, making even the pebbles in the path glisten under a light film of water. A little way off in the woods was the waterfall. She did not know whether she wanted to go there today. Some days she did not feel like going there. When you felt that way it didn't make any difference whether you went or not. Sometimes you went and afterwards you couldn't imagine how it would have been if you hadn't gone. It made a difference, too, who went with you. She and her mother came here often. The stream flowed in a narrow channel up there on the bluff, then suddenly dived between two tall, leaning rocks and fell ten or fifteen feet to a flat ledge below. That was what made the waterfall. Her mother would stand, clasping the trunk of a tree, and stare and stare until you were afraid she would forget who you were and you went to her and took her arm and said "Mama" . . . Her father had come here with them once. In the spring, soon after they bought the place. . . . He said that he would come back again some time.

Uncle Tubby had found a young beech tree whose bark shone like gray satin. He was carving LA and EM, each in the center of its own heart, but with the hearts intertwined. . . . The next time Evelyn came to visit her she would bring her here. She wouldn't say how old he was or anything about him, just "a man from New York . . ."

He had begun another carving, a very small heart, pierced by an arrow, and now he was carving tiny initials in the center.

"Who's that?" she asked.

He looked at her, smiling, like a person who knows a secret he isn't going to tell. "Imogene," he said, "Imogene . . . Marie . . . Louise . . . Lointaine. Don't you think that's a pretty name?"

"I think Lointaine's a funny name," Lucy said.

"It's her mother's family name," he said absently.

"Whose?" she said, and kicked her heels against the rocks. "Whose family name?"

"My little girl's."

"You haven't got any little girl," she said, "you're not even mar . . ." She stopped abruptly, remembering what her father had said: Ripe for a disastrous marriage. "You haven't got any little girl," she repeated to cover her confusion.

"You'd think I had if you could see her bills. The things that girl buys!"

He had finished the last flourish on the L and was putting a period beside it. "What does she buy?" Lucy asked.

"Oh . . . mink . . . and vair . . . and samovair . . . and Lucite. Let her stroll through Saks Fifth Avenue and she will order a thousand Lucite bubbles, each one in its own filigree box. . . ." He fell silent, absorbed in his carving.

"What does she do with them?" Lucy asked.

"Breaks them on people's heads. Or sometimes she lets them float out of the window and then they fall down on the heads of the people passing by and break. The police are at the door, night and day. But we pay no attention to *them*."

"Does she go to school?"

"She did, for a while, but she came home one day and said that Miss Plobscote was an old pelican. Naturally I couldn't deny that." He shut his penknife up and put it in his pocket. "How does it happen that the MacDonoghs go to school in August?" he asked.

"They start then, after the crops are laid by. And then they get out early in the spring. . . ."

"So they can put the crops in again? No wonder they get up at four o'clock in the morning. . . . And where do you go to school?"

"In town. Daddy says I'm not learning a thing."

"Well, are you?"

Lucy shook her head. "Not much," she said. "Miss Simpson is the dumbest old thing you ever saw in your life. But Mama says it's vulgar to complain about the teacher."

He looked for a second as if he were about to laugh. He said, "Your mother is a wonderful woman. Fearfully and wonderfully made. . . . I shouldn't think she'd be much help in leading your so to speak own life."

"She's got more fool ideas than any white woman I ever knew," Lucy said.

"Yes," Uncle Tubby said absently. "What are some more of her ideas?"

"She just hates Yankees," Lucy said. "She doesn't think that anything Yankees do is right."

"I've noticed that," he said before she had time to be embarrassed.

"She won't use cube sugar," Lucy said, "and she thinks it's vulgar to have your garage fastened on to your house. And Christmas wreaths! We can get 'em out of the woods but we can't buy 'em. . . . She don't like electric lights on Christmas trees, even."

They had started walking on again. "Lord, Lord!" he said. "Why, my little girl has the whole house wired for Christmas—pink and green." He pointed to a big-bellied oak that thrust its trunk out into the path, like a pompous person demanding attention, Lucy had always thought. "What's over there?" he asked.

"The waterfall," she said.

"A *waterfall!*" he said. "We'll have to see that."

They passed the pompous oak and were on a bluff overlooking the stream. The trees about them were tall and slim, second-growth her father had said, but down in the gorge were more big beeches and, glimmering as white as the water that dashed beside it, a giant sycamore that was so old its trunk had split in two.

He stood and stared. "Good Lord!" he said. "Why didn't you tell me you had this up your sleeve?"

Lucy laughed in delight. "It's not in my sleeve, it's in the woods."

But he had grasped her hand and was dragging her with him down the path, slipping, sliding, sometimes falling to their knees, rising to keep on at the same pace, until finally on the brink of the falls he caught hold of a low-hanging sycamore bough and, steadying himself, released her hand.

"There!" he said. "Look what I did for you!"

"Look what I did for *you!*" Lucy retorted.

They stood there and watched the water rushing down between the two leaning rocks to fall on the ledge below. It struck so hard that every drop of water that fell leaped off the rock again, some straight into the air, to redescend more gently, others bouncing off into spray. Lucy moved over and stood between him and the falls and felt the cold needles of spray beat against her skin. The rock showed darkest where the water was churned into the wildest froth. She put up her hand to feel how chill her cheek had grown and as she did so he raised his eyes from the water, his nostrils widening. "What's that I smell?" he asked.

She looked at her hand, from which, somewhere on the way, the crushed frond had fallen. "Sweet fern," she said, and held her hand out so that he could see the green stain on her palm. He smiled and shook his head. "I told you," he said.

"Told me what?"

"That you were a *belle dame sans merci.* Carrying *sweet fern!* Aren't you ashamed of yourself?"

"No," Lucy said, and heard her own laughter tinkle, high and frail like the spray. "No," she repeated, "I'm not a bit ashamed of myself," and she ran over and stood before the sycamore tree, not looking back over her shoulder, for she knew that he would follow.

The tree was so old that its trunk was almost hollow. It had, perhaps, been struck by lightning many years ago. That was what her father said, though her great-uncle maintained that lightning never struck a sycamore. At any rate, it had received an injury which had resulted in a cleavage of its bark and outer fibers. But time had smoothed the edges of the wound and curled them back, scroll-wise, to show the dark, decaying heart.

It was dark red and damply pitted by millions of little holes, the homes and highroads of insects. He stooped and gazed into the glistening cave, then straightened up, sighing, "*You* could slip in there," he said. "Have you ever been in there?"

She nodded. She and Ruby—the most daring of the MacDonoghs, though she had become more sedate since she had turned thirteen— had squeezed in and had stood for a few seconds with their bare feet sunk in the moist, rotting stuff that was heaped high inside. But not for more than a few seconds before Ruby had turned to her and whispered "Snakes!" and they wriggled out to stand in the daylight, with only the feel of the wet, rotting stuff still on their ankles to keep them from forgetting that they had been inside. . . . But it would be different to stand in there with a grown man beside you.

She stretched out her hand. He caught it and held it with a warm, even pressure. "This strange light," he said, "and all these great trees. . . . Everything so magical!" He looked down at her. He smiled. "You *are* a *belle dame sans merci!*" he said.

She smiled back at him. A few feet from where they stood a jewel-weed, growing on the brink of the waterfall, trembled and bent toward the water, straightened up and, trembling, bent again. The pressure of his hand on hers grew warmer, closer, then suddenly slackened. Their hands fell to their sides, as if struck apart. Mellow notes from some giant anvil were sounding through the wood. ". . . Six . . ." he said. "Good Lord!"

"Dinner won't be ready for a long time yet," Lucy said.

But he had already started up the path. "Shall we go back the way we came?" he was asking.

She looked about her vaguely and did not answer.

He took a few more steps. "This same path?" he asked.

She roused herself then. "No," she said, "there's a shortcut." She called Borcke and they walked along the stream until they came to a footlog. It was the only footlog she knew of in the whole country round. He did not notice it and she did not call his attention to it. He looked back once, toward the falls, after they had crossed on the footlog, but he did not say anything else about the falls and she did not tell him that they were passing within a few feet of where the stream sank underground.

They made their way to the top of the bluff. Up here where the ground was level there were no big trees, only third-growth post oaks, hackberries, dogwoods, gums, and a few hickories; they had been able to get wagons and saws in here and had lumbered off the whole bluff.

They left the woods and entered the plum thicket. The path was one made by small game. He pushed the bushes to one side as he went, but did not stop to hold them back for her. Sometimes the green closed in over the path so thick that she could not see his orange-colored shirt. She stopped and looked about her. The woods still blazed in the setting sun. Ahead the eastern sky was still faintly rosy from the reflection. There were no lights on as yet. The house crouched on the hill like an old gray horse lain down to rest. This was the time of day she loved best, when the sun was down but the light had not yet left the hill, the time of evening when the MacDonoghs sometimes suddenly came up over the side of the hill and without a word they would all start running through the thin, cool air while the bats veered overhead. She broke a switch from a plum tree and peeled it. The dog came panting out of the bushes and lay down in the path. She bent and brushed the top of his head gently with her switch and walked on. The edges of all the plum trees were rimmed with light, like the dew that sparkled on them sometimes in the morning. . . . *Full beautiful. . . . A fairy child.* . . . She walked more slowly, and as she went touched a leaf here and there with her wand.

. . . She would be tall, as tall as the knight if she stood up, but she would be sitting sidewise on the steed, leaning a little down. Her hair fell over her shoulder in one long wave. Her eyes were gray and shone always with the same light. . . .

"Hey!" he cried suddenly, and raised his hand high in the air.

"Come on!" he cried, and without looking around raced up the slope. Lucy ran, too. Under the willow tree her father and mother stood talking with a lady and gentleman who had just got out of a car.

"Where have you been?" her mother said. "We've been looking everywhere for you."

His eyes were fixed on the lady but he laid his hand for a second on Lucy's shoulder. "She took me to her elfin grot," he said.

The lady looked at Lucy before she looked at him. She was very tall and thinner, even, than Mama. She shook her head and her hair fell farther back on her shoulders. It was the same color as Lucy's and the same length. Her eyes were gray.

She said, "Tubby, *don't* shut your wild, wild eyes!" but you couldn't hear the rest of what she said, for Uncle Tubby had put his arm around her and was kissing her. As Lucy gazed at them she would have wept but that all eyes were upon her.

Four

A Walk with the Accuser

I

The young man who called himself Charles D'Espéville arrived early at the rendezvous. It was in the Year of Our Lord 1553 and the house he had been told to come to was on a dark street in a part of Paris with which he was not familiar. The man who signed himself Michael Servetus (but who, at present, was also traveling under an assumed name) had chosen the time and place, as befitted the one who was older and more eminent, Jean Cauvin reflected wryly.

No lights showed in the house. Young Jean Cauvin did not dare knock on the door. He stood in front of the house and waited until the sound of his own footsteps ceased to echo in his ears. The silence grew oppressive. He crossed the narrow street and stationed himself opposite the house, in the deepest shade he could find, where a plane tree reared its stout trunk up from the cobblestones, like a drunk man getting to his feet after a fall. His eyes were growing accustomed to the darkness. A strip of paler shadow, bordering the house he was watching, revealed itself as a narrow pathway. His fingers explored the wall, found the depression which must be a door. The blood was beating in his temples, loud enough, it seemed to him, to be heard on the quiet street. He clenched his fist and let it fall once against the sagging door. There was no sound within, not even the rustle of a mouse.

His temples began to throb, in a way with which he had long been familiar.

It is the wild beast! . . . The beast I have never succeeded in con-
quering. On my way here I was calm and collected, going over in
my mind, point by point, what I would say to him on this doctrine
of the Trinity. . . . But he is not here. And he may never come! . . .
That is why I feel this tightness in my temples, this sensation of
choking. . . . He did not dare to come! . . . That is it . . . he did not
DARE *to come! . . .* The pulse in his temples beat more feebly. He
drew his breath more easily. He stood where he was until the tumult
in his veins had subsided, then stole away from the darkened house.

It was late that night when he left the crooked street but he did
not seem to lack for companionship as he made his way back to his
lodgings in another part of the city. Light from houses in which
candles burned cast shadows which patterned the cobblestones under
his feet and ran past him, wavering, to mass at his back in one
towering shadow—the shadow which ever since he could remember
he had known and dreaded. When he emerged from the alley onto
the thoroughfare, his Shadow was walking at his side.

Charles D'Espéville! . . . Charles D'Espéville! Charles D'Espéville!
. . . His boots, striking on the stone, rang out the syllables of the
name he had assumed. *You must take care to remember that you are*
Charles D'Espéville!

The young man paused and turned his head to stare over his
shoulder. "I hoped never to encounter you again!"

The Shadow crept nearer. *Each time we meet you tell me that you*
do not intend for us to meet again. I am always puzzled to hear you
say this.

"You are a wild beast which I will yet conquer."

The Shadow suddenly loomed high against the wall of a nearby
house, writhing, as a man writhes, when he can hardly control his
laughter. I, *"a wild beast"! And one that* YOU *will conquer! I am*
the friend of your house!

"My father has many friends in Noyon. Some of them in high
places. The Lord Jean Hangest, Bishop of Noyon, calls my father
friend."

The Shadow flowed back over the cobblestones to resume its place
at his side. *Ah, yes, it was through his friendship with the Lord Bishop*
that your father obtained the benefice of Pont l'Evêque for you and
for your older brother, Charles?

Your father was an astute man of business, noted for his probity as much as his competence—until that affair of the will of Nicholas Obry. And was he not executor also of the will of Michel Courtin?

"My father, in his capacity as Notary, has been executor of many wills," the young man said coldly.

It was, indeed, unfortunate that he refused to render the accounts which the law demanded of him in the case of those two wills. A lifelong reputation for probity and competence destroyed in the twinkling of an eye, as it were! . . .

The young man did not answer. The Shadow moved closer. *I recall now when we last met. It was in the Chapter Room of the Cathedral when your brother Charles appeared before the assembled canons in behalf of your father. You would have acquitted yourself better than he did! It must have been hard to sit there silent while he pled your father's cause so ineffectually . . .*

"Charles, as the eldest son, was the head of our house."

There was a sound that might have been a suppressed laugh. *Ah yes . . . I attended the trial—as a friend of your house. And your house has not too many friends nowdays—at least, in Noyon. As I recall, Charles did not defend your father's refusal to give any accounting in the matter of the two wills. He appealed to the canons' humanity and sensibility. . . . Was not such a plea in itself an admission that your father was not the man of honor he had been taken for? At any rate that was the townsfolks' gossip. . . .*

"My father was buried in consecrated ground. . . ."

The young man's companion sighed. *So he was! Charles obtained the mercy and compassion he had asked for your father. Your father received the last rites, as you say, and was buried in consecrated ground. But Charles was buried at midnight, beneath the gallows. . . . Was that because he failed to render an account of your father's estate as he had promised to do? Or was it because he struck the Massier, while he was carrying the Host in solemn procession?*

The young man stretched his hands out as if to grapple with a flesh-and-blood enemy but the Shadow only laughed on a lower note and, swaying forward, enveloped him, as if in an embrace, and they walked on together like one being. Incoherent syllables fell from the young man's lips but the Shadow murmured grave admonitions.

You were wise to resign your benefice. When doubt has been cast on the father's honor, it all the more behooves the son to keep his own reputation spotless. And you did well, too, to leave Noyon. One can take little pleasure in a town once one has made the acquaintance of its jail. . . . Four months, was it not, that you lay in the prison of the Cathedral Chapter? For creating an uproar in the cathedral on Easter Eve. Not so grave as the charges that were brought against your father and brother. Still, it is known that you are infected with the new ideas. . . . Did you receive instruction in them from your kinsman Robert d'Olivétan?

"I was struck down by an irresistible grace. God, by a sudden conversion, subdued my heart, made it teachable."

God, and not Robert d'Olivétan? I have heard that Olivétan is a most persuasive fellow. And there is your old master, Jacques Lefèvre d'Etaples. A man of many ideas, some of them dangerous. But he is living his old age out securely at the court of the Queen of Navarre whilst you—I wonder what would have happened if you had not climbed out of the second-story window of your lodgings at the Collège Fortet—by means of knotted sheets, was it not?

"I have not complained of any of the sufferings I have incurred in the interest of godliness."

Again there was that long sibilance. *True godliness! I have heard that when you were four years old your pious mother carried you in her arms to view the holy relic, the jawbone of St. Eloi, when it was being carried in solemn procession . . .*

"It might as well have been the jawbone of an ass!"

So some people are beginning to say. In Noyon and in the Swiss cities I am told that the new ideas are being successfully promulgated by William Farel and Viret! . . . Both of them, like you, had Jacques Lefèvre as their master . . . Have you thought of emigrating to one of the Swiss cities? It should be easy to arrange, since you are already in correspondence with Farel and Viret. And I have heard that, young as you are, you have attracted the attention of the other Swiss Reformers, Oecolampadius, Philip Melancthon, and even the former Augustinian monk Martin Luther. They say that the Devil sleeps at the foot of Martin Luther's bed. In the form of a black dog . . . Have you ever been troubled by such phantoms?

"Not unless you call yourself a phantom."

The Shadow swayed away from his side and, as once before that night, flowed up the wall of one of the silent houses. The dreadful laughter echoed in all the air around, then shaped itself into words: *I am the friend of your house! The best of all your friends!*

The young man spoke through clenched teeth: "My friends are of a different sort."

The Shadow was again flowing on beside him. *That may be. I myself have friends of many sorts. But then I have a wide acquaintance, being obliged to travel a great deal . . . I observe that Michael Servetus, the Spaniard, did not keep his engagement with you this evening . . . I have heard that he is a very learned fellow. Melancthon said of him:* Servetus multum lege . . . di grandissime ingenio . . . gran sophista. *. . . He is said to know French and German as well as his native Spanish and he is, of course, well read in the Latin and the Greek. Hebrew, too, I have heard . . .*

"He did not dare to come here to meet ME."

And yet he is said to be a bold fellow! He himself called the attention of the Holy Office to his book, The Errors of the Trinity; *he himself sent a copy to the Inquisitor! . . . The book was burned in the public square at Saragossa and he is now in flight from the Inquisition. . . . Traveling, like you, under an assumed name. . . .*

"He is in flight from the Inquisition of the Roman Church. I have freed myself from the superstitions of the Papacy."

So you told me earlier. Would you tell me, in more detail, how this came about?

"I was obstinately devoted to the superstitions of the Papacy. Considering my age, my mind was far more hardened than it should have been. It was only with the utmost difficulty that I could be drawn out of such deep mire . . . But God, by a sudden conversion, subdued my heart and made it teachable. As soon as my mind was prepared I began to realize, as if a light had broken in upon me, in what a quagmire of errors I had wallowed. I had recourse to God's mercy. And now what is left to me, poor and wretched as I am, except to offer as my only defense my humble supplications that He will not reckon against me such fearful abandonment and estrangement from His Word, from which in His wondrous kindness He has at last delivered me?"

Hum!!! All is clearer to me than it was before. It is evident that you have a rare gift for Theology. Although I travel a good deal I do not have the company of theologians as often as I could wish. They tell me that you have corresponded with Michael Servetus although he is older than you are and—if I may say so—as yet more eminent. Can you tell me anything of the discussion that has gone on between you?

"He has proposed to me certain questions concerning the doctrine of the Trinity . . ."

As I said, a bold rogue! That is a question which has engaged the minds of many men, beginning with Augustine of Hippo, who maintained that the doctrine cannot be proved but can only be illustrated —that is to say, set forth by means of analogy. Then there is Richard of Saint Victor who held that it can be proved. And after him William of Occam, with his "Razor." The doctrine, he holds, can neither be demonstrated nor illustrated but can only be believed. The first view is the illustrative, the second view the demonstrative, and the third is called the FIDEIST. *There have been other cunning thinkers: Robert Holcott, who reveled in conundrums and enumerated sixteen contrarieties in the doctrine of the Trinity, as, for example, that God cannot be three persons because three persons would constitute three gods. And the Scholastic, Henri de Gand. In his opinion the trinitarian nature of God is necessary. Otherwise, the world could not have been created, for creation, he argued, was the work of wisdom and will and these qualities lay dormant in God until they were projected as the first and second Persons of the Trinity. . . .*

The Bishop of Hippo's view seems the one most generally accepted —until recently. They tell me that Servetus is conversant with the works of all these thinkers—but I must not let my enthusiasm for the SCIENCE OF SCIENCES *deprive me of the pleasure of hearing your views on this doctrine. You tell me that Servetus has proposed to you certain questions?*

"He asks if the man Jesus who was crucified was the Son of God and, if so, what was the nature of his filiation."

And your answer?

"Holy Church tells us that the Son was *generated* by the Father but the Holy Spirit *proceeds* from the Father and the Son."

OMOUSIOS *is the Greek word, I believe . . . Martin Luther once assured me that his soul loathes the very word! . . . But I have never considered him theologically sound. What has the Spaniard to say on the subject?*

"He maintains that nowhere in the Scriptures is there any mention of the doctrine of the Trinity."

Does he deny, then, the existence of the Three Persons?

He declares that he believes in the existence of the Father, the Son, and the Holy Spirit but he claims that God has made His Deity the property of all created things so that He is wood in what is wood and stone in what is stone . . ."

"*I have heard the same argument but it was a long time ago and in another country . . . It seems he would turn the clock back. A bold fellow, indeed! What does he argue concerning the Second Person of the Trinity?*

"The shameless dog avers that Christ is not co-eternal with the Father."

Again the air was full of that prolonged sibilance. *And the Holy Spirit?*

"He maintains that the Holy Spirit is a mixture composed of the essence of God and created force. All creatures and things are of the essence of God, he holds, and reasons that so all things are God—for he does not blush to speak and write his mind in this way."

Subtle doctrines these and ancient—but dangerous in these times, for I have heard that while Dionysos and other pagan gods are re-born and torn to pieces every spring, Jesus Christ was crucified in Jerusalem in the fifteenth year of the reign of Emperor Tiberius when Pontius Pilate was governor of Judea and Herod was Tetrarch and Anna and Caiphas high priests of the Jews . . . Does the fellow not read the Scriptures?

"He reads them and quotes them for his own purposes."

You astonish me. I had thought—but no matter. . . .

"There is matter enough in his heresies to confound the minds of the innocent, thus endangering pure doctrine."

I told you earlier this evening that you struck me as a young man of rare gifts . . . But what of this fellow? Will he continue to be allowed to disseminate his poison? Men have been burned at the stake for holding notions such as his . . . But perhaps AUTOS-DA-FÉ *are going*

out of fashion, along with the superstitions of the Papacy . . .
Erasmus, who is noted for his irenic temper, writes that the ancients
philosophized little about such matters and thinks that we would do
well to imitate them . . . As for Martin Luther, he publicly avers that
he does not believe a man should lose his life for professing heretical
doctrines. Tell me your opinion on that.

"It is clear that heresy is the worst of all crimes, for it destroys the
immortal soul. As for Servetus' ravings, I was so wounded by the
indignities which he heaped upon our Lord and Master, Jesus Christ,
that I remonstrated with him as follows: 'The Devil, then, is sub-
stantially God?' whereat he retorts, 'Can you doubt it?' and goes on
to say that his fundamental principle is that all things are part and
portion of God."

If the fellow's flesh and blood were reduced to ashes he might
come to a different opinion as to the nature of the universe . . . But
I have no doubt that you are Servetus' equal in controversy in spite
of your youth. Let me have your rejoinder.

"The true wisdom of man consists in his knowledge of God the
Creator and God the Redeemer. God's nature is manifest in His
government of all creatures."

I would take it as a favor if you would be more explicit. As I have
said, I do not keep as much company with theologians as I could
wish . . .

"God directs all creatures according to the properties He
bestowed on each of them when He created them. Man was created
in the image of God . . ."

Was he, then, perfect?

"He was made a partaker of the divine wisdom and holiness, and
being thus perfect in soul and body, was bound to render to God a
perfect obedience to His commandments . . ."

But I have heard that man fell from this high estate. . . .

"The immediate causes of man's downfall were Satan, the Serpent,
Eve, and the forbidden fruit."

Have you any idea as to the nature of this fruit which was
forbidden?

"We need to know nothing about it except that God forbade our
first parents to eat of it. The fact that they did eat of it was, as I
have said, the immediate cause of their downfall. The remote causes
were unbelief, ambition, ingratitude, obstinacy . . ."

But you hold, with the learned doctors of the Church, that man was made in the image of God?

"That image was obliterated by the Fall."

Wholly obliterated?

"When man became unbelieving, he became unrighteous and hence subject to death. As the result of the Fall the understanding of the soul in divine things is blinder than that of a mole."

You hold, then, that man cannot even see the good and therefore can do no good works?

"He can neither contrive nor desire good works. As far as divine things are concerned, man's will chooses only what is evil. The body follows the depraved appetites of the soul, is liable to many infirmities and, at length, to death.

"Ruined man can only seek his redemption through Christ. Even if he had remained in his integrity, his condition was too humble to enable him to penetrate to God without a mediator. How much less can he raise himself to such a height after being plunged through fatal ruin into death and hell?"

Ah . . . death and hell! . . .

What, then, can man do?

"The merits of Christ are sufficient to take away the sins of the whole world."

If that is true, man's situation is then somewhat altered, is it not?

"The merits of Christ are *sufficient* to take away the sins of the whole world but the merits of Christ are *effectual* only to His elect."

And who are His elect?

"Those who have been regenerated by the Holy Ghost—Who breathes His pure grace where He will."

This, I take it, is your doctrine of PREDESTINATION. *I have heard that Michael Servetus laughs at it and claims that in it you are reviving a heresy promulgated by a priest named Lucidus. That heresy was, however, condemned by the Council of Chalcedon in the sixth century . . . This Servetus is thought by some to be a very learned man. Juan da Quintana, confessor to the Emperor, with whom I have become acquainted on my travels, tells me that at the age of eighteen the range of Servetus' reading was prodigious . . . But perhaps you will further elucidate this doctrine which arouses Servetus' mirth.*

"Predestination we call the eternal decree of God by which He has predetermined with Himself what He would have become of every man. For eternal life is foreordained for some and eternal damnation for others."

And reprobate man may not question the justice of this decree?

"The fact that it is God's will is its justification. Argumentative reason may not intrude . . . God has mercy on Whom He will have mercy and Whom He will He hardeneth."

I met this God of yours once on my travels . . . But that was long ago and not among Frenchmen, or even the inhabitants of Swiss cities . . . However, there are men living today who might even choose to entertain the Devil rather than give allegiance to this God . . . I have heard that Procopius, nephew to the saintly James Arminius, has described this God as "both tyrant and executioner." Somewhat resembling your own father, as he has been described to me. But forgive me for mentioning a subject which, from its very nature, must be painful to you. . . . Your father died, deprived of the reputation which he had been a lifetime building up. I predict that it will be otherwise with you. You have gifts that assure that you will make your mark in the world.

"I am by nature rustic and shy. It has always been my ambition to live in seclusion. But God has laid certain commands upon me and allows me no rest until I have played the part He intends me to play."

Your sentiments do you credit, particularly when the circumstances are taken into account.

"My present circumstances are of little account to me."

Quite so . . . Not all young men would feel the same way under the circumstances. Another young man might have been deeply wounded when both his father and his elder brother died disgraced. I daresay that it has never occurred to you that if your father had had the proper consideration for his sons, he would have rendered to the canons the accounts of those wills that were demanded . . .

"My father showed his love for his children by seeming not to love them. From the time we were born he sought preferment for us, however . . ."

And found it—in high places. The members of your family have never been lacking in ambition. You were tonsured at twelve, were you not? . . . I have been told that it was your father who first observed your aptitude for the study of Theology. . . .

"My father early discerned my natural bent and destined me for the study of Theology."

Yet he took you out of holy orders and put you to the study of the Law?

"He observed how extensively the practice of the Law enriches its professors and suddenly changed his purpose."

That would be after his quarrel with the canons . . . Were you not grieved to have to abandon Theology for Jurisprudence?

"I obeyed the will of my father and endeavored to give my new studies faithful attention. At the same time I could not forget that Theology was my first love."

Yet your father commanded you to leave it?

"The glory of God is perceptible in all His works but His majesty is such that the religious attitude of the creature can only be one of adoration."

Quite so. Again I must say that your sentiments do you credit . . . But I hear that since your father's death you have resumed your theological studies. It seems to me that you have done wisely. As you say, Theology was your first love . . .

"I cannot remember a time when I was not preoccupied with questions of good and evil . . ."

Some people have held that from an early age your chief interest has been discerning evil in others . . . Do you remember your classmate Jacques d'Olivétan, cousin to Robert d'Olivétan? When you paced the schoolyard, conning your book, he would run beside you, saying, "Jean can decline as far as the Accusative case" and then would run away, making one of those vulgar gestures schoolboys make and calling out: "I ACCUSE YOU! I ACCUSE YOU!"

"Jacques d'Olivétan was a heedless youth. As man he has fallen upon evil courses."

Such as? . . .

"Wining, whoring, gaming . . ."

Yet he attends Mass of Sundays and will doubtless be buried in consecrated ground! . . . Do you know that in our conversation we have left one subject untouched. It is one I have heard debated during my travels: The doctrine of the Eucharist . . . The Swiss Oecolampadius holds that Christ's body cannot be in the bread and wine upon the altar since He has already ascended to Heaven and sits at the right hand of the Father . . . *Martin Luther holds that the real flesh and blood of Christ coexist along with the natural elements of the bread and wine. He has debated most acrimoniously on this subject with Huldreich Zwingli, who says that Christ warned His disciples against such notions as these, maintaining that His presence in the bread and wine is commemorative and symbolical and can be apprehended by faith alone* . . . *What is your thought on this matter?*

The young man held his clenched fist up and shook it in the air. *"A Sacrament cannot be a cause of grace!* Even instrumentally. It is no more than an outward sign by which God confirms His promise of good will toward us in our consciences in order to fortify our defective faith. And we, when we partake of the Lord's Supper, bear witness before men and angels of our faith in God."

The whole air seemed one vast sighing. Then came the whisper: *Before men—and angels, too—you say?*

The clenched hand sank to the young man's side. "If you will reflect, you will see the justice of what I have said. If a material sign is made a vehicle of grace, that part of creation would be withdrawn from its service of adoration. Similarly, if a creature were made a vehicle of grace, it would be raised to a dignity which God does not allow it to possess. . . ."

The Shadow fled away from him to dance over the walls of the sleeping houses, more ecstatically it seemed than before, then swayed back to his side, seeming to flow over him, as if in an embrace, and the airy words flowed about him, too . . . *In all my travels* . . . *the subtlest intellect* . . . *and the boldest* . . . and then a long silence and more words: *You will go far* . . . *farther than any of them!*

They had arrived at the short flight of steps which led up to the young man's lodgings: The Shadow's pace became more sedate, its words more measured: *May I thank you for a conversation which has been delightful as well as instructive?* . . . *And may I ask how you purpose to spend the rest of the evening?*

The young man silently began the ascent of the flight of steps. The Shadow made, as it were, a little bow, and remained floating beneath him. The young man gained the top step and halted. He was a little out of breath from his long walk and his recent impassioned utterances. *It was always like that!* He strove to remain calm and collected, to speak only when necessary and then succinctly, but once he began speaking, he was carried out of himself. He stood, half turned away from the threshold of the house, looking off into the night, while he mused on the mysteries of his own nature, then started as the voice came from the shadows at his feet.

Do you know, I think that of all his sons, you are most like your father. You walk with your eyes upon the ground and starve yourself until, even in anger, a blush does not stain your cheek. But you are sanguinary, like your father. A true Picard! Above all things they love contention! . . . That was a telling blow your brother Charles dealt the MASSIER, *when he was carrying the Host in procession! . . . But you will strike stronger blows before you are through! . . .*

The young man stood silent, gazing steadfastly before him until the voice rose again from the shadows: *They tell me that you read late into the night—so late that some of your friends fear that your health may be impaired . . . Would it not be wiser to exercise the virtue of prudence and mortify the flesh less—for it is obvious that you have great works to perform in the Vineyard of the Lord . . .*

"I purpose to spend the remainder of the night in study, as is my custom," the young man thought.

so *that when you meet Michael Servetus you will be able to refute him in disputation? . . .* BUT WHAT IF HE NEVER COMES? *. . . What if you never meet?*

John Calvin paused before entering the house to look down at the dark shape crouched at his feet. "We will meet!" he said, and went into the dark house and closed the door.

II

It was strange to see him standing there in the cell. He did not deign to come to our rendezvous in Paris sixteen years before but while I waited he was before my mind's eye, moving toward me along that street he never set foot upon. And ever since I have had him in my mind's eye. Standing there against the cold stone wall as I waited, he did not look as I have pictured him, as he appears now. He is only a few years older than I am but his hair is already whitened. His hair and beard have grown untrimmed during the six weeks he has been in the prison. Their unkemptness make his eyes seem to glare more wildly. But his eyes are not the eyes one ordinarily sees in a Spanish head. Or has their color altered in prison? They have a sheen on them as of silver. When I entered the room he looked up, as if I had interrupted a train of thought more important than anything I could say.

I shut the cell door behind me and approached him meekly, as is my wont. "I have been told that you wished to see me in order to beg my pardon," I said.

His eyes fixed my face: "I desire to ask your pardon and that of every other fellow man whom I have offended during my earthly pilgrimage," he said finally.

I bowed my head. "I am willing to pass over everything you have done against me," I said. "My only concern is your soul's salvation. You have blasphemed against the Father, the Son, and the Holy Spirit."

He made a slight motion of his hand. "It is not the first time men have differed in their interpretations of doctrines," he said.

"You have blasphemed against the Father, the Son, and the Holy Spirit," I repeated, "calling the doctrine of the Trinity a three-headed Cerberus of Hell! . . ."

"We have been in correspondence concerning these matters," he said, "a correspondence which you broke off."

I told him that I broke the correspondence off because I had come to regard him as a Satan bent on wasting my time."

"So you wrote Jean Frellon. . . ."

"The Huguenot publisher who would not publish your book."

"It has been published," he said.

"To your eternal discredit."

He took a step toward me. "I have a question to ask of you," he said.

I told him that I held myself ready to answer any reasonable question he desired to ask of me.

He asked me whether in the month of March I had not written by Guillaume Trie to Lyons, describing his doings. He said that he had it on good authority that Guillaume Trie had demanded that he be delivered into the hands of the Papists. And he said that, at Trie's insistence, Antoine Arneys had forwarded to Matthew Ory, the Inquisitor, the letters that had passed between the cousins.

I admitted that Guillaume Trie, knowing my concern for the things of the spirit, had consulted me, from time to time, concerning the correspondence he had with his cousin.

He gave a great laugh at this and said that some persons who had read the correspondence had been astonished by Trie's grasp of certain doctrines. They had not esteemed him so learned!

Seeing him obdurate, I remained silent, whereat he came closer to me and demanded to know how Matthew Ory, the Inquisitor, had come into possession, not only of Trie's correspondence with Arneys, but of letters that he, Servetus, had written me at the beginning of our correspondence.

I assured him that in early youth I resolved to flee the superstitions of the Papacy and that I had never departed from that resolve.

He maintained that it was I—or one of my ministers—who had placed the letters and the leaves of his manuscript of his book in the hands of the Inquisitor, with the result that he had been burned in effigy by the Papists.

"I have no ministers," I told him, "and I myself am here only a simple minister of the gospel."

He asked me whether it was the office of a minister of the gospel to make a capital accusation, and to pursue a man already at Law to his death.

I told him that it was the office of a minister of the gospel to remonstrate with any man who seemed to be in danger of losing his immortal soul, as he was.

He replied that his conscience was clear. He had not, he said, broken faith with any man or hunted any man to his death.

"You have blasphemed against Jesus Christ," I reminded him, "saying that He came in our flesh and was like to us in His human nature, thereby denying that He is a sole Redeemer . . ."

"He is the *Word of God*," he said.

"You deny that He was from all eternity the *Son* of God?" I asked the impious dog.

Whereat he twitched his snout and said, "Before his incarnation he was called the *Word*. After his incarnation with the man Jesus he was called the *Son* . . ."

"And what of the Holy Spirit?" I asked him.

He said: "There is one brightness of the sun and another of the moon, another of fire, and still another splendor of water. All these were disposed by Christ, the architect of the world. On account of him God made the world and by him the world is filled. He descends to the lowest depths and ascends to the highest heights. He walks upon the wings of the wind, rides upon the air, and inhabits the place of angels. But they have a carnal sense who—"

"Have done with your raving," I told him. "Man's only hope of redemption is through Jesus Christ and the only hope of society is through the company of the elect, who, from the foundation of the world, have been chosen to achieve God's purpose."

He said, "You are a false accuser. You are Simon Magus. I would not seem to you to rave if you were not Simon Magus. The magistrates should put you in prison alongside me, until this matter is settled."

I said, "It will be settled soon."

He said, "The sooner the better. I shall be glad to die in this cause."

"That is fortunate," I told him, "since the magistrates have already passed sentence."

He fixed his eyes even more intently on mine. I thought his eyes would run out of his head, like quicksilver, before he turned and stood with his face averted from mine. "The sentence?" he asked at last.

"Death by fire," I told him. He gave a long sigh and fell down on the floor, where he beat his breast, crying: "The sword! In mercy, the sword and not the fire, lest I recant and lose my immortal soul!"

I went and stood over him. I told him what was true, that though I had felt that he deserved death, I had requests of the magistrates that it be by the sword and not by fire. I told him also I passed over everything he had done against me and I assured him that it was not too late for him to gain salvation. If he would only deny his heresies and put his faith in Christ as the eternal Son of God. But he only beat his breast and cried out in Spanish the word "Misericordia! Misericordia!" Whereat, not wishing to be wiser than my Master, I left him writhing on the floor and beating his breast, and repaired to my chamber, where I prayed for some time for the soul of this unhappy man.

III

This house, which belongs to my godly friend Giles Fremiot, is well situated for one who loves solitude and would rather spend the moments not given to prayer in contemplation of the beauties of nature rather than the vices of men. To the north and west the mountains enclose the landscape in a sort of natural amphitheater.

My host tells me that the borders of the lake, even on rainy days, are visible. The glory of God reveals itself everywhere, the mountains echo His name, those grasses beneath my window laugh up at Him. Truly, the whole created earth is God's visible theater. But we must not take too much delight in His manifest and familiar works. For those of us who are called to election have our part to play in His theater which is not visible to the fleshy eye. And woe to us if we fail to play our parts!

The magistrates acted wisely in choosing this spot for his execution. The multitude were bound to assemble, but here in this natural amphitheater there is space for them to stand or even to turn about if anyone turn fainthearted. In October there is nearly always a faint haze in the air but today light sparkles everywhere. Yet the mountains, curving in, as if to embrace the scene, keep the air still.

The multitude stirred and murmured when he was brought into the arena but they have fallen quiet. His body is fastened to an iron stake that is driven deep into the ground. A crown of straw has been placed upon his head. The Executioner is sprinkling it with sulphur. The book in which he uttered his foul blasphemies is suspended from the stake. *Christianity Restored!* He spoke of *Christian Institutes* as an ill-composed book. He holds that infants are incapable of sin, advises that baptism be delayed until the age of twenty. In these times, when the young tend to be even more debauched than in past ages! "You are worthy that the little chickens, all sweet and innocent as they are, peck your eyes out a hundred thousand times," I told him.

The Council, when it sentenced him to death, denounced both these heresies, and a plaque charging him with Anti-Paedo-Baptism as well as Anti-Trinitarianism hangs from the stake, along with his heretical book.

I have been told that last night in his cell he declared to his jailer that today his patron, the Archangel Michael, will come to deliver him! How misguided are men, in their earthly pilgrimage, clutching the phantoms of their own imaginings.

The Executioner is stepping aside so that all the people may view him.

He is striving to raise his head but the Executioner has bound his neck fast to the stake by four or five turns of thick rope. Now that the multitude has ceased murmuring, I can hear what he says:

"I am not guilty. If I have sinned it is through ignorance . . ."

William Farel asks him: "Do you confess that Jesus is the Christ the *eternal Son of God*?" The multitude keeps silent while Servetus renders his answer:

"I confess that Jesus is the Christ the Son of the *eternal God*."

It is the same answer that he gave me for all my remonstrances. Farel turns and once again calls on him to confess Jesus Christ as the eternal Son of God. But Servetus only lifts his eyes to heaven, crying, "Jesus, Son of the living God, have mercy on me!"

The Executioner has begun piling the fagots in a circle around the heretic. Farel withdraws to a distance, then turns to the people. He is a godly man and a strong preacher. His voice carries throughout the whole arena: "Hearken! Satan is about to seize upon this soul!"

But the wood is green and the flames start slowly, too slowly for the liking of some. A man rushes forward and essays to beat them out and after him an old woman and then a boy. But they have been motioned back. The flames themselves would have rebuked them if the Executioner had not done his duty.

The fagots have at last taken fire. His head seems to swim in a cloud of smoke and sulphur. If my eyes do not deceive me, he opened his lips when the flames reached his face. "O Jesus, Son of the eternal God, have mercy on me!" It was the howl he uttered after that that made the whole multitude fall silent. . . .

I shall remain here at this window for half an hour in order to be assured that life is extinct. With his last breath he cried for mercy to Jesus the Son of the *eternal* God.

If he had called upon Jesus the *eternal* Son of God, the civil and ecclesiastical authorities would have been forced to halt his execution. But the wretch denied the Triune nature of God with his last breath.

They will be saying that I did nothing but throw Servetus to the professed enemies of Christ as to ravening beasts, that I was responsible for his arrest at Vienne in the Province of Lyons. He accused me of dictating the letters that passed between Guillaume Trie and his cousin Antoine Arneys. But Guillaume Trie has been known to me for some years. How should I properly refuse my advice when he consults me about a matter that involves his cousin's soul's salvation? As for the charge that I delivered Servetus into the hands of the Grand Inquisitor at Lyons, how should I come to have such sudden familiarity with the satellites of the Pope? It would be highly incredible, indeed, that letters should pass back and forth between those who follow Christ and those who follow Belial. So there is no need for more words to refute so futile a claim. Still, it will be well to order my thoughts—in case I am unjustly attacked.

The Olive Garden

On the way over Edward Dabney told people only that he intended to stop in Paris. He did not mention the name of the other city. And indeed, he had never actually planned to go there. It was merely that the idea, coupled with an incident from the past, had so persistently presented itself to him all that spring. An incident? The happening had not the stature of an incident. A shadow, rather, that all that spring had seemed to brush his path. The first time had been in February: a blowy day, but moist, almost sultry. He was taking the shortcut from Slade Hall to the bursar's office, in company with the dean of the Graduate School. The weak sunlight cast pale shadows of the maple boughs before them. He trod on a gray, moving shadow and thought of the time he and Joe Matthews, of the History Department, and Matthews's wife and a girl named Susan Ferris had lived in a villa at Cap Brun and of a day in October when somebody had shouted, *"Le temps fait beau!"* and he had been impelled to quit the dark, airless room in which he worked and go into the garden which sloped up the hill back of the house.

He had sat there in the arbor all morning, leaning back on the uncomfortable wooden bench, his arms folded, staring at the wall of the villa. Tawny or orange-pink roses were all about him. Yellow things, the kind that in his own country bloomed only in the spring, starred the slope below. It was at noon that the shadow of the ivy spray sprang out suddenly on the white wall. He observed that it was very dark, almost black; then looked closer and saw that the shadowy leaves were green, dark green, and saw, too, the minute serrations of each leaf quivering on the wall that on this day was whiter than ordinary. "That is the blackest, the most perfect shadow I have ever seen," he thought, but the picture went out of his memory and did not return until that day in February when the dark, perfect shadow had seemed to blow again across his path.

The dean was talking about the new faculty lounge. He had answered him with enthusiasm disproportionate to the subject, thinking, "The war is over. I can go to France now. I can go to France this summer!" And then he had put the idea out of his mind. *You would not want to go back. You could not bear it, or worse, still, you would have no emotion, revisiting those scenes. That summer you spent in the Villa Les Hortensias you were engaged to Susan Ferris. You expected to marry her as soon as you got your promotion. Provence. The Courts of Love. Arnaut Daniel. You need to be young, to be in love, to enjoy meridional sunshine. . . .* You are not in love with anybody, he told himself. You cannot be in love with trees, houses, stretches of road you walked along ten years ago, in a country that is now so ravaged that you would not recognize its face. Henry James, in spite of what you tell your students, was in many ways an old fool. And then he had seen—and this for him was the strangest part of the whole business—the roads that that summer had been all sun and sharp shadow, yawning with the cavernous holes, their edges still crumbling concrete, and had known that he was going back to Cap Brun.

The train left the Gare de Lyon early in the morning. It was almost dark when he stepped out on the station platform of the meridional city. There were not many people in the station. He walked past them, not glancing to right or left. He had been in France ten days and already he had fallen out of the habit of looking at people's faces. Across the road, partly obscured by dusty mimosa boughs, he saw a sign: *Brasserie de la Gare.* He had intended, so far as he had a plan for that first evening, to eat dinner at the Brasserie de la Gare. In the old days they always managed to eat there when they came back from trips. It was because of the miraculous squash *baignets.* They had happened on them in that dusty little hole on their first day in the city and were always, as Susan Ferris said, hoping to get them again, and probably never would, though they must, she had insisted, keep on trying. The windows were no dustier now than they had been, but he did not feel like dining there that evening and turned his steps down toward the *rade*.

He would not go to the Café de la Rade, either, this evening. He could not bear, this evening, to look at the harbor. There was only one other place for him to go: the Brasserie de la Source. They had always called the tiny *place* Fountain Square because it held their favorite of all the fountains. The fountain in itself was not remarkable, merely a shallow basin, with water gushing out of the wide mouth of the dolphin that rose out of a mound of moss and ferns in the center of the basin. But a young fig tree grew beside the dolphin, seeming to support him in his gambol. The fishmongers had used to set their stalls up alongside of that fountain. On summer evenings when you sat late over your coffee you could see the scarlet scales of the *rougets* sparkling in the light from the shop windows.

There were no stalls in the *place* now, and no water came out of the fountain. The dolphin was still intact, except for a part of his tail, which, for all he could remember, might always have been missing. He walked over in the gray light and stood beside the fountain. The basin might never have held water, and of the moss and stones that had made the dolphin's mound there was left only a little pebbly dust.

He looked about him. A black-clad old man crossed the street slowly and disappeared around a corner. A woman, black-clad, too, who had been standing in front of an *épicerie*, apparently watching the old man's uncertain progress, turned back into her dimly lighted shop. It was the only window in the street that showed a light. He entered and at first thought he was alone in the place when the black shape rose from behind the counter. "*Monsieur demand?*" a voice said. He bought a quarter of a cheese and a loaf of bread and a bottle of wine and as he paid for his purchases looked into the woman's face, wondering if he had ever seen her before. "The people who kept the Brasserie de la Source," he said. "Do you know what has become of them?" A gleam—curiosity, malice, fear?—showed for a second in the black, lusterless depths of her eyes, then she bent her gaze on the counter. "*Ils sont partis . . . Monsieur veut-il autre chose . . . ?*" "No, no, nothing else. That will do nicely," he said, and took his purchases, unwrapped, save for an inadequate scrap of paper, and left the shop.

Two streets away he boarded a tram and ten minutes later descended in the *place* at Cap Brun. It was not much changed from the day when he had stopped there on the occasion of the communal wine making. The little engine, belching black clouds of smoke, had stood in front of Monsieur Dupont's *épicerie*. Monsieur Dupont and the butcher had stood beside it in their stained aprons, and had made him drink a glass of the fiery green *marc*.

One or two dim lights showed, but most of the shops were boarded up. In front of Monsieur Dupont's *épicerie* an old man sat on a bench, his body appearing shadowy under the weight of his domed head, his hands, folded one over the other, resting upon a cane. He turned his head slowly. His eyes, pale gray, rimmed, like a bloodhound's, with red, turned, too, in their cavernous sockets and rested briefly upon Dabney's face before he resumed his stare at nothing.

Dabney walked past. That was not Monsieur Dupont. Monsieur Dupont had been old, even then. He could not have survived the first years of the war. He could hardly survive in peacetime. He was mad, Susan Ferris said. She had come to that conclusion when she was trying to help Marjorie Matthews with the housekeeping and making, doubtless, a poor job of it. She would order *tomates* and he would murmur, "*Oui, mademoiselle, des asperges,*" and when the order came you were just as likely to get *tomates* as *asperges*, she said. She insisted that he was always brooding on his past. Until his eyesight failed he had been, like his father and grandfathers before him, a painter of armorial bearings. Some of the carriages ornamented by a remote great-grandfather were in the Tuileries. Monsieur Dupont, when he turned shopkeeper, had naturally changed his name; he could not drag the family name into an *épicerie*. He had never known what the original name was, or where she got her information—from Matthews, probably. He was, in his way, a fanciful fellow.

He had made the turn. The road to the fort lay before him. It was as he had imagined it, only the holes were more numerous, more cavernous. The *camions* must have pounded along here day and night, from the time the city was first occupied.

There was a ruined house on his right, an enormous olive tree uprooted before it, but on his left the hedge rose, as impenetrable, as tall as in the old days. He stopped before a small window set high in a wall. That window opened into Madame LeClerc's bedroom. It was Madame LeClerc's other villa, Les Hortensias, which they had rented that summer. They had come here to visit her often. Madame would be sitting at the window, her tawny dog, Fifine, beside her. Once they had found Dique, the vagabond dog from the fort, sitting in the dust under the window, emitting mournful, hopeless yelps. "It is always like that," Madame had explained. "Always he is faithful to Fifine." A great one for love, Madame. On the day she discovered that he and Susan were engaged she brought them a bottle of Burgundy, and two roses from her garden, a glowing, deep-red rose for him and, as Susan commented, a small, rather worm-eaten pink one for her. The perfect rose was really a tribute to letters, he had explained to Susan; Madame had discovered at about the same time that he had written a volume of poems. But her real, her deepest admiration was reserved for the nobility. The only difference they had ever had with her was over the Comte de Garonne's eggs. She could not understand why they would not buy their eggs from the count, even if they were several sous higher than Monsieur Dupont's. They were larger eggs, she maintained, and superior in other ways. But except for that slight shadow, their intercourse that summer had been unclouded. When Madame saw them coming up the hill she would bawl at her red-cheeked orphan niece: "*Gisette! Gisette! La cave!*" and Gisette would run down into the cellar and come back with a dusty bottle and they would all take their seats at the wooden table that ringed the plane tree. Monsieur LeClerc sometimes looked down upon them from an upper window but he never joined them. He was, Madame explained, too *triste*. He had been *triste* ever since the last war, in the course of which he had lost three brothers and half a lung. Monsieur—he was employed by a naval family as chauffeur by day, but Madame would not have liked you to know that—Monsieur had been seventy-five then to Madame's seventy-three. They were certainly dead by this time, might have been dead before this war, this global war, this goddamned bloodiest of all wars began, he said to himself, his feet pounding, with his thoughts, hard on the ruined road.

He walked faster. On the right there was a break in the dark wall of shrubbery. It was down this road that he and the Matthewses and Susan had lived. He walked on, with hardly a glance for the path, so overgrown now that it could hardly have been discerned in daylight, while inside his head the tortuous way unrolled. If you took the first turn to the right you came to the villa inhabited by the famous painter, the contemporary of Manet and Monet, whose pictures you often went to look at when you were in Paris—two of them hung then in the Luxembourg. But you never took that road. You kept to the left and came in time to Les Hortensias. The bedrooms were no bigger than a rabbit hutch, there was no *salon* —a fact that Madame never ceased to lament—but the terrace held the Mediterranean framed between the squat clumps of hydrangeas, which Madame kept growing in tubs, so that the place might have a name. The garden had three terraces, each about two yards wide. From the last terrace a path led to the still tinier garden that sur- rounded the Villa Florida, where the real estate agent who had made them acquainted with Madame LeClerc lived. He, too, was *triste*, although a febrile gaiety sometimes played over his fine, aristocratic features, on a night, say, that you had dined well and were sitting on the terrace, gazing at the sea. It was on such a night that he had declared that for his part he would like to have a gramophone. "It would be so *gai*," and he turned a mournful, apprehensive gaze upon his wife. He had, Susan thought, the finest eyes and the most aristo- cratic nose in the world. His wife had fine eyes, too, of a different sort. Dark, Breton eyes, drowned, most of the time, in tears. *Et pour cause.* They had amassed a competence during twenty years of coffee planting in Madagascar and had come home just in time to lose it during the depression. And *notre oncle*—he *would* not die! The Pats—he could not, for the life of him, remember their sonorous, aristocratic name; they had always just called them "the Pats"—the Pats, Susan said, were lonely. They would have had to demean themselves a bit to run with the naval crowd—after all, *Oncle* bore one of the first names of France—but they did not have enough money to keep up with the officers, and naturally there was nobody else in town they could associate with, "except," Susan concluded, "foreigners like us." He himself had always thought that it was chiefly *Oncle*'s obstinacy that kept Madame's fine eyes clouded with tears and gave the melancholy droop to Pat's fair mustache. The melancholy always increased after the annual visit to the members of the family, made usually in July. They sent post- cards back to the quartet and to Madame LeClerc, views of the family château, with a single flowing salutation inscribed in the blank space reserved for messages. He seemed to have heard—why was it that when you thought you would never see people again you did not listen to news of them?—he seemed to have heard that *Oncle* had finally died and Pat had come into the money and the title and the château, but the money and the château were in occupied France and Pat and Madame Pat had fled to unoccupied France. Where were they now and what doing? He would not descend the winding path and ring at the door of the Villa Florida, but he would like to know.

A path branched off from the road. He followed it into an open glade, dominated by four squat fig trees. There was a rock at the foot of one of the trees. He sat down and lit a cigarette. When he had finished the cigarette he thrust his hand into his pocket and brought out the unwrapped piece of cheese. The wine bottle stood between his feet. He looked at it, wondering if the proprietress would have furnished a corkscrew if he had asked for one; then raised the bottle and with one blow shattered its neck on the stone. Wine was seeping through the laces, under the tongue of his shoe. He took a long draught, feeling the splintered edge of glass sharp against his lip, and set the bottle down and after a second laid the piece of cheese beside it. It was almost too dark to see, but he remembered this place very well. They had had a picnic here one evening, a jumped-up affair, but there had turned out to be more food than anybody had expected, and they had eaten and drunk prodigiously and were stretched out, all four of them, under the trees, when Victorine, their *femme de ménage*, and her husband, Edmond, came through the grove. They were on their way to take the tram car to the movies but they had stopped to chat. Edmond was carrying Toussaint, the three-year-old, and Victorine had the baby in her arms. Victorine had announced that they might all kiss the baby, whose face and hands were covered with a rash. Matthews —he was the kind of fellow who is always afraid he is going to catch some disease in railway stations or restaurants—had not much liked the idea of kissing Albert, but he had done it.

He got up and walked back to the road. It was dark now. The housefronts were gray oblongs, rising out of dark masses of shrubbery. There was a break in the hedge. He put his hand out and felt cold stone. Yes, the gate would be about here. There was an arch above it, with the name *Villa Agatha* in faded colors. In the old days a figurine, a blue-clad Madonna, had hung on a rusted wire from the center of the arch. It was gone, but the bell still gave its faint jangle when you pushed the gate open. The place, when they knew it, had been deserted for years. It belonged to a distant relation of Pat's, and was for sale. That was how they had first come here, armed with permission from Pat—not that they had ever had any intention of buying it. But it was fun, as Susan said, to pretend they had. They had formed the habit, all four of them, of coming back often, by twos sometimes, more often singly. "I'm going to miss the Villa Agatha more than anything," Susan said the day they left.

The paths were not much more overgrown now than they had been ten years ago. That was the beauty of this country. The hard, acid soil had been so tended, so cherished for generations that weeds dared not grow, even in an abandoned garden. He took, as he always did, the path to the right. There was another walk that was Susan's favorite: an *allée*, bordered with cypresses, with at its end two stone benches, convenient for the contemplation of the inevitable statue: a cowled Madonna, with lilies thrusting up about her feet. But he had always preferred the path that led downhill through the olive orchard. The moon was up. The silver-gray path before him was intricately patterned with the black, moving shadows of the little leaves. These trees were old. They had not grown an inch, had not spread their arms in a new gesture in the years he had been away.

There were no more trees. He had come into a little hollow. The fountain, a great, deep Roman cup, tilted a little on its heavy column, stood in an open space. Behind it laurel and olive and fig trees grew in a great tangle. He used to walk here when he grew weary of seeing precise, ordered shapes about him, when the desire to see a tree thrusting its limbs out as wildly, as uncontrollably as nature intended, came over him, as, he had been told, it came over all Americans in Europe. This tangle was the only really wild spot on the grounds. He had had a surprising thing happen to him once, here in this grove. He had been standing beside the fountain, idly remarking to himself the absence of birds. And suddenly, from the tangle, had come a burst of song. Nightingales, he supposed, who made their nests in the undergrowth.

He crossed the glade and took the path up to the villa. The ground under his feet was spongy; a chill air fanned his cheeks. It was always a little damp in here, even when *la chaleur* held the countryside in its grip. It was on this path that he had come upon the man, crouching, his back turned, behind some shrubbery. A trespasser, like himself, he had thought, only one trespassing with no good intent, and was in a mind to turn back when the fellow rose to his feet and he saw the fresh-plucked mushroom in his hand, the basket dangling from his arm. He had never seen him again, though he had told him that he came here often; it was a good place for mushrooms. A young fellow, not more than twenty-five. Some workman in the village, probably; his clothes were stained as if by grease from a mechanic's shop. That was the only human being he had ever met in these grounds, though he had walked here so often.

He stopped and looked behind him. No, it was along here that the man had risen up. He had stood beside that plane tree while they talked. His teeth had showed very white in his brown face. He had smiled all through the brief conversation and when he turned away his blunt, earth-stained fingers had sketched in the air the gesture that meant they would meet again. They were used to seeing aliens among them in those days and always smiled on them. They were kind, too, about helping you arrange your affairs, and when you made your most execrable errors invariably complimented you on speaking the language so well.

He was in front of the villa now. It had the bulk, the proportions of the houses around l'Estaque that Cézanne loved to paint. The unsheltered terrace ran the length of the façade. He took a few steps to the right. Those cypresses that lined the west wall had grown taller in these ten years. They could not grow darker. He had always thought that they were the blackest cypresses he had ever seen anywhere. He did not walk directly to the house but went instead down a path to the abandoned potting shed. Susan used to come here with him sometimes, to steal the little cactuses which grew in a solid wall below the shed. She always stopped to look at a giant nicotiana growing in a crumbling pot. There had been a rusty pair of gardener's shears hanging from a hook on the wall. He turned back toward the house. Flowers had been all along here in the old days. They were here now! The odor of phlox was heavy in the air—or was it Susan's nicotiana? Her *allée*, the one with the cowled Madonna, was off a little to the right. He would go out that way. He was at the house. The steps gave a little under his feet as he ascended to the terrace, but no more than in the old days. He crossed the terrace and looked down. Cypresses reared themselves darkly at each end of the terrace. Between them lay the sea, each wave, as it raced north, a little flecked with silver. He looked away, into the gloom of the cypresses, then turned around. The same light that edged the waves splotched the floor with silver. Something at the end of the terrace was blacker than a shadow. He leaned and touched the sagging round of an iron table. What had been two chairs lay beside it.

He and Susan had sat at that table once, to drink a bottle of wine. It was mournful, Susan said, for the chairs and table to keep on standing here on the terrace when the house had been deserted so long. That was ten years ago. The chairs and table had stayed on, long after he and Susan went away, had been there when the port was seized, had sprawled on, rusting, during the occupation, the desertion deeper than any he or Susan could have envisioned. There had been nobody—not even that young poacher—to walk in the garden then. "Nobody," he said aloud, "nobody. They are all dead."

He walked back to the edge of the terrace. He put out his hand and touched a plume of cypress. It was cool and firm and prickly to the touch. Beyond the plumes the sea still shimmered. A long way down to the sea from here. Terrace after terrace to descend before you struck the road—what did they call it? The *corniche?*—that ran the length of this rocky coast. Pirates used to frequent it; there were caves along there where they hid their stolen wares. Matthews said that there was a legend that Ulysses, in his wanderings, had taken shelter in one of those caves. A long time ago, all that. The pirates had used that road in the days of Julius Caesar. Ulysses had sheltered himself there before recorded time. A lonely time he must have had of it. But there was one hero lonelier than ever Ulysses had been on his wanderings. Deucalion, who, after the flood, walked the earth, companioned only by his wife, Pyrrha. The Delphic Oracle told them to strew the earth with the bones of their mother. Pyrrha shrank from the impiety, but Deucalion picked up stones and cast them far and wide and from those stones, just such stones as one found in this flinty soil, a new race of men had sprung up. He turned his back on the sea and walked along the moon-splotched path to the gate. He put a hand out as he went, touching a spray here, a flower

there. The garden no longer seemed deserted. He did not now wish
that he might meet somebody on its paths. Far below, in the rocky
caves, that would always furnish refuge, that could, if they were
needed, bring forth a new race of men, he could hear the heroes
murmuring to each other.

Emmanuele! Emmanuele!

Robert Heyward glanced at his watch as he closed the door behind him and walked out onto the terrace: high noon. A waiter was passing. Heyward asked him to bring him writing materials and an apéritif. Before he sat down at a table he walked over to the balustrade and stood for some seconds looking out over the sea; the Hotel Alamède sat on an eminence not five hundred yards from the beach. The gardens of the hotel consisted of a series of terraces which ended in a cliff that rose straight out of the sea. The young American's eye left the wide, blue expanse to seek and find a line of dark growth that followed the cliff's curve: the orange and lemon trees that grew on the terraces gave way at the cliff's edge to ilex and pine. A path made of pinkish gravel ran the length of the cliff. Bob had walked there yesterday with his employer, the famous French man of letters, Guillaume Fäy. At Fäy's suggestion they had left the path to go in under the shade of the orange trees. It had rained that morning and the sky was still overcast, but Bob, as he went stooping through the grove, had had the illusion that the sun shone on them: a profusion of golden globes that shone even in that dim light had hung over their heads. Fäy struck the trunk of one of the trees lightly with his stick. It was as richly colored as the pillars of the famous mosque at Córdoba, he said. A Sudanese Negro was sauntering along the path as they emerged from the grove. He was over six feet tall. The spray of white jasmine that he wore in his turban curled down over his cheek, giving him a look of languor that contrasted oddly with his brawny frame. When they came to the end of the green tunnel he grasped a handful of orange blossoms and held them in his hand a moment before he inserted the crushed petals into his nostrils.

The waiter had come back. Heyward walked over and sat down under the striped awning. He told himself that he would not touch his drink until he had written a page of his letter. But he did not begin writing at once. Instead, he stared at the door he had just closed.

It was a pale saffron color, like the walls of the hotel, but Bob fancied that the brownish yellow was here and there tinged with pink—the same pink that showed in the gravel walk on the cliff's edge. An ilex bough that drooped over the terrace cast a plume of almost black shadow on the door. A smile trembled on the young man's lips; it seemed almost incredible that the shadow should so faithfully reproduce the minute serrations that bordered each ilex leaf. He drew the sheet of paper toward him and began to write:

> My Darling:
>
> I got the job and have been at it for nearly a week. It is even easier than I had expected it to be. Fäy rises at eight every morning, drinks only a cup of tea, and is at work by nine. He is not ready for me before ten. I come in then and we work for two hours. He has an enormous correspondence, but he is already trusting me to write many of the letters, with only a memorandum for guide. He said yesterday that I seemed to know what he needed to have done without his telling me. So you see I am giving satisfaction!
>
> Promptly at noon he sends me out of the room. It is his custom to write to his wife every day at this hour. He has been doing this for thirty years, he tells me, whenever he is separated from her. I am going to follow his example and write to you, too, every day, at this hour. Don't you think that it will bring us closer together if you know that every day at twelve o'clock I will be starting my letter to you?

The sound of footsteps made him look up from his writing. Two women stood only a few feet away from him. One of them, an elderly Frenchwoman, was evidently a servant. She stood a few paces behind the other, holding in each hand a string bag from which fruit and vegetables protruded.

The other woman stood with her hands resting on the back of

a chair and contemplated the young man, her head a little on one side, a faint smile on her lips. Heyward, as he got to his feet and stood looking down on her, thought that he might have taken her for an American if he had not known that she had been born in France; she wore her broad black sun hat and gray cotton frock with a casual elegance that is not often found among elderly French-women. She was thin and a little stooped. The hands that grasped the chair back were still shapely but wrinkled and covered with sun spots. She fixed her large, gray-blue eyes on Heyward and said in a husky whisper, "And is *this* the way you work for Monsieur Fäy?"

Heyward got hurriedly to his feet. He was annoyed to find himself blushing. Mrs. Rensslaer, the widow of the historian Edgar Rensslaer, was a cousin of Guillaume Fäy's. Heyward's classmate, Forrest Blair, had taken Heyward to call upon her soon after he arrived in the city. It was Forrest who had discovered that Guillaume Fäy needed a secretary, Forrest who insisted that Heyward, with his unusually good command of French and his acquaintance with contemporary literature, was the man for the job. Mrs. Rensslaer had said negligently that she was sure that Guillaume would be fortunate to secure the services of Mr. Heyward. She would be delighted to write him a letter of introduction, but on one condition. Heyward must not let her cousin know that she was in the city. "I am not in the mood for Guillaume," she had said frankly.

Heyward, who had already written to thank her for her kind offices, told her now that he had been working for Fäy several days and found the work stimulating and delightful. He was about to say something else when Mrs. Rensslaer made a motion of her hand toward her maidservant which indicated that she was too pressed for time to share drinks with him. Casting a glance, which seemed to him tinged with mischief, at the door of Fäy's suite, she asked, "And what is Guillaume doing with himself this fine morning?"

Heyward replied simply that Monsieur Fäy was writing to his wife, adding, "He tells me that he has written to her at this hour, whenever they are separated, for thirty years."

Mrs. Rensslaer continued to eye him intently while he was speaking. When he finished she shook her head slowly from side to side, at the same time compressing her lips, then suddenly cast her remarkable eyes upward as if asking Heaven what it thought of that. An exclamation broke from her. Heyward did not think that it *could* have been "*Oo la la!*" and yet that was what it had sounded like.

"Can you dine with me tonight?" she asked. "Forrest is coming."
Heyward replied that he would be delighted to dine at Soleil d'Or
any day, any hour she named. She told him to come at eight and,
beckoning to her maid, went, with a step which struck him as sur-
prisingly light for her years, down the stairs and onto the street.

Heyward sat down again and was about to resume his letter when
he suddenly folded the sheet of paper and thrust it into his pocket.
He would have to finish his letter later in the day; the door of Fäy's
suite had opened. The great man stood for a second blinking in the
Mediterranean sunshine before he saw his secretary and came swiftly
toward him. He had been in his dressing gown when Heyward left
him a few minutes ago. Now he wore a coffee-colored suit of some
fine tropical weave and a Panama hat of equal fineness. Heyward was
struck, not for the first time, by his air of extraordinary vitality. He
wondered whether it was a family characteristic. Fäy was the same
age as his cousin, Mrs. Rensslaer, and like her was tall and thin, but
he was lither. And he came toward the young man his body actually
seemed to sway from side to side out of a superabundance of vitality.
He stopped and, settling his hat farther forward on his head, asked
Heyward if he would like to walk with him to the marketplace. He
had ordered a pair of gloves for his wife two weeks ago. They were
to be ready today.

The vitality which animated his whole body found its chief expression in his eyes, Heyward thought. They were long, like his
cousin's, capable of opening widely, and set under dark, level brows.
Heyward had thought that they were a light hazel in color. This
morning they were so lambent that they looked almost yellow. Fäy
was smiling at the young man. His smile seemed to say that he
realized that his conduct was unusual for an oldster. "But that can't
be helped," the smile also said. "Here I am. You must take me as
I am."

A scene from Heyward's childhood rose before him. A small boy,
he had been helping his grandmother's old Negro gardener cut brush,
when a snake suddenly reared itself above a fallen bough. Its body
was intricately patterned in rich shades of dark brown. Its head was
copper-colored. From under the slanted lid an eye gleamed at him.
He had put his hand out toward it when the old Negro, coming up
behind him, struck it down: "Boy, don't you know a chunkhead
when you see one?"

Heyward signified his desire to accompany Fäy to the marketplace. The two men began the descent of the long flight of steps. Fäy—who made a point of speaking English with his secretary— said that Muhammed Ali had been recommended to him as one of the best leather workers in the city. If the gloves he had ordered came up to his expectations he was of a mind to order another pair for his wife. "Her hands are one of her greatest beauties," he said. "Or were —until she ruined them with gardening—and the care of peasants— and animals." He turned his flashing gaze on Heyward. "I have seen her run out into the coldest weather, nothing on her head, a cloak falling off her shoulders, carrying a pan full of food. For whom? Stray cats, sick, mangy beasts that the farmers would let starve. In winter her hands are a pitiable sight, chapped, with raw places all over them. I give you my word I sometimes fear that she will suc- cumb to an infection."

Heyward did not answer. There was something about the scene that struck him as unreal. He, Robert Durham Heyward, associate professor of English at Bonnell College, was receiving confidences from Guillaume Fäy—*Guillaume Fäy!* He thought helplessly that things had been happening too fast. His first volume of poems had been published only six months ago. Two months after that one of the great philanthropic foundations had awarded him the fellowship that had made possible his long-awaited trip to Paris. The day before he sailed the head of the English Department had summoned him to his office and had told him that the college had recently become the beneficiary of a sizable trust fund. The proceeds from it were to be devoted to securing scholars and artists as lecturers. "While you're over there you might fix something up for us," the administrator had said with a smile. When Forrest Blair, who was attached to the American consulate in a North African port, wrote that Guillaume Fäy was vacationing in the city, Heyward had hastily reckoned up his resources and had taken the next boat for Africa; it had seemed too good an opportunity to be missed. Forrest, he had felt sure, could get permission for him to call on Fäy. He might even have a little conversation with him while he was delivering the invitation to lecture. That had been the most he had hoped for, but now—and his heart beat faster at the thought—he lived under the same roof with the great man, in an association so intimate that Fäy discussed his wife with him, complained of her to him! Madame Fäy's picture stood on Fäy's desk in a heavily wrought silver frame; a young woman in a white dress, with her hair in a great coil on the top of her head, gazing straight at you out of eyes that surely were dark. Heyward had a vision of her now, as slim as Fäy himself, her hair slipping from its coil, her cloak swinging behind her in the wind, as she ran across a courtyard, holding in her arms a great yellow cat. The Fäys lived in a château in Normandy. Mrs. Rensslaer had described it as a "cross between a museum and a menagerie." But Madame Fäy, he suddenly reminded himself, was not a young woman. Mrs. Rensslaer had told him that she was two years older than she herself was. She must then be seventy to her husband's sixty-eight.

They had come to the first landing in the long flight of steps. A narrow terrace bordered the stair on each side. At the right a marble bench stood under an orange tree. A gardener was taking oranges from the basket that he held on his arm and laying them down upon one end of the bench. There were varieties that Heyward had never seen before. One kind was as large as a muskmelon, another was shaped like an egg, and on top of the heap the gardener was scattering tangerines whose skins were a greenish yellow, faintly tinged with rose. Fäy had stopped, too. The two men stood looking down at the heap of fruit. Fäy gave a small shake of the head. "In France everything is gray," he said, "gray buildings, gray streets, gray light over everything. In Normandy we even have apples whose skin has a grayish cast!" His lean hand hovered for a moment over the heap before he selected a tangerine. It had been picked before it was quite ripe. The skin was a clear lemony green on one side, on the other a pale yellow, with a faint trace of color at the navel. Fäy held it in his hand and turned it so that it caught the light before he began stripping off the skin. "See!" he said. "The skin is as delicate, as pliable as those gloves that Muhammed Ali is making for my wife."

He sat down as he spoke. Heyward selected one of the larger oranges and sat down beside him. After they had eaten their fruit they sat on for a while, smoking. The harbor, almost elliptical in shape, lay directly below them. The sun beat straight down. The surface of the whole bay sparkled green. The depths beneath were bluer than any water Heyward had ever imagined. Fäy suddenly waved his hand.

"Does all this ever strike you as unreal?" he asked.

The young American slowly shook his head.

Fäy turned and gave him a fleeting glance. "How *does* it strike you, then?"

"Do you mean this particular scene?" Heyward asked.

"No," Fäy said impatiently. "I mean any scene, any landscape anywhere that is extraordinarily beautiful. Do you ever feel that it —does not exist?"

Heyward laughed. "No," he said. "I feel as if it had been there all along. The hell of it is that I didn't get there before!"

Fäy laughed, too. "Ah, you Americans!"

Somewhere below a clock struck. He rose and said that they must be on their way to the souks.

They left the great modern thoroughfare and turned off onto one of the older streets, cobbled and so narrow that the stick Fäy swung in his hand struck occasionally against the wall. He told Heyward that the last time he had been in the city was just after the winter rains. These walls had all been mantled in green moss. The flowers planted on the edge of the terraces had overhung them like great baskets of flowers.

They emerged from the narrow passage into a square floored with cobblestones. From the dark stone fountain in its center interlacing plumes of water jetted high into the air. They went past the arched front entrance and passed through a narrow doorway shaded by a leaning jujube tree into an alley which led, Fäy said, into the saddlers' souks.

Heyward had never been in this part of the souks before. Fäy, striking his stick on stone, told him that when he first began to visit the city the alleyways all had earthen floors. On moonlight nights Arabs and camels used to sleep against the walls of the mosque. Now the alleys all had sidewalks and policemen patrolled the square at all hours of the night. Heyward, as he walked, was gazing up over his head at the ceiling. Fäy pointed out to him the peculiar half-dark, half-luminous light that bathed the stalls, the wares heaped on them, the figures stooping behind them. It was, he said, partly the effect of the whitewashed ceiling.

They had arrived at the stall he sought. The saddler, Muhammed Ali, his long legs crossed, was seated on a leather cushion, stitching a pair of gloves by the light that came in between the half-drawn curtains at the back of the stall. He laid his work aside when he saw Fäy and came forward. He wore a not very clean burnous. His turban was of some silky material striped with rose. Greetings were exchanged. He stopped and drew a parcel wrapped in tissue paper out from under the counter. His tawny eyes rested on Fäy's face for a second before he deftly whisked the wrappings away so that a pair of gloves was revealed.

Fäy stood in silence, eyeing the gloves. The leather had been dyed a dark red, almost the color of pomegranates. The texture of the leather was so fine as to be almost silky. As if obeying the kind of uncontrollable impulse that sometimes comes to children, Fäy put his finger out and touched one of the gloves, then turned to Heyward, showing his still strong, white teeth in a delighted smile. "Feel!" he said. "It is like the skin of the little oranges," and he brushed Heyward's cheek with the soft kidskin.

Muhammed Ali's tawny eyes gleamed. He said in fluent French that he was overjoyed to know that Monsieur was satisfied with his workmanship.

Fäy had held one of the gloves up and was studying the pattern of delicate stitching that ornamented the wrist when a shaft of blinding sunlight falling between suddenly parted curtains made both tourists look up. An Arab boy about fourteen entered, bearing a bundle of hides on his arm. He laid them down upon the floor at the back of the stall and, stepping over to Muhammed Ali's side, spoke to him in a low voice. Muhammed Ali nodded impatiently and, pointing to the end of the counter, said a few words in Arabic. The boy remained standing at his side for a second after he had spoken, staring straight ahead of him, then, as if he had all at once grasped the meaning of the answer that had been given him, he nodded and went to the end of the counter and, drawing out a bulky package, tucked it under his arm and left the shop. But not before his lustrous gaze had rested first on one and then the other of the tourists. His eyes were unusually large, dark, and so lustrous that they seemed to brim in the head like water. Heyward had the feeling that some substance as tangible, as soft as the pliant kidskin had been drawn across his cheek. The curtain that had been pushed aside by the boy's entrance had not swung back into place. As the boy turned away his cheek caught the light. Under a soft down it shone copper color, flushed with rose.

Fäy was still holding the glove in his hand. He did not move until the curtain had swung to behind the boy, then he laid the glove on the counter.

"Your son?" he asked.

The leather worker shook his head. "He is no son of mine," he said in an even, uninterested tone.

"Your apprentice?"

"He has been apprenticed to me," Muhammed Ali said indifferently. "It was his father's request. But I have doubts as to whether he will ever become proficient. He is not of the *caliber*." He added that time was when he would not have had a person of such low origins about him. "But what would you?" he asked. "In these days? If Monsieur will permit me to say so, the prevalence of foreigners in the city has not had an elevating influence upon the young. The boys make money too easily. It has been years since a respectable lad applied to apprentice himself to me. In the meantime, I must have somebody to fetch the hides from the warehouse and deliver the orders when they are accomplished. Hussein does that well enough. As Monsieur sees, he is well built, with a strong body and swift legs, if not a strong brain. What he does out of hours is Allah's concern, not mine."

A short sign escaped Fäy. He picked the glove up again and held it in his hand, then extended it to Muhammed Ali. "The stitching!" he said. "It is so fine, so delicate! But would not a second row of stitching improve it?"

Muhammed Ali took the glove from him. With his finger he traced an imaginary line along the wrist of the glove, drawing his head back as if to study the effect. Finally he raised his tawny eyes to Fäy's face.

"If Monsieur wishes."

"When can I have them?" Fäy asked eagerly.

"Tuesday of next week?"

Fäy shook his head emphatically and, leaning over the counter, fixed his eyes on Muhammed Ali's face. "I leave within a week," he said. "An extra row of stitching—it could be executed within an hour. If one applied oneself. I should like to have the gloves today— this evening."

Muhammed Ali raised both his eyebrows and his shoulders. "Ah, but, monsieur . . . !"

Fäy suddenly laughed. He took his wallet out and, extracting a bill, laid it on the counter. "I should like to pay you in advance for the extra stitching," he said. "And I should like to order another pair of gloves. Exactly like these, only fawn color. Do you think you can deliver the gloves this evening?" As he spoke he raised the bill a few inches from the counter.

Muhammed Ali's brown hand shot out, closed over the bill. "At seven o'clock," he said. "Hussein will bring the gloves to the Alamède at seven o'clock. Will Monsieur be in at that hour?"

"Assuredly," Fäy told him and, crooking his stick jauntily over his arm, he laid his hand on Heyward's elbow and guided him at a rapid pace out of the great whitewashed mosque onto the square where the dark stone fountain still shot its crystalline jets into the blaze of the noonday sun.

II

"And with whom is Monsieur Guillaume Fäy dining tonight?" Mrs. Rensslaer asked.

"I don't know," Heyward said.

They had dined on an iced, rose-colored borscht, followed by breast of guinea hen basted in wine, with new potatoes the size of walnuts ranged about it, and a green salad in a great, dark wooden bowl. The dessert was a sherbet flavored with some fruit that Heywood had never tasted before. While they were eating their sherbets Marie, Mrs. Rensslaer's sharp-featured cook, had put her head in at the door to ask if Monsieur found the guinea hen as it should be. Mrs. Rensslaer explained that the *recette* was one which Forrest's aunt in Maryland had sent her at her request. Forrest must dine here often, Heyward thought, often enough, at any rate, to have his preferences in food consulted.

Immediately after dinner they had gone out on the terrace. Mrs. Rensslaer wore a long dress that she said was as old as the hills but that was the same color as her eyes. As they passed through the hall she had caught up a white shawl, saying that it was likely to turn cool—thank God!—before the evening was over. She reclined now in her long garden chair which stood always beside the fountain. The little splash which Heyward heard every now and then was her hand dipping in and out of the water. Forrest Blair sat a few feet away from Mrs. Rensslaer in the shadow of the great mimosa tree. Heyward's chair was turned so that he faced the harbor.

The lights on the water, the shadowed terrace, the excellent food and wine which he had entrusted to his excellent digestion all contributed to his impression of having before him an agreeable evening. He said lazily to Forrest, "Before I forget, Fäy has let his visa run out and only told me about it this afternoon. Is there any head you could go over to get it fixed up quick?"

"Take it to the new minister," Forrest said. "I met him at the Cortots last night. Seems a good guy."

Mrs. Rensslaer said, "Oh! Has Raoul Pleyol come? I hope he will come to see me."

"Could you take me to see him tomorrow?" Heyward asked boldly.

"Sure," Forrest said. "Eleven o'clock suit you?"

They agreed that Heyward should come to the consulate at eleven o'clock and that Forrest would then escort him to the ministry. Heyward, leaning back, felt a little of the same excitement he had felt that morning. All the world—all the world that seemed of any importance to him—knew of the correspondence which Guillaume Fäy and Raoul Pleyol, the poet-diplomat, had kept up over a period of years, in the high style so dear to French men of letters. The correspondence had ceased abruptly some years ago. It was probable that each man had become too engrossed in his own affairs to continue it. Still, it was strange that Fäy did not know that his old friend was to be the new minister.

"Is it true that Guillaume Fäy writes facing a mirror?" Forrest asked abruptly.

Heyward hesitated, seeing not only the oval mirror that hung over Fäy's desk but the face that opposed it. Fäy, he thought, was neither ignorant of nor indifferent to the deductions that might be drawn from this habit of his. "See this fellow," he had said once, pointing to the reflection of his long, saturnine face. "I have been holding a conversation with him for years. I will not say that he is always in the right, but one thing I can say of him: he never bores me," and he had struck the mirrored cheek a blow so light that it was like a caress. Heyward recalled now that the fact that Fäy wrote facing a mirror had been recorded in his published journal. There was therefore no secret for him to keep. He said gravely that in his employer's suite at the Hotel Alamède a mirror hung over the desk.

"Regular Gentleman of Shallot, isn't he?" Forrest said. "Gabrielle, what are you laughing at?"

"I was thinking of the first time we ever saw the mirror," Mrs.

Rensslaer said. "Guillaume and I spent one whole summer at Crans. I was twelve, so he must have been twelve, too. Thérèse was fourteen. So was Edmond—that was Edmond Pribeaux, our cousin on the next estate."

"Bad as Alabama, for cousins," Forrest said.

Heyward said, "Thérèse?"

"She is Thérèse Gabrielle and I am Gabrielle Thérèse. I am named for her mother."

"*He* calls her Emmanuele."

"Yes. It is a name he gave her."

"What were you laughing at?" Forrest asked.

"The time we played *Peaux Rouges* on that island in the river. It was Edmond's idea, so he got to be . . ."

"Ok-äy?" Forrest asked.

"He was Ok-äy, naturally. Guillaume could have been Oon-ca but he only came and stood on the bank and looked at us and then went back to the house. So Thérèse was Oon-ca and I was Chingach-gook, which I didn't much like; he always seemed a bit of a bore, compared to the others. Still, we had a heavenly time. It was dark when we came home. Guillaume was sitting at his desk, with a mirror hung over it! We laughed till we rolled on the floor. All that summer we would laugh whenever we thought of it."

"Thérèse evidently didn't recognize her fate when she confronted it," Forrest said. "Why do you suppose she ever married the fellow?"

"I don't think it occurred to her that she had any choice in the matter," Mrs. Rensslaer said after a slight pause.

"Did the family make the match?" Heyward asked.

Mrs. Rensslaer said, "No," negligently, and all three were silent for several minutes. In the shadows Heyward could barely make out Mrs. Rennslaer's pale form half reclining on her long chair. There was a rustle among the pillows. She was sitting upright. Suddenly his cheeks were burning. Was it because her eyes fixed on his face? Was this woman subjecting him to a scrutiny more intense, more penetrating than she had hitherto found it worth her while to give him?

She leaned forward. She said, "I tried to break the match off. I tried to tell Thérèse something that I thought I knew about Guillaume. She silenced me by telling me something that *she* knew about him."

"That nobody else knows?" Forrest asked.

"That nobody else would believe."

"That makes it impossible for her to leave him?"

"I'm sure it has never occurred to her to leave Guillaume," Mrs. Rensslaer said. "She's very *bourgeoise* and she's also very devout."

"What *is* it she knows?" burst from Heyward.

"He suffers more than most people," Mrs. Rensslaer said.

"Of course," Heyward said drily. "The man's a genius."

"I don't think that makes any difference to her," Mrs. Rensslaer said. "It isn't that his capacity for suffering is greater than yours or mine. It's that it's—inevitable."

Forrest said, "For the Lord's sake! What *is* this doom that hangs over him?"

"He is possessed by a devil," Mrs. Rensslaer said.

There was a silence; then Forrest said, "How quaint! How long has he had it or how long has it had him?"

"I knew how that would sound to you young Americans!" Mrs. Rensslaer said. "He was able to tell Thérèse the moment it took hold of him—when he was quite young."

"Probably right after he made his first Communion!"

"He has never taken Communion. The Fäys are Protestants—or were. I do not think that Guillaume professes any religion. But we Pribeaux have always been Catholic."

"So she's held to him by her religion—and her knowledge," Forrest mused. "Well, ' 'Tis certain that fine women eat a crazy salad with their meat . . . !' "

Heyward said, "I wonder what it would be like to be inhabited by a devil."

"Nothing much," Mrs. Rensslaer said briskly.

"But the Devil is the Ancient Adversary."

"A created being who chose to be nothing rather than something —if I remember my catechism aright."

"The man suffers," Heyward said. "I've known him less than a week. But I can see that."

"Those Gadarene swine that rushed over the cliff must have had it tough," Forrest said. "Did they go over because they couldn't take it or did the devils hurl them to destruction?"

"Ah, I'm out of my depth now," Mrs. Rensslaer said. "But *you* ought not to be!" She laughed. "My husband used to say that ours was the first age in all history when the educated classes had no theology."

"Why does Fäy write to his wife every day?" Forrest asked. "What can he find to say to the woman?"

Heyward had recovered his self-possession and now felt an agreeable glow diffuse itself through his whole being. All the literary world knew that Guillaume Fäy's wife's name was never mentioned in his celebrated journal except casually. Even before he came aboard Heyward had heard that there was reason for this omission. It was rumored that the letters which the great man addressed to his wife whenever he was absent from her and which were not to be published until after his death would tell the real story of their life together, would, in effect, constitute another journal, a journal that was confidently expected to be even more startling than the already published journal.

He, Robert Heyward, knew something that nobody else knew! He could not tell his own wife, for he was a little ashamed of the way he had come by his knowledge. And yet he knew that if it were to do over again he would do exactly what he had done. Fäy had been called out of the room for a few minutes. The sheet of paper on which he had been writing lay where he had left it on the desk. Heyward had stepped over and had read what was written there:

> For you know, and you alone know, that if your name is not mentioned in my journal it is because I cannot trust myself to utter it. It is fatuous to say that I love you better than my life. You are my life. I have no existence except in and through you. . . .

He looked out over the harbor. The lights of the city encircled it like a wreath of flowers flung down on the sand. The reflection of the lights extended only a little way out over the bay. The center of the vast body of water was dark blue, lusterless. From below the marble balustrade came a heady fragrance. On the terraces below the mimosas were in full bloom. When he had told Mrs. Rensslaer about seeing the Sudanese crush the orange blossoms and insert them into his nostrils she had said that once in Paris, sitting with some friends at a café, she had seen a gigantic Sudanese walk past, holding a flower in his hand, and had burst into tears. She had added that she did not know that she would ever leave this part of the world again. Heyward had reported the conversation to Forrest, who had told him how Edgar Rennslaer, in his vigorous middle age, had been stricken with paralysis while on a vacation in this city. Those had been the days before airplane travel was common. The doctors had said that the journey back to Paris might have disastrous consequences. Rensslaer would not give up his work. His enormous library had been transported at considerable cost. And just as well, Forrest had said, for Edgar Rensslaer never left his bed again except for a wheelchair. After his death Mrs. Rensslaer had closed the villa and at the solicitation of friends had taken an apartment in Paris, but in two years' time she was back in the villa. She had told Blair that she could not bear being in places where her husband had never been, meeting people he had never known.

Heyward had asked Forrest if he had known Edgar Rensslaer. Forrest had replied in his slow way that he never had but he felt as if he had. He added that Mrs. Rensslaer had been very much in love with her husband.

Heyward bent his eyes now on his friend's half-shadowed face. Why was it that some men were swept all at once out into the current of life while others seemed fated to spend their lives in the shallows? He himself, poor as a church mouse, had been married at twenty-five, a father at twenty-six. Forrest, who had always had an income sufficient for his needs, was still unmarried at thirty-three. At St. Matthew's he had been in love with Sara Hall, who was two years older than he was and already going to dances at West Point. In college he had been in love with the wife of one of his professors. It was obvious that he was a little in love with Mrs. Rensslaer. She must have been an extraordinarily beautiful woman. Even now when she turned those eyes on you it was like being proffered handfuls of violets. But even with the best will in the world what can a woman of sixty-eight do for a young man?

Somewhere within the recesses of the house a telephone bell pealed. Slow footsteps were heard in the hall. A voice said, "Madame. . . ." Mrs. Rensslaer said, "Oh . . . !" and got up and went into the house.

Heyward drew his chair up to the railing and sat leaning forward, his arms folded on the cold marble. On the terraces below the fragrance of the mimosa blossoms was almost overpowering. This villa was so high above the city that all the noises mingled to form one great humming sound—as if a gigantic bee hovered above the flowery lights. Occasionally another sound, heavy yet wailing, rose above the humming: the drums and singing from the casbah. Heyward, like all tourists, had visited the old city, strolling through it once with Forrest and going a few nights later with Fäy to a place that was half shop, half theater where pantomimes were enacted. As they made their way through the narrow streets Fäy had talked learnedly of the dances they were going to see. Obscenity was their distinguishing characteristic. They were forbidden by the police of every city except Constantinople and the city whose stones they now trod. The character whose amorous adventures constituted their subject matter appeared only at the Fast of Ramadan, when men's senses were sharpened by abstinence.

It had been, Heyward thought, a little like a New York nightclub, with its habitués, and its singer on whose popularity the show depended: a young boy who played a huge, vase-shaped drum and wore a heavy white blossom tucked over his ear. Fäy had whispered to Heyward that the shop was not a brothel but rather "a court of love." Those who made assignations here would have to go elsewhere to keep them. . . . The doorbell had rung promptly at seven o'clock this evening. The Arab boy stood there, holding a package in his hand. He had been about to pay him and dismiss him when Fäy called sharply from the inner room, "Is that Hussein? Let him come in here. I want to see him."

The passage was narrow. Heyward and the Arab boy had stood face to face before the boy slowly wheeled in the direction of Heyward's pointing finger. The Arab's eyes had been full on Heyward's face for a second and again Heyward had had that feeling of some infinitely soft substance being drawn lingeringly across his cheek.

Forrest Blair, as if he had been reading his friend's mind, asked suddenly, "Where *is* your old man tonight?"

"I don't know," Heyward said. He added coldly, "I am quite aware that Fäy's life is—irregular. At the same time I must say that his conduct toward me has been exemplary, both as man and employer."

Forrest laughed coarsely. "Maybe you don't ring his bell. I hear he likes 'em young."

"Is it because of his irregular life that Mrs. Rensslaer won't receive him?" Heyward asked after a pause.

"No," Forrest said thoughtfully, "I think it's those letters."

"You mean his correspondence with Raoul Pleyol?"

"No. The 'love' letters . . . the ones he writes his wife."

"Has she seen any of them?"

Forrest was silent so long that Heyward thought that he was not going to answer; then he said, "She thinks that the marriage has never been consummated. After all, she's in a position to know. Seems he tried to have a whirl with her after they were both married —before he began going after the Arab boys."

"Yes," Heyward said impatiently. "What's in the letters?"

"She thinks that they aren't written to Madame Fäy. . . ."

"I've never heard his name mentioned in connection with that of any other woman."

Forrest laughed again. "No . . . He writes them sitting in front of a mirror. That's what burns Gabrielle up."

"She's a charming woman who's just fed us a lot of delicious food," Heyward said hotly. "Guillaume Fäy's a genius. I don't believe she knows any more what goes into his letters than she knows what'll go into his next book."

"There she comes now," Forrest said in a low voice.

Mrs. Rensslaer emerged from the hall and stood in the doorway. *"Look!"* she said.

The moon had suddenly risen from behind a grove of ilex. It was at the full, as round as an orange and as yellow. But the light that fell upon the water was silver. In the broad track of light that it sent across the bay every wave was tipped with silver. Heyward got up and walked over to the balustrade. He was still thinking about his friend. When he had first known Forrest it was Forrest who had been the initiate and he the acolyte; it was in Forrest's rooms that he had first read Eliot and Pound and Mallarmé. But there was a gulf between them now, a gulf that was always widening. He remembered something that Fäy had written in one of his journals: "For five days now I have been *afraid* to work, yet always longing to!" Sometimes a man had to refrain from work simply because the mind was not supple enough to do what it would be called upon to do! To sit all day and look into a mirror might be the hardest thing a man was ever called upon to do. . . . Guillaume Fäy was obviously not like other men. A man, it might be, of unnatural loves. But is there not something mysterious in the very nature of love? And who is to say what love is natural, what love unnatural? *It is* they, *not* we, *who are strange*, he thought, and a sense of the almost insuperable difficulties which the artist confronts, of the immeasurable rewards he receives burst upon him and in his imagination mingled with the radiance spread upon the waters. At that moment he would not have changed places with any man.

All at once he was overcome by a longing for his wife. It seemed incredible that she should not be here beside him. Under the pretense of admiring the spectacle he walked over to the end of the terrace. At this moment she might be watching the same moon shed its rays over water. Their apartment in New York overhung the East River. After dinner he and Molly often turned off the lights and sat on the davenport to look out on the river. When he thought of her it was usually her eyes that came before him, brown eyes whose gaze was luminous but steady. Tonight he could not call up her eyes or her expression, could feel only the warmth and slightness of her in his arms.

"Gabrielle," Forrest said, "didn't you tell me that you were engaged to marry Guillaume Fäy once?"

Mrs. Rensslaer, laughing her silvery laugh, resumed her place on the chaise longue. "Don't hold it against me," she said. "Thérèse is older than I but I was—more precocious. It seemed natural that Guillaume should make love to me when we were at Crans together. And natural that I should accept him. After all, he was the first man who ever made love to me . . ." She shivered a little, as if the air had suddenly grown chill, and drew the shawl from the back of her chair and folded it about her.

"How long did the engagement last?" Forrest asked.

"A year," Mrs. Rensslaer said. "He was faithful to me for a year. At least I had no evidence that he was unfaithful."

"And yet you broke the engagement?"

"Yes," she said, and stifled a yawn. "He was keeping a journal even then."

The telephone bell pealed again. Footsteps were heard in the hall. "Bother!" Mrs. Rensslaer said. She rose and stood for a second, looking from one to the other of the young men who had risen too. "I was *gauche* in those days—heavens! But I knew that a man who keeps a journal makes a poor fiancé and a poorer husband."

"I suppose he just can't resist putting everything that happens to him into the journal," Forrest said reflectively.

"Or what doesn't happen to him!" Mrs. Rensslaer said, and went with her light step into the house.

III

When Heyward reached the consulate the next morning he found that Forrest had already attended to the matter of Fäy's visa. "But let's go over to the ministry, anyhow," Forrest said. "I called Pleyol and he said he'd be glad to see you."

When they reached the ministry Forrest stopped to talk with a friend whom he met in an anteroom. Heyward was shown into an inner office.

Blinds drawn against the midday heat gave the room a pleasant gloom. It was sparsely furnished, with several heavy leather chairs, a black teakwood table drawn up beside one of them, and in the corner a huge desk behind which the minister sat.

Raoul Pleyol's peasant origins showed in his short, stocky body and round head. Heyward thought that he must be nearing seventy; his hair and bristling mustache were white, as were his shaggy eyebrows. He grasped Heyward's hand warmly and firmly and made a gesture which indicated that he should sit in a chair which had been drawn up beside the desk, and said with a smile, "The friend of my young friend. What do you do when you are at home?"

Heyward replied that he taught English literature in a college in New York and wrote poetry "on the side."

"What is the name of your volume of poetry?" Pleyol asked, and when Heyward answered, repeated the syllables after him musingly, then, nodding his shaggy head as if in approval, rose, and, going to the window, pushed the blind aside so that he could look out on the square. "I have never been in America," he said, "but I should think that it would be good for a young American poet to live for a time in a country like this, a city like this one. Do you find that Africa speaks to you, Mr. Heyward?"

Bob said that in his mind there was no doubt that Africa spoke to him. "The trouble is that I haven't figured out yet what it's saying," he added, and then wished that that sentence had been better turned. But he found it hard to keep his mind on the conversation, he was so occupied in observing Pleyol. He was glad that the great man had risen at that moment. When he was seated at his desk he appeared taller than he actually was. Or did he give the impression that he was shorter than he actually was? His shoulders and arms were so large that the lower part of his body seemed to diminish in size when he stood. But it was the poet's head and neck that fascinated the young man. The big, round head was so set on the powerful neck that it seemed to flow out of it. One could hardly tell where the neck ended and the head began. The effect was of remarkable compactness, of leashed power. The man was, as it were, all of one piece, with all his members at his immediate disposal. Heyward remembered that in their correspondence Fäy had described Pleyol as being shaped like a hammer. He fancied that for all his age and bulk Pleyol would react in moments of stress faster than most men.

Pleyol, turning from the window, was asking him what poets he read. Heyward said that since he had been in Africa he had been rereading Rimbaud.

Pleyol nodded his head again. "When I first came to Africa to live I, too, reread Rimbaud. It was as if I had never read him before..."

Heyward said eagerly, "You feel that it was fated for him to come here. So much that he found here—the heat, the blossoms, the languors, even the diseases from which he suffered—they are all there in the early poems. It is as if he *had* to come here to find them."

Pleyol gave him a quick glance from under shaggy brows. He said, "I do not believe that Rimbaud was fated to be damned—any more than any other man."

Heyward felt the color rising in his cheeks. He spoke with the slight stammer that came over him in moments of excitement or confusion. "What I said about Rimbaud is hardly original, sir. Your confrère, Guillaume Fäy, said what amounted to the same thing the other day."

Pleyol said negligently: "Ah, Fäy. . . . There is no telling what notion will come into that head."

"You do not have any regard for Monsieur Fäy's critical opinion?" Heyward asked, somewhat taken aback.

Pleyol did not answer at once but looked at him intently. Heyward felt sweat start out on the palms of his hands. There was something minatory in the blue gaze, the slightly lowered head, the curious alertness of the stocky, powerful body. A phrase from one of Fäy's journals came into his mind: "*I wish that I had never met Raoul Pleyol!*" What could Fäy have meant by that? He pushed the question from him, heard himself talking at random: he had read the correspondence between Fäy and Pleyol, as who had not, and had been enormously stimulated by it. Pleyol must have been as pleased as he himself had been when he, Fäy, won the Monnier award last year. What made it so interesting was that Pleyol had won it the year before. Two such men of letters—men who had rendered service to letters which was at once disinterested and distinguished— had never before won the prize in two consecutive years. Did not Monsieur Pleyol regard this as a significant triumph?

Pleyol raised his shaggy head. "*No!*" he thundered. "The prize should have gone to an artist."

Heyward found himself stammering again. "You do not consider *Guillaume Fäy* an artist?"

Pleyol slowly shook his head.

"But, sir! *La Fuite de Lemnos! Le Frère Prodigue!*"

Pleyol said, "Fäy cannot read mythology any better than he reads the Scriptures. *La Fuite de Lemnos* is a fantasy of the unconscious unresolved by art. *Le Frère Prodigue* is brilliant in passages but is a failure because of its inconclusive ending. Fäy himself does not know how his story turns out! There is an American expression which, to my mind, describes Fäy: 'He does not know what it is all about.' Fäy does not know what it is all about."

Heyward forgot his awe of the great man. He said, "Is not that the very source of his strength? He does not *know* but he has never stopped seeking. His journals alone . . ."

"What do you find in his journals?"

"A moral integrity that is an invaluable example to the younger writers. In his journals he dares face himself. It is more than most of us can do. . . ."

Pleyol said heavily, "It is more than any of us can do. . . . Do you think that a man sees himself when he looks into a mirror? He sees only the pose he has assumed. If you want to see yourself look into the eyes of your friends—or your enemies—who are made in the image of God."

Heyward said stubbornly, "An artist's first duty is to confront himself."

Pleyol brought his big hand down on the desk. "An artist's first duty is the same as any other man's—to serve, praise, and worship God."

"Do you not think that a poet, like yourself—or like Fäy—has responsibilities different from those of that pretty secretary who just showed me in here?"

"We have exactly the same responsibilities. The difference is in the methods we use to discharge them."

"And you wholly disapprove of the methods which Fäy uses to discharge his responsibilities?"

Pleyol said musingly, "Fäy is a poisoner. . . . What is strange is his influence. . . ." He looked up at the young man as if suddenly recalling his presence in the room. "I used to see a great deal of Fäy. That was before I learned of—the abyss in his life."

Heyward was trembling all over. "You profess to be a Christian. Yet you turn your back on him the minute you discover that he is unfortunate!"

Pleyol bent a piercing gaze upon him. When he spoke it was as if he were choosing his words with great care. "There is a fascination in heights. Fäy is not the first created being to feel it. I gave him up when I discovered that he loved the abyss better than life."

"But if a man goes down into the abyss for the sake of his fellow men?" Heyward asked. "Does not even *your* creed allow virtue in that?"

Pleyol shook his head. "He will have spent his life for nothing. There is nothing at the bottom of the abyss. . . ."

The two men sat staring at each other. Heyward never knew afterwards what he would have said in answer. The pretty secretary put her head in at the door: Monsieur Bleeair was leaving. Did Monsieur Evard wish to accompany him?

Heyward got to his feet. He was about to leave with a murmured word of thanks, but Pleyol, making a gesture of assent to the girl, leaned over the desk to shake hands with him before letting him go. As Heyward felt the big, warm hand close over his he remembered the phrase with which Pleyol so often ended his letters to Fäy in the correspondence broken off twelve years ago: "I grasp your hand." And yet Pleyol evidently felt a real animosity toward Fäy. As he mounted the long flight of steps to the hotel he thought that it was strange that so much warmth and candor could exist side by side with envy. For in the last analysis, what but envy could have prompted Pleyol's displeasure over Fäy's receiving the Monnier award? He was still thinking of the two men as he let himself into his room. He came to the conclusion that Pleyol's attitude could only be explained by the notorious jealousy which French men of letters have always had for one another.

IV

"Her eyes have no perfume," Heyward wrote, and then crossed the words out.

Molly was not jealous by nature, but no woman, he thought, wants her husband waxing enthusiastic about another woman's eyes. Besides, when he wrote that sentence he had been thinking not of Madame Fäy's calm gray eyes but of Mrs. Rensslaer's eyes that always reminded him of crushed violets. She had spent a whole summer here when she was a girl. But that had been many years ago. It hardly seemed likely that her girlish ghost would haunt these old walls, these corridors, and yet ever since he had arrived at Crans he had found himself thinking, off and on, of Mrs. Rensslaer!

He must finish his letter! He and Fäy had arrived at Crans over a week ago and during that time he had written his wife only one short note. And yet he had written to her almost every day when he was in Africa. But it had been easy to write letters there. Every time he went out of his hotel he saw something he wanted to tell her about. It was different here. There was not much to see, and nothing going on—if there was anything going on it was not anything he could write her about.

He raised his head to stare through the open window. The view was monotonous and rather somber: wide, flat fields separated from each other by the avenues of beeches that in this region are planted to protect the houses from the winds that blow off the Channel. He had been a little disappointed, too, in the village. There were few old houses there. The dwellings were mostly cottages which had been erected a few years ago by a benevolent building association in which Madame Fäy had interested herself.

A breeze, laden with summer fragrances, came in through the open window at his back. He heard voices below. A laugh rang out. He had begun to type again, but he stopped, his hands suspended over the keys. The laugh sounded as if it might have come from a child who had laughed out in exuberance and might laugh again at any minute. He had seen only one child about the place, the cook's eight-year-old, black-haired granddaughter, who, whenever he passed her, stared at him, her finger in her mouth. He would not have thought that she could laugh with such exuberance. He got up and went to the window.

There were many magnificent trees on the wide lawn. Beech trees predominated. Some of them must be quite ancient. He had heard that the earth that surrounded beech trees was poisonous to other plants, that none except plants that were themselves poisonous would grow in their shade. Certainly, there was a wide ring of bare earth about the roots of each beech tree, but that would be the gardener's doing. He frowned. Pleyol had called Fäy "a poisoner." He wished that he had had an opportunity to know Pleyol better. He did not look like a man obsessed by jealousy—he himself had as great a reputation and had had as much public honor as Fäy—and yet what but jealousy could have inspired such a remark? Fäy, he thought, had as little jealousy as any man he had ever known, not even that jealousy which the old who are on their way out of life sometimes feel for the young who are coming into their strength.

Last night Heyward had read some of his poems aloud, at Fäy's request. In the *salon* after dinner, the old basset hound snoring in his chair, Madame Fäy, her knitting laid aside, sitting with her hands folded in her lap, her eyes fixed intently on his face. Fäy had sat a little apart from the others, beside a window. His hand shielded his eyes during the reading. Heyward had felt as if Fäy's whole intelligence was concentrated on the words that were being uttered—as if a great beacon had suddenly withdrawn its beams from the ocean to light a passer-by across a brook. When Heyward finished Fäy looked up, let Heyward have his full, burning glance, then rose and came over and laid his hand on his shoulder. "You are a poet," he said.

Heyward thought now that Fäy couldn't have said anything to him that he would have liked better. But he frowned again and put his hand up and rubbed his forehead. He had not slept well last night and what little sleep he got had been broken by a long confused dream. He had been with Fäy in Africa or in some land beside a blue sea and Fäy had asked him to undertake a commission for him. "But you will have to go to . . ." he had said, and pronounced a name that Heyward had never heard before. Heyward's way had brought him to a long avenue bordered by beech trees. There was a house at the end of it and a woman was standing at the top of a long flight of marble stairs. She was neither young nor old and in answer to his questions would only smile and shake her head. "No, Monsieur Fäy is not here. . . . He has never been here. . . . No, Monsieur Guillaume Fäy is not here . . ." "But he was to meet me here!" Heyward cried in anger, whereat the woman smiled and shook her head faster: "Not here . . . not here . . . He has never been here . . ." until Mrs. Rensslaer came and put her arm about the woman's shoulders and led her away.

"I'm a poet, all right," Heyward muttered, "or I wouldn't have such devilish dreams," and he took his handkerchief out and wiped the sweat from between his fingers.

On the right of the graveled drive a circle of fresh earth had been cut out of the turf. A man and a woman had just passed under his window and were crossing over to this bed. The man—one of whose arms ended in a steel hook—was dexterously guiding a wheelbarrow heaped high with loam. The woman who walked beside him carried a green shrub under her arm. She was not tall, rather broad in figure, and somewhat stooped. She wore a shapeless apron of some striped fabric over a black skirt and the sleeves of a gray pullover protruded from under the apron. A strand of her gray hair had come loose from the coil on top of her head and blew backward in the wind. She put a hand up to replace it and, turning to the old man, said something that brought a sour smile to his face, at which she laughed again. That, Heyward thought, was the most astonishing thing about Madame Fäy. He had become accustomed to the contrast between her appearance and that of her husband—she looked so much older than he did that he might have been taken for her son—and he no longer wondered at her rather long, weathered face whose withdrawn expression was enhanced rather than diminished by a pair of eyes of a very clear gray, but he had not yet heard her laugh without involuntarily looking around. It always seemed to him that that laugh might have come from a child hiding in the shrubbery. Or was it the laugh of an adult who remained in some ways immature? He had had an old maid aunt in North Carolina who laughed like that.

The old man took the little tree from the woman and set it firmly upright in the hole that had been made in the turf. She stooped her ungainly body and began vigorously throwing shovelfuls of earth about the shrub.

A young girl in a fawn-colored coat emerged from the house and stood watching them. Madame Fäy heard her footsteps on the gravel and, throwing one more shovelful of earth, turned and squatted on her heels to look up at the girl. "There is more consommé if the little Henri needs it," she said.

The girl shook her head and said, smiling, that Henri's temperature had been normal for two days. "The doctor says that this afternoon he may have *pommes purées*."

The girl, who looked more like a Provençal than a Norman, had an artificial rose pinned in the masses of her black hair. Heyward, noticing the awkward cut of the cloth coat, wondered if Madame Fäy had received, as he himself had received, an impression of something at once exotic and pathetic about her undeniable beauty. Just then Madame Fäy smiled and, detaining the girl with a gesture, rose heavily to her feet and went into the house.

The girl stood idly, balancing herself on shiny black heels. There was a large manila envelope under her arm. Heyward knew that it contained whatever material Fäy wanted typed that day. Soon after they had arrived at the château Fäy had informed his secretary that he was not to type any letters while he was there. "This is your first visit to Crans. Your boat sails all too soon. We will look upon you as a visitor. I know that you will not be able to work in the few days you have here. But meditation can sometimes be accomplished as well in a moment as in a month. Explore our grounds. They are not laid out on the grand scale, but I assure you they have their surprises. It would make me happy if while you are walking in our *allées* some vista down which you may gaze for years suddenly opened in your imagination. I should then feel that Emmanuele and I had our modest share in the fine poems you are sure to write."

Madame Fäy had come back. Heyward moved nearer to the window. She carried a package wrapped in tissue paper in her hand. The girl took it from her and slowly unwrapped it. Heyward leaned over farther in order to see what was in the package: a pair of gloves, dark red, almost the color of pomegranates. The girl's cry of pleasure floated up to the open window. Madame Fäy had watched the girl intently as she unwrapped the package. When she cried out she smiled, as if only now convinced that the gift had brought pleasure, laid her hand on the girl's arm for a second, shook it lightly, then turned back to her planting while the girl walked off down the drive.

A bell sounded. It was the custom at Crans, as it had been at Heyward's grandfather's house in North Carolina, to sound a "warning bell" five or ten minutes before each meal. Madame Fäy put her shovel down and, still kneeling, leaned back on her heels again. Her hands, which even at this distance showed themselves stained with earth and swollen at the joints from arthritis, were clasped in front of her. She stared off through the trees.

The gardener finished tamping the last shovelful of earth about the little tree and straightened up. He made a sharp clicking sound with his teeth. Madame Fäy started and got to her feet.

Heyward decided that he would finish his letter to his wife after luncheon and descended the curving staircase to the lower floor.

A small corridor opened off the main hall. Fäy's study was down that corridor. The door to the corridor was open. Heyward judged that Fäy had emerged for luncheon. He himself advanced up the hall and stood for a second before the open door of the *salon* for the pure pleasure of looking into the room. The parquet in here was lighter than the stair treads, almost honey-colored. The carpet was faintly colored in rose and green and fawn colors. Where the furniture was not covered with chintz it shone a dark mahogany. The *boiseries* were white.

A capacious chintz-covered armchair was drawn up to the empty fireplace. Sultan, the aged and enormously fat basset hound, was sunk, as he often was at this hour, in its depths. He raised his domed head at the sound of footsteps and stared at Heyward out of red-rimmed eyes that reminded him of his uncle, Judge Walter Abbott of Winston-Salem.

In the dining room Fäy was already seated at the round table between two tall windows. The weather had been balmy since they had arrived at Crans but he complained frequently of the cold. For the last few days he had been wearing a white burnous that he had brought back from Africa over a corduroy jacket and flannel trousers. Heyward knew without looking that he still wore pantoufles though he had been up since seven o'clock.

He looked up as Heyward entered. "Heracles is on board!" he said.

An exclamation of delight broke from Heyward as he took his seat. "Heracles" was the name of the long poem which Guillaume Fäy had been working on for years. It had been Heyward's duty to type the lines Fäy had written while he was in Africa. The work had been rather a delight than a duty. Fäy, when he turned his manuscript over to Heyward, had had more the air of one man of letters asking the opinion of another man of letters than of an employer assigning a task. When Heyward brought him back the carefully typed pages he always asked him if he had any comments to make and listened thoughtfully to whatever the young man said. And once he had showed Heyward where he had inserted an exclamation point at his suggestion.

Madame Fäy entered. She had removed her apron but she still wore the black skirt and gray pullover in which she had been gardening. Fäy half rose at her entrance, then, sinking back with a smile, let Heyward draw her chair out. The old manservant brought an omelette sprinkled with *fines herbes*, new asparagus, and a loaf of the crusty bread made on the estate under Madame Fäy's supervision.

Fäy gave Heyward a look which seemed to say that they would resume their conversation later. His dark glance flickered over his wife's face. "What have you been doing this morning, Emmanuele?" he asked.

Madame Fäy smiled and said that she and Joseph had finished planting the third *pivoine de l'arbre* only a few minutes ago.

"Where?" Fäy demanded.

"One on each side of the drive and one a little farther back where it can be seen from your study window."

Fäy looked at her again and as hastily looked away. "That was very good of you, my dear. But you look flushed. Are you sure you have not been exerting yourself too much?"

Madame Fäy's fresh laugh rang out. "You know that the doctor has ordered me to exercise for my arthritis."

"But not necessarily with Joseph." He turned to Heyward. "Have you ever watched them together? Joseph stands like a statue. It is Emmanuele who does all the stooping, the carrying, the fetching."

"Joseph has only one hand," Madame Fäy said.

Heyward kept his eyes on his plate. *He has no existence except in and through her, and yet he leans a little forward when he addresses her, as if she were a stranger he is anxious to please, and his eyes seldom rest on her face and when they do will dart aside as though that placid countenance reflects the one thing he is not able to contemplate. . . . And when she spoke to him a moment ago her voice sank, as if to soften some blow that is preparing . . .*

". . . with no education, no training, set himself up to be a veterinarian. God knows how many cows he has killed, to say nothing of dogs and cats, till he went to the war and came back with one hand—to become our gardener."

"Still, it is astonishing what he accomplishes with one hand," Madame Fäy said.

"Ah, but if he had two hands!"

"Then he could get a place anywhere as gardener."

Armand removed the larger plates and brought smaller ones. An epergne filled with apples stood in the center of the table. Armand proffered it first to Madame Fäy and then to the gentlemen. Fäy took a small, slightly misshapen apple from the dish and held it out toward Heyward. "Not much like our tangerines, *hein?* Did I not tell you that here we have apples that are of a grayness—actually of a grayness?"

Madame Fäy's eyes rested on her husband's face a moment, then sought the window.

Heyward felt a chill down his spine. *She does not see him! Is it because he is no longer there?*

Fäy's voice broke into his thoughts. ". . . Can you not show them to him this afternoon, my dear? They were, after all, planted for your pleasure."

"What is that?" Heyward asked, confused.

"*Les pivoines de l'arbre.* Emmanuele and I brought them back from China, where we went on our honeymoon. We are transplanting some of them now to other parts of the grounds. But one has to go over there to the peony garden, behind the coach house, to see them in their full beauty. You will take Robert there this afternoon, Emmanuele?"

"Oh yes," Madame Fäy said. A maid was standing in the doorway. She arched her brows and in an audible whisper said something about "*le vieux Philippe*" and "*l'autobus.*"

Madame Fäy said, "Oh! He has come to get his medicine and he has to be back by three o'clock."

Fäy made an impatient gesture with his hand. "We will excuse you, my dear."

The old woman made off to the kitchen. Fäy laid his hand on Heyward's arm and walked slowly beside him out of the room. "My wife has become the veterinarian for the whole neighborhood," he said. "Joseph's influence, no doubt."

Heyward ignored the petulance in his tone. "I am glad you had such a good morning's work!" he said warmly.

"Ah! Heracles is on board!" Fäy said. "But will he sail? Will the nymph *let* him sail?" . . . His bony fingers closed on the young man's arm. "*If I had it to do over again I would not marry. Instead, I would go around the world . . . around . . . and around . . . and around!*"

Madame Fäy was waiting for Heyward under the porte cochere. They walked past the rabbit hutches and the poultry yard and on to the old stone building that now housed automobiles but was still called "the coach house." Back of the coach house the stable stood, encircled by a high brick wall. The gate was open. Heyward caught a glimpse of Joseph standing in the runway of the stable beside a black cow.

They passed the stable and were in a small wood which he had not entered before. A path wound between tall pines. The earth was brown with pine needles, except where ferns grew. Somewhere close by a brook was running. They walked slowly past the red-brown trunks and emerged in a hollow.

Heyward cried out. Confronting him was a rampart of massed blossoms. Pure white, delicate pink and lavender, pale yellow, scarlet, vermilion shading to clear crimson, dark red, even purple. He thought that he had never before seen so many colors in one place. The hollow formed a natural amphitheater. Three of its sides were covered with peonies. Many of them grew higher than Heyward's head.

Madame Fäy had sat down on a marble bench under a pine tree that stood at the edge of the clearing. He sat down beside her. The breeze brought the indefinable fragrance of the peonies to them. Heyward was remembering mornings in his grandmother's garden when, a small boy, he used to run and pick up the peony blossoms fallen on the ground after a night of spring rain and, breathing in their fragrance, asked himself what it was that peonies smelled like.

"You can smell them from here!" he said.

She told him that sometimes, riding in the mountains of northern China, she had smelled that faint fragrance and had known that when their ponies rounded a bend they would come upon a whole mountainside covered with the blossoms. She was silent a moment, then said dreamily, "It seemed strange to think that if nobody ever came that way again they would go on blooming."

Heyward said, "Paean to the god Apollo. You spent your honeymoon in a Greek temple!"

She said, "Guillaume remembered this hillside even then. The exposure was right but the soil was not suited to them. The first trees we imported died. Then Guillaume consulted someone at the Jardin des Plantes. They told him what to do. Today, when we want to transplant one of the trees we simply provide it with an ample supply of the soil from this hillside."

"He is an amazing man!" Heyward cried warmly. "The longer I know him, the more he astonishes me. I don't believe there's anything he couldn't do if he set his heart on it."

She turned her head. Her eyes met his. In the landscape of the face an eye is set like a lake, for exploration. He thought that her eyes were like those lakes that the hunter comes upon in the Carolina marshes at the end of a long day. The dog goes ahead, parts the reeds. The body of water shimmers palely in the rays of the setting sun. What is strange is to know that all the long day it has lain here unvisited and that after dog and man have made their way back to the road it will still lie here, reflecting nothing but the reeds along the bank and the sky above.

She said, "Yes. . . . If he sets his heart on anything."

There was a rustle on the path. A black-haired child in a checked pinafore stood before them. She said, "*Joseph a besoin de Madame.*"

Madame Fäy got to her feet. "You will excuse me? Evidently I am needed."

"I'll come, too," Heyward said, but did not immediately follow the old woman and the child up the path. He went over and stood in front of the rampart of blossoms. When one stood this close the fragrance came in almost tonic gusts. But the appeal to the eyes was even stronger. It was as if the sense of sight became another organ, plunged repeatedly, drunkenly, into depth on depth of color. A sob broke from him. He had to wait a moment before he regained his composure. And after he had started up the path he stopped short to stare at the brown pine needles. He had just realized with astonishment that all day long he had had an overpowering desire to see Mrs. Rensslaer.

He had not been in his room long before one of the maids informed him that Monsieur Fäy would like him to come to the study at his convenience. Heyward, as he washed his hands and brushed his hair, was smiling. The vision of Mrs. Rensslaer had faded before another vision, one which would always bring a smile to his lips, he thought. They had found Joseph standing beside the black cow, holding a quart measure in his hand. He beckoned to Madame Fäy peremptorily with his hook and, pointing to the child, said something in French so rapid—or colloquial—that Heyward could not follow it, then handed the measure to the child.

Madame Fäy smiled indulgently. "Her hands are not large enough, Joseph," she said and, stepping to the cow's side, she inserted the thumb and middle finger of each hand firmly into the flaring nostrils and drew the cow's head steadily upward. Joseph, meanwhile, braced himself against the cow's flank. There was a soughing noise, a surging backward of hindquarters promptly checked by Joseph. The beast opened her mouth and the child poured the draught down her throat.

Heyward, as he entered the little corridor that led to the study, was still thinking of the scene in the stable yard. After the drenching there had been some discussion of the cow's condition, then Joseph had said that he had a hundred cabbage plants to set out before nightfall and could attend to them if Madame would pick the raspberries for tonight's dinner. Madame replied that she would if Josette would help her. The three had made their way companionably to the garden while Heyward went back into the house. A strange woman, he thought, as he paused before the study door. As strange as her husband, perhaps, though in a different way. Perhaps even stranger.

Fäy was at his desk in a welter of papers. The old-fashioned wooden blinds and the jalousies that covered them had been drawn aside. The midafternoon sun poured through the window and made a little pool for motes to dance in on the carpet. Heyward thought that Fäy must have undergone a sharp change of mood since luncheon. He had discarded his burnous and sat erect behind his desk, basking in the sunlight. He turned glowing eyes on the young man and said, "I have written five more lines! At least I think I have."

"I *know* you have!" Heyward said jubilantly. "I can tell by looking at you."

He had come up to the side of the desk as he spoke. Fäy put a hand out and gave his shoulder an affectionate pressure. "Would you go quickly and ask Emmanuele for the key to the secretary? There is a phrase in a letter which I wrote her the other day which I think I can use. It goes . . . But wait! You will see it in the poem."

Heyward hurried from the room. Halfway across the lawn he slowed his steps. In a few minutes he would hold in his hand the key not only to an old secretary but to a mystery. Fäy had announced years ago that the letters would supplement the mysterious omissions from the journal. What sort of man would emerge from the letters? What sort of woman? He stopped under a linden tree; a question beat in the air. He looked up as if his interlocutor were perched on the branch above his head. His lips formed words. *Yes. It is my duty to look at them if I get a chance. Surely I'll get a chance. . . .*

He ran on and arrived at the old walled vegetable garden. Joseph, squatting on his heels, trowel in hand, glanced up at him as he ran past. The child had disappeared. Madame Fäy was stooping along the raspberry rows at the end of the garden. He slackened his pace so as not to be out of breath when he approached her. He said, "Madame, Monsieur Fäy asks that you send him the key to the secretary in which his letters to you are kept. He wants to verify a phrase."

A blackbird flew down from the plum tree. Light dazzled off the raspberry leaves, a trailing branch quivered, then was still as the bird's claws took firmer hold of it. The woman's back was still toward him. The bulky body had not quivered but rather settled in on itself, as if to sustain a long-anticipated blow. She turned around. She looked at the basket she held in her hand, then up at him. She said, "I will go to him."

Was she going to refuse to give him the key? Was it possible that he might not see the letters, after all? He felt an insane desire to laugh out, to chatter nonsense. *It is not Bluebeard's key I ask for, madame! Merely the key to an old secretary.* Aloud he said, "If you could perhaps tell me where the key is kept?"

She did not seem to hear him. She had stooped clumsily to set her basket on the ground and now her hands came up to unfasten the apron that was tied about her waist. When she had untied the apron and had flung it on a raspberry bush she stood a second, looking down at her swollen, arthritic hands before they dropped to her sides, and she went with her old woman's gait down the raspberry rows and across the garden.

The blackbird left the raspberry bush and lit on the ground not far from Joseph. He made a menacing gesture with his hook and rose as the old woman approached. "*Madame . . .*" he began, then fell back as Madame Fäy walked past without looking at him.

They entered the house through the kitchen door, traversed two more rooms, and were in the back hall. Madame Fäy pushed aside the heavy velvet portieres that separated the back hall from the front and disappeared. Heyward stayed where he was. It was always dark in here. He had never noticed before what a curious smell old velvet has. *I have been here a long time. . . . How long has it been since she pushed those curtains aside?* Somewhere on ahead there was a whimpering sound, such as might be made by a dog in distress . . . *or some other beast, that has thought to escape, being forced over a cliff?*

He pushed the curtains aside and tiptoed into the hall. The door to the corridor stood open. He tiptoed past it and down the hall. The door of the *salon* was open, too. The chintz-covered chair was drawn as usual up to the cold fireplace. The old basset hound who lay in its depths raised his head and stared at the young man a moment, then laid his head down on his paws.

Heyward heard footsteps behind him. Madame Fäy emerged from the corridor, passed him with a slight inclination of the head, went through the hall and out onto the front steps. Outdoors the sun was still bright, but on the horizon a few clouds glittered darkly. She spoke without turning her head: "It looks as if we might have rain later in the afternoon." "It looks as if we might," Heyward rejoined, and watched her go down the steps.

The whimpering had started again. He waited until the woman had disappeared into the shrubbery, then tiptoed into the corridor. A splinter of grayish light lay athwart it; Madame Fäy had not closed the door of the study when she left. The wailing broke off. A voice spoke in a whisper: *"We can never get them back. . . ."* Heyward's whole body grew rigid. "She *burned* them!" the voice said. There was a sob and then the whisper again: *"She* burned them!"

The young man's hands reached out on each side to touch the cold walls. Absently he noted that the shaft of grayish light had been blotted out; inside that room a body swayed from side to side. When he had left the room a few minutes ago it had been full of sunshine. Now it was dark. She must have drawn the blinds before she left. The old man's head and shoulders would show hunched against the pale-colored jalousies. Ever afterwards he was to think of that head as hooded, but the eyes, the eyes that had gleamed so merry, so mottled! They would be black now—twin prisons in which a creature that had once sported in the sun would sit forever in darkness.

Notes and Sources

THE PETRIFIED WOMAN. First appeared in *Mademoiselle*, vol. xxv, no. 5, September 1947, pages 200-1, 308-20. Reprinted as the sixth story in *Old Red and Other Stories* (OR 6), Charles Scribner's Sons, 1963.

THE BURNING EYES. Originally published as the fifth story in *The Forest of the South* (FS 5), Charles Scribner's Sons, 1945.

TOM RIVERS. First appeared in *The Yale Review*, vol. xxii, October 1933, pages 794-815. Reprinted as the tenth story in *The Forest of the South* (FS 10), and the fifth story in *Old Red and Other Stories* (OR 5). Also appeared in *The Best Stories of 1934*, edited by Edmund J. O'Brien.

OLD RED. First appeared in *The Criterion* (London), vol. xiii, October 1933, pages 51-73, then in *Scribner's*, vol. xciv, December 1933, pages 325-32. Awarded the second prize in the *O. Henry Prize Stories of 1934*, edited by Harry Hansen. FS 9, OR 7.

THE ENEMIES. First appeared as "The Enemy" in *The Southern Review*, vol. iii, Spring 1938. Reprinted in *O. Henry Prize Stories of 1938*, edited by Harry Hansen. FS 15.

ONE MORE TIME. First appeared in *Scribner's*, vol. xc, December 1935, pages 338-41. Reprinted in *Famous Dog Stories*, edited by Page Cooper, 1948. FS 7, OR 8.

THE LONG DAY. First appeared in *The Gyroscope*, no. 2, February 1930, and then in *Scribner's*, lxxxviii, August 1930, pages 162-66. FS 11.

TO THY CHAMBER WINDOW, SWEET. First appeared in *Scribner's*, vol. xcvi, December 1934, pages 345-49. FS 6.

THE LAST DAY IN THE FIELD. First appeared in *Scribner's*, vol. xcvii, March 1935, pages 162-65. Reprinted in *Present-day Stories*, edited by J. T. Frederick, 1941; and in *Modern Short Stories*, edited by Robert B. Heilman, 1952. FS 8, OR 9.

THE PRESENCE. First appeared in *Harper's Bazaar*, October 1948, pages 175-86. OR 10.

ONE AGAINST THEBES. First appeared under the title "The Dragon's Teeth," in *Shenandoah*, vol. xiii, no. 1, Autumn 1961, pages 22-34. Reprinted as the first story of *Old Red and Other Stories*, 1963, OR 1. This is a revised version of the author's first work of fiction, "Summer Dust," which originally appeared in *The Gyroscope*, no. 1, November 1929, and as the first story in *The Forest of the South*, FS 1. It was reprinted in *The Best Stories of 1930*, edited by Edmund J. O'Brien.

HEAR THE NIGHTINGALE SING. First appeared in *Harper's*, vol. clxl, June 1945, pages 624-31. FS 2, OR 12.

THE FOREST OF THE SOUTH. First appeared in *The Maryland Quarterly*, no. 1, 1944, pages 92-111. FS 3.

THE ICE HOUSE. First appeared in *Hound and Horn*, vol. iv, July-September 1931, pages 502-7. FS 4, OR 11.

THE CAPTIVE. First appeared in *Hound and Horn*, vol. vi, October-December 1932, pages 63-107. Reprinted in *American Harvest*, edited by Allen Tate and John Peale Bishop, 1942; and in *Reading Modern Fiction*, edited by Winifred Lynskey, 1952. FS 1, OR 13.

THE BRILLIANT LEAVES. First appeared in *Mademoiselle*, vol. xi, no. 6, November 1937. FS 16.

HER QUAINT HONOR. First appeared under the title "Frankie and Thomas and Bud Avery," in *The Southern Review*, vol. iv, Spring 1939, pages 696-712. Reprinted in *O. Henry Prize Stories of 1939*, *The Best Short Stories of 1940*, and in *The Art of Modern Fiction*, edited by Ray B. West and R. W. Stallman, 1941. FS 14.

MR. POWERS. First appeared in *Scribner's*, vol. xc, November 1931, pages 545-50. FS 13.

ALL LOVERS LOVE THE SPRING. First appeared in *Mademoiselle*, vol. xviii, no. 4, February 1944, pages 102-3, 164-65. FS 17.

THE WATERFALL. First appeared in *The Sewanee Review*, vol. lviii, no. 4, October-December 1950, pages 632-65.

A WALK WITH THE ACCUSER. First appeared in *The Southern Review*, vol. xiii (new series), no. 3, Summer 1977, pages 598-619.

THE OLIVE GARDEN. First appeared in *The Sewanee Review*, vol. liii, no. 4, October-December 1945, pages 532-43.

EMMANUELE! EMMANUELE! First appeared in *The Sewanee Review*, vol. lxii, Spring 1954, pages 181-212. OR 2.